# - MASTER OF -
# THE FOUR KEYS OF TIME

## O J BARNES

*To My Sister Carol
Love & Best Wishes
Owen xx*

- CARTOON BUDDY CLUB PUBLISHING -

This novel is a work of fiction dedicated to world peace.
Names and characters are the product of
imagination and any resemblance
to actual persons, is entirely coincidental.

All rights reserved. No part of this publication may be
reproduced, stored in a retrieval system, or transmitted, in
any form or by any means, electronic, mechanical,
photocopying, recording or otherwise, without the prior
permission of the copyright owner.

The right of O J Barnes to be identified as the author of
this work has been asserted by him in accordance with
the Copyright, Designs and Patents Act 1988.

ISBN 978-0-9556880-0-3 (Paperback)

Published by Cartoon Buddy Club Publishing 2008

**Copyright ©**

# - *MASTER OF* -
# THE FOUR KEYS OF TIME

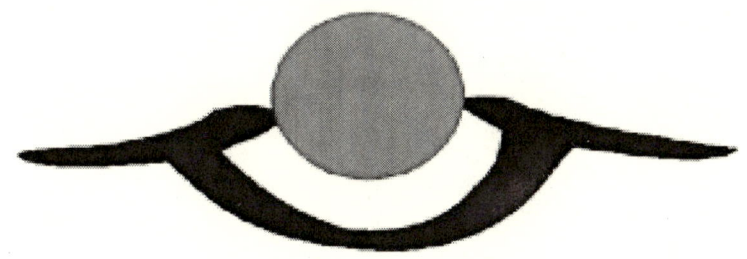

- LEGEND OF THE PENGUIN PEOPLE -
CARTOON BUDDY CLUB

O . J . B A R N E S

Book one of a serial adventure story

(-: www.cartoonbuddy.org :-)

# Contents :-)

## - Chapters -
### Finding The Legend Time Chests

*An Individual Entry Point :-)*

1. James - A Legend And The Old Dusty Box.
2. James - The Skate Park.

1. Peter - A Legend And Old Antique Avenue.
2. Peter - Sorry Your Majesty.

1. Abdul - A Legend And The Bazaar Day.
2. Abdul - The Pharaohs Tomb.

1. Sue - A Legend And The Wallaby Pouch.
2. Sue - Dingo Dogs.

### The Time Adventure Begins

*World United Time Club :-)*

1. Living Legends
2. The Evil Void Returns - (The Great Eraser)
3. Into the Void - (Fear Overcome)
4. Kids World United v Evils Black Heart Shadows - (Ultimate Football Match)
5. Times Sword Of Damocles - (Fate in the balance & The final countdown)
6. Times Planet Wake Up call - (Classroom Kids)
7. And In The End - (The Last Chapter)

- Cartoon Buddy Club Publishing -

Copyright ©

- Ye shall have Peace -
Jeremiah


( When every individual has defeated evil from within themselves )

From the west and a new world:- An individual entry point.

## *James - A Legend And The Old Dusty Box.*

James lived in an ordinary place, in an ordinary town, in an ordinary street. Every week day, travelling on the same old yellow school bus with his friends Todd and Rebecca, James made the long way home from school to his grand-parents' house, a place where he had lived for the past six months.

As the three children reached their usual stop and the large yellow bus slid to a smooth halt, James gave a cheery thanks to the bus driver.

'Bye Mr Edmund' he said with a smile. 'Thanks a lot.'

Mr Edmund nodded his head, then he waved goodbye in an age old ritual and responded with a smile of his own.

'See you Buddy!' He replied. 'Enjoy the weekend kids.'

James Todd and Rebecca quickly exited the stationary school bus, then they all laughed at the noise of whistles made from the other children passengers that had not yet reached their own stops, but who were also very much looking forward to the weekend.

Mr Edmund straightened his peaked cap and thought sadly to himself. 'Good kid that James,shame about his folks being missing on that plane in the Bermuda triangle though, it must be kind of tough on him.'

The doors of the yellow school bus closed quickly with an exhausted whoosh and the vehicle roared away down the long street.

'What are you doing on the weekend James?' Asked Todd as he watched the bus roll away into the distance. 'Want to hang out with the skate-boards?'

'That's neat!' Interrupted Rebecca before James could answer.

'Look! - Girls don't belong on skate-boards!' Said Todd indignantly. 'It's a guy thing!'

'Who says!' Rebecca turned up her nose and gave Todd an angry and very penetrating stare with her deep blue eyes.

'It's only because she's better than you Todd!' Laughed James while giving his friend a friendly pat on the back.

'Huh - Well' muttered Todd, embarrassed by the truth. He sheepishly kicked upwards at the air with his trainers and jumped forwards momentarily as if riding on an invisible skateboard. 'Are we going to hang out or what.'

'Sounds good to me' said James adjusting his back-pack and fumbling for a small front door key that was hidden somewhere in his pocket.

'Me too!' Rebecca glared at Todd in her best, smug manor.

'OK' relented Todd. 'All right, girls as well, see you guys at 11 o'clock.'

'Sure!' Replied both James and Rebecca in unison.

Todd waved goodbye as he turned left toward the short path leading to his own house. Suddenly he jumped upwards and span in the air momentarily to land gracefully with arms out-stretched as if performing a trick on an imaginary, invisible skate-board. 'Girls! - Ha!' He muttered quietly to himself.

## James - A Legend And The Old Dusty Box.

Arriving next door, James watched as Rebecca walked slowly onward toward the next house in line where she lived. He gave her a smile as she opened her front door and looked back toward him.

'Bye! - Bye!' They both shouted to each other, and Rebecca very quickly disappeared inside.

At that moment James could not help reflecting on how good it was to have his friends living right next door to himself. He considered himself really fortunate that both his classmates lived so close to his grandparents' house, the place in which he had lived ever since his parents sudden disappearance while photographing a strange, slowly moving storm that had appeared out at sea.

James reached deeply into his pocket, then he pushed the quite small and glistening golden front door key that he had found there into the lock of the very old, and very solid white wooden door of his grandparents' house.

This golden key, for some strange reason, always had to be turned twice in this ancient doors peculiar shaped lock. But this always gave James a few more seconds to examine the strangely shaped door knocker that always seemed to smile at him as he pushed open the heavy, creaking door.

After the door had swung open, James hung his backpack on the intricately carved dolphin hooks in the hallway. Skip the Labrador dog bounded towards him, tail wagging.

'Hi boy!' James petted Skip at the same Time that his grandfather appeared from the living room.

'Have a good day at school?' Asked the old man who was clutching a cup of hot coffee, and he proceeded to carefully take a sup of the steaming liquid.

'Yes grandpa' replied James, scratching Skips stomach. The dog, as usual, rolled over and over, expecting more attention from the boy.

'Done anything interesting today?' Asked grandpa smiling.

'No, nothing much' replied James.'The usual stuff.'

'OK then, better get yourself washed up' said the old man, examining his now empty cup. 'Grandma has fixed you a snack, so better hit the table son.'

'Yes grandpa' replied James, smoothing Skips head. The boy then quickly made for the bathroom to wash-up.

A little later, as James sat down at the kitchen table, grandma produced a deliciously smelling pizza, the pleasant aroma filling the entire room.

'Thank you grandma' said James, tucking into a slice. 'My favourite!'

'Remember to keep that dog away from the table!' Scolded the old lady, and she placed a long cool glass of lemonade on the table for James.

'OK' replied James, quickly flicking a piece of Pizza into Skips mouth. He winked to the dog as grandma left the kitchen.

Skip the dog licked his mouth with satisfaction, and then looked upward toward rapidly flickering images that had cast shadows all around the room.

## James - A Legend And The Old Dusty Box.

A small TV set that grandpa had recently fixed to the kitchen wall played cartoons. These were the shows that James had always liked best to watch as he ate, while Skip also looked on. But the dog had now become much more interested in other things.

Skip edged slowly, and ever forward toward the kitchen table. With his nose twitching and smelling food, Skip explored the air and accidentally knocked the TV remote control from the table edge. The small machine dutifully changed over a channel at it hit the floor with a thud.

'Oh heck!' James groaned to himself. 'Not that news channel - I hate that.' He picked up the remote control and switched back to the cartoons. 'That is much better' the boy said to himself.

While James supped from his glass of lemonade the news channel suddenly flicked back on. James looked at Skip, but the dog was nowhere near the remote control. As he watched and was just about to change the channel again, James went kind of cold inside, experiencing a strange feeling that seemed to freeze his whole body solid.

'Plane is missing,' the words from a news reader hit James hard and he could not move.

'Mum – Dad -' he muttered to himself, the memories of his past flooding back. The news itself changed quickly to other events of strife and bad things that are always happening around the world, but James was by now staring blankly toward the TV screen.

Grandpa appeared swiftly from the living room after hearing the news readers first words, and he quickly flicked the channel over at random.

'OK young-un?' Enquired the old man, as a nature programme jolted James back to reality.

'Yes... I guess,' James could hardly speak the words.

'Still miss them and always will' said grandpa, looking toward the happy family picture of James and his parents who were smiling from the wall.

'Yes' replied James, staring blankly down at his half eaten pizza. 'But why do all these bad things have to happen everywhere grandpa?'

'Don't rightly know' answered the old man, sitting down at the kitchen table. 'But it don't do to think about such things like that now.' He looked James in the eye, then looked up at the TV. 'Where is that happy smile of yours gone?' Grandpa then pointed toward a Penguin that was tottering around on the nature documentary. 'See that critter!' he said with a grin. 'Think he worries himself about such things?'

'No grandpa, of course not' smiled James.

'Well now, you could be wrong about that' replied the old man smiling back.

'What do you mean grandpa?' Asked James.

Grandpa lent forward, his voice gentle and hushed... 'Let me tell you a strange tale from my old exploring days, all about a critter legend.'

## James - A Legend And The Old Dusty Box.

The old man leant back in his chair and folded his arms. His mind became engrossed in memories, as he now entered his full flow story telling mode.

'Many many years ago, when I was trapped all alone in the barren wastes of the snow bound Antarctic, I was saved by an old Eskimo who seemed to appear from nowhere. This feller put me on a sleigh and took me many many miles to an old derelict building made from snow.'

James lent on his hand, elbow heavy against the table top.

'Yes grandpa' he sighed, as by now James was well used to the old man's far fetched fables from his exploration days.

Grandpa pointed toward another penguin that was on the TV screen, and he slowly continued his story as the nature programme came to an end.

'That old Eskimo feller told me a strange tale, a legend in fact, of how critters like that are making a documentary of our human race, much like we humans make of critters. But they have made it throughout all of Time!'

'Yes grandpa' James feigned interest. 'I really hope this is better than last weeks Alligator wrestling in the Amazon story' he thought, slowly reaching over and taking another sup from the rapidly dwindling lemonade supply which was happily bubbling from within his glass.

As Skip settled down at grandpa's feet, the old man became even more eager to tell the tale to his grandson.

'It was by now the middle of the night' Grandpa stared ahead as if visualising the scene. 'That old Eskimo had patched up the doorway with snow, and it was kind of warm inside, like a big igloo. But creepy. All kinds of strange sounds were occurring outside as a big old blizzard, in all it's fury, swept by the derelict building and high over the huge mountain range standing behind it.' The old man seemed to shiver. 'Yes sir! - Heard nothing like it in all my born days! Was as afraid as afraid can be.'

Grandpa leant forward onto the table top, feeling quite spooked as he remembered the past, and the old man sensed the hairs stand upright on the back of his neck.

'Was the Old Eskimo afraid too grandpa?' James asked, observing the old man's sincerity.

'Oh yes! - Terrified!' Grandpa replied, looking directly into the eyes of James.

The boy shuddered, feeling a little spooked himself as he listened to his old grandfather continue his strange tale.

'That old Eskimo thought that end of the world itself had come! - He plain howled that the Dark Force had released itself onto the planet, and on all of us human folks!' Grandpa raised his bushy eye brows, and then said quite softly.

'I managed to settle him down some, and that's when he told me the ancient Eskimo legend.' The old man settled back in his chair again and composed himself. 'It runs like this young feller, well least wise, the way that I can remember it from so long ago anyhow.'

## James - A Legend And The Old Dusty Box.

Grandpa folded his arms, reflecting deeply on the past as he started to speak.

'The ancient Eskimo legend says that it all started long before Time itself was born, way back, when there was nothing. And by that young feller I do mean nothing at all. Only a dark and empty, but somehow living Evil Void filled all of space. There were no planets, no stars, no people, not a thing was in creation at all.' The old man rubbed his chin thoughtfully, and spoke softly.

'But then the good and great Spirit Of Peace And Light that has always, and will always exist, did not rightly favour this state of affairs. This spirit brought about the very light of creation that was to shatter that Dark Void and it's hold on all things.'

'Yes sir-re!' Exclaimed grandpa. 'The Great Spirit created Time, all the universe, planets, stars, all that kind of stuff. It also created mankind, allowing all us people folks to slowly evolve throughout Time so that we could appreciate all that the Great Spirit had done with creation if we had a mind too.'

James again sipped more lemonade, listening attentively while watching the bottom of his glass approach from beyond the remaining drink. Skip, for his part, fell sound asleep by the boys legs.

'Also, in the beginning' continued grandpa. 'The Four Keys Of Time were created. These are the 'Past Key', that is the hour hand on any clock. The 'Present Key', that is the minute hand on any clock, and the 'Future Key', that is the second hand on any clock. And all these precious keys of Time, are held together by a creature called 'The Master Of The Four keys of Time'. Which is a kind of cute, small little round spot feller, going by the name of Tick Tock Fotherington Splotch.'

'Well I suppose this certainly beats the Amazon adventure story' thought James to himself, never ceasing to be amazed at his grandfather's tall stories.

'But that is only three keys grandpa' noted James. 'There is nothing else on the clock.'

'Yes sir, I said the same thing' replied the old man, rubbing his chin thoughtfully. 'But that Eskimo told me that a fourth key was created, and is the most important one of all. But it is not a key that all people may see on a clock face.' The old man paused for a second and smiled. 'The fourth key, is known as the 'Key To Peace'.'

'What exactly is that grandpa?' Asked James, now feeling a little surprised at his own interest in one of grandfather's tall tales.

'Well - I will tell you' said grandpa, gently pushing a deep sleeping Skip from his feet and those of James.

'That legend says that at the dawn of all Time a final symbol was created, one that everyone, big and small, low and mighty, from one end of this big old Earth to the other, would all understand to mean Peace and friendship. Well heck, the thing was even built directly into people themselves, so that it could flow natural like, from within all folks.'

## James - A Legend And The Old Dusty Box.

Grandpa out stretched his feet, pushing Skip even further away. The dog dutifully rolled over, still fast asleep.

'Yes, but grandpa' James then asked. 'What sort of key is it, there are only three hands of Time on a clock, and you have said all of those?'

'Well -' answered grandpa. 'It is both a symbol and a Peace key. The kind of thing that stares you in the face, but what most people don't really take much notice of, especially these days.'

The old man looked James directly in the eye, a serious expression on his wrinkly face.

'The symbol is just that plain old smile of happiness.' He laughed, then smiled himself. 'See!' He continued, pointing to his mouth. 'Simple, Buddy! - That is the fourth key.'

'Oh -' huffed James, who was not really sure if he was disappointed or not by this answer. Somehow he was expecting something that was far more grand and complicated than a smile. But the boy really could not help automatically smiling back at grandpa, as the old man had said, it came 'natural like, from within'.

'Now then,' his grandfather had not quite finished the story, and was still eager to tell it. 'To keep check on what mankind does with his Time, a club of strange critters was created, and these creatures live deep in the depths of Earth's snow covered wastes. The function given of these critters, is to make a documentary of things that go on throughout all of Time.'

The old man went thoughtful again and he stared hard at the ceiling, leaning back in his chair. 'Legend says, these things are a really strange kind of looking creature, penguin like things, and they can speak too!'

'Talking penguins -' James said it aloud quite sarcastically, but he didn't really mean too.

'No no, not penguins' said grandpa. 'Something, kind of different altogether. The legend says that these talking critters keep an eye on the Peace Key for The Master Of The Four Keys Of Time, and when it goes missing now and again, which it does, they can then collect their pieces of documentary. It also says, that the bad folks records, along with the good, these critters keep in a kind of celestial safe, so that the Evil Dark Void can't get it's hands on them.'

'So what is that Dark Void thing grandpa?' Asked James, feeling a little confused. 'How can something like that be alive?'

'Well now' replied grandpa quietly. 'It is plain to see that both dark and light, good and Evil, have always existed side by side, always have, always will. But when Time itself and the goodness of creation was actually made, that old Dark Void was pushed to the back of the clock of creation for eternity, to always remain in the shadows, and never be released again.'

'So, what would happen if it was released grandpa?' Asked James, taking a large bite from his pizza.

## James - A Legend And The Old Dusty Box.

'Well that is what made the old Eskimo so afraid' said the old man, gently rubbing his chin, with his mind deep in thought.

'If that Dark Void gets it's Evil hands on those records, it will release all the spirit power of bad folks and their deeds that have been made throughout History. Then that Evil force would use this bad spirit power, to free itself from the shadow of the back of every clock, and then erase all of creation, stopping all of Time itself.'

Grandpa picked up a now empty plate, as James washed the last of his pizza down with some last drops of lemonade.

'I never got to hear any more of the old Eskimos story after that though' he said sadly, and grandpa walked toward the sink and proceeded to wash the dirty plate.

After a moment of awkward silence, the old man quickly placed a now clean plate on the draining board, adding. 'I fell fast asleep, as I was plain tired out. By morning the blizzard had passed, and I was woken by the cold of an open doorway. The old Eskimo had gone and didn't even say goodbye. Too afraid to hang around I suppose?'

While Skip moaned in his sleep, and James patted the dog affectionately on the head, grandpa sat back at the table. The old man contemplated further.

'Still, it's a funny kind of way to get a front door?'

'What -' James was a little taken aback by his grandfathers statement. 'What do you mean by that grandpa?' He asked inquisitively.

His grandfather proceeded to finish his story.

'Well now, as I went out-side there was hide nor hare of that old Eskimo to be seen.'

Grandpa sat back in the chair and folded his arms. 'But may-be the strangest site in the barren snow bound wastes that anyone had ever saw before!'

James lent forward across the table, his elbows resting hard onto the table top, and with cupped hands supporting his chin while he listened attentively.

'There, lying on the snow out-side' said grandfather. 'Was that old front door. The door we now use on our own house that has a big red centre smiling door knocker. Strange, but it was just lying there, complete with lock and key, resting on top of a long, very old box.'

'Who left the door there?' Enquired James... 'Maybe it was the Eskimo.'

'I really have no idea' huffed grandpa. 'But I sure didn't get Time to think about it! - Just then a big old Polar Bear happened to pass by, a huge blood-thirsty thing. In fact, the biggest thing I ever saw running wild.'

'So what did you do grandpa?' James was just itching for one of the old man's exciting escape stories.

'Well... I saw that just past that old derelict building was a really fear-some slope. It was running downhill for as far as the eye could see, and I had to think fast, very very fast!'

## James - A Legend And The Old Dusty Box.

The old man recalled the scene from long ago, visualising it in his head.

'So I pulled that ancient door toward the edge of the slope. Slung that long old box on top to rest my back. And, hanging on to the door-knocker, pushed all kit and caboodle over the edge as the huge Polar Bear made a bee-line straight for me.'

Grandpa shook his head, remembering fondly his experiences.

'Never went so far and so fast. Heck knows how far I went down that slope, but I quickly lost that following Polar bear though. After some hour or so, I ended up a real long way off, only stopping after crashing into another expedition. They were as surprised to see me, as I was thankful of seeing them. Took the door home as a souvenir.'

'What was in the box?' Asked James, impressed by his grandfathers vivid imagination.

'I don't know' answered grandpa, holding his hands up as if he was resting something on each palm. 'Broke three whole drill bits trying to open it when I got back.'

Just then grandma had had quite enough, and she entered the kitchen.

'Stop filling that boys head with foolish nonsense!' She said impatiently, heading quickly for the sink. Grandma picked up a drying cloth and wiped the plate clean of moisture.

A booming knock suddenly thundered from the front door. It was a noise so loud that it rattled the now empty lemonade glass of James, causing it to topple forward and roll across the kitchen table.

Skip, ever alert, opened one eye, huffed, then went back to sleep.

'OK - OK' called out grandpa, heading to answer the door. 'No more stories.' The old man winked at James while he past.

'Not right now, any-how' he whispered, so James could hear.

'I really don't know where you get all those ridiculous notions from' huffed grandma, putting the plate back into storage.

'All right honey?' She asked, smiling at James.

'Yes, thanks grandma' replied James, and he smiled right back.

Grandpa opened the front door just as the smiley mouth shaped door knocker boomed loudly again. The ancient door creaked open, but the doorstep was empty. He looked back and forth, but there was no one on the path or on the street.

The old man shut the door gently, and then bent down to examine with his finger a very small hand print barely visible to the human eye, which was embedded in the paint at the bottom of the doors edge.

'Ridiculous notions! - Huh!' He said to himself... 'There's stranger things to be had in creation, than most folks give credit for.'

## James - A Legend And The Old Dusty Box.

Normally on a Friday after school, James along with friends Rebecca and Todd would be out-side playing. But this particular weekend grandma had arranged with both their parents to hold a three house garage sale, to clear out all those old things that they no longer needed any more.

Grandma felt that James would benefit from an extra play room, and the old attic at the top of the wooden staircase had not been in use for some years, having been used as just an extra storage area. Because it had amassed all sorts of junk through the years, and with grandpa's agreement, it was now decided that the Time was right for the room to be cleared out and painted.

So, just as the other kids were doing, helping their parents gather things together that Friday after tea Time. James was going to help grandpa sort through, and then move all the things from the attic that were to be sold, down-stairs into the large garage area at the side of the house.

'Well, I guess we have got a fair old task ahead' said grandpa, pushing open the attic door.

'Phew!' He exclaimed, as the musty odour of a long enclosed and forgotten room licked his nostrils, 'better open the window!'

Grandpa moved past a pile of boxes and pulled up the window sash to it's full opening point.

'Now then, where to start?' He huffed, beckoning James into the room.

'Wow!' Exclaimed James, examining the many cardboard boxes and huge array of junk that seemed to fill every part of the large room.

'We sure have a lot of stuff to move grandpa' he said, scratching his head in wonder.

'Yes sir-re, sure thing!' Replied the old man, peering into a box that he had just opened. 'A lot of this stuff came from my travelling days.' He picked up and examined an old ice pick that was sticking out from the box top.

'Maybe not a lot of call for some of this stuff round here though' said grandpa quickly putting it back. 'Suppose some of it can head straight to the junk-yard!'

James held up a pair of old skies that had been propped up against the wall behind the attic door. 'How about these?'

'Good grief!' Exclaimed grandpa, eyeing the skies nostalgically, 'I Had forgotten all about those.' He tapped one of the skies on the bare wooden floor and laughed. 'Shame there's no snow in these part's eh? - But I expect that grandma wouldn't let me use them these days anyhow?'

The old man pushed two of the boxes to one side, and peered intently toward the object laying hidden behind them.

'Well what do we have here!' He cried out in excitement.

James stood by the side of his grandfather, leaning sideways to look at what grandpa had found.

'See, told you that story was true' smiled the old man. 'There is the box that was propping up that old front door all those years ago!'

## James - A Legend And The Old Dusty Box.

James looked down and there, on the floor next to the wall, he saw a long, old and very, very, very, dusty box.

Grandpa bent down and picked it up.

'Pity we can't open it' he said, holding up the long chest shape box for James to see.

James peered at the strange object with interest. A film of fine dust blanketing the box top seemed to shimmer, bathing itself in a beam of brilliant golden light that cascaded in through the open window. It gently tempted a sneeze from their nostrils as it shone and flickered.

'Can't abide dust!' Grandpa coughed, and he blew the dust away with a big, forceful breath.

James rubbed his eyes as this fine dust swirled frantically in the beam of golden, streaming light. And, as he turned his head toward the wall where the beam of light had hit, just for a second, while his eyes were clearing. James thought he saw the shadow of a penguin reflected onto the boxes of junk stacked in front of him. 'No, it can't be?' He said to himself quietly.

'Well, here we are!' Grandpa put the box triumphantly on the ground right in front of James.

James bent down and examined the object, his eyes still watering. There was he noted, a plain oblong mirror embedded in the intricately carved swirling effect lid. A lock on the side of the equally carved base. But it was the riddle, etched on the long lid, below the mirror, which stood out and jumped toward the eyes of James. He repeated the words aloud.

***Any fool can frown at me***
***Any person can happy be***
***Stop think twice before a key you turn***
***For Time and Peace you have to learn***

'What do you suppose that means?' James asked the old man.

'No idea' replied grandpa, standing up. 'But I do know that if that things made of wood, it's the toughest I ever saw. Can't drill it, or cut it, with well, it seems like anything.' Grandpa looked around the room and sighed. 'Come on young-un, let's get a move on. There is a whole heap of work to be done yet.'

'OK grandpa' agreed James picking up the old dusty box, and he put it behind the attic door out of the way. 'Mind if we keep that box' he asked hopefully.

'Sure thing! If you want too,' grandpa nodded. 'But I don't rightly see what use is a box that you can't open. Still if you want to hold on to it, that's OK.'

'Gee thanks!' Cried James... 'Maybe one day, we can solve that riddle?'

'Ha!' Laughed grandpa. 'If anyone will solve it, I guess it will be you.' The old man gave James a hug. 'Come on, let's get these things shifted!'

## James - A Legend And The Old Dusty Box.

Later that night James was totally exhausted. He had climbed the stairs to the attic many, many Times and taken what seemed to be at least a hundred boxes down to the garage, or so it seemed, to his aching limbs. He lay there in bed pondering his bodily aches and pains, but was happy.

Pulling the warm blanket closer to his chin, James reflected on how all the many piles of Junk had been sorted and how the attic was now cleared, ready for re-painting and transformation into his new playroom.

James sighed, and his deep brown eyes grew more heavy and sleepy, with the pillow feeling as soft to his head as he imagined a fluffy cloud would be to lay upon.

Comfortably pressing his head deeper into this pillow, his tired eyes drifted lazily across the bedroom wall slowly meandering past the various sized posters of pop stars and skateboarders, family pictures, the toys on shelves. They eventually came to rest toward a comforting and soft glow of light which was emanating gently from a large globe of the world, that was etched with a crazy paving of many maps, and resting on a table in the bedroom corner.

Tonight, somehow, he noticed that the bland white Arctic and Antarctic regions at the top and bottom of the ball seemed to glow far more brightly than ever before in the dimly lit room.

James had never needed a night-light before. But ever since his parent's aircraft had disappeared in the Bermuda triangle some six months ago while they were taking photographs for a magazine on strange phenomena, he had felt somewhat insecure in the darkness. So now and again to aid a restful night, James much preferred to sleep with the soft comforting glow of this global sphere and it's light, that reflected most gently around his bed-room.

Tonight, with grandpa's strange story of a legend still rolling around his head, James blinked and slowly shut his very tired eyes.

He was not really sure how long it had been, but it was the ever gradually increasing sound of a strange howling wind which awoke James. As his eyes slowly opened, he noticed that the globe in the corner of the room was turning anti-clockwise. This blue ball was revolving unaided, very slowly backwards.

The crazy paved maps that were printed all around this world globe gradually altered formation before him and as the sphere gathered speed, thin borders changed much more quickly to those of past empires and countries that had once existed in Time. The more James eyes grew awake, the more the maps were becoming a frantic, ever altering jumble.

Many names that were etched into the various countries seemed to change now with every second that passed, and with each change the strange wind howled louder and louder. The world sphere span wildly around and around, until the very structure of the landmasses and continents that were indicated upon it finally slid to the formations that had been created many millions of years ago, long before any life had existed on planet Earth.

## James - A Legend And The Old Dusty Box.

James inexplicably thought that he could hear the familiar sound of his mother's voice, then that of his father chillingly reverberate within the howling wind that was by now travelling past his head and was whirling around the room.

'J-a-m-e-s' both the voices slowly whispered his name in anguish, and laying in his bed, James shook with a cold fear.

Finally, after a matter of seconds but what seemed an age. With an almighty crash, the blue globe exploded into countless fragments of dotted light that emulated the stars within a night sky.

James looked on his body frozen, his eyes witnessing in reverse the very dawn of creation along with the birth of endless galaxies of light that now whirled around the space where the small globe had been.

In the very centre of this light the form of a swirling black hole grew larger and larger until, with an ear shattering explosion, a darkness engulfed all of the endless twinkling lights.

James was startled, he sat quickly upright and the whole room plunged into darkness. He sat there, totally stunned.

There was a gentle scratching at the bedroom door and it opened slowly. Skip entered with nose twitching and the globe illuminated the room once more with it's soft light. James looked around the bedroom and everything was exactly as it had been before he went to bed..

'Wow! - Now that's what I call a bad dream' he whispered quietly, beckoning the dog to lie with him on the bed.

Skip snuggled down but James was by now wide awake. Thinking deeply for a few moments, James patted Skip on the head.

'Wait here boy! - I have got something that I have to do' he whispered, and the boy left his bed then put on his slippers and dressing-gown.

'I wonder...' James moved toward the globe and picked up his front door key which was resting on the table in front of it. Putting this shiny golden key in his pocket, he then very quietly left the bedroom and headed up the creaky wooden staircase toward the attic.

As James climbed the wooden staircase and approached the attic door, he could see an oblong light silhouetting the frame.

'Must have left the light on' he mused to himself, and James slowly pushed open the creaking door, trying not to wake anyone as he entered the room.

Inside, the room was empty, the shade surrounding a single gently swinging light bulb reflecting spooky shadows into distant corners.

James shut the door most carefully so as not to wake grandma and grandpa. Then he slowly picked up the old dusty box and moved to the centre of the attic, placing the long box onto the floor again directly beneath the single, brilliant light bulb.

James sat on the floor, drawing the golden front door key from his pocket.

## James - A Legend And The Old Dusty Box.

'Any fool can frown at me. Any person can happy be. Stop think twice before a key you turn. For Time and Peace you have to learn.'

James repeated this peculiar riddle in his head for a few moments as he examined the front door key thoughtfully.

'Well, no key will normally open two locks' he said to himself. 'But this is the only key that I can think of that you have to turn twice to open anything.'

James pushed the glistening key into the lock of the long dusty box, and to his surprise it fitted snugly.

'Here goes' said James quietly. He turned the key twice, but as it reached the stopping point, the key twisted back against his fingers all of it's own accord.

'Wait a minute!' Thought James, again pondering the riddle. 'Any fool can frown at me. Any person can happy be.'

James smiled, looking directly into the mirror embedded into the box lid, and then at the same Time, he again turned the key twice.

The lock clicked, and the box lid sprang wide open releasing a whooshing sound. James peered inside.

There he found an old cloth covering the contents. James lifted it up, and his eyes surged with surprise as he stared at the hidden objects beneath.

'I do declare!' He said to himself. James put both hands into the old dusty box and slowly lifted out a plain old skateboard.

'Huh?' James scratched his head in wonder. Then he noticed that a picture of the smiling mouth shaped front door knocker was etched into the top of the board. 'Strange stuff!' He thought.

Turning the skateboard over, James looked at the writing that he found inscribed beneath it.

'Cartoon Buddy Club Recorder Board Mark 3 - Non planetary use of this transportation Mark 3 device will invalidate the guarantee.'

James shook his head, trying to think what this could mean. He placed the skateboard on the floor, and again peered into the box.

Picking up the remaining contents, he was again surprised and feeling a little confused.

'An empty note book and pencil' he said aloud.

Somehow James felt that he should have been disappointed by the plain and strange contents. But then again he had managed to open this box, and the skateboard was in far better condition than his own. He slipped the notebook and pencil into his dressing-gown pocket.

'I will take this to the skateboard to the park tomorrow' he said to himself.

James put the skateboard under his arm, stood up and headed back to the bedroom.

'Better tell grandpa about opening the box tomorrow morning.' James flicked off the light-switch as he left the attic, and gently closed the door behind him.

## James - A Legend And The Old Dusty Box.

Descending the creaky wooden staircase back to his bedroom James not only felt the notebook and pencil to be quite heavy in his pocket, but also the skateboard very awkward to carry. However, he managed to reach his bedroom without waking anyone and was feeling quite glad about that.

Skip lifted his tired head as James entered the bedroom, and the dog sloped off the bed to see what he was carrying.

James put the long skateboard gently onto the floor of his bedroom, and he slipped the notebook and pencil from his pocket, placing both of these items along with the front door key, onto the table top in front of his globe.

'Shush boy' whispered James, as Skip sniffed intently, then pawed the skateboard inquisitively.

James now felt himself to be thirsty, the dusty box had dried both his throat and nose.

'Quiet now,' he whispered to Skip, smoothing the dog. 'Shush while I go get a drink.'

James left the bedroom while Skip sniffed with his wet nose, the front door knocker picture etched into the skateboard's top. A few moments later the dog playfully pawed the skateboard again, but got a shock.

'Get lost fur ball -' the door knocker etching sprang into a life of it's own, with it's large red centre becoming a nose that revolved in irritation, and the curved knocker a mouth that twisted in rebuke. 'How would you like it, if I mess with you, Buddy!' It added with contempt.

Skip stood back three steps in amazement and as he did so, the skateboard flipped over into the air flying right past Skips head. Continuing it's trajectory, the skateboard flew around in a circle and most, most gently, performed a literal nose-grind trick as it travelled down the dogs own nose.

Skip howled and ran from the room, passing James who was returning with his glass of water.

'Shush!' Insisted James, holding his finger to his mouth... 'Quiet boy!'

James watched Skip run down stairs to the safety of his basket.

'Had a bad dream too huh?' James shook his head as he quietly entered his bedroom.

Stopping beside his bed, he looked down and pushed the skateboard with his foot. James watched it roll gently backwards to where he had first left it, and then the boy took a sup of cold water. After placing the glass down onto his bedside table, James rolled into bed by now already more than half asleep.

He quickly slipped off into a gentle dreamland as he pulled the warm blanket further up toward his chin.

'Goodnight Buddy!' Quietly whispered the strange smiling mouth door knocker shape that was etched onto the skateboard top.

'Goodnight grandpa' whispered James in a sleepy automatic reply, not really realising who had said it.

## *James - The Skate Park.*

Over breakfast, James had just finished explaining how he had managed to open the old dusty box to grandpa.

The old man slowly took another sip of coffee from a steaming mug and pondered quietly the strange, but rather plain contents of the old dusty box which lay open on the table in front of him.

Behind grandpa two smiling faces appeared behind small, clear glass panes that were set in a pair of large French doors leading out to the garden.

A girl with flowing blonde hair tapped the window in front of her to gain the attention of James.

'It's Todd and Rebecca!' James called out, interrupting grandpa's train of thought. Then he waved to his friends.

Grandpa swivelled sideways in his chair, coffee cup still in hand.

'Come on in!' He said, beckoning to the children, grandpa leant forward to unlock, then pull the French doors open. 'A good bright and sunny day today for a garage sale!'

'Sure thing!' Todd replied, moving the skateboard he was carrying very carefully past grandpa and the long kitchen table.

'A great day for some skateboarding too!' Beamed Rebecca, holding her own skateboard forward and spinning the wheels with her hand as she passed the old man.

'I bet you can whoop both these guys on that thing?' Laughed grandpa. 'Don't you reckon so too Todd?'

Todd smiled as grandpa looked directly at him, because he really knew that she could.

'Maybe, sometimes' he squirmed.

'What is that?' Asked Rebecca looking toward the dusty old box and the strangely etched skateboard that lay inside it. 'Kind of old things aren't they?'

'Yes' replied James, and he started to tell his friends of the events of the previous evening, especially how he had managed to open the old dusty box.

After a short while grandma interrupted his tale, but James had just about finished anyway.

'Please take that old piece of junk off the table, and I will fix you kids some breakfast if you want some' said the old woman, putting a glass of orange juice in front of James.

'Thanks!' Todd and Rebecca spoke in unison.

'But we have already eaten at Rebecca's house as we were both up very early this morning' Todd finished, what Rebecca was also thinking and about to say.

There was a loud, booming knock at the front door and grandma left the room to answer it.

James grinned toward his friend, teasing him just a little bit.

'Might be best to get practising very early every day if you want to have any chance of winning a competition on your skateboard Todd.'

## James - The Skate Park.

Todd huffed, thinking of how he could tease James back. Then he grinned, and pointed to the skateboard inside the old dusty box.

'Well at least I don't suppose that old thing in your box will beat my board for speed!' He sneered in jest. 'Make sure you oil that old piece of junk before you use it, or it may fall apart!'

Everyone around the table laughed together and their voices echoed around the room. However, a short and particularly loud sound interrupted their voices.

It almost sounded like someone 'blowing a raspberry' or even, someone breaking wind in an altogether crude and disgusting manor at the breakfast table.

The voices suddenly hushed and everyone looked at each other, each not quite knowing what to say. After a few embarrassed moments James decided to break the ice.

'Let's get to the skate park then, if that is OK with you grandpa.'

Yes, yes, OK' replied grandpa feeling a little lost for words, which was very unlike him.

James picked up the old dusty box, and carried it out onto the patio. He put it down and removed the ancient skateboard from inside it. James noted that strangely, the smile etched into the skateboard top seemed to be smiling just a little bit more than it had been before.

'Just my imagination' he thought to himself.

'It was not me!' Todd whispered as he passed James, and headed for the back garden gate.

'Probably was' whispered a following Rebecca, and she winked to James.

Grandpa stood in the open doorway and waved goodbye. Contemplating as he watched the three children leave his garden and enter the street beyond, the old man muttered to himself.

'Could have sworn that sound came from that old smiley skateboard.'

Grandmother focussed his attention again. She entered the room in an irate mood.

'No one there again!' She said angrily.

'A strange thing' thought grandpa aloud.

'What is strange?' Asked grandma, starting to clear up the dirty dishes.

'Strange things that may be in the wind my dear!' Laughed grandpa.

'Crazy old fool' muttered grandma, and she marched past the old man who quickly took the opportunity to peck her on the cheek.

'I will help you with these dishes my dear' grandpa grinned, and he moved toward the open window to watch a gust of wind flick some fallen leaves into the air, very near to where the old dusty box lay.

The old man licked a finger, then pointed it to the sky.

'No breeze at all?' He shook his head thoughtfully, and helping grandma with the dishes he muttered, 'strange things may indeed be in the wind?'

## James - The Skate Park.

Outside the garden gate a long, flat, very quiet street awaited the three children. They all put on their helmets and protective pads, then laid their skateboard's, in Time honoured fashion, onto the concrete floor.

'Ready!' Todd looked at Rebecca who stood in between him and James.

'Steady!' All three children adjusted their feet position, so as to give them a good starting point.

'Go!' Todd pushed down hard onto the floor, sending his skateboard rolling speedily down the long concrete pavement.

James and Rebecca started almost as quickly, and all three headed toward the skate park that was situated just around the corner of this block.

'Come on!' Shouted Rebecca to both the boys, as she reached the park gate first.

Todd came next and panted, being a little out of breath when he stopped his skateboard next to the happy Rebecca.

'It must be the heat this morning' said Todd, trying to make an explanation for not beating her to the gate. But Todd was really quite satisfied that he had beaten James, as normally it was he that was last at the finishing post.

James rolled to a stop at the gate and met a sarcastic grin from Todd.

'See, told you that old thing was junk!' Exclaimed Todd. He opened a heavy, creaking gate, to let both Rebecca and James into the park. 'Don't try any fancy tricks dude, that thing may fall apart!'

James let Rebecca through the gate first.

'It just seemed to have a mind of it's own' said James puzzled. 'Every Time my foot went near the nose and smiley mouth picture the board kind of moved away all on it's own.'

'Whoo!' Todd held his hands up in a spooky fashion. 'It seems dusty old junk does not want it's little old face stepped on' he continued in his best sarcastic voice.

'Yeah - Right' replied James, moving through the open doorway.

Todd gave out a little cry of annoyance as the old skateboard James was riding on suddenly veered quickly toward him, and knocked his own skate board out into the middle of the park.

'What's the game?' He cried, and glared at James.

'Told you!' Replied James, struggling for control of the skateboard. 'It kind of moved all by itself.'

'Don't be silly boys!' Rebecca was loosing patience. 'Let's get onto the ramps before anyone else.'

'Yeah - OK' answered Todd and James both nodding, knowing that the place could be full at any Time after breakfast.

Todd regained his skateboard, then the children headed for the biggest ramp and clambered to the top, board's under their arms.

## James - The Skate Park.

Rebecca bagged the first try and rolled down the steep ramp. Her skateboard gathered speed and she shot up the opposite ramp flying quite high into the air. She brought the front end of her skateboard upward to meet her hand and completed a perfect '180 Indy' stunt. With a grin of satisfaction she rolled back up the ramp to once more stand next to the boys.

'Beat that!' She called happily.

Todd let James go next. James hoped that the old skateboard would not let him down, and he replicated the stunt that Rebecca had just performed.

The old skateboard shot down the ramp, then up the next, soaring much higher than Rebecca's had done into the clear blue sky.

Strangely, the smiley face imprinted on the skateboard top looked as if it was smiling much more than normal to Todd who followed it's path high into the air and back.

'But it can't be?' Todd said quietly to himself.

'Come on then, your turn!' James suddenly shouted to Todd as he returned back up the ramp. 'Not bad for a piece of old junk!'

Todd positioned himself and then launched his own skateboard down the ramp. Just as he reached the base of the opposite ramp, a large figure smashed into him and knocked him clean off his skateboard onto the floor.

'Time to get off my ramp's squirt!' The school bully's face was instantly recognisable to Todd as he lifted his pounding head from the floor.

'Oh no, it's 'Crusher' Grime!' Exclaimed Todd, feeling his heart sink. But he felt thankful that he was wearing all his protective padding, as very suddenly he thought he may be needing it.

Rebecca looked down at the unfolding scene from the top ramp.

'What shall we do now?' She asked, turning to James and feeling worried.

Below James and Rebecca 'Crusher' Grime picked up Todd's skateboard and threw it angrily across the park.

'That's not a deck!' He laughed menacingly. 'This is a deck!'

Grime held up his skateboard and proudly displayed the symbol of a skull and crossbones that he had painted onto the dark surface.

'Er – Yes - Nice board' Todd tried to pacify the bully who was showing off in front of his friends who were all standing by the park gate.

Todd tried to get to his feet, but was knocked down again by the large hands of 'Crusher Grime'.

'We ain't gonna stand for that, big boy!' A loud voice made both James and Rebecca turn around. But they were the only ones at the ramp top.

From the floor 'Crusher' Grime looked up at them and snarled.

'You ain't gonna stand for what Squirt?'

'Bullying is for wimps who ain't got no brains at all' came an instant, and very firm reply from the ramp top.

James and Rebecca looked at each other, mystified.

## James - The Skate Park.

Then they both looked down at the old skateboard that James was standing on, while this unknown voice continued.

'You have got no brains at all Buddy!'

'That came from your skateboard!' Exclaimed Rebecca, looking downward at the smiley mouth painted onto it's top.

James stared hard toward the smiley mouth. Then gasped as it moved and said with disdain.

'It is rude to stare Buddy!'

'What the...' But James had no more Time to speak. 'Crusher' Grime made a move toward the ramp, his anger quite apparent and his face flushed with rage.

'Time to squash squirts!' Called out 'Crusher'.

James looked up to see the large boy approaching. He tried to move, but his feet seemed glued tight to the top of the old skateboard.

'Run!' Shouted Todd, getting up from the floor.

But James could not move his feet to run anywhere. Instead, the ancient skateboard rolled forward defiantly to the ramp edge.

'Hold onto your hat!' Called out the smiley mouth. Then with a start, the old skateboard shot forward to meet 'Crusher' Grime who was by now at the ramp bottom.

'Ah!' Shouted James leaning backwards, but remaining upright on the old skateboard as it's speed and force of movement took him completely by surprise.

'James!' Rebecca's concerned voice quickly trailed into the distance while a howling wind rushed past the ears of James. Both he and the old skateboard hurtled down the very steep ramp at break neck speed.

'I can't look!' Exclaimed Todd, but who looked anyway when he reached the park exit gate. 'James must have gone nut's to take on Grime.'

In a matter of seconds the old skateboard with James aboard, and the approaching 'Crusher' Grime, would meet with a huge crash at the ramp bottom. At least, that is what everyone who was watching James and Crusher on the ramp thought would happen.

'Crusher' Grime quickly pushed his ample shoulders forward ready to 'bounce' James from his skateboard.

The school bully, who his football coach had nicknamed 'The Wall' (i.e. Tall, well built, and quite dense) then snarled and lunged toward James.

At the exact moment of potential contact the old skateboard twisted sharply to the side. So did James, who felt quite sick when he twisted with such speed that Crusher Grime missed both him, and his skateboard by an inch.

'Ouch!' Cried out 'Crusher', slamming painfully into the wooden ramp and then sliding down it, to crumple into a heap on the floor.

'Good call!' Shouted Todd from the park exit, assuming James had made the manoeuvre himself and was in total control of the board.

## James - The Skate Park.

Reaching the top of the opposite ramp at great speed, the old skateboard launched itself and James high into the air.

'I can help you - But you have got to stand up for yourself Buddy!' The smiley mouth on the skateboard top shouted to James. 'Try to keep your balance!'

James found keeping his balance a little difficult though, especially when the old skateboard twisted him upside down, and double span him around.

'A barrel roll with variation!' Whispered Todd. He was very impressed. 'Didn't know you could do that James.'

But then Todd noticed that the school bully had made it to his feet, and was heading to take another lunge at James when he finally returned to the ramp.

'Gonna get you now!' Called out Grime, sneering.

James tried in vain to effect some sort of control of the old skateboard, and this desire became more urgent when he noticed Grime at the ramp bottom waiting for him.

Suddenly he and the old skateboard stopped twisting, and headed upright back to earth, directly into the path of 'Crusher'.

'Heck!' James shut his eyes. It was all he could think of doing with the shape of Grime becoming nearer and nearer.

The school bully tried to 'bounce' James from the top of his board again. But this Time, the old skateboard flew straight up into the air and flipped James right over Grime's head.

With a yell, 'Crusher' smashed headlong into the wooden ramp. When he lifted his sore head, he could see his own 'friends' sniggering at the park entrance.

This was more than enough for Grime. He put his own skateboard under his foot, and chased after James who was by now heading toward the concrete section of the skate park. Crusher called after him.

'You are toast!'

James shouted to the old skateboard to Stop. But the board just carried on, and then, unexpectedly, it span around to face the school bully.

'Have a little faith Buddy' the smiley face made a big smile at James. 'You have found me in Time, and I have to help you out in Time.'

'What do you mean?' Asked James, but he really hadn't the Time for any sort of conversation for Grime came rushing toward him again.

Rebecca ran to Todd at the park exit and turned her head back toward James. 'Leave him alone!' She shouted at the bully.

But 'Crusher' would not listen, and just snarled in his usual unfriendly and angry manner. He kicked the floor to make his skateboard go even faster.

James looked on helpless as his ancient skateboard came to a complete stop.

'What are you doing!' he shouted to the smiley face, still unable to release his feet. 'Grime will rip me to bits!'

## James - The Skate Park.

'Take it easy there Buddy' replied the smiley mouth. 'Don't you know that the bad guys never win.' The skateboard waited for Grime to get closer.

Just at the split second that the school bully had reached James and grabbed him by the shoulders to stop him running away, the old skateboard James was riding on flipped upwards into the air at a very steep angle, and turned quickly upside down, with James still stuck fast.

It halted directly in the air above 'Crusher' Grime who was still holding onto the shoulders of James, but now the school bully's arms were suddenly reaching skyward.

'Huh?' Crusher looked upward at an upside down James, and in turn, James looked directly downward toward the open mouthed school bully.

'Um?' James was really lost for words. But the old skateboard was not.

'Fancy an anti-bully ride Buddy?' It said with a half grin.

Grime's jaw dropped open at the sight of a skateboard talking to him, and no words would come from his mouth as he tried to speak.

The old skate board whistled hard at 'Crusher', but equally, no sound had came from it's mouth. No sound maybe, but there did come a blast of frozen wind that stuck the hands of Grime to the shoulders of James, and the feet of Grime to his own skateboard.

The ancient smiley mouthed skateboard then hurtled forward, along with this strange sight attached, toward the tallest ramps in the park.

'Ah!' Called out 'Crusher'. 'Your board is haunted!'

Suddenly bullying did not seem such a good idea to him any more. Especially when the old skateboard hurtled up the tallest ramp, and as all three span around in a very quick Barrel roll, the old skateboard whistled again. This Time it's breath melted the ice that was holding James and Grime together.

Grime flew out of control over the tall fence surrounding the skate park and landed with a terrific splash, unhurt, but shaken, into an ornate pond. He sat there stunned, and while the fountain in the pond sprayed water into his open mouthed face, the wish to bully anyone again drained completely from him.

James landed upright at the bottom of the ramp and his old skateboard veered at break neck speed toward the park exit.

Just outside the exit gate cool dudes Jed and Rafe were sat on a steep grass bank chilling out.

'Check this scene out dude!' Said Jed, scratching his scraggly goatee beard. 'The kid just wasted 'Crusher' Grime!'

Rafe stopped reading his music magazine and put down the can of soft drink he was supping.

'Radical, man!' He replied in his laid back voice.

Peering through his small pair of dark sun-glasses, Rafe viewed the scene of James riding on the old skate board and Grime sitting very wet in the pond.

'Is it me dude' he asked. 'Or is that kid's board not touching the ground?'

## James - The Skate Park.

'Nope. No it ain't!' Replied Jed, scratching his head in wonder.

Todd and Rebecca both heard what they had said, and then both noticed that too. But before they could say anything at all about it, the old skateboard with James stuck fast on top reached them.

The skateboard soared vertically upward and over the surrounding fence.

'Where are you going?' Shouted James, balancing, or trying to balance, furiously on the skateboard's top.

'Save Time!' Replied the smiley mouth in a terse reply. 'Must save Time!'

Jed and Rafe both followed in amazement the path of James and his ancient skateboard as they cleared the high fence surrounding the skate park and flew directly above their head's.

Both leaned backwards, then quickly felt the steep grass bank on their back's while their head's lay at full tilt to follow this strange sight.

'Like totally awesome!' Exclaimed Jed. 'Gotta get one of those dude!'

Rafe still clutching his can, spilt the soft drink over his sun-glasses and face.

'Yeah. Cosmic!' He spluttered.

Todd and Rebecca just looked at each other momentarily stunned, then they quickly grabbed their own skateboard's and set of in pursuit of James.

Way up in the clear sky, when it had righted itself, James settled down somewhat on the old skateboard. But he still desperately tried to keep upright and find his balance.

'What is going on?' He shouted. 'Who, or what are you?'

'A friend!' Replied the smiley mouthed old skateboard. 'Your Buddy carriage, in Time and Space!'

The old skateboard turned sharply around the block corner, then hurtled up the long street toward the house of James.

'No Time to explain Buddy. Must save Time. It needs your help. You found the chest and opened it.'

'Chest?... Oh - You mean the old dusty box' said James.

James thought to himself and wondered if he should be a little afraid this strange skateboard character or not. But in his mind he remembered how his parents and grandpa had always told him...

'That it is better not to fear the unknown at all. But to take on adversity or adventure, head on, with a smile on your face, no matter what.'

So, while riding an old talking skateboard high in the sky. Which he had found in an old dusty box in grandpa's attic. A box that only he could open and one that had come from barren wastes of the Antarctic when grandpa was an explorer. James then decided that he would not be afraid of the situation. After all, when he looked downwards, James found that he really quite enjoyed the experience of a flying skateboard, most especially, one that had helped him deal with 'Crusher Grime'.

'So... What do you mean save Time?' James asked.

## James - The Skate Park.

'Only children save Time!' Shouted back the smiley mouth etched onto the ancient skateboard. 'Only the future, can save the future!'

This answer still did not make any sense to James. He turned his head forward again, to see the friendly shape of grandpa, in a very, very, rapidly approaching distance.

Grandpa was standing by an open garage door in front of his house. The old dusty box, James noted, was being held in his hand and Todd and Rebecca's parents were examining it.

The old skateboard had seen grandpa too.

'Please obtain the chest!' The old skateboard requested politely, it then proceeded to head directly toward this small group in front of the open garage.

Feeling a cool rush of wind whip around them, this small group looked toward the direction that the wind had emanated from and saw the approaching flying skateboard, with James riding on top. Grandpa and the others all looked quite astonished to see this strange spectacle.

The old skateboard slowed down as James flew right by grandpa.

James removed the old dusty box from the old man's arms, with a single, firm, but gentle movement from an outstretched hand.

'Thanks grandpa!' Called James while he sped past. 'It's a bit difficult to explain!'

'Gee-whiz!' Exclaimed grandpa, looking on while the old skateboard and James flew quickly past the solid white wooden door of his house.

The nose and smiley mouth door knocker smiled happily at the skateboard and James as they passed by. Or so it seemed to James, as he tucked the old dusty box under his arm.

'Please say the passwords for entry!' Requested the old skateboard to James.

'What?'... James was not sure what it meant.

'Passwords to effect portal entry please!' Replied the old skateboard.

The only words that sounded like passwords that James could really think of, were the ones that he had used to open the old dusty box the previous evening. So he decided to repeat them, and hoped that these were the ones that the old skateboard was talking about.

'Any fool can frown at me. Any person can happy be. Stop think twice before a key you turn. For Time and Peace you have to learn' said James aloud.

'Thank you James,' the smiley mouth responded instantly.

Inside the house grandma heard the smiley mouthed door knocker boom twice, the sound echoing very loudly through the house.

'Not again!' she thought. But this Time assumed it would be grandpa knocking.

'That old fool has probably locked the garage door behind him again' muttered the old woman, and she started walking to the door to let him in.

## James - The Skate Park.

Outside, the old skateboard turned sharply in the sky and then it unexpectedly thundered downwards toward the closed front door while James clung tightly onto the old dusty box.

James watched with horror as the solid door grew nearer and nearer, and he felt his throat gulp with anticipation when the rapidly approaching smiley mouthed door-knocker slammed down all of it's own accord, to send a deep vibrating boom along the long street.

A blinding flash, then a beam of brilliant light flowed from the oblong door shape. Then a whirling wind arose, with a strength so strong that the litter bin's across the street toppled over and rolled away.

The skateboard shouted to James in a most urgent voice.

'Here we go! - Hold on to your hat!'

James shut his eyes, for at the very last moment of impact the brilliant light grew far to strong to see properly.

Both he and the old skateboard hurtled into the doorway, and at the moment that they collided with this solid structure a huge roar shook the very ground. The wind that had come from beyond the doorway was instantly sucked backwards to it's origin, and the brilliant light extinguished to reveal the door just as it had been before.

Todd and Rebecca reached the doorway at the same moment as grandpa and both their parents.

They all stood in front of this solid white door with it's smiley mouthed, and red nosed door knocker in silence. Each one of them was watching and waiting while the door gradually and very slowly creaked open.

'What are you all staring at?' Asked grandma, appearing from behind the door. 'What is going on?'

Everyone that stood outside all looked at each other, and grandpa looked through the doorway past grandma's shoulder.

Skip slowly plodded toward the front door and edged past the old woman, pushing his nose forward to sniff the still outside air.

There was a strange calmness in the sky, and not a sign of James or the flying skateboard could be seen, inside or outside the house.

'My dear!' Replied grandpa slowly. 'I believe only James could explain.'

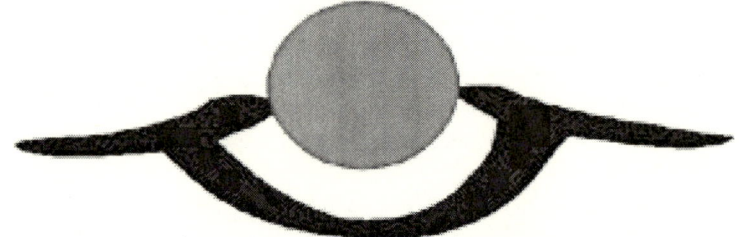

*From here you may read onward for the next individual's entry point, or just skate forwards through the book to our Living Legends Chapter.*

From the north and an old world:- An individual entry point.

## *Peter - A Legend And Old Antique Avenue.*

Peter lived in an ordinary place, in an ordinary town, in an ordinary street. This particular weekend during the Christmas holiday season, the boy had travelled from his boarding school to visit his favourite uncle Charles in London, who had recently taken lodgings in the city.

Uncle Charles was a travelling writer and performer, and he wished to show his favourite nephew the many sites of the capital to further his education.

'Look to the culture centre of the city of London and of our British Empire young man!' Ordered his uncle, waving his silver topped walking stick into the air and pointing it forward like a sword. 'Covent Garden land of the theatre, ballet and of course, market!'

Peter watched his uncle push the long black walking stick tip into a barrow laden with fruit, and then quickly flick a single red apple high into the air, catching it firmly with the fingers of his other outstretched hand.

'Have a bite!' Smiled Charles, and his nephew laughed.

The barrow owner however, was not quite so amused. Just as the Cockney market barrow proprietor handed another customer a bag of pears, he turned just in Time to see Peter take a bite from the deep red shining apple.

'Oy – you!... What's your game!' He shouted angrily.

Peter tried to speak but his mouth was full while he chewed the juicy fruit.

'I do believe the young man approves of your wares sir!' Interrupted uncle Charles and he produced a farthing coin from his coat pocket, offering it to the scowling man. 'A bag of the fruit if you please!'

The barrow owner stared at uncle Charles in recognition.

'Sorry Mr Dickens sir, didn't realise the lad was with your honourable self sir!' He put some apples into a brown paper bag. 'My deepest apologies sir!'

'The boy accepts!' Retorted uncle Charles, slapping Peter forcefully on the back as he choked slightly on the apple skin.

Peter nodded and gulped in a deep breath of air as the piece of apple finally headed toward his stomach.

Uncle Charles paid the barrow owner and placed the full brown paper bag into Peters knapsack that was loosely dangling over his shoulders and across his back.

'Onward my boy! - Ever onward!' Uncle Charles pointed his walking stick toward a side street that swirled within in a light haze of misty fog. 'Let us venture forth through Old Antique Avenue and toward Trafalgar Square.'

Within moments the commotion and hustle and bustle of raised voices from Covent Garden market had faded into a distant whisper, as the boots of Peter and his uncle Charles clopped louder and louder onto a quiet cobbled street, echoing eerily around the surrounding buildings.

## Peter - A Legend And Old Antique Avenue.

Far below a beaming afternoon sun, unlit gas lamps glistened brightly for a few seconds as the blanket of misty, swirling fog momentarily cleared. Small glass panes from these lamps instantly reflected thin beams of brilliant light that probed deeply into the angry, swirling mist continuing to shroud London's cobbled streets below.

Old Antique Avenue's long and darkened pavements could only be traced by this floating mid-air trail of lamp-post's, which to Peter now resembled rows of light house's as only the top half of these gas lamps remained fully visible in the quickly returning, dense low lying fog.

Inside the various shops on either side of the avenue candles burned, illuminating the entrances to entice passing customers to enter.

'I do so love these curiosity shops!' Enthused uncle Charles waving his cane toward an illuminated doorway. 'You can always be assured of something unusual to be had inside.' He tapped the end of his walking stick onto the pavement and the sound echoed with a metallic thud.

'May we stop and take a look inside a shop uncle Charles?' Asked Peter hopefully. 'I would most certainly like to see some curiosities.'

'Good Boy!' Exclaimed uncle Charles, and he curled the end of his long moustache. 'The best stimulation for the imagination, is curiositation!'

He pointed his walking stick forward toward the flickering lights and the swirling mist parted in front of it.

'Take your pick!' Ordered the old man.

Peter nodded, grinning at yet another one of his uncle's rather silly, made up words of which the old man was so fond of creating.

'Curiositation indeed!' Mumbled Peter, who thought for a moment. 'That one I think uncle' he said firmly, and pointed toward an open doorway that was being entered into by a small hunched figure who wore a long cape and carried a long box under it's arm.

'Yes, a good choice!' Beamed uncle Charles. 'I have visited this shop before and it's a veritable trove of Old things.'

Uncle Charles gestured with his outstretched hand for Peter to enter the building.

'After you sir, young master!'

Peter skipped up the three steps to the doorway, and just as the door clicked shut from the last small customer to enter, Peter opened it again.

The heavy door creaked slowly open and a small but loudly ringing bell sounded both in welcome, and also to inform the proprietor that someone had entered his shop.

As Peter entered the shop he became instantly in awe of the long interior. For all sorts of small artefacts crammed themselves on an endless sea of shelves, and the larger variety stood majestically in lines across the creaking, highly polished floorboards.

## Peter - A Legend And Old Antique Avenue.

   Peters eyes surveyed in wonder the many varieties of stuffed animals in cases, ancient statues from the Orient, Middle-East and Africa, old elaborately carved furniture from all areas of the British Empire, and beautiful Icons from Russia and the east of Europe. His mouth stood open at the endless variety of books and porcelain and then even more so, where, at the shop's end, Peter saw the biggest and oldest Grandfather clock that he had ever seen.
   'Make way Peter!' Ordered uncle Charles ushering the boy forward gently from the doorway. 'Fascinating is it not?' The old man closed a heavy creaking door, and the little bell sounded again.
   A portly figure appeared from the back room and the Jolly faced shop owner nodded in greeting as he brushed bread crumbs from his jacket.
'Hello Mr Dickens, nice to see you again sir.'
Uncle Charles removed his long hat in reciprocal greeting and then placed it back on his scraggly hair.
   'Greetings Mr Smythe, I hope you keep well sir!'
   'I do, I do, thank you' replied Mr Smythe, who looked down at Peter and smiled. 'And who may you be young master?' He asked, edging his portly figure forward past the shops polished wooden counter.
   'I am the Nephew of Mr Dickens sir, my name is Peter.'
   'Ah!... Your uncle has told me of your good-self before Master Peter Dickens' Mr Smythe outstretched his hand. 'A pleasure to meet such a fine upstanding gentleman.'
   Peter shook Mr Smythe's hand, and at that moment his eyes were drawn to the large Grandfather clock as the mechanism inside it chimed twelve o'clock midday.
   'It is a beauty is it not' said Mr Smythe. 'But I will never sell that old clock though, it is my most treasured possession. Some say the clock is as old as Time itself. Even older than an old fool like me!'
   The shop keeper laughed a deep rippling laugh that seemed to fill the whole shop.
   'Go and take a closer look if you wish' said Mr Smythe gesturing toward the clock.
   'Thank you sir!' Peter walked slowly toward the old clock as the chimes boomed louder with every step he took.
   'And what may I do for your good-self Mr Dickens?' Asked Mr Smythe. 'Have you come to browse, or if I may help you find something specific?'
   'Thank you sir' replied uncle Charles. 'I have just brought the boy in to view your curiosities.' He looked around the shop vainly for the small figure that had entered the shop before them. 'You may continue to serve your present customer, as Peter looks around your establishment.'
   'Other Customer sir?' Mr Smythe looked bemused. 'There is no-one else here sir... You are the first customers for the bell to ring this morning.'

## Peter - A Legend And Old Antique Avenue.

'Oh, really,' uncle Charles strained his eyes into every corner of the shop. 'It must be my mistake sir' he said slowly.

'Would you care for a sherry to warm you on this cold day?' Asked Mr Smythe, gesturing to the back room.

'That would be most agreeable, thank you' replied uncle Charles, still looking around the shop. 'Most agreeable indeed.'

'Take your Time Peter!' Uncle Charles called out as the boy neared the old clock. 'Please do not break anything.'

'No uncle, I will be most careful' Peter called back, eyes transfixed toward the strange clock face.

In the small back room Mr Smythe quickly brushed a profusion of bread crumbs that lay scattered on the table top into a bowl. He then put the bowl into a cupboard and produced a decanter of sherry and two crystal glasses from inside.

'Is there any further news regarding the young masters parents?' Asked Mr Smythe, pouring an equal amount of sherry into each glass.

'Alas, as yet no sir' replied uncle Charles, nodding in appreciation as Mr Smythe handed him one of the glasses. 'Still lost at sea as yet.'

Uncle Charles took a sip of the sickly sweet drink.

'But, as ever, there is always hope.'

'Indeed sir, there is' Mr Smythe quickly drank the glass dry and poured himself another from the decanter... 'Hope burns eternal sir.'

A small carriage clock above the fireplace chimed twelve o'clock, the clear glass front flickering with golden light illuminated by flames from a roaring coal fire in the hearth beneath.

Mr Smythe produced a pocket watch, flicked open the cover and checked the Time.

'Strange,' he muttered aloud. 'The Grandfather clock appears to be a little slow.'

Mr Smythe replaced the pocket watch and indicated for uncle Charles to sit down.

'That old clock was here well before I had become the proprietor of this establishment and indeed, the last owner before me.'

He reached over and picked up a plate containing buttered bread and ham, offering part of his lunch to uncle Charles.

'It has never been known to lose Time!'

Uncle Charles graciously declined the meal.

'I do believe a clock maker lies but three streets away' said uncle Charles helpfully. 'If the time-peace is that old it may be as well be that you need a repair of some sort.'

Mr Smythe shrugged his shoulders and his mind pondered.

'Yes Sir, but it is most strange, repairs to the clock are said to be impossible.'

## Peter - A Legend And Old Antique Avenue.

The shop keeper scratched his chin with a mystified look about his face.
'I have already tried to effect repairs to that clock many years ago and since' he continued, placing his plate back to the table centre. 'But the door to that clock refuses to open and all the clock makers have said that it will be impossible to repair as the wood is of some of the strangest and strongest they have yet seen, and the door lock of a type that no key can possibly open.'
'A dilemma sir' smiled uncle Charles, sipping from the sherry glass. 'Still it seems to remain a great source of curiosity to your customers.'
Charles placed his glass back on the table, and pushed his feet nearer to the warm fire.
'My nephew certainly seems to have taken a shine to it.'
'Yes sir' relied Mr Smythe and he nodded, rubbing his chin thoughtfully. 'How goes the young master at boarding school?'
'Excellent' replied uncle Charles. 'The boy has the best of reports, although he finds the holidays a little difficult.'
Uncle Charles sighed, and he stared into the fire, his mind deep in reflection.
'That is why I brought him to London, to further his education and relieve his mind of the heavy burden.'
'Yes, yes' frowned the shopkeeper and agreed. 'I would hope that Time will bring forth better things to the young master sir.'
'Indeed' replied uncle Charles, turning his head from the fire. 'A toast to better Times sir!'
Charles raised his glass, and both he and Mr Smythe touched glasses gently.
'Better Times!' They quietly said in unison.
At the rear of this long shop, the very last booming chime of twelve o'clock midday had long since slipped away, when suddenly from deep inside the old Grandfather clock, Peter could now hear a rushing of wind that was gradually getting louder and louder.
The boy looked upwards toward the intricately carved clock face. A large red dot at the centre circle bound tightly together the large hands, which reminded him somewhat, of fingers, that pointed assertively to the decorative numbers that circled the clock face. Around this large red dot a half-circle seemed to smile down at him almost like a happy mouth.
Peters eyes were then drawn to a thin line of light that was gradually getting brighter and brighter around the Grandfather clocks single large doorway.
A single bead of this light spread brighter through the small keyhole making it's shape larger and larger on his jacket.
Peter slipped off his knapsack as the apples inside made it somewhat uncomfortable and heavy, but dropped it onto the floor which allowed a single apple to roll out, the fruit disappearing into a corner of the dimly lit shop. The boy placed his ear to the clock's door and listened to the wind howling, then he peeped into the keyhole, but the light was far too bright for his eyes.

## Peter - A Legend And Old Antique Avenue.

It was at that moment a voice from the dark corner of the shop caught Peters attention.

'Hmm... Tasty!' Peter thought he could hear someone say in a hushed tone and his ears caught the muffled crunch of someone biting through an apple skin. The boy moved away from the clock his eyes examining the many statues that lined the wall in the shadows.

Peter suddenly noticed that beyond the Chinese statue and at the side of a large vase stood the statue of a penguin. It was about the same size as himself, but what had brought his attention to it was the fact that a large red dot seemed to protrude slightly from behind the inanimate object and that the red dot appeared to be moving, almost as if it belonged to a face that was, well, eating something, like an apple perhaps?

'Who is there?' Peter called out in the deepest most grown up tone he could muster. There was no answer and the nose stopped moving.

Peter edged forward and picked up an umbrella that helpfully protruded from a pot. He moved between the Chinese statue and a large vase holding the umbrella up in his hand like a club, and with caution Peter peeped behind the penguin statue.

The boy saw another statue that was of the most curious nature. It looked somewhat like a penguin, but had the strangest nose he had ever seen that consisted of a large red ball which reminded Peter of the Grandfather clock centre. Even more curiously, under this large red nose a long, thin and very dark moustache protruded.

This penguin like statue wore a strange hat that was flat at the top and had a yellow clock embedded in the front. The body was partly coloured in the Union Jack Flag and the feet wore shoes that had no laces.

Peter stared hard at the object and noted that although he could not seem to see a mouth, that the side of the statues face bulged with a ball like shape.

'Almost as if it had an apple stuffed in it's mouth?' Thought Peter as he reached forward and tapped the statue quite hard on the head with his umbrella.

The statue spat out an apple from it's mouth, which had mimicked the shape with which the fruit went in, and this single red fruit sailed past Peter's head.

'Ouch that really hurt!' Cried out the statue, dropping a long box that it had held under it's long arms.

Peter fell backwards in shock as the 'statue' sprang into life and moved forwards. The vase broke first with a crash, then the Chinese statue toppled onto it's side.

As Peter sat up and turned around he could see this 'statue' entering the clock doorway which had by now swung wide open. A hand waved in good-bye as the door quickly shut tightly again, extinguishing the light and sound of a strong rushing wind that flowed from within.

## Peter - A Legend And Old Antique Avenue.

Peter still sat there umbrella still in hand, as uncle Charles and Mr Smythe appeared from the back room to find out what all the commotion was about.

'Are you injured boy?' Asked Mr Smythe examining the scene.

The shop owner bent forward and helped Peter up from the cold floorboards, pushing pieces of the broken vase away with his foot as he did so.

'No sir!... I...' Peter pointed to the Grandfather clock mouth open. 'Saw... Er... Something.'

Uncle Charles gently removed the umbrella from Peters hand.

'I hope the explanation is something more than something' he said grinning to himself.

'I thought it was a statue, but it was an animal of sorts, with a big nose' replied Peter still in shock. 'It went into the clock!'

'A rodent!' Mr Smythe grabbed the umbrella from uncle Charles. 'Good boy! We shall track down the beast!' The shopkeeper turned to uncle Charles.

'I really must refrain from leaving bread-crumbs too near to the floor in the future sir.'

Uncle Charles nodded and picked up a dusty old book that had been encased for years inside the vase and now visible due to the damage.

'Of course I shall compensate for any damages sir.' Uncle Charles opened the book and the dusty pages rippled forward to an old drawing. 'Curious he said to himself.'

Peter turned around to apologise to his Uncle for the mess and saw the drawing.

'That is it! That is what I saw!' the boy exclaimed.

Uncle Charles peered toward the drawing and noted a penguin shaped creature with a large nose that appeared to be mounted on some sort of transportation device with wheels.

'You must be mistaken Peter' replied uncle Charles reading the text. 'This is a very old book of legends and that is a drawing of an ancient cave painting from the Orient.'

'But that is what I saw. I am sure of it!' Peter pointed to the picture and then to the Grandfather clock. 'That creature went into that clock!'

Uncle Charles looked bemused as his foot found and then crunched a piece of broken porcelain.

'Come, let us clean up this mess and then examine the book more closely' he said calmly, pondering the situation.

Uncle Charles placed the old book down onto the shop counter and he indicated for Peter to pick up a sweeping brush from the side wall.

'First things first... Would you not agree Mr Smythe?'

'Indeed yes Sir' replied Mr Smythe lowering the umbrella, and wondering to himself if the whole thing was just from the imagination of a clumsy child, trying to strike a rodent with an umbrella.

## Peter - A Legend And Old Antique Avenue.

The shopkeeper was a little confused as he considered Peter to be sincere, but either way, he would keep his food stock further away from the ground in future.

Peter carefully dropped the last piece of broken vase into a large metal bin standing in the back room of the shop. He then picked up the sweeping brush and shook it. With a musty odour the last bit's of porcelain and dust that were left entangled in the brush clouded the bottom of the bin and Peter quickly replaced the lid.

'It is written in an ancient dialect' Peter heard uncle Charles exclaim as he re-entered the shop. Peter put the brush back to it's correct place on the side of the wall. 'I can decipher many parts, but not all of it' continued uncle Charles peering closer at the strange writing as Peter lent on the shops counter and strained his eyes at the pages of the book.

'I wonder how it got in the vase?' Pondered Mr Smythe, rubbing his chin. 'It must have been when the vase was manufactured, centuries ago.'

'Yes!' Agreed uncle Charles turning a page.

'What does it say uncle Charles?' Asked Peter, examining the picture of the creature that he had seen enter the Grandfather clock.

'Well now,' uncle Charles put on his spectacles to make the pages more clear in the dim light. 'This particular legend refers to, well, I will read out the parts that I can understand.'

'With a click of finger and thumb The Great Spirit of Light and Peace that has many names, banished darkness and created Time.' Uncle Charles curled his moustache in thought. 'Creatures were created to document all things that start and end in Time and place them safe for all eternity.'

'Do you suppose that the picture is one of the creatures' asked Peter examining the picture.

'It would appear so' replied uncle Charles. 'But it does say here that no man can see the creatures, so the picture may only be the imagination of the cave dweller who drew the picture.' He pondered the words at the bottom of the page. 'When Time is in danger only children will see, the future of light is entrusted to those who join in Peace and harmony.'

'But I did see the creature!' Exclaimed Peter. 'So it must be real.'

Mr Smythe sipped from the sherry glass that he had brought from the back room.

'Well it really is a most curious to-do' he said putting the empty glass on the shops counter. 'But I do find it hard to believe that legends could be real, stuff and nonsense I call it.'

'Maybe so Mr Smythe' said uncle Charles, thinking back to the strange character that he himself had seen enter the shop earlier, but a character that did not seem to exist. 'But strange things have been known to happen, unexplained things' he said quietly.

## Peter - A Legend And Old Antique Avenue.

Uncle Charles moved to where Peter said he had first seen the 'creature' and he picked up an old cloak that was lying on the floor behind the penguin statue. Beneath this cloak was a long decorative box that carried a small shiny mirror embedded into it's top.
'Similar in shape to the one the figure carried?' Uncle Charles thought to himself picking up the box. He noted that this long box seemed to be fashioned from the same material as the shop's Grandfather clock, and the box lid was as equally impossible to open as was the clock's door.
'Strange things indeed' muttered uncle Charles and he placed the box onto the shops counter, directly next to the old book.
Mr Smythe, Peter and Uncle Charles all lent forward together and examined these curious items carefully.
Flickering brightly and reflecting glows of golden, burning candlelight that illuminated the dark shop, this small that was mirror embedded into the box top caught the intrigued and attentive facial images of Peter, uncle Charles and the shopkeeper.
Situated just below this mirror an inscription was etched into the wood like material, uncle Charles placed his spectacles onto the end of his nose and proceeded to read it aloud.

***Any fool can frown at me***
***Any person can happy be***
***Stop think twice before a key you turn***
***For Time and Peace you have to learn***

Uncle Charles probed a small keyhole in the box front with his spindly finger. 'Alas no key' he said thoughtfully.
Peter nodded in agreement and then, almost instantly found his eyes drawn to a square box with a small glass door fixed to the shop wall behind the counter. Inside it held many keys dangling lazily from small hooks, but one key in particular caught Peters attention.
'What about that one!' Peter pointed to a single brass coloured key which was almost hidden amongst the many, but one whose metal head held the round shape of a nose and smiling mouth door knocker, just like the patterned centre of the old Grandfather clock's face.
'That is just the key for winding the old clock mechanism' said Mr Smythe who then automatically proceeded to open the key box and remove the item. 'It could not possibly open this box!' He examined the key and twirled it slowly around with his fingertips. 'But the end does seem to be the same size as the key-hole.'
'Might I try the key in the lock sir?' Uncle Charles held out his hand and indicated for Mr Smythe to pass the brass key to him.

## Peter - A Legend And Old Antique Avenue.

Mr Smythe placed the key into the palm of uncle Charles hand.
'Certainly you may try sir! But no key will fit two locks or mechanisms.'
Uncle Charles smiled in agreement, but thought he would try anyway and pushed the key into the lock.
'It fits!' Exclaimed Peter. 'Do open the box uncle so that we may see inside!'
Uncle Charles turned the key, but the box top stayed firmly shut.
'The key appears to turn forcefully back against my finger tips!' Uncle Charles removed the key and scratched his head in confusion. 'Perhaps the box does not want me to open it!'
'Nonsense!' Mr Smythe took the key from uncle Charles and tried to forcefully turn the key in the lock adamant that he would open this silly box. 'I do declare!' he exclaimed as the key also twisted back against his own fingers. 'This is most strange!... Most strange indeed!'
'Maybe it has something to do with the inscription' noted Peter, leaning over the box to get a better view.
'Well I do not think that we have learned anything Mr Smythe!' Said uncle Charles, rubbing his chin. He tapped the inscription with a finger. 'Certainly not how to open this box! Perhaps the young master may guide us and the box be more willing to open for him.'
'Hmm' responded Mr Smythe, not really sure, but he handed Peter the key anyway. 'Well they do say that the young may teach the old a thing or two!' He patted Peter on the back. 'Best of luck young Sir!'
Peter pushed the key into the lock. But before turning it, he deeply pondered the inscription that had been placed upon this box.
'Any fool can frown at me. Any person can happy be.' Peter repeated the words over and quietly to himself. Then as Peter smiled into the small mirror on the box top, he thought of the words. 'Stop, think twice before a key you turn. For Time and Peace you have to learn.'
'Ah - I wonder -' the boy exclaimed aloud, and he turned the key twice quite forcefully in the lock. It clicked and immediately the long box lid sprang wide open with a whooshing sound, taking Peter somewhat by surprise.
'Well done!' Congratulated both uncle Charles and Mr Smythe.
Inside the box a cloth covered the contents beneath. Peter removed the cloth and put it on the counter. This box seemed to be somewhat deeper on the inside than it looked on the outside, and the items that it contained were obscured by shadows cast by the box itself and that of this dimly lit shop.
'Well -' asked Mr Smythe leaning forward. 'What does it contain young Master.'
Peter placed his hand into the box and revealed a pencil and note book. All really quite ordinary, apart from the same image of a nose and smiley face imprinted on both items. He handed them to Uncle Charles, then slowly removed the last item that lay deep within this long box.

## Peter - A Legend And Old Antique Avenue.

With both hands Peter produced a long board like object that had two sets of wheels at the bottom.

'Very much like the object in that old book uncle' he said placing the long object on the shops counter.

'Yes indeed it is!' Noted uncle Charles in amazement.

Mr Smythe pushed the board with his hand and it rolled gently to the edge of the counter then back of it's own accord.

'A strange device but of absolutely no practical use I warrant' huffed the shopkeeper. 'What possible use for transportation could this perform. It is much too small to carry any goods.'

Peter picked up the long board and placed it onto the floor.

'In the picture, the creature is standing on it!' He exclaimed, and placed both feet quickly on the board's top. The board flew forwards and Peter fell into a heap on the floor. 'Ouch!' He cried, rubbing his leg as it twisted painfully.

'I do believe balance may be a feature of this transport' said uncle Charles helping Peter from the cold floor. 'Some practise may be required before the feat of propulsion may be obtained.'

'Yes uncle!' Agreed Peter standing up again and looking down at the board, noting that the round shape of a nose and smiling mouth imprinted at the front of the device seemed to be smiling more than ever.

'Well it is of no use to me, however curious a thing' said the shopkeeper disappointedly. 'My customers would find no use for a transportation device that you can fall off so easily and carry so little on.'

'But may I keep it Uncle' asked Peter hopefully. 'I am sure that maybe with a little practise...'

'Of course! Of course!' replied uncle Charles. 'If a creature in a book can master the contraption I am sure that you can do likewise' and he winked at Mr Smythe. 'However, the force of gravity will and must always remain the master of one who falls off anything, so please do be careful.'

Uncle Charles produced two coins from his pocket and held it out toward Mr Smythe.

'I hope two guineas will be adequate to purchase this old book, box and this strange board, and also be sufficient to recompense any damage to your stock.'

'Indeed yes!' Smiled Mr Smythe taking the coin gleefully. 'You are most generous, as always sir... More than enough!'

Uncle Charles placed the note-book and pencil back inside their box and placed the cloth back on top of them.

'We shall not lock the box sir, so you may replace the old Grandfather clock key, back with the others' he then retuned the key to Mr Smythe.

'You may carry the board Peter and practise your balance with this strange device in the street outside.'

'Thank you very much Uncle!' Replied Peter, most happily.

## Peter - A Legend And Old Antique Avenue.

Peter picked up his knapsack full of apples and slung the heavy pack across his back.

He moved forward and then bent down to pick up the ancient skateboard board, quickly putting it under his arm.

'Thank you also Mr Smythe!' He said politely.

'You are most welcome young master!' Replied the shopkeeper. 'Do call again.'

Uncle Charles nodded in appreciation, and indicated to Peter with his hand that it was Time to exit the shops doorway and enter the misty street beyond.

'After you young gentleman' said the old man, opening the door for Peter.

As the shops bell sounded loudly and he walked past his uncle, Peter heard, or at least thought he heard, a quiet voice call to him.

'Thanks Buddy!' Whispered this voice and it appeared to come from the direction of the board, but Peter could not be sure with the bell ringing.

'Strange?' thought Peter, but the boy put it down to his imagination as he entered the cold air of the misty street outside.

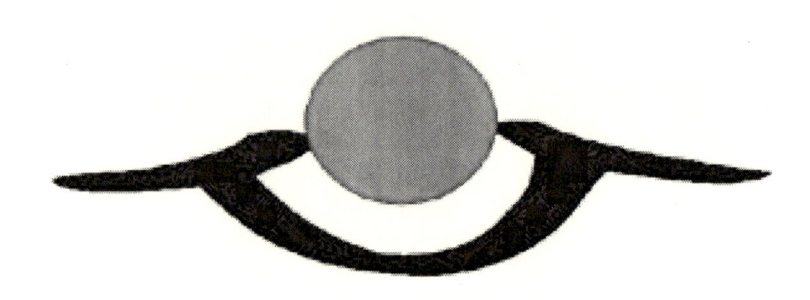

## Peter - Sorry Your Majesty.

Uncle Charles closed the shop door and followed Peter outside into the misty, fog bound street.

Peter placed his long skateboard onto the pavement and he noticed that somehow, the smiley mouth beneath the large red nose seemed to smile at him even more so than it had done in the shop. The swirling, low lying fog, whirled around this curious long board with wheels, but seemed quite disinclined to obscure it, as it had with all other objects at ground level.

'Be most careful of the cobble stones!' Said uncle Charles, tapping the end of his walking stick to the hidden stone floor beneath the misty, swirling fog at his feet.

'Yes uncle' replied Peter, placing a foot onto the long boards top and prepared himself to move forward.

A few yards away, three figures that were hiding within the shadows of a darkened doorway watched both uncle Charles and Peter. But they were all more interested in a house directly opposite the curiosity shop.

One of these figures, a consulting detective wearing a deerstalker hat, tapped out the contents of his pipe that he had been slowly puffing from, and he extinguished the smouldering, dry smoking ash beneath one of his highly polished shoes.

'Take care!' He urged quietly to the others at his side, observing that a rather dark and sinister figure had left the house that they had under surveillance.

This sinister figure that wore a black cape and top hat, observed uncle Charles and Peter, but proceeded to move quickly down the long street toward Trafalgar Square obscuring his identity with a scarf.

A police officer standing next to the consulting detective quickly placed a shiny whistle to his lips and prepared to blow.

'Now Constable!' Exclaimed the third man, fearing that this person might escape.

The whistle shrilled loudly, echoing through the foggy street and in an instant, the three figures made toward their prey, with the constable already holding a wooden truncheon in his hand.

Uncle Charles, Peter and the sinister figure all took note of where the shrill whistle sound had come from and noticed the three figures heading quickly toward them. Another shrill, high pitch whistle came from the other end of the street and two more constables loomed from the swirling fog.

'Move to safety!' Shouted the consulting detective in warning, observing the sinister figure removing a large spherical object from beneath his cloak.

He then shouted to his friend standing at his side who had produced a small revolver from his pocket and with which, was preparing to fire at the sinister figure. 'No! - You may hit the boy!'

Uncle Charles and Peter were both quite shocked by the fast moving events, and they were quite close enough to observe this sinister person.

## Peter - Sorry Your Majesty.

The obscured figure reached into his pocket and lit the end of a spherical object with the flickering flame of a match.

'Great Scott!' Exclaimed uncle Charles, moving toward Peter to pull him from the street to safety. However, the old long skateboard with a smiley grin and red nose had also noticed the events that were taking place.

'Heavens!' cried Peter, waving his hands in the air trying to steady himself as the skateboard hurtled forward.

It was all the more confusing for the boy, as both his feet were stuck fast to this boards top, and it seemed that the board had suddenly become, well, almost alive. But he really did not have any Time to consider the situation, for the skateboard jumped upward from the floor into the air, and with a piercing grind scrapped it's way along a set of railings by the very tip of it's rear edge.

Everyone watched in amazement, not least the sinister figure, while Peter and the skateboard quickly reached the spot where he stood.

'Um -' Peter did not really have any words for the sinister figure that held the spherical object in his hand and who was now staring at him in confusion and the skateboard did not have any words for him either. It span around and hit the figure square on the head, using it's rear end that had previously been grinding the railings.

'Naughty! Naughty!' Came a voice from the smiley mouth on the skateboard top while the sinister figure crumpled to the floor.

The skateboard then turned upside down and hovered in the air above this person that was now laying flat out on the cobble stones.

'Lights out!' It said, blowing a bead of thin wind toward the spherical object that was about to explode. The flame from an almost ended fuse disappeared and the skateboard righted itself again.

'You can talk!' Cried Peter, most amazed, he looked down at the smiley mouth and watched it move.

'What? - You never seen a talking skateboard before?' It replied, giving Peter a huge grin.

Before Peter could say anything else, the ancient skateboard suddenly hurtled upwards into the air and span upright again. In a breath taking instant, the skateboard unexpectedly hurtled back downwards toward ground level where it quickly righted itself just above the cobblestones, and then shot forwards at great speed to make the two approaching Constables jump quickly to one side.

'What is going on!' Shouted Peter to the skateboard, his feet still stuck fast to it's top.

'No Time to explain!' Replied the smiley mouth. 'Time is in danger and it needs your help!'

The consulting detective, his friend and the policeman reached the sinister figure at the same Time as uncle Charles.

## Peter - Sorry Your Majesty.

The Constable handcuffed the figure that was still lying on the floor whilst the consulting detective watched Peter and his skateboard hurtle into the misty fog toward Trafalgar square.

'What is going on here!' Spluttered uncle Charles, as the detectives friend made safe the spherical orb that had rolled into the gutter.

'A dangerous villain is under arrest!' Barked the consulting detective to Uncle Charles, who was observing, deep in thought, that the wheels of the skateboard Peter was riding were not actually not touching the ground. 'But it also seems, that a mystery is afoot' he added with a grin.

For Peter, who was finding it quite difficult to stand upright while balancing on top of the fast moving skateboard, the mystery was not so much, afoot, but rather, under both his feet. His polished boots, still strangely stuck fast to the top of this old board, just behind the smiley mouth and red nose, that he had assumed were painted on the top, but were in fact, the face of the living skateboard.

'So what are you -' Peter called out to the smiley mouth. The boy struggled with the straps of his backpack that was still full of apples and held tightly to the old dusty box, that somehow, he had managed to keep hold of and had kept under his arm.

'I am your Buddy carriage, in Time and space' replied the smiley mouth, it's red nose sniffing the air. It turned sharply back and forth, then entered William IV street.

'Must save Time. Time needs your help. You found the chest and opened it. Only the future can save the future!'

'What do you mean save Time?' Asked Peter, grimacing as the skateboard twisted and turned, then narrowly avoided a horse and carriage while entering Charing Cross Road. This was much to the surprise of the driver who dropped his horse whip when the skateboard and Peter flew over the top of his head.

'No Time to explain!' Replied the skateboard and it accelerated past the crowds of people walking the long pavements. The ancient board seemed quite preoccupied and desperate to reach it's destination, wherever that may be.

Peter then decided that he would not be afraid of this peculiar device. After all, it had dealt with the sinister villain and had not his parents always told him to - 'Take on adversity or adventure, head on, with a smile on your face, no matter what.'

Uncle Charles also had the same sort of positive outlook.

'To be afraid of the unknown, is only to be afraid of ones own shadow!' He would say. 'As the unknown, is only the shadow of your future!'

So, while riding this old talking skateboard that sped quickly in the air through the streets of London, Peter decided that he would not be afraid of this situation and would really try to enjoy the experience.

## Peter - Sorry Your Majesty.

'After all' Peter thought to himself. 'This skateboard seemed friendly enough, even if it was quite strange.'

The device may have previously lay hidden, in an old long box, which uncle Charles had found beneath a cloak in the curio shop, just after Peter had seen a strange creature apparently figured in old cave paintings that they had seen in a book. But only Peter could open the intricately carved box and it seemed to him that some sort of an adventure was destined to befall him.

'Take on adversity or adventure, head on, with a smile on your face, no matter what' the words echoed around Peters head and mingled with the rushing wind that passed by his ears.

Peter smiled at the open mouthed onlookers that stopped on the pavement to see the strange sight flying past them and he held on tightly to the old box as the skateboard flew past St Martin in the field Church and whizzed quickly into Trafalgar square.

The Pigeons did not care much for this large 'bird' that hurtled into Trafalgar square. They spread their wings and took flight, all rising like one huge cloud, to dissipate quickly onto the surrounding buildings and window ledges. Nelson stood atop his tall column, his one eye still eternally looking out to sea and his hat now lined with pigeons that were looking down at Peter and the skateboard.

'What that thing needs is decoration at the base!' Exclaimed the smiley mouth at Peters feet. The skateboard whizzed around Nelsons column, while the red nose sniffed the air again. It swerved sharply to avoid a white haired gentleman who's top hat fell off as the skateboard brushed it's top. 'Maybe a few lions would make it a great monument?'

'Er - Yes' agreed Peter, balancing with great difficulty, then he looked up at Nelson and noted how the fog seemed to be lifting rapidly.

'Are you all right Sir Edwin?' A Constable helped the gentleman retrieve his top hat. Then both of them looked up together and followed the path of Peter and his skateboard, who were by now heading at some speed toward Downing street. 'Never seen nothing like it in all me born days!' Gasped the Constable.

'No, I have never seen anything like it either' replied the gentleman calmly, watching this strange sight head toward Westminster. He then produced an artists sketch pad and pencil from his pocket. 'However Lions would be a rather capitol idea!'

Outside Horse Guards Parade the two horses 'on guard' watched Peter and the skateboard pass without interest. However, their shocked resplendent riders in uniform gave out a sudden yell.

'Flipping heck!' They exclaimed as this flying sight passed before them.

'We cannot go down this street!' Cried Peter to the smiley mouth. 'Not today!'

'And why is that Buddy?' Asked the smiley mouth. 'This is the right direction!... My nose tells me so.'

## Peter - Sorry Your Majesty.

'Because the Queen is visiting the new clock tower that is being built at the House Of Parliament building!' Replied Peter anxiously.

Flying straight past Downing Street Peter could already see crowds of people that were lining the street ahead.

'Clock tower?' The smiley mouth on the skateboard smiled even more. 'See, told you we were heading in the right direction!' And the board accelerated.

Reaching the back of a huge crowd lining the street and pavement, the skateboard lifted itself and Peter skyward, brushing the helmets of a line of smartly dressed soldiers wearing red tunics that were stood in front of the crowd.

Peter looked on in horror as he and the skateboard flew over the top, then turned sharply and flew up the middle of Bridge Street. They were both heading toward Westminster bridge in front of the crowds and soldiers that were lining the street, and on a collision course with an open carriage that contained two people sitting in the back.

With the fast moving skateboard and Peter flying directly at them, the soldiers on horseback escorting the royal carriage struggled to stop their horses from bolting. Behind them, a figure in the carriage stood up and looked directly toward Peter, the amazement in his moustached face quite apparent to Peter, who shouted to the skateboard.

'Stop! - We shall collide with the Queen's husband.'

Unfortunately, there was no Time to actually stop, and Prince Albert fell back into his seat when the skateboard reached him.

At the last moment Peters skateboard twisted upside down to avoid any actual contact, and it held Peter by his feet to dangle embarrassingly in front of Queen Victoria and her husband Albert.

'Sorry your Majesty!' Exclaimed Peter. 'I am having a little trouble controlling this device!'

A single apple rolled from Peters backpack and it dropped earthward, to land with a plop into Albert's open mouth. The Prince instantly turned to face the Queen, feeling quite stunned. The Queen looked directly at Albert, then smiled.

'We are most amused young man!' Victoria really couldn't help laughing, despite the strange spectacle.

An officer in charge of a very large group of soldiers behind the carriage was not so amused.

'Someone is attacking their majesties!' He shouted at the top of his voice. 'Load your arms!'

'Oops! - Better go now!' Said the smiley mouth on Peters skateboard. It wolf whistled toward Queen Victoria - 'See you babe!'

The ancient skateboard span upright again and Peter held on tightly to the old box. It hurtled forward toward Westminster Bridge in a rush of howling wind, as the apple dropped from Albert's mouth.

## Peter - Sorry Your Majesty.

The army officer and his men had quickly spread themselves across the road and all had their weapons aimed toward Peter and the skateboard.

'What do we do now!' Shouted Peter, feeling quite frightened.

'Relax' replied the smiley mouth at his feet. 'Have a little faith Buddy!' It then quickly mumbled a strange verse. 'Time will tick on, no person can stop, the eternal tock, of any clock!'

Peter could see the soldiers and their rifle's, which were aimed straight toward him growing larger by the second.

'Ah!' He yelled, shutting his eyes.

'Open fire!' The army officer barked out his order and all the weapons discharged, in a single, massive bang, releasing a huge puff of acrid white smoke that covered the entire road.

At this precise moment in Time, high above the events below, the hands of an unfinished clock tower span wildly backwards to twelve o'clock and inside, high above Bridge street, the huge bell nicknamed 'Big Ben' boomed out for the first Time across the Thames river.

Glancing at his wristwatch, which indicated that it was one o'clock, the tourist guide continued his flowing commentary through a shiny microphone and stood confidently on the breezy open top deck of the London double-decker tour bus that was now passing over Westminster bridge.

'And here is one of London's greatest sights' he continued, thinking his own wristwatch must be wrong, as Big Ben chimed it's last chime of twelve o'clock.

The tour guide turned, while still talking, then pointed toward the old clock tower of the Parliament building.

'A boy on a flying skateboard!' His mouth said automatically, what his eyes suddenly saw, but a sight his brain, could not really accept as real. He dropped the microphone and it whined over the loud speakers with a high pitch squeal.

Peter opened his eyes, just as the acrid smoke from the soldier's discharged weapon's cleared and he entered a new, brilliantly lit day, under clear blue skies.

'Ah!' He continued to yell out, heading toward the strange sight of a tall horse-less carriage heading toward him and the face of a very, very, confused tour guide.

'Up we go!' Called out the smiley face at Peters feet. The skateboard rose at a steep angle then suddenly levelled off. It then continued it's path and flew right over the bus, parting the tour guides hair into a new style, when it's wheels moved a little too close to his head. 'Oops, sorry Buddy!' The skateboard called back to the tour guide who had collapsed into his seat.

'Where are we?' Asked Peter in confusion. 'Is this London?'

Peter looked around, recognising some features of the buildings, but others were totally different. Especially a huge wheel like structure at the Thames edge, that seemed to be rotating and carrying people inside little glass eggs.

## Peter - Sorry Your Majesty.

'It is OK Buddy!' The smiley mouth on the skateboard grinned. 'I had to take an emergency Time portal. You are in the future now.'

'The future?' Peter thought and said aloud. It sounded like one of the stories Uncle Charles was so fond of. But the boy could not argue with his own eyes and the fact that he was actually flying on a skateboard. 'What could be more stranger than that?' He pondered.

'Not home yet though' continued the smiley mouth, with a huge sniff the red nose above it searched the air. 'The clock was not finished, so we entered a stitch in Time and missed the club entrance completely.'

'Club entrance?' Peter wondered what this device was talking about, but was too busy balancing, or trying to balance, to ask questions.

All along Westminster bridge, the many people of all nations walking the pavements stopped to observe this phenomenon flying before them.

Some managed to take a quick photograph, or pointed their video cameras toward Peter and some just stood and watched as the skateboard veered sharply left, flew past the art gallery and aquarium, then continued onward toward the London eye.

'It is not ready yet!' Called out the smiley mouth to Peter.

'What is not ready -' Peter replied, watching the eggs full of people get closer and observing their surprise as the flying skateboard and himself passed them.

The skateboard accelerated even faster down the Thames south bank.

'Can only be wise, if you go clockwise' replied the smiley mouth. 'Can't go back, must go forward.'

Peter thought to himself trying to understand what the smiley mouth was saying.

'Oh!' Peter then said. 'Do you mean that you have to travel around in a circle again, if you do not succeed the first Time?'

'Yes - Yes!' replied the smiley mouth. 'If at first you do not succeed, try, try again, clock wise.'

Peter looked around him at the many strange buildings, that had replaced many that he had known. But he could still recognise the dome of St Paul's Cathedral looming from behind a row of strange, rather oblong shaped buildings that tried to hide it. Peter held on tightly to the box, as the skateboard swerved again to avoid a lamppost, then rose up into the air again, to fly over the head of two, brilliantly yellow jacketed figures.

The policemen were amazed at this spectacle. But reacting quickly, one of them called into his radio.

'We have a situation on the South Bank' he said calmly, following Peter and the skateboards path as they headed toward Tower bridge. 'There is a flying skateboard, with a child on top holding a box!'

At the control centre a voice replied, somewhat sarcastically.

'Yeah, right pull the other one!'

## Peter - Sorry Your Majesty.

But then, observing through one of many small televisions linked to security cameras, the voice coughed an embarrassed and rather confused cough.

'I have it on camera!' the voice continued. 'Red alert being initiated!'

Within minutes a senior police officer had entered the control centre and was viewing Peter and the skateboard on the many television screens.

He watched intently as they passed City Hall, then was quite amazed when the skateboard and rider veered sharply left and rose high into the air, to ride across the upper walkway of Tower Bridge.

'This really is quite extraordinary!' He muttered.

The ancient skateboard and Peter continued their journey through the skies of the capitol city. They flew past the Tower Of London, rolled over St Paul's Cathedral dome and flew low over Covent Garden, to rise high again over Trafalgar Square.

Passing over Nelson's Column, Peter noticed that these brightly jacketed figures now seemed to be practically everywhere. One held a device in his hand which amplified his voice.

'Land immediately, or we will be forced to shoot you down!' The voice boomed out.

The skateboard plummeted toward the ground, but Peter was now balancing much better and smiled as the wind rushed past his face.

'They have placed Lions at the bottom of Nelsons Column!' He exclaimed.

'Yeah!' Replied the skateboard. 'Cool.'

On top of the London tour bus reaching Trafalgar Square, a shaken guide had composed himself, combed his hair and continued calmly his commentary to tourists.

'And here we have...' He did not finish his sentence. The tour guide turned quickly around when he heard the policeman's voice on a loud-hailer. His eyes met Peters for a second, just as the skateboard flew over the top of his head and parted his hair again with it's wheels.

'Sorry!' Shouted Peter turning his head to watch the guide faint and fall back into his seat for the second Time.

Inside the control room a firm voice came over the radio.

'Shall we open fire sir?'

The senior police officer watched his TV monitor while deep in thought.

'No!' He replied. 'Await my order!'

Quickly the police chief magnified an image on his monitor and the decorative box that Peter was carrying filled the screen.

He examined Peters Victorian clothes closely on another screen. The officer suddenly moved quickly to his office and pulled an old book from a shelf.

It was the very same book that uncle Charles had read aloud in the curiosity shop, and one that had been left in the senior officers family for generations.

## Peter - Sorry Your Majesty.

'I thought so!' Exclaimed the senior police officer, examining a very old photograph that had been placed inside the books cover. It was a photograph of Peter with uncle Charles. 'But that is impossible!' He whispered.

With a huge grin, the smiley mouth accelerated back to Westminster, over the bridge and rose high into the sky over the art gallery.

'Here we go!... Hold on to your hat!'

'Here we go, where?' Shouted Peter, gripping the old box tightly.

'Home!...' The smiley mouth grinned and the skateboard headed toward a single glass egg, that lay empty at the bottom of the big wheel at the River Thames edge.

Suddenly, as they grew nearer, a wind howled and brilliant light beamed from this capsule, forcing Peter to close both his eyes.

The attendants ushering people into the empty eggs stopped immediately, then all stood well back.

Both Peter and the old skateboard hurtled through the open doorway of the glass egg and with a huge roar, the wind that had come from it, was sucked back in and the light went out to reveal the empty capsule just as it had been before.

Policemen standing nearby rushed to the open doorway and examined the interior.

'Empty sir' one called through his radio.

Back at the control centre, a stunned senior police officer sat down in front of his TV monitors, and he looked deeply into the faded photograph of his long past on ancestors.

'Good luck Peter' he whispered, so no one else could hear.

*From here you may read onward for the next individual's entry point, or just skate forwards through the book to our Living Legends Chapter.*

From the east and an old world:- An individual entry point.

## *Abdul - A Legend And The Bazaar Day.*

Abdul lived in an ordinary place, in an ordinary town in an ordinary street. Today was the weekend and as usual, he and his friends were playing football in the waste ground past the town.

The children had marked out the area with lines as carefully and as straight as they could on the dry sandy dirt. To finish off this makeshift pitch they had placed broken sticks for goal-posts at either end. It was all rather basic, but to the children playing football it may as well have been a grand, grassy pitched stadium, with an important cup to win at the end of each game.

'Over here!' Everyone shouted at once, all wanting the ball to be passed to them. The football was then kicked high into the sunny sky.

Abdul was small, but threw himself into the air quite gracefully, to fly past a much bigger boy's shoulder's and hit the spinning football squarely with his forehead. The ball ricocheted in a straight line toward the goal and the big goalkeeper lunged with a loud grunt, sideways and at full stretch.

'Goal!' Cried Abdul's side in unison as the opposite sides big goalkeeper scraped the ball lightly with his finger tips and then saw the ball fly past him and into the net. The big goal-keeper disappeared into a huge cloud of dry dust as he hit the floor heavily. At the very same moment, Abdul did likewise, as the players on his side leapt on him for joy at scoring the goal.

'Two minutes to go and the scores are three each!' Someone shouted, pretending to be like a commentator which they had seen on TV.

Suddenly the roar of engines drowned out his voice and just after this Abdul appeared again from beneath the crowd of happy players that had quickly cleared away. He stood upright and rubbed the dry dust from his eyes.

With his vision quickly restored and through strained eyes due to the brilliant sunlight, Abdul could see the boys hastily scrambling back toward the town, turning quickly he saw a large vehicle approaching him followed by two others.

The first vehicle stopped suddenly in front of Abdul, spreading dust high into the air. A soldier stepped from the cab and walked forward to where Abdul was standing. The man lent down and picked up the football from the ground.

'As from now this area is to be cleared' he said, in a flat unfeeling tone. The soldier threw the ball to Abdul. 'No more football here!'

Abdul instinctively headed the ball back, his mind still on the game. The soldier caught it, slightly taken aback.

'But we have no-where else to play!' Said Abdul firmly.

'Orders are orders!' Snapped the soldier, as other soldiers left their vehicle's and started to unfurl coils of barbed wire and carry them past the pitch and nearer to the town.

'Well they are very silly!' Snapped Abdul right back. 'This is our football pitch and I am sure you had one like it when you were my age!'

## Abdul - A Legend And The Bazaar Day.

The soldier forcefully threw the ball back to Abdul and this Time the small boy caught it with his chest, dropping the leather sphere downwards. Abdul quickly flicked the football skilfully back into the air.

'This is our stadium!' He stated firmly, keeping the football bouncing up into the air with his right foot five Times in a row. Abdul then stopped and held the ball under his arm, glaring with contempt toward the soldier.

'Your stadium!' The soldier laughed sarcastically, and he looked around at the shabby dusty football field. Then without saying anything, the soldier pointed toward the town, indicating for Abdul to go home.

Abdul instantly turned around, and walked dejectedly back to the town.

With a grin, the soldier watched the small boy walk away and he pulled a map from his tunic pocket.

'Sergeant!' He barked aloud.

'Yes sir!' Came an instant response.

'It would seem that our wire is being placed too near to the town!' He said looking at the map. 'Withdraw it to beyond this Stadium!'

'Stadium sir!' Asked the sergeant looking at the dusty football pitch.

'Yes!' Said the officer thoughtfully. 'This may be a waste area to us but it is a huge stadium in a small boys imagination!' The officer placed his map back into his pocket. 'I think we all had those when we were young' he said smiling.

'But the orders sir!' The sergeant attempted to remind his officer of what orders he had written down.

'My responsibility!' Retorted the officer sharply. 'And my orders are, to bring the wire back!'

'Yes sir!' Giving a sharp salute, the sergeant obeyed immediately.

The officer watched Abdul through his binoculars as the small boy reached the town and into the crowd of boys standing beside a building wall.

'Hooray!' Shouted the boys, watching the soldiers clear the barbed wire back from the football pitch. 'Well done Abdul!'

Abdul turned around as the boys patted him on the back. Watching the pitch being cleared he nearly waved to the officer who he could see looking directly at him, but decided against it and just smiled back instead.

His grandmother's voice interrupted the celebration and parted the clamour of boys.

'Come on Abdul, it is Time to go to the Bazaar, enough of football for today.'

'Yes grandmother' replied Abdul, throwing his football high into the air and to the side.

The crowd of boys hurried toward the spinning ball, their feet sending a dust cloud into the sky.

'See you all tomorrow!' Cried Abdul and he and his grandmother started a long walk to the Bazaar.

## Abdul - A Legend And The Bazaar Day.

Palm street was, as always, busy and quite dusty as motor cars whizzed by at a frantic speed. A cloud of dust flew into the air as Abdul's grandmother stopped to talk on the pavement to Mrs Haggi, who then called for her son Yaz to come out and say hello.

From an open gate-way Yaz rolled from the courtyard beyond, while balancing gracefully on top of his skateboard.

'Hello Abdul' he said cheerfully. 'Been playing football today?'

'Hello' replied Abdul responding with a nod. 'Yes for a while, but grandmother wants to go to the Bazaar now.'

The two women were already deep in conversation and the boys lent against the low wall.

'I have this this new board!' Exclaimed Yaz excitedly. 'Want to try it out?'

'Well OK' replied Abdul. 'But I'm not much good on these things.'

Yaz rolled his skateboard toward Abdul with his foot, and Abdul picked it up quickly examining the complicated but colourful design that was printed onto the skateboard's bottom.

'Nice board!' Observed Abdul, putting it back on the ground.

His eyes suddenly caught a discarded drink can that lay on the floor by the gutter, blown there by a passing car. He picked it up and placed it on the far edge of the skateboard.

'See that bin across the road' Abdul pointed to an open bin on wheels that lay on the other side of the pavement. He then pointed to the can and indicated that he could place it in the bin with his foot.

'No chance' laughed Yaz.

Abdul prepared himself, and with a hard stamp of his foot on the skateboard's end tip, sent the can flying directly upward into the air. As the can returned to Earth, Abdul judged the exact point at which to strike the can and then hit it full force, as he would a football, with his foot in the direction of the bin.

With a thud the can hurtled straight toward the open topped bin and as it reached the far end of the road, sped through both open windows of a passing Police car, flying past the startled drivers head, to plop with a clang into the bins bottom.

'Oops!' Exclaimed Abdul, as the mouth of Yaz opened wide in amazement at such an accurate shot.

The Police car screeched to a halt and spun around in the road to stop at the pavement directly in front of Abdul.

'You are for it now!' Cried Yaz, looking in the direction of the still chatting women, but they hadn't noticed what had happened yet.

A policeman left the car and walked slowly toward Abdul, shaking his head equally as slowly.

Abdul gulped a breath of air hard and blurted nervously.

'Sorry Mr Abaas, that was my fault.'

## Abdul - A Legend And The Bazaar Day.

A stern looking policeman bent forward and looked Abdul straight in the eye.

'You could have caused an accident kicking a can across the road like that young man!' He said firmly.

Abdul gulped another breath of air and swallowed hard, looking sheepishly toward his grandmother who was still deep in conversation with Mrs Haggi.

The policeman unexpectedly smiled and continued.

'But that was one heck of a shot Abdul,' he patted the boy on the back. 'Maybe one day you will be a football star!'

Abdul's grandmother turned around, as another car spread a haze of dust into the air from the road as it sped by.

'Is there any trouble Mr Abaas?' She enquired, observing the policeman who was also her neighbour, talking to Abdul.

Abdul felt his body sinking into the floor in anticipation of what Mr Abaas would say.

'No no' replied Mr Abaas. 'I just came to congratulate Abdul on his anti-litter technique!' He grinned toward Abdul. 'Well done for keeping the street clear of litter' and then he winked an eye.

'Oh!' Exclaimed Abdul's grandmother, wondering what he was talking about. But before she could say anything else Mr Abaas had opened the door to his police car.

'If you are going to the Bazaar this morning can I offer you a ride in the car.' Mr Abaas smiled. 'I am going in that direction anyway.'

Abdul's grandmother was grateful for the offer of a lift as the Bazaar was quite a long walk for her aged bones to cope with. She nodded in appreciation and replied.

"Thank you Mr Abaas - Most kind of you.'

Yaz picked up his skateboard, looked at Abdul and let out a silent whistle of just air in thankfulness that the policeman did not take a harsh attitude toward the flying tin can incident, Abdul just looked back at him and grinned.

'See you later Abdul' Yaz said aloud. Passing Abdul and heading back toward the courtyard he whispered. 'That was close!'

'Mm!' Agreed Abdul quietly. 'Goodbye Mrs Haggi. See you Yaz!' He called out.

Mrs Haggi waved goodbye as Abdul and his grandmother entered the police car. Mr Abaas slammed his door shut, started the engine, then drove the roaring car forward toward the bustling Bazaar.

Reaching the Bazaar's entrance, Abdul noticed a Police officer that was waiting patiently for Mr Abaas to arrive, and this officer waved his hand as the Police car rolled to a stop in front of him.

The policeman moved forward and opened the car door to let Abdul and his grandmother exit the vehicle.

'Hello Abdul' he said cheerfully as the boy left the car, and quickly added a 'Good morning' to Abdul's grandmother.

## Abdul - A Legend And The Bazaar Day.

Slamming the back door shut, the friendly policeman then opened the front door and sat next to Mr Abaas.

'Thanks very much!' Shouted Abdul, while his grandmother waved to both the officers.

'A Quiet day today' said the policeman to Mr Abaas. Then acknowledging Abdul and his grandmother with a nod, he slammed the door shut.

'Good, good' replied Mr Abaas, pressing down on the cars accelerator to move the vehicle forward with a loud roar.

The policeman watched as Abdul and his grandmother grew distant within the cars rear view mirror, and then saw both disappear into the crowded throng of the Bazaar.

'That is a strange case regarding Abdul's parents' he said thoughtfully. 'How can two Archaeologists disappear in a Pyramid's sealed room with only one exit?'

Mr Abaas turned the cars steering wheel and re-entered Palm street, heading back toward the Police station.

'Well we searched the place for hours' said Mr Abaas shaking his head. 'It just does not make sense!' He braked, allowing a pedestrian to finish crossing the road. 'It is a funny thing though, that strange smell and the room being pitch dark until we actually entered it and then all the torches were burning brightly!'

'Yes!' replied the other policeman, scratching his head thoughtfully. 'I had heard about that.'

'We were there in seconds' continued Mr Abaas, reflecting back to that Time. 'A roaring, howling wind blew out of the Pyramid and right through the tunnel that three of us had been guarding while the Archaeologists did their work!' He suddenly started to feel the hairs stand up on the back of his neck. 'We rushed in, but they had gone!'

'The mysteries of the Pyramids eh?' Pondered the other policeman.

'Downright scary!' Replied Mr Abaas. 'I have seen some strange things in this job, but that! - It was almost as if the darkness swallowed them up!'

'Woo! - Ghosts!' Joked the policeman making fun of Mr Abaas.

'Not funny!' Mr Abaas was not amused and held his finger up to rebuke his fellow officer. 'That boy Abdul does not find it funny either!'

'Yes,' replied the officer sheepishly. 'Sorry!'

With a pall of dust swirling high into a sunny blue sky, the Police car entered a police station compound while, at the same Time, Abdul and his grandmother reached the centre of a bustling Bazaar and found themselves immediately surrounded by all sorts of smells of both freshly cooked and raw food-stuffs.

The Bazaar centre was an extremely busy and colourful place, with all manor of stalls, shops and people bustling with activity in a long narrow street.

Abdul noticed a small elegant bird frantically jumping about within it's cage as people passed quickly by, and was most concerned for it's welfare.

## Abdul - A Legend And The Bazaar Day.

The bird cage was situated on the floor directly outside a shop which sold many types of things, and Abdul's grandmother had stopped to examine fruit piled high onto a stall next door to the entrance.

The boy stood in front of this cage and held out his arms so that any passing people could not walk so near to the small bird, which finally rested thankfully upon it's perch.

'A beautiful bird is it not!' Said a voice from behind Abdul.

'Yes' replied Abdul in a concerned voice, his eyes transfixed toward the bird. 'But all these passing people frighten it, this bird should not be left so low to the floor!'

'Ah! - Excuse me' the shop owner picked up the cage and held it high. 'So, I think you are correct young man!' He agreed, placing the bird cage onto a high piece of metal which protruded from the shop wall, above a small window.

'What are you doing Abdul!' Exclaimed his grandmother, looking at him, while holding an orange and squeezing it to see if it was firm.

'The boy has just saved my bird from harm!' Interrupted the shop owner, smiling toward Abdul's grandmother.

'Oh! - Well, well done Abdul!' Complemented his grandmother.

The shop owner thought for a moment.

'I have seen your face before young man. Are you not the son of those Archaeologists that have disappeared?'

'Yes sir' replied Abdul, not really wishing to be reminded of the past as he felt his heart sink.

'Well maybe you can help me!' Said the shop owner. He then turned to Abdul's grandmother and asked. 'May I reward the boy with something from my shop?'

'Of course, most kind' replied Abdul's grandmother nodding in appreciation.

'Come inside the shop and you may choose any item you wish Abdul.' The shop owner gestured to the shop entrance.

'I shall be along in a few moments' called Abdul's grandmother. 'Go ahead.'

Abdul entered the shop through the narrow doorway and moved to one side allowing the shop owner to enter. Two tourists were already inside and they were examining pieces of ancient artefacts, both pondering whether or not to make a purchase.

'Cheap rubbish!' The shop owner whispered to Abdul, then he winked an eye at the boy. Abdul smiled and looked closely around the shop's interior. There seemed to be all types of everything in the shop, clocks, statues, furniture, jewellery, paintings, clothes, in fact anything that you could mention and in all the colours of the rainbow.

'Firstly' said the shop owner hopefully to Abdul. 'Do you know how to read hieroglyphics?'

'Yes' replied Abdul, his eyes still wandering around the shops interior.

## Abdul - A Legend And The Bazaar Day.

'Well mostly I do, but not all... I was taught some.'
'Excellent!' Beamed the shop owner, moving behind the counter. He produced a deep cardboard box from beneath the shelf and quickly placed it on the top.
'See if you can read these!' He pulled out two old and fragile scrolls from the box, both of which had the remains of wax seals to keep them closed, but which the shop owner had broken open to examine the contents. He handed one of the scrolls to Abdul and placed the other on the counter.
'The seal is of the Pharaoh called Nefelkheres' said Abdul looking at the wax seal picture and instantly recognising it as one of the things that his parents had taught him about. 'This is a scroll from his personal library.'
The shop owner was most impressed.
'Can you read the contents?' He asked Abdul hopefully.
'I will try!' Replied Abdul, gently unfurling the delicate parchment and placing it onto a flat table. He placed four small statues that were on the table on each edge of the parchment to flatten it out and proceeded to decipher these small Hieroglyphics pictures into words for the expectant shop owner.
'At the first rising of the sun and cooling of the night, The Great Spirit Of Anger and Hate was banished, to remain without power and forever lie in a Void of stillness.' Abdul pointed to each picture as he read them out, so as not to lose his place.
'Peace reigned happily, and drawn creatures of Time were created to collect a library of all things.'
The tourists in the shop put down the things they were looking at and moved closer, watching, as Abdul read the story.
'It is a scroll of legends' noted Abdul smiling at the shop keeper.
'Please continue!' The shop owner was eager to find out what the rest of the scroll contained and produced a note book from behind the counter to write down what Abdul was saying.
'Through many sun rises and sunsets, all was well and Time was happy' Abdul continued. 'But as great Kingdoms and Countries formed, the anger and hate of peoples grew stronger with war and greed, feeding the great spirit of anger and hate with power.'
Abdul scratched his chin, wondering what all this meant and read onward. 'Fed with this new power and lying deep within the Void of stillness, the Evil Spirit reached forth, wishing to return and prevent the rising of the sun and cooling of the night.'
Abdul took a deep breath, feeling the air within this shop suddenly grow cold.
'It wished to destroy all, especially that which had been created in the Spirit Of Good and Peace forever.'
The shop owner wrote as fast as he could to keep up with Abdul's reading, but stopped momentarily to look around his shop, as he could also feel a cold chill and wondered where it had come from.

## Abdul - A Legend And The Bazaar Day.

'From above the Kharga Oasis, a dark circle became larger as the Spirit reached forth. From the sky this dark circle descended to Earth, to both spread and devour all that would stand in it's path.'

Abdul looked up to the shop owner and asked for a glass of water which was produced very quickly, as the shop owner wanted to know what happened next.

The two tourists were also provided with a glass each, as the midday sun made the interior of the shop quite humid.

'The Great Pharaoh was troubled and sent forth his mighty army of the most loyal and fearless to defeat the Spirit. Multitudes of Archers, Chariots and Swordsmen were sent in abundance to do battle. But all were swallowed by the Circle of Darkness.'

That piece started to upset Abdul a little, but curiously the legend interested him and he decided to finish reading it for the shop owner.

'That is the end of this scroll' said Abdul. 'May I have the other?'

'Of Course!' Said the shop owner and gave Abdul the second scroll, while rolling up the first, then placing it back into the cardboard box.

Abdul, as with the first scroll, rolled out the parchment and placed a statue at each edge, to hold it firmly in place on the table top. He then started to read aloud the second scroll.

'None could with-stand The Great Spirit Of Anger And Hate as it was released further from the Void of stillness.'

Abdul, still thirsty in the humid shop, licked his dry lips. Then once more tracing his finger slowly over the Hieroglyphics, he reached slowly for the water glass with his other hand.

'The Powerful Spirit rejoiced and feasted upon the very anger and hate that was sent to destroy it. Mighty Pharaoh watched helplessly as it's powerful darkness spread over the land and lay waste to the fruit's of the Kingdom. All was deemed lost.'

Abdul took another sip of water from his glass, while the shopkeeper smiled and wrote quickly into his notebook.

'From the skies, arose the strange creatures of Time. Joined with a host of children, speaking many tongues and carrying within them the Peaceful Spirit Of Charity Toward Nations. They did battle with the Evil Spirit.'

Abdul put the glass back on the table top, being very careful not to spill the water onto the parchment.

'Riding their flying chariots and armed only with the flaming red sun ball of history and wisdom, the creatures and children lit up the Great Circle Of Anger and Hate with the Sun Flame Of Faith and Hope. Fire raged within the darkness. Creatures and children entered the Great Circle. A howling of wind and mighty roar arose. The Great Circle that had spread across the land was vanquished. It returned to the sky and disappeared back to the stillness.'

## Abdul - A Legend And The Bazaar Day.

'A moment please!' The shopkeeper turned a page in his notebook as the other had quickly filled. 'Please continue!'

'Mighty Pharaoh rejoiced and proclaimed that a monument be built to the saving of the Land. A Pyramid was built, so that if the creatures should return they could balance in the sky upon it's summit and Great Pharaoh himself could keep watch for their return there-after and throughout all eternity from within the monument.'

Abdul rolled up the scroll and handed it back to the shopkeeper.

'That is where the scroll ends' he said, happy that he been able to translate so much.

'Excellent! - Excellent!' Replied the shopkeeper, thankful that Abdul could be so helpful. 'Would you please be so kind as to interpret this also?'

The shopkeeper produced a long decorative box, that had lay hidden deep within the cardboard box.

Abdul examined the curious object intently. Fashioned from some sort of wood, inscribed with a complex swirling pattern, it had a mirror embedded on the top and directly below that, a verse in neat, but quite small hieroglyphics.

'Do you have the key?' Asked Abdul, looking at the small keyhole on the side of the box.

'No, I am afraid not!' The shopkeeper held up his arms and shook his head.

Abdul removed the long box from the shops counter and placed it on the table. Although it felt weightless and empty, Abdul could not help thinking that something interesting lay await inside.

'These Hieroglyphics are small, but I think I can understand them' said Abdul, looking very closely at the long box.

The two tourists bent forward toward the table. The shopkeeper did likewise from behind the counter. But only Abdul could see and translate the verse embedded on the box top. He read it aloud for all to hear.

> **Any fool can frown at me**
> **Any person can happy be**
> **Stop think twice before a key you turn**
> **For Time and Peace you have to learn**

'That does not sound Ancient Egyptian' said one of the tourists.

'It's a shame you do not have the key to open the box!' exclaimed the other tourist. The shopkeeper nodded in agreement.

'Yes. It is a most strange verse. It would also seem that the contents will also remain a mystery. Not even a locksmith can open the box' said the shopkeeper scratching his head. 'It is made of the hardest of materials and cannot even be broken open with a hammer or crowbar!'

## Abdul - A Legend And The Bazaar Day.

Abdul examined the small lock. Then he noticed that etched into the metal surround, almost invisible to the human eye, was a tiny symbol that looked like a rather peculiar smiling nose and mouth.

'Well it is not the Eye of Re' he said to himself, but it does look very similar.

'What!' Exclaimed the shopkeeper, thinking that the boy may have discovered something important.

Abdul glanced at a statue standing upright on the table. One that he had used to keep the parchment held down. It crossed his mind that if they were genuine, it would be around the same age as the scrolls that he had interpreted.

'Well,' said Abdul. 'That statue,' he pointed to it. 'Has the same symbol etched onto it, as does this box around it's lock.'

'What?' exclaimed the shopkeeper again, who was slightly bemused. 'I do not see the relevance. How does that make us able to open the box?'

Abdul picked up the statue that had caught his eye. It was a small effigy of a Pharaoh, that was pointing it's arm out and a finger forwards. The thumb of the statue, protruding slightly up and to one side, was carved intricately at the side of the pointing finger.

'The symbol is also carved onto the top of this statues hand!' Observed Abdul.

The shopkeeper tried to look closer. Abdul held the statue forward for him to see. Abdul then pushed the pointing hand of the statue into the small lock, his face taught with concentration.

'I believe the hand may be a key!' He turned the statue to one side, to attempt to open the lock.

'Please don't break the statue!' Exclaimed the shopkeeper. 'It is one of the oldest things in my shop!'

The lock, however, would not budge with the turning of the statue. Abdul felt the small statue turn back against his twisting hand.

'No sir, I will be careful' said Abdul who then contemplated the verse silently in his head, before he tried again, gently, to open the long box. 'Any person can happy be?' He thought deeply.

Abdul smiled into the mirror embedded onto the box lid and gently twisted the statue like a key, twice, around in the lock.

'Wow!' Exclaimed Abdul, along with the shopkeeper and the two tourists as the long box lid flew open with a whoosh of wind.

Abdul moved forward and peered into the open box.

Abdul re-placed the old statue carefully back on the table top. Then, slowly, removed the old cloth that covered the box's hidden contents. He placed this cloth on the table top next to the statue, then placed his hand inside.

The shop owner moved eagerly from behind the counter for a closer view. 'Well – Well -' he exclaimed in excitement. 'What is inside the box?'

## Abdul - A Legend And The Bazaar Day.

Abdul produced a plain old note book and pencil from inside. Really rather ordinary things, but both contained a nose and smiley mouth imprinted on both items. Just the same symbol that was etched into both the box's metal surround and statues hand.

'These!' Announced Abdul, holding them up and handing both to the shop owner.

With a stunned look, the shop owner quickly flicked open the note book.

'No writing inside?' He said, disappointed. Then he rubbed the pencil across the pages, but no lines of any sort were produced by the tip. 'Useless he said aloud' and threw both objects onto the table top.

'There is something else!' Exclaimed Abdul, this instantly brought back the shop owners interest.

From the boxes dark bottom, Abdul, with both hands, produced a long skateboard and held it up for all to see. This also contained a symbol of a nose and smiley mouth etched onto the long boards, top front end.

'That looks kind of modern to me!' said one of the tourists with a grin.

'Yes - Well - I - Er?' The shop owner did not know what to say.

'Looks like fake stuff to me' said the other tourist shaking his head.

'Oh dear' the shop owner realised his 'find' was of no value whatsoever and one of the tourists broke his embarrassed silence.

'Well I would like to buy the objects we examined earlier!' The tourist then gestured to the 'cheap rubbish' that the shop owner had whispered to Abdul about earlier.

'Certainly sir!' The shop owner sprang back to action. 'Would you like them gift wrapped?' He enquired.

'Sure why not!' The tourist nodded a yes.

'And as I promised young man!' The shop owner turned to Abdul. 'For your kind help with the bird out-side and with the scrolls and box!' He gestured with both hands to encompass all areas of his shop. 'What of my many items would you care to choose for yourself?'

Abdul looked around the shops interior at the vast array of merchandise that surrounded the walls.

'Well?' he said thoughtfully. 'I would like this skateboard please!'

The shop keeper laughed. 'Well of course, if that is your wish!' He patted Abdul on the back. 'Take that and the long box and scrolls with you!' He smiled at the tourists about to buy his 'cheap rubbish'. 'I sell only quality items in this store!' He exclaimed and winked at Abdul, when the tourists were not looking.

Abdul smiled back at the shop keeper and just then his grandmother entered the shop from out-side.

'Are you ready to leave Abdul?' She enquired.

## Abdul - A Legend And The Bazaar Day.

'Yes grandmother!' Smiled Abdul. He put the scrolls into the old box and put it under his arm. The skateboard he picked up and placed onto the floor, hopping on board to roll out of the shop.

'Goodbye!' The shopkeeper shouted, he smiled, then waved goodbye.

As Abdul followed his grandmother into the bustling noisy street out-side and rolling from the small shop doorway, the boy thought he heard a small voice say...

'Hello Buddy!'

Abdul looked around, but the voice seemed to come from the direction of the skateboard itself that he rode upon. Abdul just shook his head and put it down to his imagination and the noise of a crowded Bazaar.

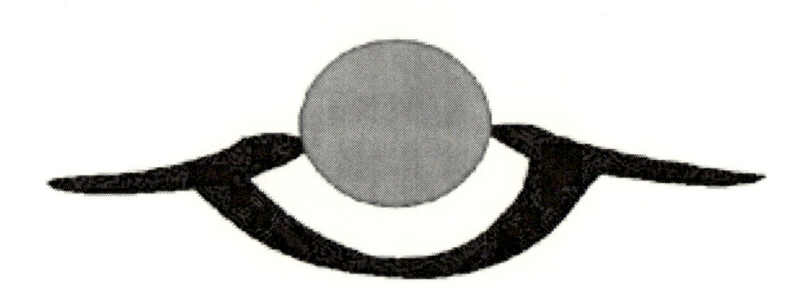

## *Abdul - The Pharaohs Tomb.*

There were far too many people walking around the Bazaar for Abdul to comfortably ride the skateboard without bumping into anyone. At least, that is what Abdul's grandmother thought and told him.

'May I take the skateboard outside the Bazaar, near to the sand dunes then grandmother?' Asked Abdul.

For a little Peace and quiet, to carry on with her shopping, grandmother agreed.

'Stay away from the Archaeological diggings though!' She added.

'Yes grandmother!' Agreed Abdul and he disappeared into the throng of bustling, busy, people.

He emerged into the fairly quiet back streets of the town and put the skateboard down to rest it's wheels onto the hard, but unsurfaced ground.

'Don't like the dusty ground huh?' Muttered Abdul automatically, talking to himself, as much as the smiley mouth on the skateboard top, which had seemed to stop smiling for a second. Then he looked around, to make sure no-one had seen him talking to himself. But the street was empty.

Abdul stepped onto the skateboard, held on to the old long box and pushed hard with his foot. The skateboard rolled quite gracefully along the dusty road and both Abdul and it appeared from the last building of the town, to stand in front of the deserted road that led downward, to a tall Pyramid, surrounded by sand dunes and other Archaeological diggings.

Abdul's eyes sadly surveyed the scene where his parents had disappeared. The Pyramid of an unknown Pharaoh had been found buried beneath the sand dunes, in a valley, hidden for centuries. Much of this area had been uncovered by many bulldozers, which stood resting for the next days work all around the diggings.

'What the -' Abdul's thoughts of happier Times, was very rudely interrupted by a quickly moving Khamseen sand storm, that rolled low across the sand dunes and seemed to be heading directly toward him.

'Time to get out of here!' Said Abdul, watching the Khamseen pick up the surface dust of the desert and throw it ever higher into the air. He stopped for a few seconds though, because to his eyes, this Khamseen seemed quite different to any he had seen before and it started to spread an eerie orange glow, that gradually turned to a quite deep red, throughout it's sprawling, tumbling length.

'Yes! Time to get out of here!' A voice made Abdul look quickly around, but the street remained empty.

'Wow!' Abdul gripped the old long box tightly, as the skateboard beneath his feet hurtled forward. 'Hey!' He shouted, finding his feet stuck to the skateboards top and Abdul struggled to balance. 'What is going on?'

The skateboard and Abdul moved at lightening speed, down the deserted road, past the static bulldozers and toward the ever increasing in size Pyramid.

## Abdul - The Pharaohs Tomb.

Abdul looked downward, trying unsuccessfully to free his feet. He noticed how the smiley mouth on the skateboard top seemed to, well, smile even more at him. Then, for a moment, he thought the large red nose above it sniffed the air, like it was searching for something, it reminded him of grandfathers dog, when it could smell supper coming.

'Must save Time!'

Abdul was amazed. The smiley mouth moved as he looked at it and had spoken words.

'What?' Was all that would come from Abdul's lips, his brain feeling quite confused.

'No Time to explain!' Continued the smiley mouth. "Must save Time. Time needs your help. You found the chest and opened it. Only the future can save the future!'

The confusion of how a skateboard could talk, was only matched by the sheer horror that met Abdul's eyes, when an awesome roaring noise made him look upwards.

'Ah!' He yelled, watching the massive, rolling, deep red and very angry Khamseen moving forward to engulf him.

'Relax!' Shouted the skateboard above the awful noise. 'Have a little faith Buddy! Things will turn out OK.'

Abdul still could not believe his ears, but he believed his eyes and shut them very tightly, a split second before the hellish wind struck him and the skateboard.

The howling wind rushed past Abdul's face. He clenched his teeth together tightly, expecting the sand thrown up by the Khamseen to flail his skin painfully.

'But just a moment?' He thought to himself, feeling very puzzled. 'This wind feels just like a cool breeze?'

Abdul opened one eye, then both. Then Abdul found that he was still travelling very fast on the skateboard, only through a long triangle shaped tunnel that was brightly lit with a line of electrical light bulbs.

'Inside the Pyramid!' He exclaimed aloud.

Abdul turned for a moment and saw the furious Khamseen reach toward him from the Pyramid's entrance. The redness of the sand however, quickly evaporated the further it was whipped into the brightly lit tunnel and then, as the wind reduced in power, the sand fell to the ground, quite gently.

'What are you?' Asked Abdul to the smiley mouth on the skateboards top. 'Are you some sort of magic, or what?'

'No! - No!' came the firm, but polite reply. 'I am just the means created to help and protect you, while you are transported to the place that you must be.'

'OK!' Said Abdul, not really understanding the answer. He was about to ask another question, when the skateboard suddenly veered to the right and hurtled downward.

## Abdul - The Pharaohs Tomb.

Abdul held on tightly to the old long box and tried to keep his balance, or at the very least, stay upright on the skateboard that was stuck to his feet.

The skateboard hurtled down another long corridor that was elaborately decorated with Hieroglyphics and entered the burial chamber of the unknown Pharaohs tomb.

Inside, the archaeologist's light bulb's shone brightly, illuminating the square shaped room, but casting shadows into the corners. Just for a moment, Abdul thought he saw the shape of a penguin cast across an exquisitely decorated wall as he passed by. He had seen them in books at school, but then he put the shadow down to his own fertile imagination. This shadow seemed to have a large nose on it's head, which penguins do not, besides there were no statues of them in the room to cast a shadow anyway.

Above the open sarcophagus, that lay in the centre of the chamber, hung a rope ladder that dangled from a hole that had been cut into the roof. The sarcophagus, that the archaeologists had removed and found empty, except for a large amulet, that pictured the Sun and a curved half circle that was embedded into the bottom, was littered with plaster and stone that had fallen from the ceiling.

'That looks like you!' Noted Abdul, looking at the amulet while the skateboard circled the sarcophagus.

'Not as pretty!' Replied the smiley mouth on the skateboard top. The skateboard then suddenly rose up toward the hole in the ceiling. 'Hold on to your hat!' It called out, then accelerated through the opening.

Beyond the opening that had been crudely made in the chamber roof three figures stood examining the treasures that they had found in the room above and were about to steal.

'Quickly!' Said one, help me remove these Jewels. He produced a knife and proceeded to remove a ruby that was embedded into the wall as part of a hieroglyphic story.

'A pity to ruin such an old picture!' He said sarcastically. One of the other thieves moved to help him.

The third thief picked up a heavy sack and turned, just in Time to see Abdul and the skateboard rise up through the large opening, that the thieves had made in the chamber ceiling.

Abdul was really amazed by this hidden and quite large room above the chamber. While the skateboard quickly climbed higher through the opening made in the floor, then slowed down. His eyes automatically followed the many beautiful wall paintings, that were, at certain points, encrusted with colourful jewels which glistened under the golden light of flickering lamps illuminating the room.

Abdul and the skateboard turned. His own eyes then met, with quite some surprise, the eyes of the thief that had picked up a heavy sack.

## Abdul - The Pharaohs Tomb.

With a sudden lunge, the third thief dropped the sack and tried to grab Abdul.
'Got you!' He shouted, reaching out with both his hands.
Unfortunately, for him, the skateboard was somewhat quicker in motion. It moved Abdul almost to the top of the room in a split second. The thief, with hands still outstretched, fell downward through the hole in the floor and landed painfully, in a crumpled heap onto the floor of the chamber below.
'Oops!' Called out Abdul, looking down through the hole at the man laying stretched out and dazed.
'What the -' the second thief looked toward the hole. His mouth fell open when his eyes looked up to see Abdul, who was now almost at ceiling height, standing on the hovering old skateboard. He tapped the first thief on his shoulder. This thief was engrossed in the act of removing the shining ruby and was very annoyed at being interrupted.
'What is the problem?' He asked angrily and turned to the open mouthed person who had tapped his shoulder.
'That is the problem!' The second thief stood up and pointed to Abdul.
The two thieves looked at each other in confusion, both not really accepting the sight of a boy flying, or at least hovering, on a skateboard high in the air above the ground.
The old skateboard suddenly accelerated forward, heading directly toward the two thieves.
'Wow!' Exclaimed Abdul, gripping the long box that was tucked under his arm.
Both thieves moved to one side and fell flat on the floor.
'It is the Pharaohs curse!' Shouted one of them, with a frightened look on his face.
The other looked upwards from the floor and saw Abdul smiling down at him.
'It is some sort of trick!' He said. 'It is only a boy!' He then reached for his knife that had fallen on the floor.
In a second, the old skateboard flipped Abdul upside down and blew an icy blast of air from the smiley mouth. The red nose twirled in agreement as the knife stuck fast to the floor, in a glistening, frozen pool of ice.
'Now that's not nice Buddy!' Said the smiley mouth with a grin. 'So have some ice!' It blew an incredibly icy blast toward the two thieves and both their head hair and moustaches, froze into a solid mass of freezing ice.
'It is the Pharaohs curse!' Both the thieves now howled together, recognising the smiley mouth that talked to them from the skateboard bottom, as being the same symbol as in the sarcophagus bottom.
They scrambled to their feet and headed toward the hole they had made in the floor, all thoughts of loot now very far from their minds.
'Curse! - Smirk!' said the smiley mouth, quite offended. It then span back upright, with Abdul balancing furiously on top.

## Abdul - The Pharaohs Tomb.

Then, accelerating quickly, it helped the thieves exit the room, the rapid way, by tapping them both on their back's.

The two thieves fell, with a clash of head's, through the hole in the floor and landed next to the thief, who was already in the chamber below, rubbing his own sore head.

'It is coming again!' Shouted one of the men, looking up to see the skateboard and rider appear in the hole that was made in the ceiling.

The old skateboard tilted Abdul forward.

'Hold on to your hat!' Ordered the smiley mouth grinning. 'Time to clear the trash from this room!' The old skateboard then hurtled forward through the hole, directly toward the three thieves who sat on the floor looking upwards with strained eyes.

With a look of horror on each of their faces, the three men scrambled in panic to their feet. Each ruffian pushed the other violently, in their hurry to exit the chamber of the Pharaohs tomb and escape it's 'curse'. There was now no honour or friendship amongst these thieves, as each was now only concerned for his own safety, whilst running away in fear.

Above them, Abdul clutched the long box under his arm and felt a cool, but howling wind rush past his ears as the skateboard flew through the hole. But somehow, strangely, this wind did not prevent his eyes from seeing clearly and in fact, did not seem to touch them in anyway.

'Most peculiar for a wind' he thought momentarily, remembering how wind usually made his eyes stream with tears.

'Get out of my way!' Shouted one of the thieves, now reaching the chamber doorway, pushing another man to one side.

'Me first!' Shouted another thief, who followed close behind. He grabbed the man in front and threw him against the wall.

'Oh dear, oh dear!' Shouted the smiley mouth on the skateboard to Abdul sarcastically. 'As thick as thieves, must mean they are stupid.' It laughed - 'Fancy running away from a smile!' The skateboard then accelerated toward them, but stopped just as it reached the doorway that they were all fighting each other to get through.

Flipping Abdul upside down, the smiley mouth gave another strong blast of icy air. It was a blast strong enough to force all three thieves to exit this small doorway opening at the same Time.

'Ah!' they all bellowed loudly, momentarily hitting the outside wall and falling into a heap toward the floor. The thieves scrambled back to their feet and quickly ran up the corridor toward the Pyramid exit.

The skateboard and Abdul accelerated forward and followed them through the doorway, with the howling wind rushing up this long corridor and making the hairs on the back of the thieves necks stand up, tingling with fear.

## Abdul - The Pharaohs Tomb.

Outside this impressive, intricately decorated set of corridors and way beyond the Pyramid entrance, the red Khamseen had passed over the Bazaar, causing everyone there to seek shelter inside the many shops. Although this sand storm had hit with an enormous and raging ferocity, angrily turning over stalls and sending things tumbling about all over the place, it then, strangely, disappeared as quickly as it had come.

With one hand slipping the sun glasses over his eyes as the sun shone brilliantly behind the Pyramid tip, Mr Abaas turned the wheel of his police car with his other hand and his foot applied the brakes. In a pall of dust, the car pulled up to halt in front of a bulldozer at the archaeological dig. He and another police officer left the vehicle, slammed the doors shut and headed toward a figure that was sat slumped, in the bulldozers cab.

Mr Abaas had driven his police car here to search for Abdul. For, at the Bazaar and after the Khamseen had struck, Abdul's grandmother had become concerned for him. She had asked the police to search for Abdul, but, Mr Abaas had now found something completely different to the small boy that he had been looking for. The two policemen opened the bulldozer cab door and helped the slumped figure remove the tape that had been placed over his mouth.

'They hit me from behind!' Said the policeman, who was tied up in the cab. 'There were three of them and they entered the Pyramid.'

Mr Abaas moved quickly toward the Pyramid entrance, leaving his college to radio for help and untie his fellow police officer that still sat in the bulldozer cab.

Mr Abaas, reaching the triangular doorway, removed the pistol from it's holster that was now dangling loosely from his belt and moved slowly inside.

The wind that howled up the long corridor, suddenly blasted a very surprised Mr Abaas who was not expecting wind to come from a Pyramid. This wind was followed very closely by the terrified howling of the three thieves who knocked Mr Abaas to one side, completely ignoring the fact that he held a pistol in his hand.

'Save us from the curse!' Two shouted and grovelled at the feet of Mr Abaas.

The police officer reacted very quickly and handcuffed these thieves together, while loudly calling for the other police officer to arrest the third criminal who had ran very swiftly in a state of complete panic down the long corridor. Mr Abaas moved toward this long corridor, while his college handcuffed the last thief.

'Thank you! Thank you! - Get us away from here! - Take us to prison! - Anything! - But save us!' The third thief pleaded.

'First Time I have heard that' said the college of Mr Abaas in surprise.

'But what makes them so afraid?' Replied Mr Abaas, noticing that the howling wind now seemed to be sucked in, rather than blown out of the doorway. He looked down the corridor to see Abdul and the skateboard turn sharply and head back toward the Pharaohs tomb.

## Abdul - The Pharaohs Tomb.

Swerving back into the Pharaohs tomb, it suddenly struck Abdul that flying on top of a talking skateboard was not really the normal sort of thing for people to be doing. He had heard of other kinds of magic happening in stories, flying carpets and things like that, but a flying and talking skateboard, well that was quite strange.

But Abdul now decided that he would not be afraid of the situation, after all, he really quite enjoyed the experience of riding a flying skateboard, even if he could not control it. The smiley mouth seemed friendly enough and it had dealt with the very bad people trying to rob the tomb.

'Always take on adversity or adventure, head on, with a smile on your face, no matter what' were the words that his parents always used and they now echoed around Abdul's head, as the skateboard rose into the air and quickly circled the chamber. That, decided Abdul, is exactly what he should now do.

Outside, high above this Pyramid, a scorching midday sun beamed downward and the skateboard seemed to sense it.

'Light is good, light is fine, shine on us, for all Time!' It said, the smiley mouth beaming it's best smile. After it's words were spoken, thin, but brilliant rays of sun light suddenly pierced the Pyramid, being channelled through many tiny corridors in the stonework that had been carved countless centuries ago.

Within seconds, these rays of golden sunlight touched the colourful jewels that were embedded into the wall as part of a hieroglyphic story in the hidden room above the sarcophagus. The skateboard took Abdul higher, right up to the ceiling and Abdul could see the hieroglyphic story much more clearly in the previously, dimly lit room through the large hole in it's floor.

'There was only a very small hole here!' Said the skateboard, it's smile disappearing. 'But Evil deeds have made it larger!'

Abdul continued to read the hieroglyphics, while also trying to listen to the skateboard, but found doing both things quite difficult, as the hieroglyphics were very complicated things to translate.

'This is a similar story to the legend told in the scrolls' replied Abdul, only half listening to the skateboard. He carried on reading about the eternal battle between light and darkness, good and bad, that was written on the wall. Abdul found it quite fascinating, then, he read.

'Mighty Pharaoh rejoiced and proclaimed that a monument be built to the saving of the Land. A Pyramid was built, so that if the creatures should return they could balance in the sky upon it's summit and Great Pharaoh himself could keep watch for their return throughout all eternity from within the monument.'

It was at that point, Abdul realised, that this was the actual Pyramid that was built after the battle mentioned in the scrolls and that was written on the wall.

'Incredible!' He exclaimed aloud. 'But I wonder what happened to the Pharaoh?' Remembering that the mummy had not been found.

## Abdul - The Pharaohs Tomb.

The many beams of sunlight became stronger. Brighter and brighter they came from the sun outside, flowing toward and then from the jewels, forcing Abdul to squint, then shut his eyes.

With his eyes closed, he did not notice the sarcophagus bottom open, like a lid, and a brilliant beam of light flow from it, that met the light from the sun and jewels, to form a single, corridor like beam.

'Time to fly!' Exclaimed the smiley mouth on the skateboard top. It banked sharply and accelerated in a rush of wind down the corridor of light and both the skateboard and Abdul disappeared into the sarcophagus bottom.

Mr Abaas puffed as he ran down the Pyramids corridor, chasing Abdul to make sure he was safe.

'I am too old for this at my age!' He thought to himself, reaching the tomb's entrance.

He stopped suddenly in the corridor, looking through the tombs doorway, being just in Time to see Abdul disappear and the sarcophagus bottom close to extinguish the beam of light that flowed from it.

Speechless, Mr Abaas moved to go through the entrance. But as he did so, the light from the sun extinguished, at the very same Time as a deep rumble arose from the ground.

'Ah!' Mr Abaas yelled. The corridor wall collapsed at the side of him, to allow the mummy of the Pharaoh to lunge forward and block the policeman's path. Both mummy and policeman fell to the floor with a thud.

Mr Abaas quickly pushed the mummy to one side and raced toward the sarcophagus. He leant forward, moving over it's side and shouted toward the amulet that smiled at him from the bottom of the ancient box.

'Abdul! -'

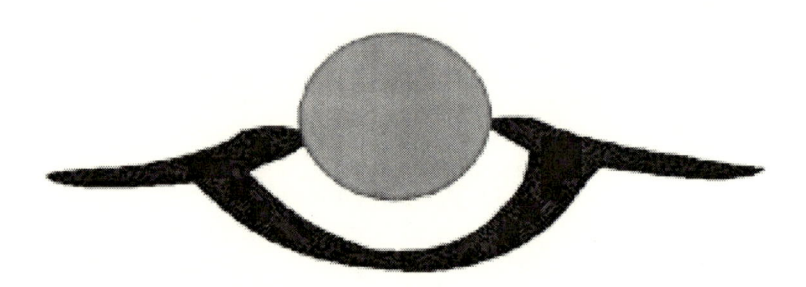

**From here you may read onwards for the next individuals entry point, or just skate forwards to our Living Legends Chapter**

From The South And A New World:- An Individual Entry Point.

### *Sue - A Legend and The Wallaby Pouch*

Sue lived in an ordinary place, in an ordinary town in an ordinary street. Today was the weekend and she had just finished washing and dressing upstairs after getting up quite early in the morning.

With a brilliant ray of golden sunshine streaming through the large living room windows, and standing at the bottom of a long twisting staircase, Sue adjusted her eyes to the light of a new morning.

A loud noise reached out from the kitchen.

'Whatever is that!' Sue called out, and she hurried forward and beyond the doorway separating both rooms. Sue found that a large figure stood in front of an open refrigerator door.

'Hoppy!' Sue moved forward and quickly shut the refrigerator door. The small Wallaby moved back and licked Sue on the face. 'Good morning' laughed Sue. 'You had better scram!' She pointed to the open door leading to an outside patio area. 'Grandmother will not be so happy to see you in the kitchen!'

Grandmother was not very to happy to see the small Wallaby in the kitchen, and screamed while entering the doorway.

'Get that beast from this kitchen at once!' Grandmother's arm's were waving in all directions.

'What is going on?' Grandfathers voice boomed from the staircase.

'It is that Wallaby!' The old lady shooed Hoppy from her kitchen.

Hoppy bounded quickly toward the open doorway and out into a warm and clear morning light.

'Ah!' A voice outside cried in surprise, and was knocked into silence by Hoppy who hadn't been able to avoid an unfortunate collision.

Sue rushed outside immediately.

'Are you hurt?' She asked, helping a stunned figure stand up from the ground.

'No?' Guess not said Charlie pulling himself upright. 'You really are on form today Hoppy!' The boy shouted toward a concerned Wallaby.

Hoppy moved forward and licked the boy on his cheek.

'OK OK!' Charlie pushed the apologetic Wallaby back. 'Take it easy!'

Grandmother emerged from the doorway and Hoppy quickly headed toward the safety of the trees.

'Would you like some breakfast Charlie?' Asked grandmother.

'No thank you' the boy replied, rubbing his sore back.

'Well come on in and have a cup of tea!' Smiled grandmother.

'Thanks, that would be nice' replied Charlie and he followed grandmother and Sue into the kitchen.

'Hello Charlie,' grandfather had just finished wiping Wallaby footprints from the fridge front. 'No damage done here love!' He called to grandmother.

## Sue - A Legend and The Wallaby Pouch.

'Sit yourselves down and I will make some tea and breakfast!' Called the old lady, and she disappeared into the pantry.

'Have you solved the puzzle of Ghost Rock yet?' Asked grandfather sitting on one of the four chairs of a large kitchen table.

'Well no, not really,' Charlie handed grandfather a newspaper that he had come to deliver.

'What is that?' Asked Sue.

'Oh sorry!' Charlie smiled. 'You are new here.' He sat back somewhat uncomfortably in a chair, still quite sore after being knocked down by Hoppy. 'It is an old aborigine cave and legend, would you like to hear about it?'

'Yes it sounds cool' replied Sue, putting both elbows on the kitchen table and cupping her chin in her hands. 'Please tell me about it.'

'OK' said Charlie. 'Well it started a long Time ago.'

Grandfather rested a pair of spectacles on the end of his nose as Charlie continued.

'The old aborigine legend says that Ghost Rock is a hidden entrance to the home of the creatures of Time.' Charlie felt the soreness of his back ease a little and he rested more comfortably on the wooden chair.

'Creatures of Time?' Asked Sue. 'What are they?'

'Well,' continued Charlie. 'In the legend when Time and light came into being during the first sunrise, these creatures, being neither human or animal were born. They make written records of what happens within Time and keep these records safe for all eternity.'

'Do you know what these creatures look like?' Asked Sue, resting her head on a single palm of her hand.

'There are some paintings of them in a cave up at Ghost Rock, weird looking things' smiled Charlie. 'Maybe you would like to see them?'

'You bet!' Exclaimed Sue.

Grandfather looked over the top of his newspaper.

'After breakfast I will take you home Charlie.' He turned a page over. 'Perhaps we will stop off at the Rock for a look at the paintings and Sue can see them too.'

'Thanks' replied Charlie, who was not really looking forward to riding his bike the long way home and would be glad of a lift.

'So what is the puzzle of Ghost Rock?' Asked Sue.

'Ah -' Charlie smiled. 'In the legend, as one of the very first aborigines was on walkabout, he went to the Rock.' Charlie scratched his chin in thought. 'The legend says that he found a bent stick, one that this aborigine had seen the creatures of Time use to stop a follower of the Dark Spirit running away with some of these creatures records.'

'Dark Spirit -' Sue was fascinated. 'What is that?'

'Well that is the main part of this legend' replied Charlie.

## Sue - A Legend and The Wallaby Pouch.

'When Time was first started and light created by the Good Spirit, an Evil Dark Void that occupied space was banished forever. But this Dark Void was a bad spirit that has always wanted to return, but cannot generate enough energy.'

'Energy -' Sue wondered how darkness could have 'energy'.

'Yes, it is a battle between good and Evil legend' said Charlie. 'Sort of like, well,' he tried to explain. 'Evil cannot exist without people doing bad things, and Good cannot exist without people doing good things.' He thought for a moment. 'So the more bad things people do, the stronger the bad spirit gets. That is it's energy.'

Grandfather put his paper down and interrupted the conversation.

'The bent stick was the first boomerang. That is the real puzzle.'

'Why is that a puzzle?' Asked Sue curiously.

'Well,' answered grandfather. 'A boomerang was unearthed recently at the Rock that was reckoned to be buried around the Time of the dinosaurs.' The old man shrugged. 'But people haven't been around nowhere near that long!'

Grandmother appeared from the pantry and placed some eggs near to the cooker.

'I hope you haven't been telling those old ghost stories and upsetting Sue!' She snapped angrily, breaking an egg into a hot frying pan.

'Just getting Sue acquainted with the history of the area' replied grandfather, watching the egg sizzle and flick spots of fat high into the air.

'It is very interesting grandmother' said Sue, standing up and moving forward to help her cook.

'Really!' Replied grandmother, giving grandfather a stare of disapproval.

The old man picked up his newspaper and hid his face behind it sheepishly, then he said.

'Sue would like to see the paintings in the Rock, and I said I would take her there later while running Charlie home.'

There was an awkward silence, and grandmother turned around. Steam from a kettle drifted lazily into the air, and the old lady switched off it's power button.

'You know I do not like that place!' She snapped, lifting containers off a shelf and then noticing they were empty. 'Oh darn it' grandmother muttered, shaking her head. 'Come on Sue, lets get some tea and sugar from the pantry!'

'OK grandma' agreed Sue, and both left the room momentarily for supplies.

When they had gone, grandfather lent across the table and whispered quietly to Charlie.

'Grandmother does not like Ghost Rock, because that is roundabout where the helicopter lost contact and disappeared.'

'Oh – Right -' whispered Charlie right back. The disappearance of Sue's parents while they were travelling in their police helicopter was well known, but Charlie had no idea it had been near the Ghost Rock area.

'Maybe I should not have invited Sue to visit that place?' Sighed Charlie.

## Sue - A Legend and The Wallaby Pouch.

'Nonsense!' Replied grandfather. 'Besides, with that archaeological dig going on I expect there will be a lot of interesting things to see up there, as well as those paintings.'

'Yes, there sure is -' blurted Charlie in sudden excitement. 'Dad's team have unearthed some new artefacts near to the old boomerang that they have found, and I would really like to go up and see them myself.'

'Sounds good to me!' Agreed grandfather, looking toward the pantry. 'They are coming back now!'

Before Sue and her grandmother entered the room, Charlie whispered very quietly.

'Do you think they have any hope of finding the helicopter and Sue's parents?'

Sue's grandfather looked him straight in the eye and winked.

'There is always hope son, always hope.'

'We have the tea and sugar!' Announced Sue re-entering the kitchen. She started at once to make four cups of the brew.

Grandmother moved quickly toward the cooker and proceeded to produce fried sausages to go with the eggs. She then placed three large sized plates of the breakfast onto the kitchen table.

'Are you sure you would not like any thing to eat Charlie?' Grandmother asked again politely.

'No thanks!' Charlie accepted a cup of warming tea from Sue, but declined a breakfast. 'Already had mine earlier.'

Grandfather, grandmother and Sue then tucked into the delicious breakfast while Charlie decided to wait outside on the patio.

After a few minutes the empty plates and cups were placed into the sink for washing.

'I will get on with these' said grandmother, turning on the hot water tap.

'Well come on then!' Grandfather stood up and put on his bush hat. 'Let's get moving folks!' He kissed grandmother on the cheek. 'See you later love.'

'Do be careful up at the Rock!' Warned grandmother, and she gave a quick smile toward Sue, who smiled right back.

'No worries!' Exclaimed grandfather as he walked toward his small Jeep that stood outside on the dusty driveway. 'Everybody in!' He gestured toward the doors. 'Your carriage awaits.'

With Charlie's BMX bike stowed safely in the rear of grandfathers Jeep, the small vehicle speed along a straight, dusty highway toward Ghost Rock with it's engine roaring loudly.

'We have company!' Noted grandfather, looking into his rear view mirror. Charlie and Sue looked backwards, while the old man released foot pressure on his accelerator pedal and slowed the vehicle down.

## Sue - A Legend and The Wallaby Pouch.

From her hideaway in the trees Hoppy had seen the children enter the Jeep, and this small Kangaroo followed it and them at full bouncing speed, all the way to Ghost Rock.

Arriving at a winding clear stream, Ghost Rock laying beyond it looked like a single, vast, red painted boulder pushing ever skyward.

Grandfather stopped his Jeep and stepped out. He then helped both children disembark, while Hoppy of course made straight to the stream for a drink.

'I Guess that is petrol top up for animals' laughed grandfather.

Both Sue and Charlie walked up to Hoppy and patted the friendly Wallaby while she drank.

'Hello there!' A voice sounded from a group of tents gathered at the base of Ghost Rock.

'Hi dad!' Charlie waved to his father.

'We did not expect to see you guys up here!' said Charlie's surprised father as he shook grandfathers hand.

'Just visiting while I take Charlie home' replied grandfather. 'Sue would like to see the paintings, if that is possible.'

'Sure, of course.' Charlie's father pointed to a hole at the base of Ghost Rock. 'Best way in is there' he said, adjusting his hat to keep the hot sun from his eyes. 'Come on then!'

Walking up a steep hill and past a small encampment of tents, greetings were given from all the various members of Charlie's fathers team of archaeologists who were hard at work.

'We have found some interesting artefacts this week' Charlie's father proudly announced to grandfather. 'Come and take a look while Charlie shows Sue the paintings in the cave.' The old man nodded, and he and Charlie's father entered a large tent.

Charlie and Sue walked onward and upward into the narrow, round, and very dark opening of Ghost Rock.

'Wait here!' Ordered Charlie to Hoppy who had followed them. 'You are not allowed in the cave.'

Hoppy huffed her disapproval and hopped to one side, stopping quickly to sniff the lush green leaves of a large bush that grew outside and partially hid this sinister looking cave entrance.

'This is a spooky place!' Exclaimed Sue, entering what seemed an endless and very dark corridor that was surrounded by cold rock.

'Perfectly safe' replied Charlie, his voice echoing around the tunnel. 'Been here many Times.' He pointed to a light that grew ever brighter as they walked each step. 'See - There is the cave, there are electric lights set up inside.'

Suddenly, a gentle, but strangely howling wind whistled toward the pair and it made the hairs of both Charlie and Sue's neck stand up as it flowed right past them.

## Sue - A Legend and The Wallaby Pouch.

'Um, I don't like this much!' Cried Sue, but this strange howling wind stopped as suddenly as it had started, and both the children continued forward.

'Wow!' Exclaimed Sue entering the brightly lit cave. She rubbed both her eyes to adjust them from the tunnels darkness.

'Excuse me' said Charlie moving past her. Charlie moved a cable that he knew was laying on the floor and one that most people who visited the cave tripped over. 'Darn thing!' he cursed, pushing it safely to one side.

Sue gently opened her eyes.

'Fabulous!' she blurted, looking around the large interior of the cave. 'But what is that?' Sue pointed to a most strange object, the outline of which was brush painted with a light yellow ochre colour onto one of the grey rock walls of this large caves interior.

'They think it is a painting of one of the creatures of Time' answered Charlie, walking up to the artwork. He pointed at it, but did not touch the old and delicate outline of the cave painting. 'Looks kind of an ugly bug don't you think?'

Sue examined the painting carefully.

'Well if I did not know better' she pondered.. 'That looks something like a Penguin, with a rather large red nose.'

Charlie looked closer, although he had seen the outline many Times before he hadn't really thought of it that way.

'Well -' he thought. 'I suppose it might -' He then pointed to the head. 'But what about that huge plumage? - Penguins do not have anything that shape.'

Sue thought for a moment.

'If you ask me' she said, examining the picture. 'That plumage looks really like a hat.' She laughed and her voice echoed around the cave. 'It looks like a Penguin, with a large red ball nose, wearing a hat.'

'Don't be silly!' Replied Charlie, feeling somewhat offended. 'It's well OK, strange, I do admit that.' Charlie moved aside and pointed to the rest of the artwork. 'You can see that this one, and all the other creatures are riding clouds, and, all are accompanied by children which appear to be in human form.' Charlie remembered the rest of the legend which the archaeologists had deciphered. 'The follower of Evil is being struck down by a bent stick, thrown by one of the creatures.'

Sue looked again at all the interesting paintings.

'Why do you think that all those creatures and children are smiling, except that single creature behind the one that is throwing the bent stick?' Asked Sue.

'Oh yeah - I hadn't noticed that replied Charlie'. He laughed, taking the drawings far less seriously. 'Perhaps they ran out of paint?'

'Very funny!' Said Sue, as she quietly observed how much the 'clouds' that these creatures rode upon looked rather more like skateboards to her eyes. With a sudden howling, but gentle rush, the wind that they had experienced on entering Ghost Rock returned, echoing around every area of the cave.

## Sue - A Legend and The Wallaby Pouch.

'That is why they call it Ghost Rock!' Said Charlie, pretending not to be afraid. 'The wind comes from nowhere. Not from any single place that anyone can find that is.'

Sue did not care much for the wind either.

'Let's go now!' She muttered, moving toward the exit tunnel. With Charlie following close behind and the lights starting to eerily flicker on and off, Sue glanced behind her to take a last look at the paintings.

The strong lights flickered again, and Sue momentarily thought that a shadow cast large across the rock face behind them as a light went out, formed the shape of one of the creatures in the painting.

It sent a chill down her spine. But she just put it down to Charlie's own moving shadow and her imagination as they both passed beyond the lights.

Sue moved forward quickly into the long narrow tunnel, and was thankful for the warm embrace of the sun as she and Charlie walked outside.

Hoppy had been foraging in the undergrowth and had, as always, placed any things she found into her pouch.

The Wallaby looked up instinctively listening for sounds and movement. She twitched her nose and ears, then welcomed both children as they exited the tunnel.

Sue and Charlie quickly appeared into warm, still air outside the dark cave entrance of Ghost Rock and patted the awaiting Kangaroo.

'Come on Hoppy!' Called Charlie, walking straight past the Wallaby and he headed toward a group of tents at the bottom of the slope. 'Let's see what is new at the diggings.'

Sue and Charlie walked quickly down the hill, trying to slow down their momentum as they walked. Hoppy had no trouble though, as she bounced happily behind the children.

'Come on in' shouted Charlie's father from the interior of a large tent.

Grandfather who stood next to him, picked up the large long box that he had been looking at.

'It is really well sealed!' He said looking underneath the object and then placing it back onto a trestle table that also contained many other items from the archaeological dig.

'That is a nice thing' observed Sue, entering the tent and noting many intricately carved swirls on the box top.

'Probably belonged to a female' replied Charlie who was standing directly behind Sue and staring hard at a small mirror embedded on the box top which glistened in the sunlight amidst a sea of carved swirls.

'It was found inside the cave' explained Charlie's father.

Grandfather nodded, peering at the long box.

'Do you think it is all that old?' asked grandfather. 'The key hole on the front makes it sort of modern doesn't it.'

## Sue - A Legend and The Wallaby Pouch.

'Yes it is a rather peculiar find' replied Charlie's father. 'But the age is certain due to the depth in the ground it was buried, and other artefacts found along side it.'

'The boomerang being one?' Asked grandfather.

'Yes, it is really odd' Charlie's father scratched his head. 'There is no way of opening the box as it is made of the most peculiar and hard material, but it does feel very light.'

He picked up his bush hat and placed it firmly atop his sweating brow.

'Come on' he said grinning. 'I will show you where we found it.' He then turned toward Sue and Charlie while pointing to his backpack which lay on a rickety chair. 'Have a look at the things on the table while we are gone, there is some lemonade in that backpack if you are both thirsty.'

'Thanks!' Replied both Charlie and Sue together, but with their eyes, the children were already contemplating this mystery of a decoratively carved long box.

Sue moved slowly forward to examine the item more closely and Charlie followed her.

Picking up the long box and jiggling it back and forth, Sue spoke with a hushed tone.

'It feels empty -'

The contents, if it had any, made no sound. But just below the embedded mirror on the box top, a piece of rock that had been stuck fast finally fell off with the movements Sue had made.

'There is an inscription here!' Exclaimed Sue, placing the box on the table top.

Charlie moved forward and picked up a large magnifying glass to get a clear look at the small writing.

'This is written in old English' he said. 'Most odd.' And he read aloud the inscription.

> ***Any fool can frown at me***
> ***Any person can happy be***
> ***Stop think twice before a key you turn***
> ***For Time and Peace you have to learn***

'What do you suppose that means?' Asked Sue, also peering through the magnifying glass.

'I Don't know' replied Charlie. 'But dad will be disappointed that this box is not as old as he thought.' He put the magnifying glass down and looked at the small key hole. 'A pity they have not found the key.'

'Yes, a shame about that' replied Sue. 'What do you suppose those little pictures are.. The ones that are surrounding the keyhole.' Sue picked up the magnifying glass that glistened within a beam of streaming sunlight.

## Sue - A Legend and The Wallaby Pouch.

'Some sort of Symbol' said Charlie, stating the obvious.

'Looks like a large nose and smiling mouth to me!' Noted Sue, moving the magnifying glass back and forth to get a better look.

'Maybe -' Charlie was mystified, but suddenly remembered. 'That symbol is also painted on the cave wall inside Ghost Rock.'

'That is interesting' replied Sue, trying to look through the keyhole.

A sudden loud crash attracted both the children's immediate attention.

'Hoppy!' Cried Charlie and Sue together.

The Wallaby had been as curious of the contents of the archaeologist's tables as the children had been, and this small Kangaroo stood motionless as the entire contents of an adjoining trestle table slid to the floor, it's supporting legs having been moved to collapse by her big, protruding feet.

Both children moved forward and put the table back to it's original position. 'It's OK Hoppy, nothing damaged here!' Said Charlie picking up both the tools and artefacts and putting them neatly back onto the trestle table top.

Sue patted the Wallaby and reassured her everything was all right.

'What have you got here -' Sue looked at Hoppy's pouch. 'Did you get that from the table top, or outside -' She put her had into the pouch and removed a most curious object. 'What do you make of this?' Asked Sue, carefully removing the object.

Charlie lent forward and observed a thin metallic necklace which Sue was holding in her hand.

'I do not remember that being on the table' said Charlie.

'Neither do I' replied Sue. 'Hoppy must have found it outside the cave entrance.'

Charlie thought to himself for a moment, and then said softly.

'Is it me, or does that medallion hanging from the chain look like a sort of key.'

Sue picked the small medallion up with her fingers and the metallic chain drooped gently toward the floor.

'Yes, I think it does!' She exclaimed quite excitedly, and looked at it more closely. 'And the handle has the same shape as a large nose and smiley mouth.'

'I reckon that it will fit the box -' Charlie thought the very same thought as Sue.

'Let's try it then' she said, moving toward the other trestle table where the box lay.

Charlie and Hoppy followed her instinctively.

'Keep your blooming big feet away from the table Sport!' Charlie looked disapprovingly at Hoppy. 'Don't want you knocking this table down again.'

Hoppy hopped back one step and then strained her neck forward so as not to miss anything.

## Sue - A Legend and The Wallaby Pouch.

Sue adjusted the small medallion and pushed it's shaped end into the key hole of the old long box.

'It fits!' She exclaimed.

'See if it turns' replied Charlie. 'Be careful though, don't break it in the lock!'

'OK' said Sue, and she turned the key gently around with her fingertips. The key revolved fully around in the lock, but the lock and box did not open. Sue was quite puzzled as she felt the key revolve backwards against her finger tips, and then return to it's original position.

'It will not open -' Sue looked at Charlie in disappointment.

'Maybe it's something to do with that inscription' Charlie said hopefully.

Sue thought about it for few moments, then gave her opinion.

'Well it is really sort of a riddle isn't it.' She contemplated the words in her head. 'Any fool can frown at me. Any person can happy be.' Sue then muttered quietly. 'I will try smiling into the mirror.'

'Stop, think twice before a key you turn. For Time and Peace you have to learn.' These words rolled around in her head, and triggered an automatic response from Sue's fingers.

Sue turned the key gently around twice in the lock while still smiling into the small mirror embedded into the box top.

With a sudden whoosh of cold air which flew past Sue's head from the long box, the lid sprang open to reveal that the box was not empty after all.

'Wow!' Charlie moved forward, leaning on the table to get a better view.

Both children peered into the open box. Then Sue slowly removed an old cloth that was covering the contents.

She placed her hand inside the box and very slowly produced a plain old notebook and pencil. Very ordinary things really, apart from the symbol of a large red nose and smiley mouth imprinted on the notebook cover and stem of the pencil.

'It is the same symbol as on the box and key' noted Sue, somewhat surprised by the plain contents.

Charlie was not overly impressed.

'Not exactly cave man stuff' he moaned, peering into the darkness of the box. 'Anything else in there -'

Sue put the notebook and pencil onto the table top and placed both hands into the box.

'Well, there is this!' Sue lifted a long skateboard from the box. 'It has also got that symbol on top of it.'

Charlie shook his head.

'I don't think dad will be too impressed by this.'

'Not too impressed with what?' Charlie's father entered the tent with Sue's grandfather trailing behind him.

## Sue - A Legend and The Wallaby Pouch.

The children quickly explained how the rock had fallen from the box. The riddle. Hoppy having the key in her pouch. Being able to open the long box using the mirror. Solving the riddle. Finally ending this barrage of words with the discovery of the plain contents of the box itself.

'Looks like these are not so ancient artefacts after all then' mused a disappointed Charlie's father after both children had finished and finally paused for breath.

'Not unless the first cavemen rode skateboards' laughed Sue's grandfather.

Charlie's father thought for a moment.

'It looks like someone must have buried this stuff here and forgotten about it.' He looked at the old boomerang that was also on the table top. 'Guess that things fairly modern as well.'

'Guess so!' Replied Grandfather.

Charlie's father picked up his backpack and slung it across his shoulder.

'We still have to finish the excavation of those dinosaur bones though.' Then he pondered. 'Whoever buried that stuff managed to do it right between the feet of that old T. Rex without even disturbing the skeleton.'

'At least that is one good thing' mused grandfather positively. 'You will get an undamaged new exhibit for the museum.'

Charlie picked up the boomerang.

'And we solved the puzzle of Ghost Rock!'

'So where did all these things come from?' asked Sue.

'Doesn't really matter now' replied Charlie's father, looks now like they are recent burials, so they can be put in the bin.

'Do you mind if I keep them?' Asked Sue hopefully. 'I rather like them.'

'Sure thing' replied Charlie's father, heading toward the open tent doorway. 'They are of no use to us.'

Charlie put the boomerang into the long box, along with the notebook and pencil. He left the key in it's lock, and the lid open.

'Just in case it wont open next Time!' he said, picking up the box and carrying it back to the Jeep for Sue.

Sue's grandfather and Charlie's father shook hands outside the tent, while Charlie walked back to the road and placed the objects he was carrying onto the back seat of the small Jeep.

Meanwhile back at the tent, Sue placed the skateboard onto the floor and rolled it forward with her foot to see if the wheels were working correctly. The long board rolled elegantly forward across a dusty, uneven floor, and at this very same Time, Hoppy bounced forward heading toward the open doorway jumping over the moving skateboard.

'Me first big ears!' Sue thought she heard a small voice call out, and she noted that it seemed to be coming from the symbol on top of the skateboard itself, but that was quite impossible.

## Sue - A Legend and The Wallaby Pouch.

The long skateboard suddenly shot forward to exactly the same spot as Hoppy was about to land on. Instead of her feet hitting the floor, the Wallaby's feet landed on top of the board and her feet stuck fast. Both skateboard and bemused Wallaby rolled quickly from the tent entrance, and flew straight between Charlie's father and Sue's grandfather.

'Now that is something you do not see everyday!' Commented Sue's grandfather as both his and Charlie's fathers eyes followed the progress of Wallaby and skateboard which were heading quickly toward the stream next to the road.

Charlie looked up and also saw them coming, he jumped to one side as this odd sight of a skateboard riding Wallaby passed him by.

The skateboard stopped very suddenly in front of a gently flowing stream, and Hoppy felt her feet just as suddenly come unstuck from the boards top. With a subdued plop, the Wallaby slid into the cool clear water of the stream. She stood upright, pricked up her ears and took a drink from the stream.

Even carried here by the strange means of her transport, the Wallaby was still glad of a drink on this hot day, but she would however be a little more cautious of this strange long object in the future and try not to hop over it again.

'Nice riding!' Called Charlie when both Sue and grandfather reached his side. Charlie and grandfather entered the small Jeep.

'Go home now Hoppy!' Ordered Sue, moving forward and picking up the skateboard. She walked back to the Jeep and turned to see if Hoppy was indeed going home. As she did so, Sue thought she heard a small voice call out to her.

'Hello Buddy!' It seemed to say.

But with grandfather's turn of the ignition key and the roar of the Jeeps engine, Sue just put it down to her imagination.

'Come on then!' Shouted grandfather. 'Let's get Charlie home!'

Sue put the skateboard onto the back seat of the Jeep along with all the other objects and climbed aboard.

With the little vehicle spreading a dust cloud high into the air from a dirt track road, Sue watched and smiled as the small Kangaroo bounded into the trees heading homeward.

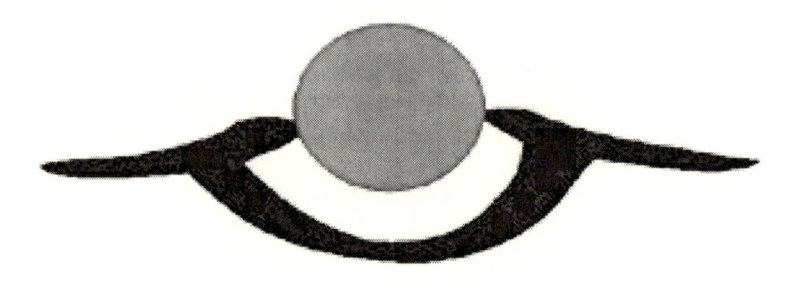

## Sue - Dingo Dogs

Taking the North track around Ghost Rock and heading back toward town the Jeeps engine roared in complaint as the little vehicle bounced over this rutted dirt track of a road.

'Hey!' Cried Charlie, looking toward a figure that was sat down at a small clearing on the roads edge. 'It is old Ben!'

'Who is old Ben -' asked Sue, watching this person become larger through a dusty windscreen.

'He is kind of a legend around here' said Charlie holding on tightly to the back of the front seat headrest. 'Old Ben's a kind of witchdoctor, a little weird but harmless, everyone likes him.'

Grandfather slowed the speeding vehicle with his brake pedal, then pulled up beside this old Aborigine who, grandfather noticed, seemed to be sat in some sort of circle that was etched into the dusty ground.

'Strange -' he thought to himself, but old Ben was a mysterious sort of fellow who was prone to doing things modern folk thought quite odd.

Old Ben nodded his head in greeting, then smiled at the Jeeps occupants.

'G'day!' He called, recognising grandfather.

'G'day mate!' Replied grandfather pushing back the peak of his bush hat from a sweating brow. 'Want a lift -'

'Na - Thanks!' Old Ben held forward a long stick that he held in his wrinkly hand, and momentarily stopped a drawing that he had been making with this white dotted and decorated piece of wood. He looked across at Sue who was sat in the front seat.

'That your grand daughter that I heard about.'

'Yes, sure is. Say hello to Ben Sue' said grandfather. Then he winked at the old man. 'He's the expert in these parts. Bet you could even teach those young archaeologists at Ghost Rock a thing or too, eh Ben?'

'Yep!' Agreed Old Ben, accepting with a nod Sue's wave of hello. 'How is your old man doing up there Charlie?' He asked.

'Not so good today' replied Charlie. 'Thought they had some real finds, but all turned out to be modern stuff buried there.' Charlie tapped Sue on the back and indicated for her to show Old Ben the skateboard. 'Like this skateboard' he said, as Sue held the board up and span the wheels with her hand.

Old Ben's eyes opened wide as he examined it with interest, and noted the smiley mouth and nose etched onto the skateboard top.

'It came from an old box that we had to solve a riddle to open!' Sue blurted, interrupting Charlie before he could speak and mention the other items himself.

'But dad says even the boomerang is fake now' Charlie as always, tried to have the last word.

The old Aborigine grinned.

'Well, I guess the archaeologists are the experts.' Ben held up his long stick to rest it on his shoulder. 'What do you think of those things Sue?' he asked.

## Sue - Dingo Dogs.

'Well I like them' replied Sue. 'They have a happy face on them, and I like that.'

'Good on yeah!' Replied the old aborigine. Old Ben looked Sue directly in the eyes. 'Bet you have the spirit of happiness strong inside yeah girl.'

'Er, thanks -' answered Sue, feeling slightly embarrassed.

'What are you doing there mate?' Asked grandfather, most curious about why Ben should be sat in a circle at the roadside.

Old Ben tapped his long stick on the dusty ground.

'There's darkness about' he said and motioned the stick to point out and follow around the circles line. 'This is a kind of talisman circle to ward off the Evil spirit.'

'Another old tribal custom?' Asked grandfather.

'Turn on yeah radio!' Replied old Ben.

Grandfather followed the aborigines somewhat strange request. The Jeep's radio burst into sudden life after he pressed the on button.

'This strange weather phenomenon continues to spread in all directions!' The newsreader, with a rather serious voice over the radio continued her report.

'The unusual phenomenon, that has been spreading from the Bermuda triangle area since early this morning, has been blamed for a serious disturbance in orbiting weather satellite systems that has made tracking the storm impossible.'

Everyone listened with interest as she continued.

'There has been no contact from military aircraft investigating the storm and it has been reported that two ships and a submarine are also missing at this Time.'

'See!' Told you darkness is about, interrupted old Ben.

Grandfather turned off the radio so as not to upset the children.

'How did you know that was on the Jeep radio Ben?' He asked ever in awe of Ben's supernatural abilities.

Ben produced an old, folded cloth from behind him, placing it on the ground so everyone could see.

'Magic!' He said, drawing everyone's eyes to the mysterious package while he slowly opened it. 'Well, at least the magic of a wristwatch and radio listings!' Ben laughed as he produced both items from the unfurled cloth. 'Knew your radio is always set on that channel.' Old Ben put the shining wristwatch around his very wrinkled wrist. 'What - You think I should always be looking up at the sun for Times' he laughed at grandfather. 'Very bad for the eyes mate!' He then picked up a small battery operated pocket radio, that was also hidden in the cloth and placed it's small headphone that dangled from a very thin wire into one ear.

'Well, take it easy mate!' Laughed grandfather, winking at the old aborigine and smiling. 'Let's hope that things improve on the darkness front!'

## Sue - Dingo Dogs.

Old Ben waved goodbye as grandfather pressed the Jeep's accelerator, moving the vehicle down the dusty track.

'I just reckon it might?' Said Old Ben to himself aloud, watching Sue and Charlie wave at him through the Jeeps rear window as it moved away. He placed the cloth to one side, stood up, then moved out of the circle that he had been sitting in.

'Just reckon it might -' He said thoughtfully again, while beneath a second, much smaller circle, that had been drawn and hidden directly under his bottom, Old Ben drew a smiley mouth with the decorated long stick. The picture in the dirt, now matched the face on Sue's skateboard.

The old aborigine suddenly looked up, as a howling wind rose up and rustled through the trees, throwing strange shadows to fall in all directions. This howling wind then blew directly toward him and fell downward to the large drawn circle at his feet. The outer rim gently dissipated under it's force, but the smiley mouth and nose remained ingrained in the dusty soil. Old Ben smiled back at the picture and whistled a happy tune as he turned and walked away, heading home.

After just a few minutes and with the last cloud of choking dust being thrown high into the clear blue sky, the wheel's of grandfather's Jeep spun furiously, as they left the dirt track road behind them and reached a modern, bending highway, that twisted gently around ghost rock.

This new and fairly wide road very quickly led to the small, but sprawling town, which Grandfathers house bordered and where Charlie lived, near to the sweeping Ocean coastline and seemingly endless Tasman Sea.

'You can just about see Sydney from the harbour!' Said Charlie, leaning forward and pointing toward a very distant skyline of tall buildings down the coast, while the Jeep speed past the towns old school house building. Sue strained her eyes, but could not really see anything much, except maybe, the odd shadow of a tall building through the heat haze.

'There you go!' Said grandfather, suddenly pulling up in front of a building with a large, 'Store' sign painted outside it. The owner, Charlie's mother, waved from the window and came out onto the porch to say hello.

With a smile, she said 'G'day!' to grandfather and Sue.

'G'day!' Replied grandfather, smiling right back. 'Just dropping Charlie home, to save him some peddling on this hot morning.' Grandfather removed his bush hat, throwing it on the back seat, then mopped dripping sweat from his brow that was now being cooled by a breeze coming from the ocean.

'Can Sue stay for a while?' Asked Charlie hopefully. 'She can come and see dad's boat, it's just been repainted.'

'Oh, yes! - Can I?' said Sue. 'We can try out that old skateboard we found too!' Sue held the skateboard up and span the wheels with her hand.

## Sue - Dingo Dogs.

'The ground is much better around here!' She observed, looking at the flat, concrete pavements.

'Well, we should be getting back' replied grandfather thoughtfully, but not wanting to disappoint the children.

'Do stop for a drink' Charlie's mother said, swaying the decision. 'I have cold lemonade, if you would like some.'

'Okay doke!' Grandfather looked at the kids faces. 'Thanks! - Seems like these guys need a pit stop anyway.'

Grandfather removed Charlie's BMX from the Jeeps rear. Then while he and Charlie's mother disappeared inside the store Sue and Charlie moved off to look at the boat.

'Why don't you leave that box in the car?' Asked Charlie, wondering why Sue had bothered to take it with her.

'I think it could do with a bit of a wash!' She replied, holding the long box under her arm. Sue pushed the skateboard forward with her foot and it glided gently forward. 'We can do that in the sea!'

Charlie peddled his bike and led the way. Sue followed, trying to get used to the feel of this old skateboard, which, she noted, seemed to ride the pavements remarkably well, considering it had been unused for so long.

Reaching half way across a long, wooden jetty, that reached out to the Ocean and that held many types of bobbing boats in place at either side of it, Charlie turned, just in Time to see what the sudden, roaring, screaming noise was.

'Ouch!' He cried out. The sight of a fast moving jet ski machine and rider jumping over the wooden decking just in front of him had caused Charlie to fall off his bike. Sitting up on the wooden floor and holding his painfully bruised leg he watched three other jet skies and riders follow the first. 'Oh no!' He exclaimed, recognising the gang who had painted their nickname onto each jet ski. 'It's the Dingo Dogs!'

'The who?' Sue followed the jet skies path as they carved a wide arc in the water and then turned sharply, heading back toward the jetty.

'It's The Dingo Dogs!' Repeated Charlie. 'They are a nasty minded gang of bullies, that are a real big pain around here!'

Sue helped Charlie to his feet, then watched the 'Dingo Dogs' gang accelerate their jet skies directly toward the jetty again.

'Let's get out of here!' Sue said, stepping onto the old skateboard, while Charlie started to get back onto the saddle of his bike.

However, the first jet Ski and rider hurtled forward and again launched themselves over the wooden jetty before Sue and Charlie could get off it. The jet ski and rider passed by in the air, very close to Sue and Charlie covering both the children in a pall of salty water.

'Get off our jetty!' It's rider snarled in a most unfriendly manor.

## Sue - Dingo Dogs.

'Yuck!' Exclaimed Charlie, while the salt water drenched both him, Sue and the wooden decking. When this sea water hit the old skateboard under Sue's foot, the most peculiar thing happened.

Using one hand to clear her stinging eyes of the salty sea water, Sue then opened them, one at a Time. Then, looking downward to allow the sea water in her hair to drip away, she noticed that the nose above a smiley mouth painted on the old skateboard's top, seemed to be, well, growing. This spherical red nose on the skateboard appeared to be moving too, sort of sniffing the air, while it grew steadily into the size of a small football.

Behind Sue, with a sudden, screaming roar, the second jet ski passed quickly over the wooden jetty very close to where Charlie stood.

'Take your Sheila with yer kid!' Shouted it's rather coarse and rude rider.

'Your not going to put up with that sort of behaviour are you?' Asked a firm voice, while this second jet ski again hit the sea water with a huge splash.

Sue was quite taken aback. The voice had come from the smiley mouth on the skateboard top, just below the bulging red nose.

'I – Er -' Sue was a little lost for words to reply with, after all, she had never had a skateboard talk to her before.

'No - I thought not!' Replied a grinning smiley mouth on the skateboard top. 'Hold on to your hat!'

Before she could gather her thoughts, both Sue's feet stuck fast to the skateboard top.

'Wow!' She shouted, as the skateboard started to move quickly backwards.

Charlie had finished clearing the salty water from his eyes, just in Time to see Sue pass by, now heading at some speed back across the jetty out toward the sea.

'What are you doing?' He called out in panic. 'The other jet skies are coming!' Charlie looked toward the remaining gang members who were already taking their run up to the jetty and each blowing a huge plume of water into the sky from the back of their machines.

'I can't control it!' Sue shouted. 'It's alive!'

'Alive?' Charlie wondered what Sue was talking about. 'She's gone nuts!' He thought, watching Sue and the skateboard now hurtle toward the jetty's end.

The remaining Dingo Dogs jumped over the wooden jetty and their jet skies roared in anger, causing a huge wall of water to fly in all directions, while they accelerated to meet the others preparing to take another run.

'Stop!' Shouted Sue to the skateboard, watching with horror the approach of the sea water beyond the last wooden planks of a rapidly shrinking jetty.

'Hey Buddy, relax!' Replied the skateboard, it's calm voice rising above the awful high pitch noise of engines. 'Just have a little faith! - Things will turn out OK.' The old skateboard suddenly accelerated, causing Sue to lean backwards and clutch the long box under arm even more tightly.

## Sue - Dingo Dogs.

She felt the most powerful wind rush past her face and shut her eyes, expecting a rather wet landing at any second.

'Heck!' Exclaimed Charlie, watching Sue and the old skateboard zoom off the jetty's end, but, to his surprise, the old skateboard just skimmed the surface of the water, acting like a sort of self propelled surfboard. 'Wow!' He said in wonder as the board tilted slightly back, causing a huge wake of water to rise behind it. 'That thing's better than a speedboat!'

Sue opened her eyes, not feeling the sudden splurge of water that she had expected to engulf her.

'See!' Said the old skateboard rather smugly. 'Not bad for a Buddy Board huh?'

Sue really hadn't the Time to reply. In front of her, the Dingo Dogs watched her quick progress across the water heading toward them with a great deal of surprise, with roughly the same amount of surprise, that Sue felt as she also watched them grow closer. Sue, who was furiously trying to balance and just stay upright on the old skateboard, found this was made even more difficult when this strange device that was stuck to her feet had almost reached the jet skies.

'Now then!' Called out the old skateboard from it's grinning smiley mouth. 'Time to teach bullies some manners!'

Charlie, watching from the jetty, shouted out in concern.

'Sue!' Just as the old skateboard and rider hurtled skyward from the sea trailing a solid wall of water behind them.

Watching Sue and the old skateboard take off from the sea and following their path to fly directly over them, the Dingo Dogs gang really could not believe their eyes. They all sat open mouthed on their now stationary jet skies, looking skyward, an act which, unfortunately, did not allow the gang to notice, or brace themselves, for the impact of a solid rushing wall of water that followed the old skateboard skyward.

'That's incredible Sport!' One managed to mutter, seconds before his and all the other gang members mouths, were engulfed by the deluge of very salty sea water.

While all the Dingo Dogs spluttered and spat out the ocean that had washed out their mouths, each one still clinging desperately onto their bobbing jet skies, whose engine's still buzzed on, despite the Ocean deluge. The flying old skateboard banked sharply in the clear blue sky, then flipped over, to leave Sue upside down and looking directly Earthward at the hooligans.

'N – ice - To meet you!' grinned the smiley mouth on the old skateboard top. From this smiley mouth there suddenly came a well directed thin blast of icy air, that froze solid the sea water surrounding the jet skies. The machines engines still all buzzed like angry bees, but they were stuck fast to this thin, but very strong ice shelf.

## Sue - Dingo Dogs.

'Let's get out of here!' Cried one of the Dingo Dogs, trying to accelerate his machine forward. But his machine's engine, although it roared, could not move the jet ski forward. 'I'm stuck!' The rider said angrily. Each of the gang then tried to release themselves from the ice shelf, but found that their own jet skies were also frozen solid.

'Hey! - My hands and feet are stuck too!' The gang all shouted together.

'Er - Sorry!' Was all that Sue could think of saying, as she was always told that it is good to be polite.

The old skateboard in the sky flipped Sue back upright, then headed toward the jetty again, at a very fast speed.

'What's going on!' Exclaimed Sue, quite confused. 'What are you?' She gripped the old box under her arm and struggled to balance. 'Are you an alien thing from another planet or what?'

The old skateboard laughed.

'No! - No! - That's silly - But no Time to explain!' It banked sharply downward and the red nose seemed to tense itself. 'Time needs your help. You found the chest and opened it. Only the future can save the future!'

'How can I help? - What do you mean save the future?' Sue was feeling a little confused, but what seemed to be an imminent collision with the wooden jetty cleared all thought's from her head. 'Stop!' She shouted.

Swooping low and levelling off at the last second, the old skateboard's wheels brushed the wooden jetty just long enough for the bulging red nose to sweep a coil of rope from in front of a boat. Charlie ducked as the old skateboard took off again without stopping and flew low over his head, to then bank sharply back to sea heading toward the stuck Dingo Dogs gang.

'Time to go - Have a tow!' The smiley mouth on the skateboard top said with a snuffle, almost as if it had a heavy cold. But this was not really surprising, as the small, bulging red nose was now quite full of the long rope, which the old skateboard now used to lasso the frozen Dingo Dogs gang and accelerate at high speed down the coastline, with the unwilling block of ice water-skiers, while still sat on their machines, in tow.

'Where are you going?' Shouted Sue to the smiley mouth that now seemed to smile even more than before.

'Home!' Was the short and very happy reply.

Sue felt a howling, but surprisingly cool breeze rush past her while trying to balance on this old talking skateboard, that now sped very quickly in the air beside the Australian coastline.

Not really quite sure what to make of the strange events that had taken place, she looked downwards, to see the Dingo Dog gang that were all still sat on their jet-skies, leave behind a large wake in the water that came from the shelf of ice that encased them.

## Sue - Dingo Dogs.

Sue then decided to herself, that although it had turned out to be a rather peculiar day, she would not be afraid of the situation, besides, Sue quite enjoyed the experience of a flying skateboard.

'After all, it had dealt with the bullies' she thought to her self. 'And this old skateboard seems friendly enough, even if it is quite strange!'

Interrupting these thought's, the fast moving skateboard suddenly turned somewhat sharply and Sue looked up, then around, to see many Sydneysiders look up in amazement from a huge array of sailing boats that crowded the waters of Sydney harbour. The sudden, strange appearance of a skateboard flying low across the water, was obviously not a usual sight here, or indeed anywhere else that could be mentioned. But with the sight of Sue, riding at high speed across Port Jackson waters while towing via a rope this group of jet-skies, complete with their riders encased in a shelf of ice.

Everyone's attention was brought skyward and many boats collided together, that were not now being guided properly by the stunned onlookers.

'Ethel' said an elderly tourist, quite calmly to his wife, as he looked out into the harbour while standing in front of Sydney Opera house. 'Could I have the camera dear?'

'Just one moment John!' Replied his wife. 'I have a great view here!' She adjusted her camera lens to focus on the impressive white, sail like structures of the Opera House in front of her, that she had noted, were made up of over a million separate tiles. The camera clicked, then auto wound the film. Ethel turned eagerly, her eye still looking through the lens, to take a snap of her husband. 'Smile!' She called out, and clicked the camera. This was just in Time for Sue and the skateboard, with Dingo Dogs gang in tow, to fill the camera screen behind her husband while they all hurtled skyward from the water and flew directly over the top of Sydney Opera House.

'Ah!' All the Dingo Dogs were really quite terrified at this point. Especially, when the old skateboard and Sue flew gracefully across the metalwork, right up to the top of Sydney harbour bridge and the tow rope was released. They looked down at an extremely large drop to the water and thought they were about to fall off. But at the last moment the old skateboard flipped Sue upside down and blew a thin blast of very icy air, to stick the rope end, Dingo Dogs and their jet-skies to the bridge top.

'G'day mates!' Said a cheerful bridge Painter watching this peculiar scene unfold in front of him. Unruffled and casually having his packed lunch, while sitting on a painting gantry at the very top of Sydney harbour bridge, he added. 'Don't usually get many visitors way up here during lunch.' The bridge painter recognised the Dingo Dogs gang as hooligans, who regularly visited Port Jackson and other areas to annoy people. He smiled at their terrified faces. 'Got your comeuppance then boys.'

## Sue - Dingo Dogs.

Watching Sue and the skateboard turn very quickly and fly off into the distance, the painter picked up a radio that was stuffed into a large pocket on the front of his paint splattered overalls.

'Come in control!' He called out, while continuing to nibble his sandwich. 'Do us a favour sport, send help up here - There's some garbage to remove from the bridge top!' But then the painter watched the shelf of ice start to slip slowly forward and the Dingo Dogs look at each other in panic.

'Ah!' Was all they and the painter could muster when the ice shelf slipped even more and then fell from the bridge, heading straight downward toward the water. However, the long ropes end was held very tightly in place by ice and the Dingo Dogs gang, rather like bungee jumpers, had their descent stopped suddenly by the stretching, elastic like rope. Now laying suspended beneath the bridge, the ice shelf and Dingo Dogs gang swung like a clocks pendulum over the water.

'Phew!' The gang gave a huge sigh of relief, but the rope twanged and stretched under their weight, then stretched some more, until it suddenly snapped. The Dingo Dogs finally fell the last few feet into the water, to re-emerge and bob up and down in their inflated life jacket vests. When they were picked up by passing boats, they had all decided that their hooligan days were well and truly over.

Flying further away into the City from these event's, the red nose on the skateboard top sniffed the air, searching for something.

'It is close now!' Said the smiley mouth.

'What is close?' Asked Sue, looking downward toward George Street and all the modern buildings.

As the skateboard flew directly above, then past the old St Andrews Cathedral, the nose twitched and sniffed the air.

'The Clock is close!' The old skateboard had found the Town hall and now headed directly toward it.

Sue held on tightly to the long box under her arm and watched the large clock face that was embedded into the tall, decorative tower above the town hall start to signal twelve o'clock midday. A brilliant, startling light started to emanate from a cylinder like dome above the clock and the old skateboard headed directly toward it.

'Here we go! - Hold on to your hat!' Shouted the smiley mouth.

Both the old skateboard and Sue disappeared into the light above the clock, which extinguished on the last chime of twelve.

## United Time Club - Living Legends

This doorway portal that lead to who knows where, was an extremely brightly lit twisting tunnel which seemed to roar very loudly with a powerful wind that howled fiercely through it. But surprisingly, this wind was found to be quite gentle to the touch, rather like a calming, cool breeze.

In what seemed to be a matter of seconds, suddenly and very unexpectedly, the old skateboard and rider banked sharply upward then quickly levelled off.

A small doorway could just about be seen through the blinding light, which quickly grew larger the closer the fast travelling old skateboard got to it. This door evaporated immediately when the old skateboard shouted it's own portal exit passwords.

'A stitch in Time! Saves nine!' It said happily, coming back to it's home.

The skateboard and rider hurtled through the exit of this bright, twisting and very windy portal, flying directly toward two very strangely shaped figures that stood talking to each other, standing in the middle of what seemed to be a large, ice walled cavern.

Simultaneously, three other fast moving shapes appeared. Coming from three separate squares of light, situated high in the cavern walls, three more skateboards and their riders also headed on a collision course from the back and either side, of these two strange figures that stood quite still, in the centre.

All four old skateboards, with their riders, collided with a fairly painful crash, knocking the two strange figures that stood in the centre of the cavern to the icy snow that blanketed the ground.

'Are you all right -' Called James, sitting up and brushing snow from his t-shirt. 'Hey -' He then said thoughtfully. 'This snow is warm!'

'You are right' said Peter, picking up a single apple that had rolled from his backpack into the snow.

'Warm snow' pondered Abdul, picking up a handful and making it into a ball. 'We do not get this where I come from.' He threw the ball toward the girl who was looking at him, so she could catch it. 'Warm snow, that is impossible, isn't it?'

Sue caught the ball and examined it.

'Quite impossible!' Agreed Sue, and she examined the round, warm snowball, feeling quite mystified as to why it should not be cold.

'Hello, my name is James' said James, deciding introductions were more important than warm snow. 'Did you find these talking skateboards too?' James pulled his skateboard from the snow and held it up for the other three children to see.

'My name is Abdul' said Abdul. 'Yes, I also have the same sort of skateboard' and he held his up.

'Hello, my name is Sue' said Sue. 'I found this skateboard in an old long box.' She held her skateboard up for the others to see.

'And my name is Peter' said Peter, putting an apple back into his backpack.

## United Time Club - Living Legends.

Holding his old skateboard up for the others to see Peter announced proudly.

'I had to solve a strange riddle, which allowed me to open an old long box from which I have obtained this device!'

'Me too!' The other three children replied together.

All eyes then turned to two strangely shaped figures that appeared from under a mound of snow, where they had been suddenly buried by the crashing four skateboards and riders.

'I say!' Cried one of the figures sitting upright. 'What an interminably bad show!' This figure then noticed that four human children were all looking directly at it.

At that moment the other stunned figure also sat upright.

'Gosh darn it!' It spluttered, clearing snow from it's mouth and very small eyes. 'Can't you watch where your going!' It was then that this figure also noticed the children staring.

'Kids? - Human kids!' The creature exclaimed with astonishment.
The other strange penguin shaped figure bearing a large red nose, directly under which lay a long dark moustache, straightened the peculiar hat that it was wearing.

'By Jove - What are they doing here?' It muttered discontentedly.

'Is that a clock on your hat?' Asked Abdul, observing a small yellow Time-piece on the front of the creatures hat.

'Heck Buddy!' The other penguin shaped figure turned it's head toward it's friend. 'That kid can see you Monty!'

'Don't be ridiculous Patriot!' Replied Monty, struggling to his rather small feet. He looked at the human children one by one. 'Of course they cannot see us, no real person can.'

'Well I have seen you before!' Peter said firmly. 'Entering into the large clock at the shop' he continued while Monty looked up at him, calmly brushing the snow from his flag coloured jacket. 'And in the old pictures of cave paintings from a book!'

'Me too!' Announced Sue. 'There are pictures on the wall of you at Ghost rock!'

'And I have seen you in the old scrolls from the Pyramids' interrupted Abdul.

James looked down at these strange penguin shaped, but human person like figures. Both were almost the same in general appearance, but each displayed a different oval flag of the world on their jacket front.

'You must be the folks in the old Eskimo legend -' James scratched his chin thoughtfully. 'When grandpa used that old front door with the smiley mouthed door knocker, to get away from a fierce Polar Bear all those years ago.'

'Yes sir - They can see you Buddy!' Replied Patriot, removing a large piece of snow from his red spherical nose. 'And me too.'

## United Time Club - Living Legends.

James looked more closely down at the strange characters that stood in front of him, and he noticed that they both had an identification card printed onto the top of their hats. James read aloud some of the words.

'General Monty Knowledge. So that is your name huh?'

'Yes! Yes!' snapped the Monty penguin like person creature, looking for his notebook that had fallen somewhere in the snow, then finding it.

'And this is General Patriot Knowledge.' Monty held out one of his quite long arms, and pointed to the figure next to him.

'Friends just call me Pat' nodded Patriot, smiling toward James.

Monty brushed the cold crisp snow from his note book and pressed the small clock embedded on the front of his Hold All Things receptacle. The H.A.T flipped open, and he placed the notebook and pencil carefully inside.

'So why do they call you guys General then?' Asked James picking up the skateboard and putting it under his arm. 'Are you the leaders or what -'

Monty's nose twitched in agitation and his monocle revolved in disgust.

'I say! Don't be absurd old fruit - Such titles are strictly for you silly human things!' This strange creature shuffled snow from his lace-less shoes and with a twitch of a rather large red nose continued. 'One Penguin Person better than the other! - The very thought, how quite absurd human child.'

Monty looked closely toward the bemused human children's faces, and his monocle glistened with a shimmering golden light reflected from the cavern walls. He decided to elaborate further, as these children looked somewhat confused by his reply to the question James had posed.

'I say, well it is jolly well like this old fruits' he said, pondering for a moment. He twitched his large red nose and the long moustache under it did likewise. 'We Penguin Person chaps were all born, or to be rather more precise, drawn, at the very initial stage of all creation and Time, so therefore, we have been existing for far longer than your 'new' human race.

So such titles that may exist today, along with any related powers that they may hold, are really just trivial entities that only you human being things place importance upon.

As for ourselves 'old fruits', we are initial, that is, existing at the very beginning, before, well, anything else at all really.' Monty tried to explain his own Penguin People club world in simple terms, as best he could for the children.

'Therefore -' He continued while his large red nose twitched again. 'It is only the initials that we use to identify ourselves, or to be more defined, the very first letters of our very own function within creation. We are **G**et **E**very **N**ew **E**vent **R**ecord **A**nd **L**og / **K**eep **N**otes **O**f **W**orld **L**ife **E**ach **D**ay / **G**uard **E**ternally / Penguin People, and make general knowledge notes of all human events that exist within Time.

## United Time Club - Living Legends.

'Yes sir!' Agreed Pat. 'We much prefer to use the shorter initials **G.E.N.E.R.A.L.** as it fit's better on our identification tags now that we have added human style names within the initials. More and more of us have became drawn throughout Time and the new system allows our notes, or **P.P.** pages as we prefer to call them, to not get confused and be easier to file.'

With another twitch of his long moustache and flicking snow from his Union Flag jacket, Monty then pressed the small clock again and his H.A.T closed quickly. 'Time for ice-tea I think' he said thoughtfully, 'fancy a cup?'

'Sure thing!' Replied Pat. 'Come on kid's lets go to the Great Hall.'

'This really is a most peculiar event' muttered Monty, while the four children, each carrying their skateboard's, followed his and Patriot's small shuffling, penguin like hunched figures. 'We must consult The Master of The Four Keys Of Time about this!' He made a decision. 'Time to go and see him! - Please keep a cup of ice-tea cold for me, while I go to the Great Hall of Time.'

'That's odd?' Noted James, clutching his skateboard and old dusty box under each arm while he slowly followed the Patriot and Monty Penguin Persons.

James had observed a rather strange sign post, made of the same glistening ice, as was a large frost encrusted staircase, that now stood imposingly and quite impressively, in front of the group.

'That down arrow is pointing upwards and that up arrow is pointing downwards.'

Monty stopped directly in front of the signpost.

'Mm -' he muttered thoughtfully. Then Monty twitched his large red nose, which made his hat bobble about a small head. 'Of course it's quite simple!' He replied to James, a spherical monocle glass filling with an open eye. 'It all depends where one is standing! - For example - If you are in Australia you go down to Europe, and if you are in Europe you go down to Australia. But you cannot have two downs, or two ups for that matter, that is impossible! - Up and down is really all in the mind dear thing, The Earth is a very round ball you know.'

'Thank goodness for gravity!' Interrupted Patriot Penguin Person, shuffling forward to step onto the shining staircase. 'Kind of keeps your feet on the ground.'

To all the children's surprise Patriot lifted the bulky bottom of his coat, to reveal thin, stick like hairy legs protruding from a pair of lace-less shoes.

'Quite - Quite' muttered Monty, who also stepped onto the staircase in the same way. 'Do follow!' He beckoned to the children.

James, Peter, Abdul and Sue stepped onto the now crowded staircase. The children looked at each other, all wondering how these creatures could possibly climb the endless number of steps that led in both directions, up and down, or was it down and up? - It was all a rather confusing situation.

'See you later!.. Tally ho!' called out Monty, interrupting the children's thought.

## United Time Club - Living Legends.

Monty tapped his right foot. 'Up we go for Time to know!' he said nose twitching.

The steps under his shoes started to move quickly downwards and Monty waved goodbye.

'Down we pass for a chill out glass!' Replied Patriot, the steps under both his and the children's feet proceeding to move in the opposite direction, upwards.

'An escalator -' James said aloud.

'Made of ice!' Exclaimed Abdul.

Sue shook her head, 'I don't believe this can be real.'

Peter looked downward at the ice step and kicked it rather hard with a foot.

'Ouch!' He felt a toe inside his boot throb.' It feels real enough to me!'

'Here we go!' After a few moments, Patriot stepped off the ice escalator and the children followed him, into a long, ice clad corridor.

'The Chill Out Hall?' Sue read the blue sign that stood above an impressive, but closed, double doorway.

'Yes sir!' Here is the rest hall. 'You kid's can wait here till Monty gets back!' Said Patriot, and he motioned for the children to follow him as the double doors opened and he proceeded to step inside.

'And just where do you think you are going?' Called out a rather stern voice.

At that precise moment both doors suddenly slammed shut again catching Patriot's nose, then releasing the red ball quickly again as the Penguin Person tottered backwards into the corridor.

Just beside this double doorway lay a long table made of ice. This stern voice that had emanated from the top of this table made all the group halt behind Patriot before entering the Chill Out Hall.

Peter looked curiously down at the table top, as he was nearest to it and noticed that this voice seemed to come from a single book that lay open on the table top. There appeared to be no writing on the pages of this book, only a uniform set of ruled lines.

'What -' Peter stepped backwards as a piece of this paper ripped itself from the book and formed itself into a talking creature, complete with tongue and eyes which then bobbed about on the table top.

'Rule fifty one million two hundred thousand!' The paper creature continued. 'All travel devices shall be returned to their own rest area before entry to the Chill Out Hall.'

'What is that -' All the children said together.

'It is a Gobby!' Replied Patriot holding his nose. 'A Gobby rules and regulation page.' The Penguin Person lent one arm on the table top, rested his head on his hand, then stared hard at the paper creature.

'See here Buddy' Patriot Penguin Person placed a small notebook that he had been carrying in his other hand onto the table top and gently rubbed a throbbing red nose beneath his cap. 'Everyone knows that you gotta follow the rules Mr Crinkly lined page dude!'

## United Time Club - Living Legends.

He sniffed the red nose back into shape. 'But shutting a persons nose in the door, ain't a really nice thing to do!'

'Rule fifty one million two hundred thousand!' The paper creature continued, repeating itself. 'All travel devices shall be returned to their own rest area before entry to the Chill Out Hall.'

As this rather strange creation spoke, above the rather pompous bobbing up and down rule Gobby and the table top on which it stood, a large set of square fronted pigeon holes suddenly appeared in the icy wall. At first they seemed to be just an ever thickening set of thin drawn lines in the ice, but each then projected themselves gradually forward to reveal that on the inside, they were actually oblong receptacles. Some of these long boxes the children noticed, already contained a skateboard resting upside down within them.

Patriot turned his head and looked toward the kids. His nose twitched in disgust.

'Some things make you want to throw the rule book out of the window - Don't they!' He snapped in annoyance while quickly turning to indicate the small window carved into the corridor wall. 'But you know -' He then said thoughtfully. 'You gotta follow as best you can whatever a set of rules says! - So long as they are light rules and not dark rules.' Patriot pointed to some empty slots in the boxes which were marked skateboard rest area in small neat lettering. 'Put your travel devices in there, please kids.'

'What is the difference between a light rule and a dark rule?' Asked Peter, placing his board and box into one of the slots.

'You will know what the difference is when you come to it yourself' replied the Penguin Person, shuffling forward toward the Chill Out Hall. 'But what rules say to do good are light. What rules say to do bad are dark.' Patriot pushed the doors open again and waved to the children to enter the chamber. 'There's a book of good and one of bad for practically everything you know!'

The four children, with all their skateboard's and old boxes placed in the rest area, stepped slowly forward to enter the Chill Out Hall. James, walking past the Penguin Person shook his head.

'This is one weird place!'

'Most interesting though' replied Peter. 'My Uncle Charles would be fascinated by these things.'

'I still can't understand why the ice is warm' called out Abdul, after taking a last close up look at the Gobby.

Sue was the last to step into the Chill Out Hall.

'But I think it's great to have an adventure!' she said, rubbing Patriot Penguin Person on the chin. 'I think these things are really cute!'

While the small Penguin Persons cheeks suddenly went quite red and flushed in embarrassment, a thin arm and small hand reached from behind the table and tried to fumble for the notebook Patriot had left on top of it.

## United Time Club - Living Legends

The Gobby's eyes looked toward the fumbling hand.

'Rule one hundred and twenty three!' It 'gobbled' - 'All notebooks shall be kept in their hold all things receptacle while in transit to the great safe!' The Gobby then proceeded to bite, quite hard, the hand that unfortunately reached toward it.

'Ouch!' Came a stifled cry from beneath the table. A little rush of unfortunate wind also came from this character that was hidden there, trying to steal pages from the notebook.

Sue turned, just missing the hand as it disappeared back behind the table.

'You have left your notebook!' She said pointing to the object.

'Oh yes!' Replied Patriot Penguin Person. 'Thanks! - I forgot!'

Patriot shuffled back to the table, quickly pressed the small yellow clock that was embedded in front of his hat and, just after the hat top few open, he picked up the notebook and placed it inside. Patriot's nose sniffed the air while the hat lid flicked downwards and shut.

'Can you smell a little something in the air?' He asked.

Sue sniffed the air also.

'Yes I can!' Sue replied, quite disgusted and stared hard at Patriot.

'Er -' The Penguin Person went flush faced all over again. 'Wasn't me!' He said shuffling past Sue, who followed him into the Chill Out Hall. 'Lets shut the door eh?'

'Wow!' Blurted Sue, as Patriot closed the doors to stop the smell entering Chill Out Hall. 'This is one heck of a place.'

This is starting to be a darn regular occurrence now!' said Patriot thoughtfully. He quickly pressed the yellow clock button and produced from his hat a small sign, which he then proceeded to hang on one of the two smiley faced door handles that were paced on the inside of the doors. It read -

'Do not enter. A slightly Evil smell in progress.'

With a satisfied nod, the Penguin Person turned around, with nose twitching, then shuffled forward, muttering to himself quietly.

'Really must see about getting the drainage system fixed around here!'

Outside these now closed double doors, unseen by those in Chill out hall, a furtive and rather sinister character emerged slowly from behind the table.

'Curses!' He exclaimed, blowing on his hand to relieve the pain that a Gobby bite had inflicted. This nasty person, who kept his face hidden by the lapels of a long dark coat, straightened his large brown hat and shook his hand back and forth to blow on it again while staring in anger at the Gobby.

'Rule sixty nine billion two hundred and twenty two thousand!' Snapped the rule page Gobby, smelling the breath of this character, even from the table top.

'Teeth must be cleaned regularly to avoid bad breath and decay of enamel and gums!' The furtive character looked downward, then moved slowly toward the table top, pulling up the lapels of his coat to obscure an Evil face.

## United Time Club - Living Legends.

'Von Flatulence must obtain more notes for his master the Dark Void!' He snarled toward the Gobby in a very sarcastic tone.

'So, I have bad breath! - Yes! - So what?' He blew more of this bad breath toward the Gobby, which spluttered and coughed as it smelt it.

'But now, Von Flatulence has less notes thanks to you!'

The sinister character suddenly bashed the spluttering Gobby on it's head, then roughly grabbed this rule paper and crumpled it up into a ball. He picked up the book that the Gobby had come from and threw both onto the floor and stamped on them, hard.

'No one shall stop Furtive Von Flatulence! - Or The Dark Void!' He laughed, turning furtively to creep back down the long corridor.

The escalator was a mere few steps away when Von Flatulence heard the dry ruffling of paper pages behind him. He turned, furtively, to see the book that he had stamped on open and many pages rip themselves out of it.

'Oh no!' He exclaimed, watching each page form a separate Gobby.

The Gobby that he had stamped on quickly unfurled itself and joined the rest bobbing up and down on the corridor floor.

'Time to get out of here!' Von Flatulence ran as fast as he could away from the rule pages.

The Gobby's however, all bobbed forward along the floor, each muttering in unison..

'Must not break the rules!' And they chased Furtive Von Flatulence both down and up and up and down the ice escalator staircase.

Meanwhile, inside Chill Out Hall, the four amazed children were all stood in line, looking around at the many circular faces in this strange chamber that were, by now, looking at them also from the comfort of their seats. An ice chandelier suspended from the ceiling flickered a relaxing light all around the large cavern, which Sue noted, looked almost like twinkling stars, as the light reflected from the icy walls.

'There are more of these creatures!' Sue said excitedly. 'A lot more!'

'Hi buddies' Patriot shuffled forward past the stunned children. He twitched his large red nose in greeting toward a collection of plain, light blue sofas and comfortable seating arrangements. These many small pieces of furniture were spread in quite an orderly fashion around the chamber and although some were empty, most were inhabited by an array of relaxing Penguin People to which Patriot spoke. 'We have unexpected guests!'

'This is really weird' blurted James, who noticed, as did all the children, that each Penguin Person around the chamber wore a different flag emblem on their jacket fronts. But something else, rather different, caught his eye.

'That looks really cool' said James, pointing to a sign etched high onto the ice wall face in the large chamber corner that read 'Tiddler Snowball Bar' and he laughed. 'I wonder if these things serve real snowball ice cream?'

## United Time Club - Living Legends.

'Yes we do' replied Patriot. 'Well spotted young human James!'

The small character moved forward and indicated for the children to sit on a collection of high stools in front of a long ice formed bar beneath the sign.

'We also serve ice tea, milk shake, sea salt shake and a collection of fish cakes!' He turned and looked James in the eye. 'As well the snowball ice cream in five different flavours.' A large smile appeared from beneath Patriot's large red nose, which to James, seemed almost too large for the creatures small face.

'Seems good to me!' Noted Abdul, sitting on one of the high stools and spinning around on the small seat top.

'Yes most agreeable!' Peter sat next to Abdul, while Sue sat on his other side.

'Er - Thanks!' Said James, watching Patriot, who, quite elegantly for his shape, picked a high stool and sat on it. 'I think I will sit here.'

James sat down, then looked even more bemused, as a small hat appeared immediately from behind the bar. It was obviously on the head of someone rather small, as no-one on the children's side of the bar could see who was actually under it.

'What can I please serve you with?' Asked a small, squeaky voice from beneath this hat.

'Thank you Tiddler!' Called Patriot right back. 'An ice tea each for Monty and myself.' He thought for a moment. 'Keep Monty's on the cool counter, he will return soon.'

Then Patriot raised a long arm and his pointed to a menu carved onto the ice wall behind the equally icy counter top.

'And what would you children like?' He asked.

Before anyone could answer, a huge, frightening shadowy shape came from behind the children and filled the wall behind the bar. As the children looked at it, the shadow was followed by a deep, rumbling growl from behind them.

'Pat -' Sue asked quietly, who, like the other three children watching this ominous shadow grow even larger on the wall in front of them, really did not want to turn around just yet. 'Does that shadow belong to a very large creature?'

'Yes mam!' Replied Pat, accepting a cup of ice tea, that was carefully lifted upwards from behind the bar by the very short Tiddler.

'And does that creature that the shadow belongs to, have a lot of fur?' Asked Peter, gulping with a little apprehension.

'Yes sir - Sure does!' Said Patriot.

'Would the shadow belong to a creature that has very, very, sharp teeth Pat?' Asked Abdul, also feeling a dry, spontaneous gulp, reach his own throat.

'Yep!' replied Patriot, lifting his nose to take a little sip of ice tea from the cup.

'So Pat - Would it be large furry creature, with very, very, sharp teeth that could possibly, say, eat a person?' Asked James, who suddenly felt a dry lump form in his throat.

## United Time Club - Living Legends.

'Yes folks!' Replied Patriot, putting his cup back onto the saucer top. 'Reckon it could.'

Pat looked at the kids, who had all turned to look at him, but had dared not turn around.

'Not scared of an old shadow are you?' asked Pat. 'Don't never be afraid of shadows kids, there ain't no danger in reflections of light!'

Pat span around on the stool to face this 'frightening creature' that had cast such a large shadow.

'See, it's only our pet splodge!'

The children turned around and confronted a huge Polar Bear, that growled menacingly at them.

'Ah!' The children yelled in unison.

The huge Polar Bear took two steps backwards and looked at the children in a slightly confused way.

'It is OK Splodge!' Said Patriot. 'The kid's didn't mean to frighten you.' He turned to the children. 'You are sat in his seat's, that's all.' Pat twitched his red nose. ' Splodge just asked if you could move to the side a bit. See, he needs a few stools for his big bottom.'

The Polar Bear nodded, much to the children's surprise, in agreement. Then the huge animal moved forward and looked Sue right in the eye. Sue shut her eyes and could feel the Polar Bears slightly fish tainted breath, roll up her nostrils. Her eyes sprang open quickly.

'Yuck!' She exclaimed as Splodge licked her face.

'Yuck! - Yuck! - Yuck!' James, Abdul and Peter also received the friendly greeting.

'See!' laughed Pat. 'He likes you. No need to be afraid of any old shadows after all.'

James wiped his face.

'Is that the Polar Bear that grandpa escaped from all those years ago?' He asked. 'When he used that front door with the smiley faced door knocker to escape.'

A little voice rose from a sofa that was near to where the bar stood.

'I wondered what had happened to that' it said, the Penguin Person suddenly waking. 'I was going to paint it, but I left for a little Siesta, when I came back it was gone.' The little voice then snored back to the sleep it had been enjoying.

'Thanks Buddy' called out Pat. 'It would seem that your grandpa took Pancho Siesta's door.' Pat lifted his cup again. 'He is our Penguin Person Buddy that likes to take notes on Mexico.'

The children quickly stood up and moved to one side, allowing the large polar bear called Splodge to sit down.

## United Time Club - Living Legends.

'Well anyhow!' Said Pat, being elbowed off his stool by the large pet Polar Bear. 'Let's get you Kids some drinks and sit down on the comfy seats!' He pointed to the menu on the ice wall. 'Pick a drink number!' Pat turned to Sue. 'Ladies first!'

Sue examined the drink list, declining the Sea Salt Shake, that sounded awful, but choosing the drink next to it on the list. 'A strawberry milk shake please!' she said with a smile.

'Sure thing!' Replied Tiddler's squeaky voice.

The small and still unseen Penguin Person moved toward the wall, lifted a small hatch, which to the children's surprise, revealed the udders of a cow that stood unseen, behind the ice wall and Tiddler then proceeded to obtain milk from these udders, directing them into a tall glass.

When the glass was almost full Tiddler opened another hatch, next to the first, which dropped three strawberries into Tiddler's hand. He squashed them and put them into the glass. Tiddler put a single finger into the glass and stirred the concoction faster than, so Sue thought, the mixing machine in grandmother's kitchen.

'Perfectly hygienic!' Said Patriot, looking at Sue's stunned face, as the glass was put on the bar counter in front of her. 'Tiddler always washes his hands before preparing anything.'

Abdul, James and Peter also decided to have the same strawberry milkshake, all three wanting to see the small Penguin Person produce them in the same strange fashion.

'Come on!' Said Patriot. 'Let's leave Splodge to have his drink'. Pats nose twitched. 'He tends to be messy drinker anyhow!'

The four children followed Patriot toward a set of five empty arm chairs, which had a long flat table in front of them. The seating arrangements were situated near to what seemed to be a large fireplace, flickering gently with a warm light and they looked most inviting.

'Make yourselves comfortable over here!' Said Pat and he pointed to the seats, while putting his cup of ice tea down onto the table top.

James sat on one of the seats and also placed his glass onto the table top.

'Nice seat!' He said, feeling the chair instantly change comfortably to his own contours. 'So Pat' he asked, as the others sat down. 'Grandpa said the Legend about you odd creatures was real. So what is all that about taking notes and stuff.'

'Odd creatures -' Pat muttered disdainfully. 'Humans are the only odd creatures about on this Planet.' Patriot twitched his large red nose and took a sip from his cup. 'It is like this Buddy -' He tapped his chin thoughtfully. 'Things all started at the very beginning of Time, when all of creation began its great forward journey into the clock circle.' Pat placed his cup back onto the table, where the small saucer was waiting.

## United Time Club - Living Legends.

'Of course, Penguin People were only just born about then, but our own legend says that when Time itself began, the 'Great Balance of Existence' continued onwards, from where it had always been.'

Pat looked at the Kids slightly confused faces.

'Er - That's what you would call Good and Evil folks, that's the balance, always been around, always will be around!'

The children thought for a moment, then nodded in understanding and each took a sip of milkshake from their tall glasses. Pat also nodded, then continued.

'In the Great Balance of Existence, or beginning, Legend says, The Great Good Spirit of Peace and Light banished The Evil Black Shadow Void to the back of Time and that's where it is still trapped today.'

Pat scratched the bald head beneath his cap.

'Um - Like, the front of a clock is good and the back is bad, just shadow, no use at all.' He looked at the kids. 'Do you folks understand that?'

James contemplated for a moment.

'So,' he said in deep thought. 'When you look at a clock on the front, you see creation and good, moving forward, when you see the back, you see creation stopped and just a bad shadow?'

'Spot on Buddy!' Smiled Pat, nodding his large round head in agreement.

'It's pretty simple really. But of course mankind like yourselves -' Patriot looked at Sue. 'Sorry - And Womankind too! - Have been given the special honour of the great balance of choice.'

'What is that?' Asked Sue, quite interested. Pat continued.

'Well, you probably know it's not all that easy to be good. But that it is really easy to be bad.' The Penguin Person rubbed his chin. 'The thing is, each and every human person has the choice to be whichever they want to be, good or bad. Most folk though, seem to just balance between the two. That's the choices.'

Abdul interrupted Pat.

'Surely it would be better to be good though?'

'Yes sir!' Said Pat agreeing. 'But like I said, that's a choice everyone has to make for themselves.'

'So how does your taking notes apply to this?' Asked Peter.

'Well, it's kinder simple really' said Pat, twitching his nose. 'We write down and keep notes to up-date, a kinder, well, historical documentary of this Planet Earth, while you odd', he looked directly at James and sniffed with his large red nose, 'human things, make your own decisions in the great balance of choice.'

Pat took another sip of ice tea.

'We work for a great groovy dude, his greatness, Master Tick Tock Fotherington Splotch, the Grand Master and very centre of the Eternal Circle, Keeper of the Four Great Keys of Time and whose kinder mysterious and ever changing face features in the centre of everyone's clock's, as a very small dot.'

## United Time Club - Living Legends.

'Wow!' Exclaimed the children together.

'But what do you do with the notes and when do you get them?' Asked Sue.

'We have a great wall and circle of Time, within one of the cartoon Buddy clubs grand halls' continued Pat. 'On this wall, there are what we call great clocks, each one representing each single country that's been formed or reformed by you human folk. If something important happens somewhere in today's Time, sometimes, the Peace key goes missing from one of those clocks and a cartoon Buddy has to go and take notes of why that would be.'

'What is the Peace key?' Asked Peter.

Pat took another sip of ice tea to wet his dry mouth, making a rather loud slurping nose as he did so.

'You see - There are four keys on every clock' replied the small Penguin Person, putting the now empty cup down. 'The past key, guess what you folk would call the small hour hand. The present key, what you folk would call the larger minute hand. The future key, that's what you human folk would call the second hand, and then there's the most important key, the fourth key.' Pat lent back in the comfortable chair and crossed his shoes. 'Now that is the Peace key, which you human folk don't always see.'

'But what actually is it?' Asked Abdul, stopping Peter, as he was about to ask the very same question.

'Now that's the key, that all you human folk keep hidden inside and was made at the very dawn of Time!' Said Patriot quite smugly.

'It is a happy smile!' Interrupted James. 'Grandpa told me so!'

'Gosh darn it!' Exclaimed Pat. 'I was just about to say that myself!' He thought for a moment and continued. 'Guess most all you human folk know that a friendship smile, is the most important key of all to Peace, even if you do forget it sometimes?' He composed himself. 'Well anyhow, when a key, the smile that is, fades and vanishes from one of those clocks, as I said before, a Buddy goes and takes notes.' Pat stretched his legs outwards to get more comfortable in the chair. 'When he has obtained the notes and returns, they are put into the celestial safe.'

'What happens to them after that?' Asked Peter.

'I don't rightly know' replied Pat. 'But our legend says that at the very end of Time, the notes may be used for the final reckoning of the balance between good and Evil. Something like, well, the more good notes there are, the better on the weighing scales.'

'When is the end of Time?' Asked Sue.

'Whenever you human folk want it to be!' Replied Pat. 'See, it's like, well, this simple. That big old sun, the ball of fire that practically helps all the life on this planet Earth to exist and lights your Time, will eventually burn itself out. But don't you go worrying, that's almost an eternity away yet -

## United Time Club - Living Legends.

And if your 'humankind' folk, have not all, eventually, joined together in a lasting Peace, with the help of that old key and made mostly the right decisions, using your Time in the balance well, the many basic tools that have been created in very earliest Time, will have all long run out.

Things and tools, which mankind and womankind too, can use to firstly survive and then, adapt, to travel outwards into space, spreading all the written messages of good. Tools like the sun and oil of course, all stuff like that.' Pat's nose twitched and he shrugged his curved shoulders.

'Of course, in the end, if Evil does win because of human people's bad balancing, by the Time leaving planet Earth becomes a necessary reality for humans' said Pat sadly. 'Then humanity will still be just living on this planet anyway, only waiting around both patiently and, sad to say helplessly, for all the lights to finally go out on them sometime.'

'That does not sound too good?' Said James.

'No' replied Pat. 'I would not like to think that all the things that have been created since the dawn of Time on this planet would be lost and forgotten, just because some of humanity made the wrong choices and chose to be bad.'

'Definitely not!' All the children replied together.

'Good!' Replied Pat, with a huge grin. 'There's hope for the future yet.' He heard the huge doors suddenly creak open. 'Hey folks, here comes Monty.'

Everyone turned around in their seats, to watch the slow moving Penguin Person shuffle forward through the double doors and head directly toward their seats.

'Well -' asked Pat. 'What did the great master dot spirit, Fotherington Splotch, have to say about our visitors?'

'It is just simply not cricket old thing!' replied Monty, twitching his large red nose. 'The masters dot is still in the eternal circle keeping the keys of Time, but it seems that the grand master is not home at the moment and may be out to lunch.' Monty pressed his yellow clock button on his hat front, then, after the lid flew open, produced a rolled up sheet of paper from inside. 'However - The grand master has left a note for us.'

'So how long is lunch?' Asked James, also wondering to himself what sort of lunch, a dot at the centre of a clock could possibly eat.

'Difficult to say' replied Monty. 'Could be a matter of seconds, minutes, hours, months, years, centuries or even a millennium - Depends really.'

'That is some weird lunch break!' Noted James. 'Couldn't you just ask the grand master to come back and give you some advice?'

'No - No!' exclaimed Monty, unfurling the rolled up sheet of paper. 'Not for us Penguin People to tell Time.' His monocle rolled slowly around, as he read the strange, hieroglyphic writing on the paper. 'That is simply not cricket old thing!'

'What is the message Buddy?' Asked Pat, sniffing toward the paper.

'See for yourself!' Replied Monty holding the message up for Pat to examine.

## United Time Club - Living Legends.

The children also looked at the paper, which was an incomprehensible mish-mash of strange animal and plant life pictures.

'Well -' Huffed Abdul. 'I can read Egyptian Hieroglyphics - But I can't read that!'

'Oh! - Sorry old thing!' Said Monty apologetically. 'I forgot that only a language transferred by mouth can be universally understood in this Time club.'

'What do you mean by that?' Asked Sue.

'It is quite simple!' Interrupted Pat. 'Everyone here, or mostly everyone, speaks a different language.' Pat then smiled. 'But in and around the cartoon Buddy Time club everyone understands each other, because of our spirit of Peace and friendship.'

'Yes!' Said Monty, slightly sarcastically. 'Thank you for your interruption.' He turned toward Sue. 'As Patriot said, you may see that around here, no matter what different language you may speak, so long as it is spoken in Peace and friendship you will all be able to understand the same words.' Monty looked around the room. 'Also my dear old things if you look around you will notice, that although every Penguin Person here may wear a differently coloured flag jacket, so that we can tell each other apart and which part of the planet we like, we are all the same under our coats just like you real human people.'

'Yes sir re!' Agreed Pat, leaning forward to take the paper from Monty. 'But while I read out this message.' He pointed toward Tiddler's Bar. 'You had better get your ice tea from the cool bar.'

'Oh dear!' Exclaimed Monty, handing the paper to Pat. 'Not the cool Bar, how demeaning!'

'What does he mean by that?' Asked Abdul, watching Monty shuffle away.

'You will see in a moment folks!' Said Pat grinning. 'Anyhow, lets read this note.' Pat lifted the paper and spoke the words aloud as he read them.

'From the grand master of Time Fotherington Splotch. Penguin People. I have to leave for a while. Expect visitors, as indicated in the club legend, page nine million four hundred and twenty nine thousand. Make them welcome, assist and protect. Time out.'

'So Time knew we were coming?' Asked Sue, feeling quite surprised.

'Guess so' replied Pat.

'But what is that bit about your legend?' Asked Peter.

Pat thought deeply.

'As I recall, in that bit of the legend it mentions that the Dark Void, one nasty dude, tried to touch the pure hearts of those that would eventually join together and destroy it's resurrection.' Pat put the paper down onto the table. 'Kinder creepy huh?'

'Look here!' Monty's voice made everyone forget the legend and turn toward the cool bar. 'Let me have my ice tea!'

'What is going on -' asked Sue.

## United Time Club - Living Legends.

'Monty's trying to get his drink from the cool bar!' Laughed Pat. 'But the cool bar don't think he is cool enough!' Pat shuffled off his seat and stood up to get a better view. 'This should be fun kids, take a look!'

'Hey dude, keep your karma, like, cool man. Take a break and chill out, o hair faced daddy-o!' Replied the long and very icy cool bar to Monty, while the four children looked on. All were quite surprised that an ice bar could talk, especially as not one of the children could actually see a mouth on the thing.

'You know you gotta be kind of cool and with it yourself, to get your drink from me baby!' It continued.

'This is simply not cricket old thing!' Exclaimed Monty, feeling his cheeks grow a little flushed with embarrassment and shaking his head slowly back and forth. 'Do we really have to suffer this confounded reject from the sixties!'

Monty then looked downward at his ice tea, which glistened seductively upwards from inside the cup. Red lips below his large, equally red nose, formed quite suddenly from Monty's bland circular face and they pouted longingly toward the drink, even more so, as the Penguin Person lent forward to try and take a sip from the cup.

'Now you know? - O vertically challenged one' said the cool bar, while moving the cup slowly away from Monty's lips. 'That you ain't acting cool today baby, no, not one little itie bit, daddy-o!'

Monty huffed a heavy sigh of disgust, observing the cup and saucer twist in a circle, then move slowly away from his face.

'We should never have let Groovy Love Thang install this Cool Bar in the first place!' he said dejectedly.

'Who is Groovy Love Thang-' whispered James, smiling at the rather strange, but comical scene.

'Our music Penguin Person note keeper' replied Pat, twitching his large red nose, then forming a wry grin below it. 'Groovy is OK, but tends to be a little stuck with the sixties frame of mind. He invented and installed the cool bar and it seems to have inherited some of his style.'

Monty stopped stretching forward over the bar top and retracted his lips. The Penguin Person had by now given in to his craving for the ice tea and as he knew that releasing the cup and saucer by hand from the icy surface was impossible, decided to give in to the cool bar.

'So, how are ones things, um, grooving?' Monty asked, in a rather upper class English accent. 'Er – Um - Baby?' He added.

'Now that's quite smooth man! - Positive Karma! - I bet that didn't hurt one bit daddy-o!' Laughed the Cool Bar in satisfaction. 'A little bit more though, if you please, oh head capped and very short dude!'

'Hmm!' Monty stifled his discontent, twitched his nose, then continued.

'Please hit me with the, um, er, cosmic circle of smooth niceness! - Um – Man – etc.'

## United Time Club - Living Legends.

'Better!' Called out the cool bar. 'Much better!' Then the cup and saucer, slid slowly toward Monty.

'Thank you!' Snapped Monty, raising his long arm and picking up the cup and saucer. 'Ridiculous procedure!' He mumbled under his breath as he turned and walked toward the children and Pat. 'Utterly ridiculous!'

Pat sat down and chuckled to himself, watching Monty shuffle with his cup and saucer back toward the table.

'Having to act cool really gets to Monty's stiff upper lip' he said smiling. 'Which is more than the ice tea does, if he don't.'

The children looked at each other and shook their heads in disbelief, but all were smiling in amusement.

Sue, as she looked across at Pat, was quite thoughtful at all the events that had taken place that morning.

'If you creatures have been around for so long taking notes and keeping them from Evil.' She asked. 'Are you a group of, kind of like, well, sort of angels?'

'Huh -' Pat reached forward to pick up the note paper from the table top. He then pushed the small yellow clock on his cap and placed the paper inside after the lid had sprang open. 'No – No - Well at least I don't think so' he said, as Sue watched the lid thud back downward and close. 'We ain't that kind of bird people!' His nose twitched and moved around. 'I mean, they got their own functions to do and we got ours!'

'So does that mean that they really exist then?' Asked James, wanting to know more.

'Er - Guess so -' Said Pat. 'But never seen or met one though' he added thoughtfully. 'Then again, never seen or met human kids in this club before and, never seen one anywhere that can actually see Penguin People.'

Monty placed his cup and saucer carefully onto the table top and sat in a comfortable chair next to Pats.

'But they are mentioned in our own legend book old things,' he interrupted. 'So I suppose it is possible. But human types with wings? - Not very likely is it.'

'Almost as unlikely as talking Penguin People?' Laughed Abdul.

Monty lifted his cup and the red lips returned, to take with a slurp, a sip of the ice tea.

'Er - Yes, quite right old thing. I suppose it proves that anything is possible in Time and creation. Even if you cannot actually see it.'

'Yeah - Right' agreed Pat, who then pressed a button on his chairs arm. A small hatch raised from the arm and an equally small radio appeared on the end of what seemed to be an ice finger.

'Listen buddies!' Pat poked a button on the radio set. 'It's Time for Groovy Love Thang's radio show!' He looked at the children. 'You folks want to listen for a while?'

## United Time Club - Living Legends.

'What is a radio?' Asked Peter, peering at the small box. 'I have never seen one of those.'

James, Abdul and Sue looked at Peter, each suddenly realising that Peter was dressed in Victorian Style clothing.

'Yes sir re!' Pat's voice stated, what the three children were all thinking. 'Peter is not from your Time, not judging by the clothes that he is wearing.' His nose twitched toward Peter. 'Is Queen Victoria your monarch?' he asked.

Peter nodded in agreement, while the three other children just looked at each other in bemusement.

'Really most odd' replied Monty. 'Must be some sort of breach in the space and Time flow?'

'The skateboard -' blurted Peter, a little bit embarrassed that everyone was now looking at him. 'It saved me from danger!'

'Yes of course, it is designed to protect the rider' said Monty, nodding. But he was still mystified as to why the skateboards had brought the children to the club and Peter, it seemed, forward in Time.

The radio burst into sudden life, interrupting the conversation.

'Good afternoon Buddy land!' Came a loud and excited voice from inside the little speaker. 'Time to get on down with the best sounds around!' The voice then seemed to change character, very suddenly, to reveal a really mellow, hippie like voice. 'And now to chill and groove, to Groovy Love Thang!'

Everyone looked to the small box and Peter's face was quite a picture.

'How does someone fit inside that small box?' He asked.

'It is only a machine that can transmit ones voice and sound, through the use of electromagnetic wave signals!' Said Monty shaking his head. 'There is no one really inside the box!'

Peter strained forwards to get a closer look.

'And for all you resting Buddy Penguin People out there!' Bellowed, or rather, mellowed, the radio. 'Here is a tune from a human group, who's words still mean such a lot to whoever who may sit on the honour couch! - We can work It out.'

The strains of a song vibrated through the radio and Pat bobbed his head in rhythm with it.

'Honour couch?' James looked around the room. 'What is that?'

Monty finished the last traces of his ice tea and placed the cup back onto the saucer.

'Well that is over there old thing!' Monty pointed toward a far corner of the room, where a flickering fire glowed brightly and covered the walls with it's golden glow.

In front of this relaxing to the eye and slowly flickering golden light, a long and quite large couch lay shimmering with an icy, crystal hue.

## United Time Club - Living Legends.

For all those that were now looking at this peculiar piece of furniture located in the far side of chill out hall, the thing that most caught their attention was an unusual, upturned smiley mouth and red nose motif that was etched onto this piece of furniture's curved back.

'Why is that mouth not smiling?' Asked Abdul, observing the difference between this motif and the happy ones that he had seen so far.

'Well,' answered Monty, his moustache twitching beneath his large red nose. 'The couch of honour, is also, unfortunately, the couch of much sadness.'

Pat put his now empty cup back onto his saucer and his nose twitched sadly toward the couch.

'Yes sir!' He said quietly. 'It is for the most hard working Penguin People to rest on, after a really hard days note making.'

'Quite!' Replied Monty. 'But, unfortunately, to be the most hard working Penguin Person also means, that more bad events may be taking place in the areas that the Buddy has been covering.'

Pat nodded, his hat bobbing back and forth as he did so.

'We have all been there at some Time or other,' he then shook his head. 'It is not a place that any Cartoon Buddy Club member wants to be.' Pat placed his cup and saucer onto the shiny table top. 'And to be there, on that couch' he continued. 'Makes us really quite sad.'

'Hence the unhappy mouth' interrupted Monty, feeling his throat suddenly dry in emotion.

'What is that bucket for?' Asked Sue. She pointed to the large, cylinder like receptacle, that seemed to be very out of place next to a piece of furniture.

Pat and Monty, along with the other children looked downward toward the bucket that now and again became half obscured by flickering shadow.

'It is the bucket of tears' said both the Penguin People together.

'Yes, yes!' Continued Monty. 'To catch the sadness of those that are sat on the couch.'

Noticing a thin tear, well up and roll slowly from beneath the cap that obscured the Penguin Person's very small eyes, Sue reached out and patted Monty gently on the back.

'There there!' She said affectionately. Sue raised her finger and wiped this single tear from the strange creatures face. 'Oh?' Sue looked at the very cold bead of water now on her fingertip and was quite taken a back, as it suddenly formed into a very small smiley mouth shape and then slowly evaporated into a thin mist of warm steam.

'Pull yourself together Buddy!' Drawled Pat, twitching his nose toward Monty.

Monty observed the thin mist of his tear disappear from Sues finger tip and inside he felt much better.

'Thank you my dear!' He said, reaching out and holding Sues hand very gently.

## United Time Club - Living Legends.

Monty then bent forward and two large pouting lips formed beneath his large red nose, which then kissed her hand most gently.

'Only kindness of spirit can make tears go away!' He said, the lips then forming a wide smile.

'Er - Right -' Replied Sue, feeling a little embarrassed and looking at Pat, who gave Sue a sudden thumbs up sign and then smiled himself.

'Human kids are A.O.K. by me!' Said Pat.

James looked hard toward the couch.

'Why is there no Penguin Person sat there right now?' He asked, observing that the couch appeared to have no one sat on it, as the golden glow from the fire illuminated that sad little corner of the room.

The radio interrupted him quite rudely and, before anyone could answer brought everyone's attention, again, toward it. Groovy Love Thang's voice trailed from the small box, still mellow, but somehow louder and it seemed a little concerned.

'Like – Um - Lend me your small ears good buddies!' A muted shuffling of paper could be heard, as if Groovy had just received an announcement written on paper. 'We have – Like – Um - A situation -' More shuffling of paper could be heard. Then Groovy Love Thang read out the message in front of him. 'Would all Cartoon Buddy Club members please go to the hall of vision – Like – Um - At once!'

'What on Earth is going on?' Exclaimed Monty looking toward Pat. As Pat looked back and shook his head, giving a stifled.

'No idea bud -'

Groovy Love Thang continued, with the short and somehow very ominous words.

'The Dark Void has returned!'

Monty fell off his chair and his bottom gave a loud, painful thud as it hit the floor.

'Goodness gracious me!' He exclaimed.

'This does not sound very good' observed Peter.

The four children looked around and watched the room erupt and buzz with Penguin People figures, that now seemed to appear from all over the room and each shuffled quickly toward a half obscured archway carved into the wall.

'The Great Eraser!' Gasped Pat standing up. 'The Great Eraser has returned!' He then looked down at Monty and twitched his nose. 'You going to just sit there Buddy.'

Sue and Abdul helped Monty up from the floor.

'What is the Great Eraser?' Asked James, speaking the words that all the children were thinking, but he was the first to ask.

'You know' answered Pat. 'The bad thing, that feeds on bad things, the opposite of light and good!'

## United Time Club - Living Legends.

He looked at the four kids who seemed a little stunned by all the commotion. 'The darkness, that wants to rub everything out!'

'Like in the legend?' Said Sue, dusting ice from Monty's arms.

'Quickly then!' Monty composed himself. 'We must go to the hall of vision, right now!'

The Penguin Person shuffled forward and everyone followed this rather strange creature to the archway, into which all the other creatures had by now disappeared and, entered into another hall of ice beyond it.

'Now - This is really weird!' Exclaimed James, poking his head through the archway and surveying the scene beyond it.

'Let me see!' Abdul put his own head past the shoulder of James. 'Yes you are correct!' he spluttered.

Sue smiled at Peter, then pushed the two boys in front of her gently forward 'Let us see too!' She laughed as two boys fell forward onto the floor and slid on their bellies into the other room.

Peter peered into the room and was quite amazed by what he saw.

'This is incredible!' He said looking up, his mouth falling open. 'I have never seen anything like that before!'

'Excellent belly flop technique young Master James and young Master Abdul' quipped Monty, as both the boys slid forward, at some speed, into the huge room beyond the small, icy archway. 'But it is really not the kind of thing that is allowed in the vision hall' he continued, watching the boys slide past him and come to an abrupt stop directly in the centre of a huge clock face, that was embedded into the ice floor.

'Cool -' Exclaimed James, rolling himself over onto his back, to see an equally huge map of the planet embedded in the ceiling directly above the clock.

Rolling over at the same moment Abdul repeated the sentiment of James.

'Cool -' He said quietly, looking around the hall. 'This must be like a Penguin People mission control.'

'Yeah - Just like NASA on TV - The space thing' replied James, observing two huge half circular bank of separate TV screens, behind which, sat on ice seats he noted, were a huge array of Penguin People all wearing jackets each coloured with the design of a different flag.

'There are things moving and living in that huge box!' Peter called out in excitement. He marvelled at the sight of a single large screen, situated at the end of the wide and long room and in which many different pictures were flashing and moving.

'That is just a large television screen' laughed Sue. 'Oh but of course' she thought for a moment. 'You have not seen one of those coming from Victorian Times.'

'Yes of course!' called out Pat, shuffling toward his seat.

## United Time Club - Living Legends.

'The screen merely reflects the image of objects and living things, like the radio reflects the sound of a voice.' His nose twitched with thought. 'It's like, moving pictures or paintings.' It was the best description Pat could think of, to someone who had never seen it before.

'Amazing!' Cried Peter, his eyes still transfixed.

'Everyone please be seated!' A stern voice called out from a speaker system on the ice walls.

Sue noticed how the front of the ten or so speaker boxes that she could see from where she was standing, contained a smiley mouth motif and this mouth was the thing that was actually doing the speaking.

'Bizarre -' Sue thought to herself as the speakers 'spoke' again.

'All Cartoon Buddy Club geographical members have been recalled and are now sat at their viewing areas. We shall now begin.' The words boomed around the icy walls.

'What about the guests?' Called out Monty. 'They have nowhere to sit.'

'Er -' The speaker system fell silent for a seconds. 'Er – Well -' It seemed that the system was not really used to any guests and could not think of what to say.

'How about the kids sitting on the clock centre?' Interrupted Pat. 'They will get a good view from there.'

'The guests now will sit in the clock centre!' Boomed the speaker system again, then added a polite. 'Please.'

Peter and Sue moved to the centre of the clock that was embedded into the icy floor, (where Abdul and James were now sitting upright) and sat down themselves.

The four children looked around at the half circular banks of TV screens that now surround them, and smiled at the many kinds of Penguin People that were sat behind these TV screens, and who were, by now, poking their noses over the top of their TV's to get a better look at the children.

As each child smiled, so they received a large smile back, from the large array of very strange Cartoon Buddy Club Penguin Person creatures.

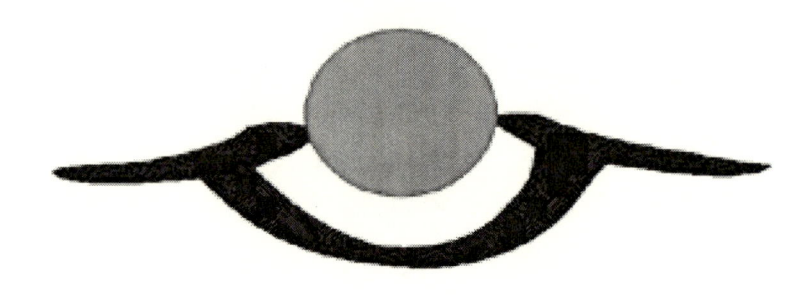

## *The Void Returns - (The Great Eraser)*

Within the Great Hall Of Vision all had suddenly fallen quite silent. The glowing light that had reflected into every corner of this large, icy room, dimmed slowly, while the single large television screen situated at the end of the Hall of Vision, grew steadily brighter. The smiley speaker system, embedded within the shiny walls, broke this uneasy silence and it's voice echoed around the hall.

'With his greatness Tick Tock Fotherington Splotch, Grand Master of the Four Keys of Time, unfortunately not in attendance at this extraordinary meeting of the Cartoon Buddy Club,' it boomed. 'I shall chair the meeting, as stated in the Club rule book, one billion, two hundred and twenty two thousand, three hundred and seventy one.'

All of the numerous and rather strange creatures surrounding the four children nodded silently in agreement. James watched in amusement while observing their red noses bob up and down, beneath the long brim of their hats.

'They sure do have a lot of rules here' he whispered quietly.

Abdul, who sat next to James, nodded himself. Then he looked toward the centre of the huge clock that lay embedded into the icy floor, on which all the children were sitting.

'I think that is where the Tick Tock person is supposed to be' he said, following the direction and to the spot that the Penguin People seemed to be looking toward. Abdul, while looking downward, observed that the circular clock centre seemed to be slowly revolving anti-clockwise. He also noticed, that this circle held the markings of a compass, although it did not appear to have any point marked that was relative to North, South, West Or East, as was marked on the usual compasses that he had seen before.

The small letters N, S, W and E, on this compass span very slowly around and around, making him feel quite dizzy the more he looked and stared at it. Peter peered downward too and then, feeling dizzy himself, shook his head, then rubbed his eyes. He tapped Abdul gently, to break his transfixed gaze, while also struggling with his own.

'There is no point in Time' said Monty, twitching his large red nose and speaking toward the children when he noticed what they were looking at. 'Unless the Peace Key is present.'

Sue lifted her arms and flicked the right ears of both Peter and Abdul with her finger tips, quite hard.

'Ouch!' Both the boys cried together painfully, their dizziness suddenly evaporating.

'Listen up and concentrate!' Whispered Sue forcefully. 'You too!' - Sue then flicked the ear of James in the same manor.

With an air of authority, although sounding concerned, the speakers boomed again.

'This newscast was received today, and is the reason why this meeting was called.'

## The Void Returns - (The Great Eraser)

All the small smiley boxes fell silent for a moment while the large television screen flickered with the single image of a lady newsreader. Suddenly, from these many speakers, the newsreaders own voice trailed forth.

'The strange weather phenomenon that had formed late last evening over the Bermuda Triangle area continues to puzzle meteorologists.' The newsreader's voice read the words on the auto cue in front of her with a steady calm.

'It has been reported that two aircraft from the American aircraft carrier USS John F Kennedy sent to investigate the phenomenon are missing at this Time. It has also been reported from news just coming in, that contact with a Naval vessel has also been lost, although this has not been confirmed.'

A small, hazy and somewhat fuzzy, satellite picture of an enormous swirling dark blob on the Earth's surface flicked onto the screen, encased in a small box, next to the newsreader. The overall picture on the television screen then started to crackle and break up with fuzzy lines while the newsreader continued.

'It has been confirmed, in a series of other incidents related to this weather phenomenon, that contact has been lost with a British Navy submarine and that both commercial aircraft and shipping are reporting interference with guidance and radio transmissions near the affected area.'

A subdued 'Hmm -' hummed around the hall as everyone listened intently in thought.

'Satellite systems operating in space and tracking this weather phenomenon are malfunctioning. Transmission has been interrupted for the Time being and no pictures or data are available. Other satellite systems orbiting the Earth are now also experiencing various degrees of interference and, contact with the international Space station has also temporarily been lost.'

Another subdued 'Hmm -' hummed from the Penguin People watching the large TV screen.

'An unusual Electromagnetic pulse that is emanating from this weather phenomenon has been blamed and, due to the most unusual aspects of this particular weather event, a joint task force of both United Nation ships and other guest nations have been invited and will be forming shortly to investigate this phenomenon.'

The newsreader read out the last piece of her newscast just as her own picture disappeared beneath a haze of interference.

'No government at this Time has explained why a joint investigation of this weather phenomenon by a coalition of all nations has been deemed necessary.'

With the end of this signal, a sudden, eye straining light, illuminated brightly the Great Hall of Vision and the large TV screen dimmed to darkness, with a small white dot remaining and centring the screen.

The speaker system quickly boomed into life again and demanded everyone's attention.

## The Void Returns - (The Great Eraser)

'The Void has returned!' It stated in a very serious, curt and very low tone. 'Members! - We must decide what shall be done!'

As the speaker system echoed around the hall and it's voice had just started to trail away, there was a low, ominous rumbling noise, that seemed to come from behind a set of huge ice doors embedded into the wall. All the children and Penguin People looked toward the direction where this strange sound was coming from.

'Oh dear!' Sue heard Monty exclaim in a hushed tone.

This strange rumbling then grew very, very quickly, to an unearthly roar, that shook the very walls of the hall and made the ground tremble.

'Ah!' All four children cried out in fright, as the two huge doors suddenly sprang open and a violent, dark wind blew through the opening.

The lights in the hall flickered and then dimmed. From beyond these huge doors a dark, sinister shadow emerged and slowly moved forward through the opening. It seemed to be a huge and frightening figure, carrying some sort of long stick, with a blade on the end, the shadow of which bounced off the walls as the light flickered.

'It is the Grim Reaper!' Cried James, his jaw dropping open.

The children looked at each other, then looked at the ever growing shadow emerging from the other room, each wondering what was going to happen next.

'This is jolly frightening!' Exclaimed Peter, as the dark and sinister shadow grew ever larger. He shut one eye, but kept the other half open, just to see what was happening.

'Ah!' Shouted James Sue and Abdul, the huge shadow finally reaching them, blocking out what was left of the rooms light and then it engulfed the horrified children.

Monty, who was still half obscured behind his TV screen had seen enough, he suddenly stood up and in an unusually loud and forceful manor the Penguin Person shouted a single.

'Stop!'

With the call of Monty's voice echoing around vision hall, the dark, howling wind died as quickly as it had come. The strange sinister shadow stopped moving. Then it grew ever smaller, while the lights of the room grew steadily brighter, casting a warm glow around the icy, shiny walls.

'A grand entrance as ever' snapped Monty. 'But you are spooking the children old thing.'

The dark shadow retreated further with the brightening lights, to eventually reveal a small, rather Penguin Person like form, that was now standing in front of and looking down at James.

'Pardon me' came a small voice emanating from under a black, coal scuttle shaped hat that the creature was wearing. A large red nose, half hidden under this hat twitched in thought. 'You all right pal?'

## The Void Returns - (The Great Eraser)

'Er -' James looked at the strange creature and was not sure if he was 'all right' or not. He noted the gravestone and sand of Time picture painted on the creatures jacket and spluttered. 'Well – I – Er -'

'Grimley Reaping is the name' interrupted the creature, a thin smile appearing from under the large red nose. 'And not so much of the Grim Reaper if you please young sir.' The creature moved forward slightly. 'What's to do?' It asked cheerfully, handing the stick that it was holding out toward James.

James held out his own hand and took the stick.

'What's to do? - What?' He replied, slightly confused.

'Grimley means what is happening' called out Pat, his voice booming from behind his own TV screen.

'I do' called out Grimley. 'There are a lot of human folk now missing on this planet, that are not on me lists, for up or down!'

Producing a black covered notebook and flicking through it's pages, Grimley continued.

'Most irregular, I say, most irregular!'

James looked at the stick Grimley had given him to hold and noted the long shiny blade. He touched it with his finger and felt the blade spring downward. 'It is made of rubber' he whispered to himself in a low voice, but was actually, just loud enough to be heard.

'Eee - That's right. Might hurt though-self, if that t'were made of metal' said Grimley whilst examining his note book carefully. He shook his head and the black coal scuttle hat bobbed up and down. 'Not part of Times procedure this. Nowt is right in me notes today.'

'I should explain' said Monty, twitching his red nose toward the children. 'That Grimley keeps note of all human people who are passing through the mortal coil of life. Both the good and bad people, recording where their soul spirit's go afterwards in the end. Mainly after wars and such, but everyday too.'

'That's right!' Agreed Grimley, still engrossed in his notebook. 'Up or down!' his nose twitched in thought. 'Good go up, bad go down.'

Sue put her hand up in the air to ask a question.

'What about -'

'Hold on there sweet thing!' Pat interrupted Sue's question. 'If you ask a question of Grimley, it cannot be personal.'

'Oh -' Sue put her hand down, but Grimley seemed to read her mind and feel her inner sadness.

'Nowt in my notes about any one of your folks kids' he said flicking through the notebook pages. 'They are not listed anywhere here and are missing from the planet, just like a load of other folk.'

'By Jove!' exclaimed Monty. 'I wager it's to do with that dastardly Void chap.'

A low hum of hushed voices could be heard amongst the Penguin People.

'Yes of course!' Monty spoke to those who were whispering near to him.

## The Void Returns - (The Great Eraser)

'It would seem that each of these children present, have been saddened by the Voids badness to others.'

Monty like all of the other Penguin People in the Hall of Vision, thought of the Club Legend book and the words it contained.

'Four in future Time, those that came, will fight the Void and defeat it's Evil Spirit, in loves own game.'

'The Void has returned?' said Grimley, quite surprised, bringing everyone's attention back toward him. 'The Great Eraser is back?'

'Yes sir' said Pat curtly. 'Looks like the big bad one has now captured both spirit's and human folk.'

Sue suddenly felt angry, which was really not in her nature.

'Do you mean that Eraser thing might have our parents in some sort of prison or something?'

Grimley rubbed his chin thoughtfully.

'Makes a lot of sense lass' he said, closing his notebook. 'Not listed, not gone.' He continued. 'Not gone - Hidden by the Void!'

The children all stood up in unison.

'Lets get that thing!' Shouted James.

'Yes!' replied Abdul, shaking his fist. 'It must be stopped!'

Peter looked at Monty.

'So how do we defeat this Void monster?' He asked.

'Yes!' Shouted Sue angrily, banging her fist against the open palm of her other hand. 'How do we crush it. You creatures must know?'

Monty was quite taken aback by the attitude of the children, but understood the young humans feeling of anger.

'Well,' he said softly. 'Anger is not really the ticket old things!' Monty shook his head. 'The Void only feeds on that sort of emotion.'

'It is what gives it it's power!' Interrupted Pat.

'Hmm - Nowt can see into the Void' said Grimley, adding to the conversation. 'And nowt can enter it either, not even me!' But he then thought and remembered. 'However, the legend book does say that the only way to destroy the Void is from within it.'

'Yes' said Monty. 'And turn bad into good.'

'So there must actually be a way into it!' shouted Sue. 'An entrance - Surely you Penguin People can think where that would be.'

There was a thoughtful silence in the hall of vision and rather a lot of negative head shaking.

'Then maybe we kids can think of a way' said James. 'We have to!'

Before anyone could say anything else, an extremely brilliant light, like the ray from a huge torch suddenly shone from the doorway that Grimley had used to enter the Great Hall Of Vision. This made both the children and Penguin People momentarily shield their eyes and cut short their conversation.

## The Void Returns - (The Great Eraser)

'Well your faith that good will triumph over Evil is certainly strong!' Called out a voice that gradually got louder the more that the figure that it emanated from entered further into the room.

Peter squinted his eyes and looked toward the light and figure.

'I do not believe it! - It's an angel' he blurted, feeling quite shocked.

'Well not quite dear heart' the figure replied, as the other children also squinted and made out it's form, all noticing the large wings that protruded from the figures back, glistening in the strong light.

The brilliant light abated quickly as the figure moved toward Grimley and the children.

'Hello Peace Faith' said Grimley, nodding his head in greeting, so that his hat slipped back and forth over his large red nose. ' What's to do?'

'Hello Grimley - Hello People' replied the figure, that the children could now see was also in the same shape of the other Penguin People. 'One has come to see what one can do, to facilitate assistance, in all that you may, or may not do.'

Grimley looked toward the children and said with a dry whit.

'Look out Kids - He never uses one word, when twenty will fit into a sentence!'

'Are you a real angel?' Asked Peter, who just felt he had to ask.

'No no dear heart!' Replied Peace Faith, a large smile appearing from under his large red nose. 'My wings are really only for decoration and identification.' He made the wings move backwards and forwards, by pulling a piece of string that dangled from his jacket front. 'Penguins and Penguin People do not fly dear heart!'

'Unless they have the skateboards of Time!' Interrupted Grimley.

Peace Faith smiled.

'Yes quite' he agreed and nodded.

Monty's nose twitched.

'Peace Faith takes note of your human faiths and is rather an expert on the battle between Good and Evil that has existed throughout Time.'

'Thank you Monty dear heart' responded Peace Faith. 'I do just hope that I can possibly help in some small way.'

'We need to get into that Void' said James, looking toward the strange creature.

'Yes!' Agreed Abdul, his voice sounding concerned. 'We must get inside to free our parents and destroy this Evil.'

Sue nodded in agreement.

'We cannot let this bad thing win and destroy the Earth!' She said, hitting her fist against her palm again. 'It has got to get crushed!'

Peter also agreed and smiled.

'Can you think of a way to enter that Void?'

Peace Faith thought for a moment. Then the small strange Penguin Person creature said quite slowly.

## The Void Returns - (The Great Eraser)

'It must be remembered that the Void of darkness actually comes from inside all of you human people. That is where it draws it's own power. That is where it feeds on mankind's ability to hate. That is where it will attempt to erase light to darkness. And, that is where it will attempt to erase mankind too, by mankind's own actions.'

'That does not answer the question' said Grimley, grimly.

'Well -' Peace Faith thought for a moment. 'If you look toward the Cartoon Buddy Club Crest, which is mounted in the caves Library room, you will see that it shows the words, 'Time Peace, Faith, Hope and Charity', and that is what you will need to have inside yourself, to be able to enter and overcome the Void of Darkness.'

'What do you mean old thing?' asked Monty, who had himself seen the Crest throughout all of Time, but had never considered it's actual usage for something.

Peace Faith looked to the children.

'You have to carry the spirit of Peace in your heart, not just in your words. Faith, that the spirit of good and light will always triumph over the spirit of Evil and darkness. Hope, that you will always have the strength to think positively and, finally, to hold the spirit of Charity. That is, to try and help all others, in no matter how small a way or form, when you have the ability to do so.'

The children looked at each other and each considered his words.

'If you really want to fight this Evil Void' continued Peace Faith. 'Then your anger may actually be your own worst enemy.'

'What about those ships' said James, remembering that the military of practically all the worlds nations were now heading out toward the Void. 'They are bound to be angry at the Void. What if they attempt to destroy it.'

Peace Faith scratched his head.

'I fear' he said calmly. 'That all they may do is to accelerate the Voids growth and to help in it's mission, to destroy your Planet and the light of good.'

'We must see what is going on with those ships!' Called out Pat from behind his TV screen.

'Yes, pray do let us use Times Powerful Oracle of Light and Vision Monty' said Peace Faith. 'We could use that device to see 'what in the world' is happening now that the human satellites have stopped transmission.'

'What do you think Times Powerful Oracle of Light and Vision is?' Asked Sue whispering to Peter, then looking around the hall for what it might possibly be.

Monty's nose twitched and he slowly removed his monocle.

'Catch!' He called out, and threw the small monocle toward Peace Faith.

The other peculiar Penguin Person creature caught the monocle first Time with it's arm out stretched, the small glass device flopping directly into the palm of his hand. 'Thank you dear heart!' Exclaimed Peace Faith who quickly placed the small monocle into the small white dot at the centre of the TV screen.

## The Void Returns - (The Great Eraser)

'That is it?' questioned Sue, expecting something much grander than a small glass eye-piece.

The glass monocle fitted perfectly into the white dot and the Penguin Person stepped back from the TV screen.

'We would like to ask a question of Times Powerful Oracle of Light and Vision' he said, red nose twitching.

With a flash, the monocle illuminated like a strong light bulb and a very small, squeaky voice, came from the small eye-piece.

'OK Buddy, what have you got to say?'

The children looked toward each other, each wondering what the others were thinking. But Sue whispered her thoughts first.

'Not exactly what you would expect of something called Times Powerful Oracle of Light and Vision' she muttered quite sarcastically.

'We do not all have to sound like some deep voiced great speaker to be of any importance' quipped the squeaky voice, hearing Sue's remarks and responding to them.

'Indeed, indeed!' Peace Faith agreed. 'We would like to ask of Times Powerful Oracle of Light and Vision what is happening with the ships on the human Planet that are heading toward the Evil Void?'

The TV suddenly burst into light and pictures of a fleet of huge of ships crackled onto the screen.

'Take a look!' ordered the squeaky voice of the small monocle.

'Oh dear' said Monty, sounding quite concerned. 'That really does not look the ticket.'

'No' agreed Pat. 'Looks like all those ships are getting ready to attack the Void.'

'The Evil Void will grow and approach first landfall in approximately twelve hours and fifteen minutes!' Squeaked the Oracle.

'What will happen then?' Asked James, turning his head to see all the Penguin People whisper amongst themselves.

'Then!' The voice squeaked again. 'Everything that the Void touches will be erased!'

'Erased' said Abdul. 'Do you not mean destroyed.'

'No replied' the Oracle. 'The Void Erases totally all light. There is no destruction, as creation itself is reversed into an absolute Void of emptiness, with no feelings spirit's or soul. All things will be Erased.'

'Can we enter the Evil Void to destroy it?' Blurted Peter.

'Yes' replied the Oracle curtly.

'But how?' Asked Sue. 'Please tell us what to do.'

'You already know the answer to your own questions that you ask of Times Powerful Oracle of Light and Vision' the squeaky voice replied. 'Look to your own abilities and powers that are already within yourselves.'

# The Void Returns - (The Great Eraser)

The TV screen faded and the Oracle returned from a bright light back to clear glass.

'I am sure that was all very helpful' said Peace Faith, removing the monocle and handing it back to Monty.

'Not really sure how though' replied Monty, replacing his eye-piece and twitching his nose. 'We will have to consider what the Oracle has told us.'

'Well, whatever!' Interrupted James. 'Fact is - It is up to us to stop this Evil Void and we have got to think how to go about it.'

'Can we ask the Oracle again, to give us a better answer I mean?' Asked Sue.

'No' replied Monty - Afraid not.' The Penguin Person looked toward the children. 'When you have your answer to what you ask, then it is up to you to make up your own minds.' He nodded. 'The Oracle cannot do that for you, or anyone else for that matter.'

'It is up to us then!' Exclaimed Peter. 'Should we not try to stop those ships from attacking the Void, as a first measure?'

'Yeah right' replied James. 'How are we kids going to do that?'

'Well, we could try and see the most important people we know about' said Sue. 'Explain to them what this Void is.'

'Like who?' Asked Abdul.

'Well, I guess the most important person in my country is the Australian Prime Minister - I think he would listen - At least we could try to see him.'

'Good idea sport!' Came a voice from behind one of the TV screens. 'Maybe I could help you there!'

Sue looked sideways as a peculiar Penguin Person waddled toward her.

'I'm Ozzy Dinkum' the creature said, raising it's strange hat upwards with one hand in welcome. 'G'day to you.'

Sue looked down at this rather strange creature whose jacket bore the emblem of the Australian flag. She then smiled as the Penguin Person replaced his hat, while the waddling Ozzy smiled back.

'Yes' said Monty, fiddling with his monocle. 'Ozzy does know the area well, he has been covering the notes on it for some Time.'

'Sure thing!' Replied Ozzy. 'We will have to use our Time wisely and use one of the doorway short cuts to get there today!' He continued, waddling up to Sue and then holding her hand. 'I do not think you human people can use the Master Blaster exit tubes.'

'Um - Don't Know? - What are those?' Asked Sue, looking around the room.

Ozzy waddled forward toward the large television screen situated at the end of The Great Hall of Vision, gently pulling Sue forward as he went.

Ozzy stopped in front of this screen, which to Sue now seemed huge, and he pressed the small clock button on the front of his hat, the lid of which then sprang open.

## The Void Returns - (The Great Eraser)

'The exit and entry points are behind here' explained Ozzy, producing a small, TV remote control from his hat. He pressed a button and the huge TV slid slowly down the shiny ice wall, stopped at the floor then twisted on it's side to form the shape of a doorway.

Each of the children were quite impressed by this strange action, but then as the TV screen doorway opened, each of them said together, with open mouthed shock.

'What is that?'

Ozzy moved forward, placing the TV remote control back into his hat, the lid of which then sprang downward and shut.

'That guys and Girls' he said moving through the doorway. 'Is the Grand Master Blaster.'

Sue nodded and then gave a polite.

'Hello.'

There had been many strange things to see in this Club, but so far this had been the strangest of all. Sue watched as a rather large Penguin Person, well in fact, a quite huge creature, in the overweight sense of the word, sat eating the remains of an enormous can of baked beans, on what appeared to be, but what Sue thought could not be, an equally small toilet.

'Hello!' The Grand Master Blaster put the can of baked beans down and wiped the dripping remains from beneath his large red nose. 'Anyone needs the tubes, i am all topped up and ready to fire!'

'Fire what?' Asked Sue, looking toward a set of thin, torpedo tube like devices that lined the ice walls of this huge room, each marked with a separate map symbol.

'The tubes are used by the Penguin People to enter the Ocean with their skateboards, to gather notes' explained Ozzy, moving into the room, that to Sue, whose own nose twitched, suddenly seemed to emit a strange odour. 'And The Grand Master Blaster produces the propulsion system energy in a quite natural form.'

'You mean -' Said Sue, not feeling that she really wanted the answer. 'From his bottom.'

'Yep' replied Ozzy, waddling past Grand Master Blaster and toward a set of doorways on the opposite side of the room that also contained separate map symbols painted onto them. 'Maybe that's why our noses twitch so much' he laughed.

Sue held her own nose momentarily, to stop it twitching.

'But we cannot use the tubes for you' said Ozzy. 'The water will be a bit too cold outside for human people.' The Penguin Person moved to a doorway that had the Australian map painted onto it. 'Just as well, eh?' It added.

'Yes, just as well' replied Sue, smiling at the huge Grand Master Blaster. 'No offence.'

## The Void Returns - (The Great Eraser)

'None taken!' The huge creature smiled back, reaching for another can of baked beans.

Ozzy pressed a button at the side of the doorway, that to Sue looked rather like a doorbell. But no sound came as this button was pushed, instead a hatch opened and a skateboard popped out, smiley face first.

'Hello again' said the smiley face to Sue. 'Want to ride again?'

Sue recognised the board as the one she had found and entered the Club with. 'Er - Yes please' said Sue. 'We have to try and see the Australian Prime Minister.'

'Sure thing!' Replied the smiley mouth as Ozzy removed the skateboard from it's hatch. 'G'day Ozzy.'

'Same on yer!' Replied Ozzy, putting the skateboard onto the floor and stepping onto it. 'Come on Sue, no Time to waste' he said, pulling Sue forward gently. 'You stand on the front and I will hold onto your legs.'

Sue stepped onto the skateboard and felt her feet stick to it's top instantly.

'We will try to stop the ships' she shouted back to James, Abdul and Peter.

'Best of luck!' Everyone in the other room all called out together, watching on as the doorway in front of Sue opened and both riders of the skateboard hurtled forward and disappeared into a brilliant shining light.

'Well I don't suppose we are just like the four musketeers in that book' quipped James. 'But having to fight the bad guy has to be a good thing.'

'Absolutely' agreed Abdul and Peter, both nodding in agreement.

'But what do we do next?' Continued Peter.

'The TV is functional again' interrupted Pat, watching the screen in front of him light up and start flickering. 'The Voids power must have just experienced a disturbance and weakened!'

'Let us see' called out the children and they, along with Monty, moved to Patriots seating point and watched with interest as the events in the Bermuda Triangle unfolded.

While the skateboard flew faster and faster, this thin tunnel of light was practically blinding. Ozzy handed Sue a pair of sunglasses to put on, they were of the same type that he himself was wearing.

'What is this thing we are travelling through?' Shouted Sue, holding on tightly to Ozzy with one hand, while putting the dark glasses on with her other hand as the cold wind continued to howl fiercely past her face.

'We are travelling through the Wind Of Change in the Light of New Events' replied Ozzy, hanging on tightly to Sue's legs. 'Nothing to be scared of - We do this all the Time!'

'Look, there is the exit now' noted Ozzy, pointing to a small doorway that was growing larger in front of them.

Meanwhile, far away, in a Parliament building Australia's Prime Minister was watching a television with baited breath.

## The Void Returns - (The Great Eraser)

The large Dark Void was practically filling a Satellite photograph on screen and it was very clear that it was now heading directly toward landfall.

'Do you think it will work?' Asked an aide hopefully.

'It has got to work!' Snapped the Prime Minister. 'If it doesn't, that thing will swallow the whole planet.

They all watched the TV screen, as did most of Earth's entire population, while the Aircraft carrier moved into position, directly in front of the massive, swirling, all consuming Evil.

The countdown ended, and with a roar and huge plumes of smoke two nuclear missiles were launched from the vessel, flying directly toward the centre of this swirling Dark Void.

'Yes!' Someone in the filled room cried out, watching both missiles strike the swirling darkness.

However, the room suddenly went very, very, silent. Both missiles were sucked harmlessly into the Void and were then spat straight back out, to harmlessly fall and drop onto the deck of the large ship. The most powerful weapons in humanities arsenal were sucked clean of any destructive power and lay there as large lumps of scrap metal.

Back in the Cartoon Buddy Club house, Patriot twitched his nose in agitation at the TV screen.

'Always knew those things were a heap of cr -'

'Children present!' Ordered Monty. 'None of that here please!'

'OK OK!' Replied Patriot sheepishly. 'Wonder how Sue and Ozzy are doing.'

'Indeed!' Agreed Monty. 'I wonder.'

Back at the Parliament building the Prime Minister retired to his office and sat down at his desk. He looked around the large room and contemplated the hopelessness of the situation. His eyes finally rested on a map of the Globe which hung from the wall, and he watched it curiously, as the map seemed to be emanating some sort of gradually increasing noise and vibration.

'Ah!' The whole room suddenly became filled with swirling light and wind. The Prime Minister fell backward and off his chair and onto the floor, as something had flown right past him and knocked him over. He started to pick himself up from the floor of his office, and then he heard someone exclaim.

'Whoopee! - Brake dancing!'

The Prime Ministers head finally reached the desk top, and his eyes met a most curios sight.

Ozzy was spinning around and around on the desk top, the place where he had landed from a wall map entrance and was enjoying his momentary 'brake dancing' spinning experience.

'What the -' The Prime Minister was lost for words.

'No Time to explain!' Sue interrupted the Prime Minister, before he could say any thing else. 'We know how to defeat the Void!'

## The Void Returns - (The Great Eraser)

Sue picked up her skateboard, and the Prime Minister sat back down on his chair, feeling quite stunned.

'But everyone has to work together!' Sue exclaimed, waving back dust that had clouded the room and made her throat almost too dry to talk.

With a swift movement, the Prime Minister quickly pushed a small red button on the telephone of his desk top.

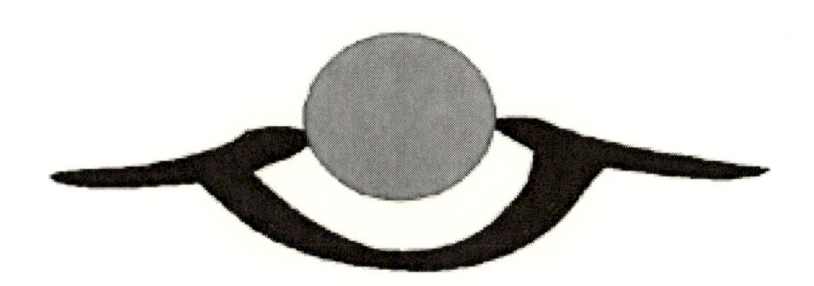

## *Into The Void - (Fear Overcome)*

While Ozzy span around happily on the office desk top with a bemused Prime Minister watching on, finger on his red button, and while Sue brushed a layer of fine dust from her blue jeans and long, blonde hair, very, very, far away, deep within the swirling Evil Void, a lone, furtive and rather sinister figure muttered to itself.

'Gobbys, Gobbys' it fumed. 'I do hate them!' The character moved forward quickly through a maze of dark and chilling corridors, holding it's hand painfully, just one of the places, where a Gobby paper rules page had bitten him.

Furtive Von Flatulence moved deeper into the Evil Void, ignoring the many dark doorways that lined this section of long corridors, but he noted while shuffling forward, the equally dark signs that lay above each doorway.

'**P**repare **A**ll **I**ntercontinental **N**egation' he said to himself, in his deep, furtive voice, reading a sign that was replicated above each doorway.

'Yes Master! - Create **P.A.I.N** - Cause conflict to erase mankind, and then all of creation' he muttered. Von Flatulence then listened for a moment, to many voices that were trapped behind a doorway and he smiled to himself, pulling up the collar of his long coat to shield himself from the chilly, ill wind that blew from under each doorway.

The sinister character then moved quickly forward into a small opening at the corridors end and entered a huge dark cavern that lay beyond it, his eyes transfixed toward the thinly red outlined face, of a swirling dark mist, the face of the Evil Void.

An enormous burp, suddenly erupted from this contorted face, the force of which blew Von Flatulence backward and made the sinister character hold onto his hat.

'I do so enjoy human hate wrapped in a tin can' quipped the Evil Voids face, digesting the remains of the Atomic explosion that had passed harmlessly into it. 'It does so increase my vitamin and growth levels!'

Von Flatulence shuffled forward toward the face and then was thrust backward again, by the power of a sudden, violent rant, from the contorted features of his master.

'And what have you got for me, menial?' The face grew eyes, that positively glowed with Evil. 'Feed me with notes - Now!'

'There has been an um, er, development' stammered Von Flatulence sheepishly and holding up his bitten hand, to show his master. 'The Gobby rules stopped me from obtaining notes again oh master, and they have injured me.

'So! - What of it!' Raged the Evil Void quite angrily, the eyes looking even more Evil than normal. 'You have failed me again!'

'But! – But! -' Mumbled Von Flatulence, emanating a little puff of something unpleasant from his bottom in fear. 'There are human children in the Cartoon Buddy Club!'

## Into The Void - (Fear Overcome)

'What!' Yet another burst of rage forced back Von Flatulence and he held onto his hat, again. The Evil Void contemplated for a few moments.

'So it seems that Time and Light has something in store for the Evil Void' it said slowly. 'This is a most unusual event.'

The Evil Void mellowed to Von Flatulence and it's eyes widened.

'Get back to the Cartoon Buddy Club and find out what is going on!' Snapped The Evil Void. 'This Time, do bring me some notes to feed on also if you do not find that too much of a trouble' it added sarcastically.

'Yes - Yes oh master!' Spluttered Von Flatulence.

The Evil Voids eyes formed to their most menacing and Evil form.

'You do know the consequences of failure, do you not' it sneered, and then glanced toward a long, schoolroom blackboard situated on the Cavern wall.

Von Flatulence also glanced toward the blackboard. He noted in it's centre, the shape of a person similar to himself, chalked in a painful pose.

'Yes oh master!' He gulped, looking at all that remained of his predecessor that had failed the Evil Void. 'I will return there right away!'

'Good' replied the Evil Void, watching Von Flatulence shuffle toward the cavern exit. 'Ah!' It shuddered in happiness. 'I feel another that another meal may now be on order from the humans.' It then sneered. 'Their anger is overflowing at the moment at the failure of their device.'

Von Flatulence turned and bowed at the cavern Exit, to disappear into the long corridors of Evil. As he did so, at the same moment, far away in Australia the doors to the Prime Ministers Office burst open and two uniformed security guards, in response to the push of a red button, entered the now quite dusty room.

The fierce wind and light that had billowed around the room stopped quite suddenly, as the two security guards entered quickly through the office doorway and the map entry portal situated on the office wall closed.

Both the guards moved swiftly toward the Prime Minister, reacting to the now strangely dusty, untidy room, by each withdrawing a pistol that dangled within their hip holsters.

The Prime Minister, still looking and feeling stunned, was quite bemused as the guards stood either side of him and pointed their pistols toward Sue. He bellowed in alarm.

'Not the Girl you dopey clots!' Then the Prime Minister pointed toward Ozzy, revolving on the desk top in front of him. 'That thing!'

Within the blink of an eye, both guards pointed their pistols immediately toward the desk top.

'Er - What thing sir?' They both asked, looking toward the empty desk top.

'That! - That!' The Prime Minister pointed straight toward Ozzy, who had stopped revolving and sat upright, twitching his nose in disgust.

## Into The Void - (Fear Overcome)

'Now come on sport!' drawled Ozzy, quite annoyed. 'Sue has only come to help you.'

The Prime Minister looked at the guards, who could not see or hear Ozzy speak.

'You cant see that!' he exclaimed.

'Um – No -' The security guards looked bemused, and wondered what was going on as the desk top was empty.

The Prime Minister looked at Sue, who clutched her skateboard and just smiled back at him.

'No – Well -' He spluttered. 'That will be all guys!'

The security guards both looked at the Prime Minister.

'Are you all right sir?' One of them enquired.

Looking toward Ozzy, who twitched his nose again, the Prime Minister gave a polite but curt.

'Of course boys! - On your way!' And he motioned for the guards to leave his office.

Both men replaced their pistols and left swiftly, closing the door behind them.

'Well -' Huffed the Prime Minister sitting back in his chair. 'I don't know what is going on here?' He nodded his head, looking directly at Ozzy. 'But it has been one heck of a strange day, and I hope you can give an explanation lady.' The Prime Minister looked toward Sue. 'What do you mean about defeating the Void. Whatever that is?'

Sue moved toward the desk, checking that Ozzy was unharmed.

'That is not a weather phenomenon sir!' She said firmly, while tickling Ozzy under the chin and receiving a large smile back from beneath his large red nose. 'That is the Evil Dark Void. A thing that wants to destroy everything!'

'Yes - I suppose' agreed the Prime Minister. 'That this thing out there may destroy the planet is something that practically all the worlds governments agree upon. Which is why we are attacking it with everything we have.'

'But attacking it will only make it grow!' Exclaimed Sue, and Ozzy nodded in agreement. 'You have to work together and fight it, but not by attacking it through anger and hate.'

The Prime Minister though for a moment, slightly confused.

'So how do you destroy it, if not through the use of weapons young lady?' He asked, rubbing a thin bead of sweat from his dusty forehead.

'From within it' replied Sue quickly.

'And how do you suppose we do that?' Laughed the Prime Minister. 'We have lost a lot of ships and planes that have got too near to that thing already!'

'You don't!' Replied Sue. 'My friends and I will get inside it.'

'You mean that -' sneered the Prime Minister, pointing toward Ozzy.

'Yes – That! - And others' replied Ozzy, quite offended at being called 'That'.

## Into The Void - (Fear Overcome)

'You may find entering and defeating this, well, Evil Dark Void, a dangerous and perhaps impossible task young lady' said The Prime Minister thoughtfully. 'What makes you think that that you can do it, and that the fate of this Planet should be placed in your, if you don't mind me saying, children's hands, without the use of weapons?'

'Well,' said Sue respectfully. 'Two of us have entered your own office and are speaking to you right now!' She tapped the skateboard, whose own smiley mouth moved, much to the surprise of the Prime Minister, in agreement, it added.

'Yes sir - Kids can do anything sport!'

'If you attack this thing' reiterated Sue. 'It will only grow more quickly.'

The Prime Minister looked at Ozzy, who smiled at him. He looked at the skateboard, whose smiley mouth smiled at him. He then looked at Sue, who also smiled at him.

'I must be going nuts' he whispered, standing up and then going to the office doorway.

The Prime Minister opened the door and called to those who were still sat in front of the television screen.

'What is that things status?' He asked.

'It is growing quickly sir, and almost over landfall' came the concerned reply. 'The fleet and air arms are almost prepared to hit it again in a massive, single attack.' There was a seconds silence. 'We have just lost live transmission again now sir.'

'Right - OK' replied the Prime Minister shutting the office door. He moved back to his desk and sat down, pondering the whole situation. 'Right!' He then said suddenly, watching Ozzy twitch his nose on the desk top. 'I will try to give you as much Time as I can and hold back the attack.' He picked up his telephone. 'But I cannot promise anything as everyone has to agree.'

'Good on yeah sport!' Replied Ozzy holding out his long arm.

'Yes thank you sir!' Added Sue, watching the Prime Minister shake Ozzy's hand.

'This is one heck of a day' said the Prime Minister, looking again at Ozzy. 'May I ask what you are?'

'A friend Buddy' replied Ozzy. 'Just a friend!' He shuffled from the desk top and motioned for Sue to place the skateboard onto the floor. 'See you around sometime sport!'

Sue stepped onto the skateboard and waved her hand in goodbye, just at the same Time as Ozzy grabbed hold of her legs. The office wall map portal suddenly opened up again, and a strong blast of wind and light again entered the office blowing papers and dust high into the air. Both skateboard and riders flew quickly upward and disappeared into the illuminated opening, which suddenly shut as quickly as it had appeared.

## Into The Void - (Fear Overcome)

With papers and dust settling downward and the office returning to normal, the Prime Minister looked at his hand that had been automatically raised in goodbye. He composed himself, then moved his hand toward the telephone phone on his desk top. Pressing a button, his voice did not sound quite as mixed as his thoughts.

'Get me the joint Nations Operations room!' He barked. 'Right now!'

Heading back toward the Cartoon Buddy Club, Sue and Ozzy whizzed through a brilliant light and cold wind that continued to howl fiercely past their faces within the travel portal as they surfed the skateboard. Replacing the sunglasses had made their eyes more relaxed to the light, but had also made the many strange streaks of darkness that now travelled the portal walls more evident.

'There is an ill wind -' Ozzy pointed toward the dark streaks, still holding on to Sue's legs with his other arm. It is trying to flow through the wind of change and is somehow entering into the light of new events. 'That is not very good!' He added, shaking his small head.

Within seconds the shape of a portal exit and small doorway back to the Club came into view.

'A stitch in Time! - Saves nine!' Whispered the skateboards smiley mouth and with it's password spoken, both skateboard and riders then flew through the portals exit as the doorway evaporated.

Beyond this exit and entrance lay a furtive and sinister figure that had entered the Club while surfing the Evil streaks of an ill wind, that lurked, almost hidden, mixed amidst the wind of light and change.

Von Flatulence clutched in his Evil hand a handful of notes that he had just acquired, which had been left on a table in Chill Out Hall while the Penguin Person collector and reader of the notes, had been called in a great hurry to the Great Hall Of Vision. Very happy with himself, the Evil and sinister character had decided to return these notes to his master at once, to then return again and spy on both the children and Penguin People.

Unfortunately of course, a collision and mix between the two winds of good and bad change that vastly different minded characters always rode, was as inevitable as the collision that now took place beyond the brilliantly lit portal exit. Sue, Ozzy and the smiley mouthed skateboard hurtled through the portal exit and back into a Club doorway entrance.

'Ouch!' Von Flatulence was quickly floored by the incoming force of the skateboard riders, who sailed straight past him as he toppled to the icy ground, still clutching his ill gotten notes. 'Curses!' He cried out, loosing a sheet of paper that flew into the air.

'Sorry!' Called out Sue, as the smiley mouthed skateboard ground to a halt.

'Hey!' Demanded Ozzy. 'Who are you?' The Penguin Person looked down at Von Flatulence who had quickly struggled to his feet, and was horrified.

## Into The Void - (Fear Overcome)

'There is a stranger in the Club!' Cried Ozzy. 'He has stolen some notes!'

The huge form of the Grand Master Blaster that had had his back turned to these events, heard what Ozzy had cried out and turned to see what was going on.

'That is disgusting!' He belched. 'There is a thief who has stolen notes that are to be put in the eternal safe!'

James, Abdul and Peter appeared from the large TV doorway exiting the Great Hall Of vision.

'Hey!' Called out James. 'What are you doing there!'

Von Flatulence, still clutching the notes, pulled from his dark coat a long skateboard of his own. He threw the skateboard to the floor and the long, night black skateboard hit the ice with a thud.

'Take it easy' a skull and crossbones face painted on the front of Von Flatulence's skateboard contorted with discomfort. 'Don't be so rough' it added.

'Silence!' Snapped Von Flatulence. He stepped onto his skateboard and then turned his head toward both the children and Penguin People who had now also entered the tube room.

'You will never defeat my master the Evil Dark Void!' He snapped again, in his best, Evil henchman tone. 'It will erase you all' and he laughed an Evil laugh. 'I must now feed my master with the notes that you have made of bad deeds and happenings!' Von Flatulence let rip a bottom burp that made even the Grand Master Blasters nose twitch in disgust.

'Stop you bounder!' Demanded Monty who shuffled forward. 'Stealing and Evil is simply not cricket old thing!'

Von Flatulence laughed again and he quickly pulled forward one of the many smiley mouthed door knockers that stood proud on the set of icy portal doorways. He lifted the door knocker until it was upright and was now giving a frown. The doorway portal opened and an ill wind reached into the Club whipping beneath the skateboard of Von Flatulence.

'You are all doomed!' Sneered the Evil character who hurtled through the doorway, and sailed far out into the ill wind.

'We can't let him get away! - After him somebody!' Ordered Pat.

Monty moved forward and stretched toward the doorway. He pressed the large red nose on the now frowning door knocker, which sprang open to reveal a small clock beneath it's bulbous surface. Monty turned the delicate hands of this small clock backwards and stood back in satisfaction.

'That should disrupt their Evil game' he muttered, moving backwards and turning toward the children. 'The travel portal has now become a Time portal.'

'Good Call Monty!' Congratulated Pat. 'We can chase the guy now and he will find it a lot harder to get back to the Evil Void.'

Groovy Love Thangs voice interrupted the conversation and flowed from the speaker system in the Great Hall of Vision.

## Into The Void - (Fear Overcome)

'Radio reports have just come in, they say that the humans have suspended their attack on the Void for the Time being.'

'Well done Sue and Ozzy!' Called out Abdul.

'That at least gives us some Time to fight this thing' chipped in James.

'Time to follow that Evil Character!' Peter motioned toward the open portal with his finger. 'I warrant that he may lead us to effect some way into the Evil Void.'

'We shall escort you' said Monty, and he stepped forward to press a small doorbell that had a map of the British Isles above it's doorway. No sound came from the bell, but as with Sue's experience, instead a hatch opened and a skateboard popped out, smiley face first.

'Come on!' Monty ordered, placing the skateboard onto the floor. 'Let us go!'

Pat pressed a doorbell that had a map of the United States above it's doorway, and as had happened with Monty and Sue, a smiley mouthed skateboard popped out of a hatch.

Abdul moved forward to press his own doorbell, but a small hand suddenly reached from the ground in front him and beat him to it.

'Allow me to assist' came a gentle, mysterious voice. The skateboard popped out of the hatch and the Penguin Person placed it on the floor in front of Abdul. 'If you please' the small, well spoken character motioned for Abdul to step onto the smiley mouthed skateboard. 'My name is Sandy' the character continued, as Abdul found his own balance on the skateboard. 'Allow me to escort you.'

'Fine – Er - Fine' replied Abdul looking down at the strange Penguin Person creature. 'Pleased to meet you.'

'Likewise, nice human child' the Penguin Person bowed and then stepped onto the skateboard holding onto Abdul's legs.

'OK everyone!' Monty pointed to the open doorway and the ill wind that flowed within the portal. 'Tally ho!' He called out. 'Stick together People! - Lets go!'

One by one, the smiley mouthed skateboards and their riders hurtled forward, to disappear into the Club exit and ill wind that howled from the portal doorway.

Beyond this entrance, the skateboard riders found the extremely brightly lit, twisting tunnel, now flickered with streaks of dark ill wind. It still roared very loudly, with the powerful wind of change that howled fiercely through it. But now, the wind was not quite as gentle to the touch, rather like a calming cool breeze, as it had been before. It now felt quite chilly, and more than a little spooky.

'There is a junction up ahead!' Warned James, watching the tunnel split into four separate directions ahead.

'Yes sir re!' Pat could now see the four separate tunnels, looking through the legs of James he pondered the options. 'Left tunnels or right?' He asked, looking toward the other riders who flew side by side while surfing the long tube.

## Into The Void - (Fear Overcome)

'Should we split up?' Asked Sue.

'No!' Ordered Abdul. 'But whatever we should decide - We stick together!'

'Yes that would seem most agreeable' nodded Peter, looking toward Abdul, who smiled as Sue and James also nodded in agreement.

'Excellent - Excellent!' Monty muttered to himself, as all the children started to work together.

Within a split second, a huge, unexpected ripple coursed through the tunnel and wind of change. This sent the four skateboards and riders slamming into the circular wall and spinning almost out of control around it.

Sue had now become just ahead of the others who had spun into single file. The skateboard beneath her feet shuddered and the smiley mouth sprang into life, it's red nose twitched.

'Which way would you like to go?' It asked, sniffing the air with it's nose. 'I cannot find any sense of direction with this ill wind, it's affecting my sinuses.'

Sue looked toward the four tunnels and then noticed something. 'That is strange' she thought to herself.

Sue had noticed a fifth tunnel that lay directly ahead, but a tunnel that was smaller than all the others, which looked quite dark inside it. With the glare from the portal reduced by her sunglasses Sue noticed a strip of yellow warning tape across this particular entrance.

'Closed mind - Do not enter here' Sue read aloud the words written in bold lettering on the tape and she shouted back to the others.

'Do you all think that an open mind is better than a closed one?'

'Yes!' Everyone agreed and shouted back automatically, each having no Time to ponder why Sue had asked the question while struggling to stay upright on the skateboards.

Sue then made her split second decision. She pushed gently downward with her foot and the smiley mouthed skateboard veered into the smaller dark hole, splitting the yellow tape, that very suddenly shattered into many small fragments of brightly lit crystal, which bounced around the dark tunnel walls.

'Hey!' Called out James, quickly following Sue into the once darkened tunnel. 'These crystals are like light bulbs!'

The whole darkened tunnel filled with light and Abdul reached for a crystal. 'That is because they are light bulbs!' He shouted back, looking at the crystal light bulb that he now held in his hand.

'Where is the power source of that device?' Asked Peter, who had never actually seen a light bulb before, but was inquisitive.

'The power of the thought bulbs are in your own mind!' Replied Monty holding tightly onto Peters legs. 'Humans can make them real, if only you are willing to try hard enough.'

'Watch out!' Warned Sue as a doorway appeared up ahead. This doorway stood very solid and forbidding, as her skateboard approached.

## Into The Void - (Fear Overcome)

'Say the exit passwords!' She shouted to the smiley mouthed skateboard at her feet.

'I cant!' Replied the smiley mouth. 'This is a Time portal.' The skateboard front tilted upwards ready for impact. 'Only the rider can give the passwords to a Time portal exit, and that is different words for everyone!'

Sue watched the doorway hurtle closer and closer, fearing a collision.

'What do I say?' She turned and asked Ozzy.

'I don't know' replied the Penguin Person, 'It is different for everyone - Just say what you feel or think - Don't be afraid.'

Sue looked to her front and replied.

'OK sport!' While trying hard to think of some sort of password type words.

But to her surprise, as she uttered those words and half shut her eyes, when the doorway was seconds from impact, the doorway exit evaporated and her skateboard followed by the three others, shot forward through it.

'Well done Sue!' Congratulated Ozzy. 'Looks like friendly spoken words are your own human passwords to the Time portal exit.'

'There he is!' Observed James while following Sue, who by then had opened her eyes fully and looked downward toward a mass of green land and volcanoes simmering in the distance. James pointed toward Von Flatulence who was riding his skateboard up ahead and moving toward a dark area in this veritable sea of green.

'After him!' Demanded Abdul, following James and feeling Sandy grab hold even tighter on his legs, while the smiley mouthed skateboard lunged forward. Exiting this Time portal with Peter, Monty also looked downward toward the massive expanse of lush, green forest and then looked upward, his eyes drawn toward a huge fireball that was heading Earthward from Space into the thinly clouded sky.

'I remember this in some old notes!' He muttered to himself, thinking of long past events, even before he, or any of the other Penguin People had worn his brightly coloured flag jacket.

Then Monty shouted in concern.

'Quickly! - We do not have much Time!'

Peter looked skyward to the huge fireball that grew even larger by the second.

'What is that?' He asked, feeling the smiley mouthed skateboard at his feet tilt downward and accelerate even faster, to then head directly toward a distant Von Flatulence.

Monty held more tightly to Peters legs.

'It is a huge meteorite!' Exclaimed the Penguin Person loudly. 'It has been sent to seal the entrance and exit to the past Evil Void and create future Time. It will create evolution of a new dominant species, that will have the free choice between Good and Evil, to hold the Great Balance of Time and manufacture the Keys of Peace.'

## Into The Void - (Fear Overcome)

Monty held on to his hat, while strong winds whipped past him and continued.
 'But most important of all, the meteorite will stop the very first escape attempt of the Dark Void from it's banishment.'
 James looked across at Monty. 'Are you saying -' He shouted, trying to get his voice heard above the wind. 'That this is the same meteorite that caused the extinction of the Dinosaurs and led to the evolution of Mankind.'
 'Bang on!' Replied Monty. 'Absolutely correct.'
 'We will never catch him in Time!' Sue shouted, interrupting, while she watched Von Flatulence almost reach the Dark Area that now seemed to be gradually expanding, erasing the lush green of the forest ahead.
 'Lets try a smile!' Ozzy called out.
 Abdul looked across at the Peculiar Penguin Person who was holding tightly on to Sue's legs.
 'What -' He said, a little confused. 'You cannot stop him with a smile.'
 Ozzy gave a half smile back toward Abdul. Then Ozzy did something that the boy did not really expect anyone, or anything, for that matter to do. Ozzy let go of Sue's leg with one arm and raised a hand to his mouth. He ripped the half smile from under his bulbous red nose, which twitched a little as he did so and threw the half smile toward Von Flatulence.
 'Wow!' Exclaimed Abdul, watching the half smile whiz forward like a boomerang, to follow, then hit Von Flatulence on the back of his Evil head.
 Just seconds before he could reach the Dark Void, a slightly dazed Von Flatulence crashed his skateboard into a tall tree, while the boomerang, made of a smiley mouth, dropped to the forest floor.
 'Good shot!' Noted James. 'But how did you do that?'
 Pat gripped firmly the legs of James, then shouted in the wind.
 'Because Penguin People are drawn in Time!'
 Pat and James then watched Ozzy press the small yellow clock on the front of his own hat, the top spring quickly open and Ozzy remove a pencil from inside his hold all things receptacle (initial:- Hat).
 Ozzy then used the pencil to quickly draw a smile back onto his face and then replaced the pencil back into his hat, the lid of which then sprang shut.
 'You mean -' asked Abdul, watching this with an open mouthed surprise. 'That you are like, um, cartoon things.'
 'Of a sort!' replied Sandy, standing behind the boy and gripping his legs.
 'But throughout Time, we are drawn, to prepare our notes for use in the future.' Sandy then looked forward, from behind Abdul's legs. 'It might said to be wise young sir, if you do not wish to catch flies, to place your lips back together.'
 'Yes my little friend!' Abdul laughed, and quipped. 'But it is not everyday one experiences living cartoons!'
 'Look!' Warned Sue again, cutting short the conversation for more important matters. 'He is getting back onto his skateboard!'

## Into The Void - (Fear Overcome)

Von Flatulence was indeed stepping back on to his skateboard, rubbing his sore head, while the skull and crossbones painted onto the Dark surface, moaned after hitting the tree.

'Maybe you had better let me navigate?' It said, with a sore front section.

Von Flatulence turned to see the children heading straight toward him.

'Silence!' He ordered in rather a nasty tone. The Evil character shook his fist toward the children, the ill gotten history notes fluttering in his hand. 'You are too late!' He sneered, manoeuvring the skateboard up from the ground and turning it toward the very close Void. 'You cannot stop me now!'

James, Abdul, Peter and Sue, along with all their Penguin people passengers, in their heads actually agreed with the Evil character, as they were still, just too far away.

But with their eyes, they all watched while a large, dark shadow formed above Von Flatulence and then circled the ground around him as it headed Earthward.

'What -' Von Flatulence looked up and just managed to make out the form of a huge Tyrannosaurus Rex Dinosaur foot, that very suddenly stamped above him, downward toward the ground. 'Ah! - Ooph!' He yelled, as the foot pressed the skateboard and himself, into the soft Earth, to leave just his arm, hand, and also the notes that they held visible.

Sue seized the moment.

'Quickly, between the legs!' She shouted, avoiding an immanent collision. All four skateboards and riders followed her downward, to then veer up and through the legs of the enormous creature, who snapped angrily at the children, with it's razor sharp teeth.

'Yuck!' Shouted James, while watching Sue grab the notes from the hand of Von Flatulence as she hurtled forward. 'That thing has bad breath!'

'Heck!' Sue gave out a yell, as the huge Tyrannosaurus Rex clipped the back of her skateboard with a single flick of it's huge head. The flying device veered around the head, but then seemed to stall momentarily in the sky.

'Are you damaged?' Yelled Sue in concern.

'No Sport!' Replied the skateboard, suddenly hurtling forward, heading back toward the club entrance. 'I just lost an egg!'

'What -' Sue looked down to see a very small, but long box land by parachute next to the smiley mouth boomerang. 'That's a funny shaped egg.'

'Give it a few centuries or more' the smiley mouth on the skateboard grinned. 'And the skateboard inside that box will be all grown up.'

Sue momentarily contemplated, thinking back to how the box in which the skateboard she now rode was found.

'Next to a boomerang?' She whispered quietly to herself. But there really was no Time for thoughts now.

## Into The Void - (Fear Overcome)

Looking downward and now backward toward the others who followed her toward the club entrance, leaving the Tyrannosaurus Rex to snap angrily, but impotently back at them, Sue then saw the Tyrannosaurus Rex, lift it's foot to follow them and Von Flatulence, hat crumpled, fly out unharmed from beneath the creatures foot and disappear into the spreading Dark Void.

'Faster!' Monty demanded, watching the huge fireball almost strike a pool of sea water at the forests edge. 'We have only seconds!'

Just as all four children reached the club entrance and portal situated in a rocky cliff face, a huge explosion ripped the Earth's surface as the meteorite struck. The force of this blast sent a huge tidal wave and massive pall of dust spreading quickly across the entire planet, to engulf the spreading Evil Dark Void, which suddenly thinned and dissipated.

'Rather like a blob of paint' Peter noted, as the Ocean washed into it.

'Look out!' Warned James, feeling the full force of this huge meteorite blast and flash of strong light strike his skateboard, sending it spiralling out of control. But, within a split second, all the other skateboards and riders were also carried away by the events of Time, in an uncontrolled spin. With an enormous roar, the blast from this single huge meteorite sent all four children and their skateboards tumbling through the Time portal. Following them closely through the small portal doorway a beam of almost blinding light and howling wind trailed behind the children, to suddenly diminish, as this force met the now dark streak free, wind of change, in the light of new events.

James quickly reached out both hands and grabbed Abdul by the arm, who in turn reached out to grab Sue with one of his arms. The momentum of their spinning, immediately, started to thankfully, reduce.

When Peter and his own smiley mouthed skateboard, suddenly crashed into this now linked chain of children, they all quickly grabbed him and clinging together, the spinning finally stopped and each skateboard surfed more steady on an even keel.

'Not a bad ride folks' James joked, grinning.

'If my head was not still spinning so much' replied Sue. 'I would probably be sick.'

'Indeed' chipped in Abdul. 'But what a rush!'

Peter looked down at the Penguin people still clinging to the children's legs. 'Are you chaps still all right?' He enquired.

The strange creatures all straightened their caps and Monty spat out a small leaf that had entered his mouth.

'Tickety Boo old thing!' Monty quipped, his moustache twitching, quite as much as his large red nose was. He looked forward, past the legs of Peter and along the windy tunnel. 'I say old fruit!' He exclaimed, watching what appeared to be a solid brick wall approach rapidly as the skateboard riders all neared the tunnels end. 'Looks like our numbers up!'

## Into The Void - (Fear Overcome)

James, Abdul, Peter and Sue, with arms still linked, looked forward toward the tunnels end, while their skateboards formed a straight line. There was a single, large number four painted in blue onto this solid brick wall and this single number, increased in size rapidly, while all the children hurtled toward it.

'We are going to strike it!' Called out Sue, thinking the wall seemed rather too solid to her.

'Pull up!' Ordered Abdul looking down to the smiley mouthed skateboards.

'Yes! - Stop! - Or slow down!' Demanded Peter.

The smiley mouthed skateboards however, just all uttered the same words at the same moment, while increasing their speed.

'Passwords for exit please!'

With just split seconds to spare, James uttered the words that seemed to flow instinctively into his head, a product of natural children's curiosity.

'What is that - for?' he asked looking toward the now large number four. The brick wall evaporated in an instant and all smiley mouthed skateboards and their riders, in line, hurtled through the portal exit.

'Good Call Buddy!' Called Pat in satisfaction, clinging hard to the legs of James.

'Good show old thing!' Agreed Monty, nose twitching, while all four children exited the portal.

'Ah!' Exclaimed Sandy in satisfaction, looking around from behind the legs of Abdul. 'A most interesting and historical Time.'

The small Penguin Person watched the huge form of a newly built Pyramid loom into view directly in front of the skateboards, it was an almost mirror image of the older Pyramid that the children had just exited, where the Time portal lay.

'Where are we?' Asked Sue, looking around, while the skateboards flew over the top of this huge smooth sided Pyramid. 'Egypt – Right?' She added.

'Ancient Egypt to be precise!' Replied Sandy, with a smile forming under his large red nose and between his beard. 'Are not these building structures most impressive.'

'Sure are!' Replied James, looking downward at a mass of construction workers building another Pyramid Tomb. 'Never thought I would see them as brand new though.'

'Most of the Planets humans elsewhere still live in crude huts at this Time' said Pat, pointing toward an elegant and bustling town edging the vast desert. 'Goes to show how different things can be!' He added, looking toward shipping on the river Nile.

'The Void is here!' Warned the smiley mouthed skateboard at Abdul's feet and it sniffed the air. 'Do you wish to follow?'

Abdul looked to the others, who all nodded.

'Yes!' Said Abdul, also nodding. 'Let us remove this Evil once and for all.'

'Let it be so!' Agreed Sandy, patting Abdul's leg.

## Into The Void - (Fear Overcome)

'Onward!' Ordered Peter, who looked toward Sue and James.
'Yes!' They both nodded. 'Onward it is!'
With a last sniff, the skateboards accelerated high above the banks of the river Nile and followed the long flowing river to head in the direction of the Evil Dark Void.
'It is amazing when you think about it' mused Sandy, looking down at the large, sprawling and elegant Ancient Egyptian cities that edged and were sustained by this flowing, majestic river. 'That mankind, even with their most primitive beliefs can create such wondrous architecture and order of life.' The small Penguin Person then sighed. 'It is just a pity that they cannot all live together in Peace and pass their Great Test of Time.'
The four skateboards all suddenly veered away from the river far below them and headed toward the vast expanse of desert laying like a huge carpet, as far as an eye could see, beyond the Nile banks.
Looking ahead, Sue could now see a vast swirling Dark mass, it was the Evil Void.
'There it is!' She exclaimed, pointing with her hand.
'Look at the size of that thing!' James was amazed by how large this Dark Void now seemed to be, almost swallowing a flat, golden desert in the far distance.
'Yes indeed' said Sandy in a concerned voice. 'It is forming over the Kharga Oasis, and would appear to have gained an enormous degree of anger and hatred power to now be so large!'
While the four skateboards drew nearer and nearer, Peter looked earthward.
'There is a large army on the move down there!' he exclaimed, watching dust fly into the air from many small figures far below walking the sand.
'They are attacking the Void' noted Abdul. 'Look!' Abdul pointed toward thousands of little dots of soldiers far ahead, that moved at the Dark Voids edge. He shook his head as dot after dot disappeared into the swirling darkness. 'How can we fight that thing?' He sighed.
'Courage old thing!' Said Monty, turning to smile at Abdul. 'Never let the bad guy grind you down!' The Penguin Person twitched his large red nose, his moustache doing likewise, while his monocle twinkled and shone in the sunshine. 'Sure you young bod's will think of something!' He added, smiling under his large red nose. 'Chin up!'
'Well, we are here!' Called out James after a few moments, his skateboard slowing down before the swirling, angry, Evil Void. 'What do we do now?'
The other three skateboards suddenly stopped in the sky next to a now stationary James and the four children examined their options.
'We could just fly into it' said Sue. 'But it might just capture us, like everything else it touches.'
'What if we should attempt to go under it?' Thought Peter and said so aloud.

## Into The Void - (Fear Overcome)

'But we would have to dig a tunnel under it, and to do so in the sand would be most difficult.'

'What do you suppose that is?' Asked James, pointing to a small red object, swirling within dead centre of the Evil Dark Voids exterior shell. Looking much harder at this object, he observed - 'It appears to be the shape of an animal.'

James felt himself becoming a little confused by the presence of this thin, red, swirling picture.

'That looks like the shape' said Peter curiously. 'Of an amphibious fish eating mammal, a member of the family Phocidae.'

'You just mean a seal' huffed Sue, looking toward the swirling red shape.

'Absolutely!' Agreed Peter.

'That is it!' Exclaimed Abdul suddenly, looking toward the shape. 'That is the safe entrance, that has been sealed.' And as he uttered these words, a howling, ill wind swept from behind the picture and battered the skateboards.

'What the -' All the other children looked toward Abdul.

Abdul stood thoughtfully on the skate board while Sandy held tightly onto his leg.

'It seems to me that we have to break the seal to enter' He said, pointing toward the very centre of the vast, swirling circle of darkness.

James nodded in agreement. 'But how can we do that?'

James pulled Patriot back up by the scruff of his neck, the small Penguin Person loosing a foot hold on the bobbing skateboard.

'Well think rather quickly!' Exclaimed Peter, watching the sprawling darkness gather in momentum.

'Can't you think of anything?' He asked, tapping Monty on the head.

'Yes!' Shouted Sue. 'You must know how to get into this thing!' She held on tighter to Ozzy, while her skateboard flipped sideways in the strong howling wind.

'Rule Five Billion Six Hundred Thousand and thirty two!' Replied Monty. 'Penguin People may not enter the circle of darkness unless retrieving a lost personal possession.'

'That means that you can gain entry!' Called out James so that his voice could be heard above the wind.

'But we have never lost any thing!' Shouted Monty right back. 'Certainly not in the Dark Void anyway! - None of us has ever entered that!'

Abdul remembered the scrolls.

'The flaming red Sun ball of History and Wisdom!' He shouted at the top of his voice.

'What -' Everyone replied in unison.

'You are cartoons right!' Abdul asked the Penguin People. 'And cartoons do not get hurt!'

## Into The Void - (Fear Overcome)

'Correct!' Sandy looked up. 'But what has that got to do with breaking the seal of the Dark Void?' He asked, holding on tightly to the boys leg.

'This!' Shouted Abdul, and reached forward to pull with quite some force the large red nose from the Monty Penguin Person.

'Ouch!' Cried out Monty, in a snuffled voice. 'I say old thing that is simply not cricket!'

'No! - Sorry!' Apologised Abdul. 'But this is football.' And he put Sandy on top of his shoulders, taking steady aim with the red nose.

Abdul kicked the red 'ball' as hard and as straight as he possibly could. The nose headed directly toward the very centre of the swirling Dark Void.

Far below the children on a sea of golden sand, Mighty Pharaoh of Egypt had watched his army angrily attack what he himself had called The Great Spirit of Anger and Hate. Pharaoh, worshipped as a living God by his people, looked on in despair as his huge fighting force became totally ineffective against the swirling, Evil darkness that had spread over his land and he looked to the sky in utter despair.

'Flying chariots -' He suddenly exclaimed. Through a fierce heat haze lifting skyward, he watched the four skateboards and their occupants move toward the Void. Mighty Pharaoh observed the red nose football, hurtle forward against an ill wind, that tried with all it's might to force it back. The red nose football glowed and flamed, as the meteorite had done entering Earth's atmosphere, to fly straight and true through this ill wind, to strike the seal picture with a direct hit.

'Good shot, young human sir!' Called out Sandy, seeing the seal break into many pieces.

'A cracking shot!' Agreed Peter.

Within a split second, a beam of brilliant light formed where the picture had been and it illuminated a circular area of the sprawling darkness. Mighty Pharaoh followed the track of these 'flying chariots' while they moved forward against a mighty roar of wind which came from this opening. He looked on open mouthed, as each skateboard entered this beam of light and disappeared into the Evil Void.

A small fly flew straight into his mouth while it lay open, but did not care for his bad breath that much and flew straight back out again.

'Bah!' Spluttered Mighty Pharaoh and this brought him 'back down to Earth' to focus on his army. 'Withdraw!' He ordered his troops. 'Fall back - Follow me!' Mighty Pharaoh then retired a safe distance while his remaining troops followed him.

High above the sands, each skateboard moved forward into the beam of light and entered the Evil Dark Void. With a last rush, the ill wind disappeared, almost as quickly as the beam of light, while darkness again fell over the entire swirling mass.

## Into The Void - (Fear Overcome)

'It seems the entrance has closed chaps' noted Monty, pressing the yellow clock button on his hat front. The top sprang open and he removed a red coloured pencil from it's interior, using it to quickly draw another nose onto his face.

'Yep!' Replied James, looking back. 'But that means the exit is closed too!'

'You are not scared are you -' Sue glared toward James, but was actually feeling a little uneasy herself.

'No!' Snapped James. 'Of course not!'

'Me neither!' Said Abdul looking around the darkened interior for the red nose football.

'Well - Not all that much!' Agreed Peter.

'As I once heard' chipped in Patriot. 'Courage is not the absence of your fear, but the conquering of it. Or well, it goes something like that.'

'Indeed' agreed Monty, new red nose twitching above his moustache. 'It seems that you children are doing that magnificently.' He looked around as his small eyes grew accustomed to the dark interior. 'It seems we are now in the bowels of the Evil Dark Void' he said, looking at a small sign that lay straight ahead.

'Bowel and digestion area' James read aloud, shaking his head while also looking at this sign. 'Crazy -'

'Yes!' Ozzy looked around at the huge dark cavern, that grew more clear as everyone's eyes adjusted. 'But it makes sense - The Evil Void gains power from within human people, so would have some human characteristics inside it, until of course, it eventually erases everything!'

'So like it would have a brain area' said Sue thoughtfully.

'One doubts' said Sandy. 'There is probably a soul area though, a reflection of it's Evil. As there of course, no brains within Evil itself.'

'Well whatever!' Quipped James. 'Lets take a look around and see if our parents are in this thing and maybe we can do something about getting rid of this Evil Void! - OK?'

'OK!' Everyone agreed.

High above the bowels of the Evil Dark Void, Von Flatulence had moved into the dark chamber, to again confront the wrath of his master.

'Oh dear -' he muttered to himself . 'No notes or information to give. It will be most upset!' He stopped at the thin red face, which seemed to be a little preoccupied. 'Oh master!' Said Von Flatulence.

'Silence!' Snapped the thin red face angrily. 'I have an upset stomach!' It's face contorted in pain. 'Something good has entered my digestive system!' The face grew Evil eyes and glared at a cowering Von Flatulence. 'Take my most Evil Anti Bodies and remove any good Bodies that you may find there! - I really cannot stand to digest anything good, I like only to taste horrible hate and anger.'

## Into The Void - (Fear Overcome)

'Yes Oh master!' Grovelled Von Flatulence, bowing deeply. He then pushed a finger up into his nose and flicked the rather horrible mess, that he had obtained there onto the floor.

Within a dark flash, six dark shadows formed from the floor and stood to attention waiting for instructions.

'The bogey-men are ready oh Evil master!' Creeped Von Flatulence. 'I shall take them to the digestive area at once, to remove any good that should be found there!' He again bowed, as he backed away from his master and headed toward where the four children and Penguin People lay.

James rolled his skateboard slowly forward, heading directly toward an opening he had noticed in the wall of this huge dark cavern. All the others followed him, rolling their own smiley mouthed skateboards slowly forward.

'Vitamin Power Library Room -' James read aloud a small sign hanging above this opening and peered into the equally gloomy and dark cavern room, that lay beyond it. 'Let's take a look inside!'

Pat looked forward from behind the legs of James.

'Be careful and Cool Buddy' he said, large red nose twitching. 'You never know what may take shape in the Evil Voids lair!'

'Quite!' Agreed Monty, holding onto Peters legs, while their own skateboard followed James into the very ominous and dark room.

'This is most curious place?' Noted Abdul, who rolled just behind James and Peter. He looked toward the dark cavern walls and then to a huge spiral staircase, that followed these walls closely skyward. Many large books that the boy could now observe, were placed in neat wallpaper like spiral rows all around this very high and long tube like cavern room.

'It is like a sort of library or something' observed Sue, also rolling her skateboard forward following behind Abdul.

'Some library!' Exclaimed James looking at the books and some of their titles. 'Who would want to read a book just called A or B, C or D' he said, examining the single, large red letters, placed on some of these dark book edges.

'It would appear' said Sandy looking at this huge library. 'That as Evil is both brainless and spineless, maybe certain events and thoughts contained within these dark books may give the Dark Void it's power.'

'Ah yes of course!' Agreed Monty, his nose twitching in the dusty dark cavern room. 'A vitamin source for the build up and Power increase, of this Evil Dark Void.'

Peter removed the book he had seen marked simply 'A' from it's shelf, and containing many many pages it felt very heavy and cold as he held it in his hands. Peter opened the cover to examine what was written inside.

'But!' He exclaimed. 'There are no words on these pages!' Peter was a little confused as to why a book should have no print inside it. 'The only word printed in this book is on the first page.'

## Into The Void - (Fear Overcome)

'And what is the word?' Asked James, removing another book from it's shelf that was simply marked 'B'.

'Anger' said Peter, examining the large red print.

'This one is the same!' Replied James. 'Just one word, only the word is, Bad.'

'This one has Destruction' said Abdul, picking a book at random from the shelf and choosing the one marked simply by the letter 'D'.

'By Jove!' Said Monty, his monocle glistening. 'I would hazard a guess that each book contains no writing, because it contains the actual spirit, of some very nasty things that have happened in the past.'

'Yes sir re Buddy' Pat agreed, nodding his head. 'Maybe some of our stolen notes have been pasted into these books for Evil purposes.'

'The absolute cad!' Exclaimed Monty, moustache twitching. 'No wonder the Void thing has been gathering in strength throughout history!' He looked around, at the vast selection of differently inscribed books. 'There must be an enormous amount of bad thought and deed energy stored here!' Monty picked up a book marked with the two replicated letters, 'DD'. 'This one is marked as the Dark Voids Dark Diary' he said, flicking through the books pages. 'This particular book does contain writing in it' his nose twitched, in some disgust. 'It is a wish diary, of things that have not actually happened, but contains listings of dark and Evil thought possibilities.' Monty replaced the diary back to it's dark shelf. 'Best not read by human folks' he muttered.

'Let's move on!' Demanded James, eager to explore. He put his book back onto it's shelf and rolled his skateboard forward again. 'There is another room over there' he observed, and the boy quickly moved toward yet another, dark doorway.

'Your Fate and Time is in the balance room' read Peter, looking at a small dark sign hanging above this doorway, as he too, replaced the book he had examined and moved his skateboard forward. 'I wonder what is in there?'

'Look!' Shouted Abdul, poking his head into this room and seeing another huge, darkened cavern. 'The red nose football is over there - I can see it.'

'Yes! - There it is!' Observed Sue, moving into the room past Abdul. She quickly rolled her skateboard forward, with Ozzy still clinging tightly to her leg, both heading toward the red nose football.

The small red sphere of a soccer ball nose, was hovering above the ground in what appeared to be a shimmering hologram picture of a weighing scales. This shimmering picture form, Sue noted, was of a rather stern looking lady, who held the scales in place with the aid of an outstretched arm, her other arm holding an upright sword. A chain was held by her tightly gripped hand, linked to two cups, in one of which the red nose ball rested, the other cup being empty, but still, strangely, Sue noted, both remained perfectly balanced and level.

'Is it just me -' Sue asked, looking around the dark cavern. 'Or does this place look like a soccer pitch?'

## Into The Void - (Fear Overcome)

'The scales of Justice!' Murmured Monty, gazing at the hologram figure through his monocle. 'Most peculiar! - A ball of History and wisdom, that balances the scales - Most odd.'

Abdul suddenly pointed with his finger.

'Hey, take a look at that!' He called out, indicating in the direction of a large, soccer goal post sized and shaped doorway.

The boy then read a small sign placed above this rather peculiar, doorway shape.

'Tip the Scales un-balance Time?' Abdul shook his head. 'A most strange place' he said thoughtfully. 'I wonder what that could mean?'

Pat twitched his red nose.

'I guess?' He said, scratching his round chin. 'That the Void has to, maybe, score bad points to get ahead in the game.'

'And it would be reasonable to assume' remarked Sandy. 'That the books stored within that library, have firstly to come through those goal posts to score seconds of Evil un-balance Time.'

'I say!' Exclaimed Monty. 'A ripping thought Sandy.' His moustache twitched. 'It all adds up! - Every book and page of those bad thoughts and deeds must equal a second erased from the clock. Every second lost and the Void grows larger as it turns back Time, to move the balance back it's own way, to an un-balanced creation - But, perhaps?' He said, thoughtfully. 'We could remove all of those books the same way they came in, to take back the minutes erased and thus remove the Voids power source.'

'How could we few folks remove all those books?' Asked James. 'There must be hundreds of them.'

As he spoke, an ill wind suddenly and quite rudely, rushed into this huge, dark cavern, interrupting everyone's thoughts. This wind whizzed past the children and fizzled out, as suddenly as it had arrived.

'It would seem!' Snapped a small and sneering voice. 'That we have guests!'

All four children and skateboard riders turned toward this voice and observed the shape of Furtive Von Flatulence. He had entered the dark cavern through another soccer goal post sized and shaped doorway cut into a gloomy wall, directly opposite the other, but above this particular goal-post entrance hung a different small sign with the words. 'Hold the scales and balance' painted upon it.

'My friends!' Sneered Furtive Von Flatulence, waving his six rather sinister bogey-men shadows forward into the cavern. 'We figures of Evil shall now commence and engage in our game to tip the scales of Peace and Justice!' Von Flatulence swiftly shuffled his small frame forward toward the awaiting children and Penguin People.

'We shall finally remove all good, once and forever, from the Dark Voids playing field!'

### *Kids World United V Evils Black Heart Shadows -*
### *(Times ultimate football match)*

With a low ominous rumble, the ground started to tremble beneath each skateboard while the four children and Penguin People curiously and somewhat apprehensively, observed Furtive Von Flatulence and his six bogey-men anti bodies who moved menacingly forward toward them.

'I really do not like the look of these guys!' Commented James, trying to steady himself on his vibrating skateboard.

As he spoke, emanating upward from the ground, a deep creaking sound quite suddenly accompanied another, violent shake from the Earth and the entire cavern vibrated violently.

'Those things must weigh a ton each to make the ground shake so much' quipped Sue, holding out her arms to steady her balance. She watched Furtive Von Flatulence and the strange, human like, but non-featured dark shadows move slowly forward.

'I do not think so' mused Peter turning toward Sue. 'Even strange creatures such as these, could not possibly effect movement of the ground.'

Monty tapped Peter on the leg, to gain his attention.

'Quite right old thing!' He agreed, and the Penguin Person nodded. 'It would appear though, that we may have given the bally old Evil Void a rather sudden bought of indigestion!'

'Well Buddy' added Pat, grinning. 'It obviously can't stomach any good folks!'

'Whatever!' Abdul reached toward the weighing scales and gripped the red nosed football, tightly, in his outstretched arms. He looked up to see the rather stern looking lady, who held the scales in place, smile at him gently.

Abdul automatically smiled back, then composing himself, he pulled the red nose from the scales and toward his chest and stated firmly.

'Those things are not going to get this soccer ball and score goals against us!'

Immediately following Abdul's removal of the red nose ball, a small white dot painted exactly in the centre of this huge cavern, and lying directly beneath this shimmering hologram picture weighing scales, started to grow larger and larger.

'Hey!' Cried Abdul, noticing this, but also observing another interesting development. 'Look...' He pointed with a finger toward the scales, that were now both empty. 'Those scales' he pondered. 'They are both still equally balanced.'

'By Jove!' Exclaimed Monty. 'It would seem that all of you human children have an equal chance of both winning, or losing.'

'Winning or losing what?' Asked Sue, looking toward the small Penguin Person, whose long moustache twitched beneath his large and very new red nose.

'Your goals of Peace in Time!' Young miss, chipped in Sandy.

As the small Penguin Person spoke, a single blast of cool wind followed closely by a whistling breath of fresh air, whipped upward from beneath Abdul's skateboard.

## Kids World United V Evils Black Heart Shadows -
## (Times ultimate football match)

The hologram picture, under the force of this wind suddenly evaporated, it's smiling form now heading like a semi transparent puff of steam ever skyward.

'I do declare this is most curious!' Gasped Peter, who watched this steam stop as abruptly as it had started and form a small transparent cloud.

In an instant, this grey cloud exploded in a single, brilliant flash of light, directly above Abdul's head. After the strange, silent flash of light had gone and when everyone's eyes, again adjusted to the dark cavern, a veritable mass, of swirling, brightly lit dots of light, could be seen hanging in the air.

These dots started to swirl, very, very quickly, around and around in a circular motion. They reminded James, who watched these things hover overhead, of a picture that he had once seen in a text book, reflecting a distant universe of small stars.

'Cool' he muttered. 'Just like the big bang.'

'Indubitably' replied Monty. 'The beginning of all creation was also a silent event, as sound is merely a result of air vibration.'

This mass of expanding, small lights hovering directly above all the children, suddenly stopped rotating. Everyone watched most curiously, then were very surprised, as another single flash of light made all their eyes blink rapidly.

The small dots all whirled chaotically upward and embedded themselves, like a shimmering carpet, over the ceiling of this huge, dark cavern.

There they shone brightly, like stars looking downward in the night sky, twinkling most gently, from the dark, Evil walls, into which they had now become embedded.

'Hey -' Called out James, looking around the cavern as his eyes adjusted. 'Would you look at that.' He observed every area of the dark cavern, that now glowed, with a soft light. 'Those star dot things, are all acting like sets of weak floodlights.'

Peter, as his own eyes adjusted, also observed the illuminated cavern. He found himself staring down at the now more shadow like, than dark field, that lay under his skateboard.

'Yes - Light does appear to have been cast into the darkness' he mused while scratching his chin... 'But what are floodlights?'

'Wow!' Exclaimed Sue, before she, or indeed, anyone, could answer Peter.

While Sue and everyone else now peered around the cavern, the full layout of a yellow lined, gently illuminated soccer pitch formed, gradually drawing itself from beneath the ground.

The small centre circle dot in front of Abdul grew rapidly larger. He looked down at it and watched as another, much larger circle drew itself around it.

'Now that is what I call a pitch!' He said grinning.

With a dull creaking sound, this larger circle opened slightly, to form two smiley mouth pictures in the pitch centre.

## Kids World United V Evils Black Heart Shadows -
## (Times ultimate football match)

Or rather, as the children all noted, a smile, or a frown, depending on which side of this pitch that a person actually stood.

'Watch it folks!' Cried Ozzy, looking toward the Evil figures approaching rapidly from the other side of the pitch. 'Here come the bad guys.'

Furtive Von Flatulence shuffled forward across the markings of this peculiar, new football pitch. He stopped just in front of the four children and Penguin People, his small, beady eyes, burning with rage.

'Firstly!' He demanded, staring at Abdul with an decidedly unfriendly stare. 'You will give me that ball, repulsive human child.'

The six very sinister bogey-men figures also accompanying this angry creature stopped just behind Furtive Von Flatulence, and they looked rather menacing while they moved, billowing back and forth, within a non existent wind.

Abdul stared back, undaunted, but in contempt of the attitude of these Evil creatures.

'Not so much of the repulsive human child, shorty!' He span the red nose ball on a single finger tip and it swivelled, almost contemptuously, before the eyes of these Evil Voids hench-beings. 'You cannot have our ball Buddy!'

Von Flatulence sprang upward slightly in anger, a faint, but audible rippling of wind heard emanating from this loathsome creature.

'Then we must take it!' He threatened, in an aggressive tone.

'What is his big deal about the ball?' Asked James, huffing in contempt at the attitude of this bully.

'The ball is also a Peace key' said Monty, looking at Von Flatulence from behind the legs of Peter. 'It enabled you human children, through your teamwork and friendship, to enter the Evil Voids thick skin.' His nose twitched above his long moustache.

'Those Evil bounders know that the ball must be used to score against you. To be placed in the Goal of Evil, not the Goal of Peace.'

'You mean that -' Asked Sue. 'It is like a sort of football game.'

'Sure is' chipped in Pat. 'You decide yourself on which side you want to be, Good or Evil, then play the game.'

'What if one does not wish to play on either team?' Asked Peter thoughtfully. 'To be a spectator or such like.'

'Well -' said Sandy, looking toward Peter from behind Abdul's legs. 'To just be a spectator in the eternal battle of Good and Evil would mean that you would just have to accept the consequences, whoever it should be, that may win in Time.'

Abdul looked at the Penguin People.

'Can you creatures play football?' He asked, looking at their small bodies. 'Otherwise it's four of us kids against seven of those things.'

## Kids World United V Evils Black Heart Shadows -
## (Times ultimate football match)

'Sadly' huffed Monty, shaking his head. 'We cannot interfere with human events. We must only take notes and observe your history, we cannot take part in the future of mankind game.'

'That is right' agreed Pat. 'We can only follow and note, not get involved with your actions.'

'Oh -' said Abdul, feeling his stomach churn a little in disappointment. 'Looks like we might get beaten then.'

'Hey!' Called out James. 'We will not let them cream us Buddy!' He smiled and looked toward the others.

'Right -' Nodded Sue. 'We will try our best.'

'Yes!' Peter also nodded, and he turned toward Abdul, 'Good will always triumph over Evil, no matter what!'

'Good show!' Exclaimed Monty. 'Good show!'

Ozzy scratched his chin.

'Hey' he said, remembering the words of a note that he had heard Monty read out in Chill Out Hall. 'The Grand Master of Time said in his note to assist and protect the children.'

'Ah -' Thought Sandy and he spoke aloud. 'To assist, maybe means to play the football game with them, would it not?'

'Er -' Monty thought for a moment. 'Well, possibly old fruit, but...'

A very sudden, loud chiming sound cut short the conversation and brought everyone's attention directly upward, to the dark cavern ceiling. Looking upward and all straining their necks, everyone present could see a large dark circle form high above them, to spin gently around and reveal a plain, ordinary, clock face.

'That sounds like Big Ben' muttered Peter, as he heard the last chime of twelve o'clock boom around the cavern. As it did so, the most extraordinary thing happened.

Above this large clock circle, a small hatch unexpectedly appeared and an equally small, silver skinned Cuckoo bird sprang forward, heading very quickly, the long distance earthward.

This bird stopped quite abruptly, suspended by a large thin coil, directly between the faces of Abdul and Furtive Von Flatulence.

'Cuckoo!' It bellowed toward the face of Abdul, who raised a lip in stunned surprise. Then, with a ruffle of metallic feathers, the silver bird suddenly turned and bellowed the same, single - 'Cuckoo!' Toward a bemused face of the Dark Voids Evil hench-being.

With a twang that echoed throughout this large cavern, the coil suspending the bird retracted, to leave a bouncing silver Cuckoo bird hovering just above the surprised onlookers heads. As everyone watched, a wing from the bird twisted forward, moving up toward it's head.

## Kids World United V Evils Black Heart Shadows -
## (Times ultimate football match)

'Now that is really weird!' Noted James, watching intently as the silver bird placed a shiny whistle into it's beak.

The red nosed football Abdul was holding suddenly shot downward with some force, from his arms.

'What the -' He exclaimed in surprise, watching the red ball hurtle toward the pitch and stick directly to the centre spot. A mere split second later a very loud, ear hurting single blast from the silver birds whistle, made Abdul automatically reach up with his hands, to cover his ears.

Furtive Von Flatulence saw his chance and wasted no Time. He lunged forward to kick the red nosed ball with as much force as his Evil frame could muster. His strange large hat bobbed forward, rocking with the force of his kick that sent the red nosed football shooting past Abdul, and toward the goal marked 'Tip the Scales un-balance Time.'

Von Flatulence laughed an Evil laugh as he sped past Abdul.

'Evils Black Heart Shadows will annihilate you all' he shouted, pushing Abdul roughly as he past him.

Monty was quick to react and lifted his jacket upward with both hands. The result, was much to Sue's surprise, as she watched this creature reveal two hairy, thin, chicken like legs attached to it's lace less shoes.

'You bounder!' Exclaimed Monty, stretching one of these hairy legs forward and into the path of a quickly moving Furtive Von Flatulence. 'Kids World United will spoil your Evil game!'

James also watched, as Furtive Von Flatulence tumbled over Monty's hairy leg and collapsed into an Evil heap, with his large hat now covering a stunned face. In this course of events, both Monty and Peter fell from the skateboard on which they were standing and landed with a thud onto the pitch.

'Was that not a foul?' Enquired Peter, sitting up from the floor and looking directly toward the new red nose of Monty who also sat up, his hat tilted to one side.

'Only if one is actually standing on the pitch at the Time dear boy!' Laughed Monty, his moustache twitching and a glint shinning from his small monocle. 'We were standing on the skateboard!'

'Come on!' Ordered Abdul, leaping from his own skateboard. 'Let's get the ball, quickly!' He ran as fast as he could toward the red nosed ball that he could now see beyond the collapsed frame of Furtive Von Flatulence.

Sue also leapt from her skateboard and ran toward the ball. She did not get very far though, as the six sinister shadows following their master, headed quickly toward the ball and pushed Sue roughly to the ground, while they all barged past her.

Ozzy too, tumbled to the ground, while the small Penguin Person tried to stop the bogey-men from getting past Sue.

## Kids World United V Evils Black Heart Shadows -
### (Times ultimate football match)

He fell backward onto the skateboard from the force of collision, and both he and the skateboard rolled backward along the ground to slam, painfully, into one of the dark cavern walls on the edge of this strange soccer pitch.

Abdul sped quickly past Furtive Von Flatulence and had almost made it to the red nosed football when he felt a rough push from behind.

'Ah!' He yelled, falling forward and tumbling over the football.

With a crash, he hit the floor, hard, then while spinning around in a circle he saw the six bogey-men who had pushed him reach the red nosed ball first. He looked on in horror as one of these strange shadows lifted a foot and struck the red nosed football with all it's Evil force. The red nosed ball hurtled forward heading upward in the air and Abdul watched helplessly, as it passed directly over his head toward an open Evil goal.

'Stop it someone!' He demanded desperately, reaching up with one arm to reach the ball as he sat on the floor. 'It is going to go in!'

The red nosed football continued in it's upward trajectory to sail past Abdul's outstretched fingertips, while he himself bent backwards, to painfully hit the hard ground, trying desperately to stop it's path.

'Ouch!' He cried out, his head thumping onto the pitch.

Von Flatulence stood up, pulling his Evil frame from the ground and adjusted a tall, crumpled hat.

'Excellent!' Flatulence bellowed, watching with glee the red nosed ball hurtling directly toward the long goal mouth.

Pat, standing behind James, quickly jumped from the smiley mouthed skateboard and lifted his jacket. In an instant, the small Penguin Person lifted one of his thin, hairy, chicken like legs and stamped onto the back of this skateboard as hard as he could. His lace less shoes thudded downward onto the back of the skateboard and it's front end lurched upward and back toward him.

The resultant and quite sudden sea saw effect propelled James upward and into the air, to pass way above this small creatures head.

'Ah!' Cried James, who was now flying through the air and found himself, quite unexpectedly, heading directly toward the goal in a direct collision course with the spinning red nosed football.

With a clang James looked up to see his helmet make contact with the ball and send it flying away from the goal mouth, heading backwards and upwards into the air.

'Good header!' Commented Abdul, who followed the path of James. He gave a short - 'Ooh!' As James returned quickly earthwards to thud in a crumpled heap onto the hard pitch. 'That must of hurt!' He added.

'Good on yeah!' Called out Ozzy, sitting upright from the side of the pitch and adjusting his hat.

## Kids World United V Evils Black Heart Shadows -
## (Times ultimate football match)

'Ace Buddy!' Congratulated Pat, lowering his jacket again and shuffling forward to help the boy up.

Sue watched the football strike the twinkling cavern ceiling and silently followed it's decent earthwards again. The red nose football fell very quickly and suddenly struck Peter on the head. He was still sitting next to Monty and Monty also observed the red nosed ball, as it rebounded off Peters head and flew toward Sue.

'Kick it!' Demanded Abdul, who saw the six bogey-men shadows frantically heading toward the girl.

Sue hit the ball as hard as she could with her foot and sent the ball sailing down the pitch. It headed skyward, flying high toward the other goal and over the head of Furtive Von Flatulence.

'Come on!' She ordered the others, running after the ball and away from the bogey-men as fast as she could.

'Curses!' Von Flatulence followed the red nosed balls flight above his head and then he looked across and seemed very cross, as Sue ran past him. The Evil little character barged Sue sharply with his arm as she past and Sue tumbled forward, but did not stop.

'That really is no way to treat a lady' shouted Peter, who was by now on his feet and running after the ball. He bumped Von Flatulence quite hard when he past him and the Evil henchman span around, tottering out of control on his large feet.

'Yes - Correct!' Agreed Abdul, bumping the spinning Von Flatulence very hard as he also sped past him. Von Flatulence fell to the ground and still spinning, sat, almost break dancing, on the cold cavern floor.

'Stop them!' He spluttered, calling on his Evil, black heart shadow bogey-men team angrily. 'They must be stopped!'

James staggered to his feet and watched Sandy, Pat and Monty block the bogey-men's path who were quickly following Sue, Abdul and Peter. With a thump and force of collision, he saw the three Penguin People collapse to the pitch floor, along with three of the sinister shadows.

Ozzy jumped from the skateboard at the pitch edge and rolled on his belly across the ground, to scatter like skittles, the remaining three shadows who all bounced in separate directions.

Von Flatulence was by now absolutely furious. He had stopped spinning and watched the children with his angry eyes as they headed toward the red nosed ball and their Peace goal.

The Evil Dark Voids henchman suddenly shoved a single finger, up each of his nostrils, and produced a large glob of repugnant mess on the tip of each.

'You will never score!' He cried, and flicked both his fingers to propel this entire mess toward the other end of the pitch in two separate, horrible blobs.

## Kids World United V Evils Black Heart Shadows -
## (Times ultimate football match)

'Shoot! - Kick it!' Ordered Abdul, watching Sue reach the red nosed ball first.

Sue tried to trap the bouncing ball beneath her foot, but winced as it flicked just out of her reach, while bouncing uncontrollably back into the air.

'What's that?' Sue called out, seeing Von Flatulence's mess fall from the air just above the red nosed ball. She followed their track and uttered a sharp, 'Yuck!' As she saw both blobs strike the ground in front of her.

The ball also fell Earthward at the same moment and stuck solid, into the two blobs that now stuck in a mess to the pitch.

'Wow!' Exclaimed Sue as she looked down, to observe the most peculiar thing happening.

It was bad enough for her to note these two horrible nasal bogeys strike the ground in front of her, but to see them start to bubble, divide and then multiply underneath this red nosed football, was really quite repellent. Then watching these things start to grow larger and larger upward and form into many more dark shadows of the opposite, Evil team, Sue found it all very disturbing.

'Um – Guys -' Sue said slowly. 'I think we may have a slight problem here.'

The shadows that now stood in front of Sue had arisen very quickly, and linking together they formed a solid wall of twisting, threatening Evil anti bodies that blocked the entire Peace goal mouth in front of the children. The red nosed football lay static at the feet of a particularly large and horrible shadow, that stood defiantly in front of Sue.

With a howl of ill wind, this creature bent forward menacingly, then struck the ball hard, to sail past Sue and head very quickly in the opposite direction.

'The other way!' Shouted Abdul, watching the football rocket firstly over Sue's, and then his head.

Peter, running behind Abdul, jumped as high as he could into the air, but missed the red nosed ball by a matter of a hairs breadth.

'Yipe!' He cried out, returning to Earth with a crash.

Furtive Von Flatulence watched the red nosed football continue on it's path and fly high above his long hat.

'Much too far you fool' he sneered, observing the ball hurtle high over his Evil Black Heart Shadows that were chasing behind the children. The bogey-men all stopped suddenly, turned and chased the red nosed ball back along the strange football pitch.

James gulped in apprehension, but stood firm, as he saw the red nosed football, followed quickly by the approaching Evil team, head directly toward him.

'Oh boy!' He muttered, closely following a perfectly straight, high track of the ball. James watched the ball start to fall and rushed to meet it. 'Ye - ha!' He yelled in defiance while running, though quite expecting, to be bowled over by the approaching hoard of shadows.

## Kids World United V Evils Black Heart Shadows - (Times ultimate football match)

'Onward my Evil beauties!' Cried Von Flatulence, seeing that only a single child now lay between his team and the Evil 'Tip the Scales un-balance Time' goal mouth. 'We have this game in the bag!'

James thundered toward the red nosed football as fast as he could. Judging his opportune moment he leapt into the air, striking the ball with the front of his skateboard helmet.

It proved not to be the best method of sending a small sphere in the direction that a person wanted, but the helmet launched the ball high into the air again and sent it flopping over the line of oncoming bogey-men.

The creatures crashed into James, sending him flying backward toward the Evil goal mouth. He slid quickly along the pitch, to stop abruptly by crashing into the side of this long goal mouth carved into the dark cavern walls.

'Just as well I am still wearing my pads' he muttered, sitting upright and shaking his aching head.

Peter, who watched the red nosed ball descend from the halfway line ran at full speed toward it. He jumped high into the air but found his upward path greeted by a sneering and also jumping, Furtive Von Flatulence.

'Mine!' Demanded the loathsome little creature, elbowing Peter painfully in the ribs.

'Ouch!' Peter crashed into Von Flatulence, but just managed to deflect the red nosed football with his head, away from this Evil creature, who was trying to push him from it.

'Good header!' Shouted Abdul and Sue agreed. However, both children who by now were running up to Peter, felt slightly less confident as the ball hurtled back down the pitch toward James.

'Not again!' Retorted James, seeing the red nosed football head back in his direction. 'Oh no!' He suddenly blurted, observing the ball fall from the sky, directly into the clutches of the Evil Black Heart Shadows team. James quickly scrambled to his feet and stood directly into the Evil goal mouth centre. 'There's no choice now!' He said to himself. 'I have to stand my ground!'

James watched the line of Evil and imposing shadows grow closer and closer by the second, he felt a bead of sweat on his brow, and the hairs on the back of his neck, stand up in anticipation.

On the sidelines, and twitching his long moustache in frustration, watching the hoard of Evil shadows rush forward toward James, Monty yelled out to Ozzy, Sandy and Patriot.

'Quickly!' He bellowed, monocle glistening under the twinkling ceiling lights. 'Let us help James stop them before they can score, and seal the fate of an unbalanced Time!'

## Kids World United V Evils Black Heart Shadows -
## (Times ultimate football match)

Looking both quite large and menacing, the Evil Black Heart Shadows rushed forward with the red nosed football, trying their best to intimidate James, by waving their spooky arms into the air and howling like a fierce, ill wind.

James straightened his helmet and bent forward, readying himself, to make a sudden leap for the ball.

'Here they come!' He said to himself and bobbed about, trying to make himself look and be, as large as possible in the goal mouth he was defending.

'Shoot! - Shoot you fools!' Ordered Furtive Von Flatulence, standing to his feet, then stamping his foot sharply to the ground, trying to hit Peter, who now sat a little dazed on the pitch after his collision. He missed, and Peter quickly reached out his arms to hold Von Flatulence firmly by the foot.

'I say old chap!' Barked Peter, a little annoyed. 'That is not very good sportsman-ship!' Peter stood up and quickly swung the Evil little character around in a circle, still holding onto his foot.

Von Flatulence tried to keep his tall hat in place with one hand and remove Peters grip with the other. However, while balancing on a single remaining foot, that still made contact with the pitch, removing Peters hold proved impossible.

'Take that, you rotten egg!' Cried Peter and he suddenly let go of his firm grip.

'Oops!' Called out Von Flatulence, the Dark Voids Evil henchman now spinning uncontrollably and at full speed backwards. He continued, like a frenetic ballet dancer, to spin all the way down the long pitch, only stopping when he crashed into a painful heap, between the 'Hold the Scales and balance' goal posts.

At the other end, Sue and Abdul tried to push past the line of dark shadows that they had now reached, but both found it quite impossible to move around them.

'Ouch!' Cried Abdul, trying to put a foot between the shadows and reach the red nosed football. With a single swipe, a shadow hand had reached back and struck Abdul, knocking him off balance.

'Ouch!' Agreed Sue as another shadows hand, reached back and swiped her away sharply.

With a single yell - 'Charge!' Coming from the sidelines, all the Evil Black Heart Shadows turned their heads, to see the four Penguin People sliding on their bellies toward them.

Monty was still shouting as his quickly moving group made very sudden contact with the Evil anti body team.

'Ouch!' He also agreed with the children, when his - 'Charge!' Yell ended in a painful collision with some of these Evil Black Heart Shadows.

'Strike!' Noted James, watching the Evil team become bowled over by these sliding creatures - 'Well' He added - 'Almost.'

## Kids World United V Evils Black Heart Shadows -
## (Times ultimate football match)

James noticed that one of the shadows, tottered, but remained standing. This creature had the red nosed football at it's feet and after regaining it's balance, suddenly launched the ball toward James.

'Humph!' James exclaimed, leaping for the red nosed football as it headed on a direct path toward the goal.

'Look Buddies!' Called out Pat, spinning to a stop on his belly. 'Hey - Catch it James!' He added, looking on, while the red nosed football span through the air and headed toward the boy.

'I cant look!' Exclaimed Ozzy, crashing into both Sandy and Monty, beyond the now entirely floored, Evil Black Heart Shadows team.

James was just that little bit too far from the football and reached out with both arms at full stretch. He thought quickly, clenched both his fists and just managed to strike the red nosed football to send it spiralling away from the goalmouth, back out into the pitch.

Sue saw the ball coming and also the remaining bogeyman who immediately chased after it.

'Take that!' She cried, barging this creature fully in the ribs while the ball sailed past her head, and the dark shadow tottered sideways, falling to the ground.

Abdul watched the ball fall towards him and as it reached waist height, the boy span around, to strike it, as hard as he could, in the direction of the 'Hold the Scales and balance' goal posts.

'Excellent shot!' Commented Peter, as the rapidly moving ball roared past him. He turned while it rocketed bye to see Furtive Von Flatulence stagger to his feet at the pitch end.

The ball flew straight and true, directly on a collision course with the small Evil creature, who looked up at the very last moment to see it approaching.

'Ouch!' Cried Von Flatulence, tottering backwards, the red nosed football striking him directly on the centre of his forehead.

He fell on his back to the floor and dizzily observed the ball flying high into the sky, then drop, directly earthward above him. The ball hit Von Flatulence on the top of his long hat, then rolled slowly down it, to drop into and beyond the goal mouth.

'Goal!' Shouted Abdul. 'He scored an own goal!'

As the boy spoke, the clock above this peculiar soccer pitch again chimed, echoing around the large cavern. The silver skinned Cuckoo bird, springing forward, suspended by a large thin coil, headed very quickly the long distance Earthward. With another ruffle of metallic feathers, the silver bird blew it's whistle, to loudly signal the end of this rather peculiar soccer match.

Peter looked up, while the silver bird disappeared back to the ceiling. 'Look!' he shouted. 'The clock!'

## Kids World United V Evils Black Heart Shadows - 
### (Times ultimate football match)

Sue also looked up and saw the clock as it was before, only this Time, a smiley mouth and large red nose had become drawn at it's centre.

'Cool' she muttered. 'Very cool.'

However, the Evil character that had inadvertently let in an unwanted own goal, was not so happy. Furtive Von Flatulence stood to his feet and bellowed toward his team.

'Get them!' He demanded. 'Remove them from the pitch!'

But for these Evil Black Heart Shadows, it was already to late in the game to have won.

High above the head of Von Flatulence, the dark ceiling started to rumble and dust fell downward from the twinkling lights. Removing some of this dust from his large nose, the Dark Voids henchman looked up to the ceiling and now saw, that his own Time had come.

'Oh dear! - Oh dear!' He exclaimed, watching the clocks glass start to crack and the circle that formed the clocks shape high above him, begin to rotate.

'This is most distressing Time for Evil.'

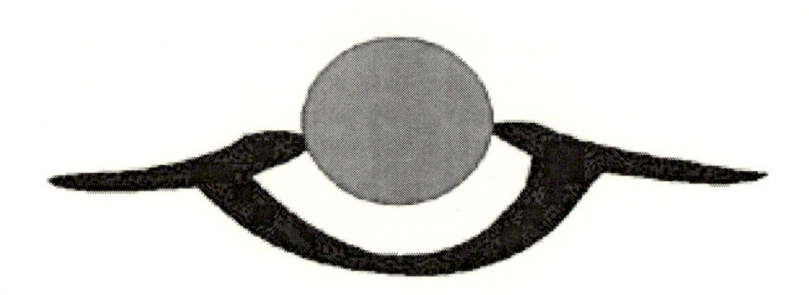

## Times Sword Of Damocles -
## (Fate In The Balance & The Final Countdown)

Behind the shuffling, concerned Evil figure of Furtive Von Flatulence, something rather strange was now taking place. After the red nosed football had entered into the goal mouth, and while everyone's attention had been drawn to the cracking ceiling clock, the most peculiar roar of a very loud, but strangely gentle wind of change started to bellow from the long, soccer goal post sized and shaped doorway cut into the gloomy cavern walls.

The goal post shape now changed to resemble a large book, that seemed to have been laid onto it's side and which now started to brighten and shine into a strong, golden yellow hue of light.

This peculiar, warm light, flowed very quickly outward, spreading forward onto the football pitch, to frame, then envelope the dark Voids Evil henchman who stood in front of it.

Flickering while it travelled forward and followed closely by the loud roar of a gentle wind of change, this golden light illuminated high into the dark cavern, to flow serenely across the quickly cracking clock face glass, that was embedded into the dark, but twinkling with many brightly dotted lights, cavern ceiling.

'Oh dear! - Oh dear!' Muttered Von Flatulence, releasing a little wind of his own in agitation. He looked down along the long soccer pitch toward his dark shadows football team, who were still looking as sinister as ever, and moving quickly forward toward the four children. The children, for their part, looked at him also, then each turned to see what he was looking at.

'Run!' Cried Abdul, observing some of the dark shadows nearing Sue.

'I concur!' Replied Peter, who grabbed Sue by the arm and pulled her roughly forward, to just remain out of reach, while a lunging dark shadow just missed grabbing her.

James, watching at the other end of the soccer pitch, took a deep gulp.

'Er – Guys -' He shouted, looking wide eyed, as a line of bogey-men moved toward him. 'What do you reckon we should do now?'

'Better think of something - Fast!' Called Abdul in reply, moving away from a Dark Shadow that headed toward him.

A small figure sat upright at the edge of the long football pitch and adjusted his hat, while twitching his long, crumpled moustache back into shape.

The Penguin Person quickly brushed some fine dust that had fallen from the cavern ceiling from his glass monocle, that was by now enveloped in the spreading golden stream of light. Brushing more dust from his large red nose, the Union Jack jacketed Penguin Person creature watched most curiously as light and wind flowed from the goal posts.

'Most interesting!' Mused Monty, looking past Furtive Von Flatulence. He had also noted a loud, audible, buzzing sound emanate from the 'Hold the Scales and balance' sign painted above the long strange doorway and watched intently, as this sign flashed gently on and off, like a flickering neon banner.

## Times Sword Of Damocles -
## (Fate In The Balance & The Final Countdown)

It was to signal the end of this rather peculiar football match, and as a relieved Monty recovered himself more fully from Ozzy's crash he shook his head back and forth, twitching his large red nose in thought.

'I do seem to have developed!' Exclaimed Monty. 'The most awful ringing in my temporal lobes.'

Patriot sat up and pushed Ozzy's large red nose from his own face. Ozzy groaned and also sat upright, brushing dust from his green hat.

Pat looked at Monty and twitched his own large red nose.

'That is your mobile phone ringing Buddy' Patriot tapped Monty's hold all things receptacle quite hard with his hand. 'From inside your hat.'

'Yes of course!' Spluttered Monty, who then pressed the small yellow clock on the front of his hold all things receptacle. The hat top sprang quickly upward and Monty removed a ringing mobile phone from inside it and pressed the device to his very minute ear.

'Hello old thing! - Monty here!' He answered firmly into the device while twitching his long, dark moustache.

James looked toward the Penguin People as the dark shadows grew ever closer. He was a little stunned at observing Monty using a mobile phone

'Hey!' He called. 'Excuse me!' And then his voice grew more urgent. 'I really could use some help here folks!'

'Be with you in a sec!' Replied Monty, waving toward James.

James huffed, then hit a fist into his other palm.

'Well, I suppose this is it then' he muttered and prepared to scuffle with the oncoming bogey-men.

Pat, Ozzy and Sandy rose to their feet, looked around the soccer pitch and wondered who to help first. The dark shadows chasing Peter, Sue and Abdul, had at that moment grabbed each of the three children by the scruff of their necks. At the other end of the long soccer pitch, James, with his fist still hitting out, disappeared under a line of Dark Shadows, who had now jumped on top of him.

'By Jove!' Monty exclaimed, shuffling to his feet, an ear still pressed to the mobile phone. 'It is all the other chaps from the club! - They are outside, every one of them!' He looked at Pat and the others. 'And each one has a human child visitor accompanying them.'

'More kids!' Exclaimed Pat. 'How?'

'No Time for explanations!' Interrupted Sandy, most concerned at the events happening upon the soccer pitch. 'Tell them to immediately enter the Void!'

'Yeah sport!' Agreed Ozzy. 'These guys need sorting out.'

The Penguin Person creature waddled onto the pitch and headed directly toward Sue, who was being held uncomfortably and roughly, up in the air, by the long arm of a Dark Shadow.

## Times Sword Of Damocles -
## (Fate In The Balance & The Final Countdown)

'Bang on Chaps!' Agreed Monty. 'Will do!' He looked upward to the quickly cracking clock in the cavern ceiling. 'Listen old things!' Monty shouted into the mobile phone. 'Bring everyone you have out there into the Void. There may be an entry point opening up at any moment.'

As Monty spoke, the glass face of the ceiling clock suddenly shattered into a billion sparkling pieces. These pieces whirled forward, then formed into a spiral that span wildly around and around. Within an instant, the pieces headed back toward the shattered clock, exploding into a single brilliant flash of light. After this blinding flash had gone, a large, swirling dark circle, remained where the clock had been.

'It is a black hole!' Monty cried excitedly into the mobile phone. 'The clock has formed an entrance hole in Space and Time - Use it to enter the Void.'

At the other end of the soccer pitch Furtive Von Flatulence grinned an Evil grin, while he watched the children being caught by his Dark Shadows. But his half smile of badness, was very soon wiped from his Evil face, when he looked again toward the cavern ceiling.

Where a clock had once been embedded the large black hole now swirled frantically around and around, spreading outward, in ever enlarging circles, within the cavern ceiling. From the ground, Furtive Von Flatulence looked up at it in horror. He could now see numerous dots of light that grew larger and larger within this strange sphere, hovering directly above the centre of the long soccer pitch.

With a subdued growl of annoyance, the Dark Voids Evil henchman, while still looking skyward, started to shuffle slowly sideways toward the Vitamin Power Library Room.

While Sue, Abdul and Peter struggled to get free of the Dark Shadow Bogey-men who held them roughly by their necks, there came an enormous, single crash, directly above their heads.

Everyone looked instinctively upwards, to see the swirling black hole fill with the ever enlarging shape of many smiley mouthed skateboards and their riders, who suddenly thundered through the large opening.

'Looks like the cavalry has arrived Buddy!' Quipped Patriot, tilting his head as far back as he could to get a better look, his hat slipping forward across his large nose.

'Charge!' Ordered Monty, waving his hand toward the Dark Shadow football team and encouraging the skateboard riders to assist the roughly handled children. However, not much encouragement was needed, as everyone who had entered through the large black hole could see what was happening to the children below.

Sue looked up, quite amazed to see such a huge array of strange Penguin People creatures approaching from above.

## Times Sword Of Damocles -
## (Fate In The Balance & The Final Countdown)

The girl was even more surprised, when she suddenly noted that these odd creatures, each one wearing a different individually designed flag painted jacket and rode smiley mouthed skateboards, were not alone.

She automatically smiled toward the huge array of children, consisting of all shapes colours and sizes, that accompanied their own particular Penguin Person Buddy.

Sue struggled with the bogeyman who held her and was also now pulling her hair painfully.

'Let go you horrible thing!' She demanded, elbowing the shadow as hard as she could.

The Dark Shadow just wailed an eerie reply in Sue's ear and twisted her hair more painfully than before.

'Wow!' Exclaimed Abdul excitedly, watching a skateboard fly quickly downward, then, veer suddenly up and across the pitch, flying like a rocket just above his head. Another and yet another passed over him, but one smiley mouthed skateboard and it's riders suddenly came from the side to clip the Dark Shadow holding him on the side of it's Evil head.

The Dark Shadow twisted and turned in anger, but it had let go of Abdul. The boy dodged the Shadow Bogeyman and grabbed Sue by the arm, just as another skateboard hit the dark shadow that had been restraining her.

'Come on!' He shouted, dragging Sue away, toward the other end of the soccer pitch.

Sue grabbed Peter by the arm while she past him and the force of two, running, linked armed children, ripped Peter away from the clutches of his own Bogeyman.

The Dark Shadow lunged back at Peter but was floored by a low flying skateboard that smacked the Bogeyman squarely on the back of it's head.

'Thank you!' Called out Peter to Sue and Abdul. 'You also!' He added, shouting politely toward the passing skateboard and riders who had now veered back upwards toward the ceiling.

'I say old thing!' Cried Monty watching the events unfold on the soccer pitch. 'This is most Ding Dong!'

'Ding what?' Asked Patriot, twitching his large red nose.

'Tickety Boo!' Said Monty, turning to Pat. 'Bang on!'

Patriot turned to his small Penguin Person friend and gave him a hard stare.

'I sure wish these human folks would all speak the same language Buddy!' He said, shaking his head. 'Monty - Sometimes I still don't know what the heck you are talking about!'

'He means that events at this Time are all right!' Interrupted Sandy. 'Or AOK as American humans would say it.'

# Times Sword Of Damocles -
## (Fate In The Balance & The Final Countdown)

'Well maybe Sport!' Chipped in Ozzy, observing Sue, Peter and Abdul speed down the pitch. 'But those kids are still in some heavy trouble!'

Reaching the mound of Dark Shadow Bogey-men that still covered James, Sue, Abdul and Peter each grabbed a Dark Shadow by it's collar and hauled it away from the pile, as roughly as they themselves had been treated.

Within a few moments, James was free and stood to his feet.

'Thanks folks!' he spluttered, straightening his helmet. 'Thought I would never get out from under there!'

James suddenly looked past the others and up at the soccer pitch. His eyes were wide enough to make Sue, Abdul and Peter look around also.

'Oops!' Commented James. 'I think we might have upset those guys!'

For heading quickly toward them he could see all the Evil Dark Shadow Bogey-men team combined. They were running in a long, single and very frightening row, each wailing loudly at the children angrily.

Sue, Abdul, Peter and James all moved and prepared to make their escape. But then, each realised that there was nowhere that they could actually escape to, as the Dark Shadow Bogey-men were by now, far too close.

'This is it guys!' Observed James. 'We all have to fight these things!'

Ozzy shuffled as quickly as he could manage back toward Sue who now stood with the others, somewhat concerned, in front of the 'Tip the Scales unbalance Time' marked goal posts.

The children had all ran quickly past the small Penguin Person in their hurry to help James, and Ozzy twitched his nose in the air, while his lace less shoes scurried forward to meet them.

'Look out!' Warned Sue to Ozzy, as he neared the children.

'What's up Sport!' Called Ozzy right back.

'Behind you!' All the children then shouted together at the top of their voices. Ozzy turned and just had Time to make out the form, of a tall line of wailing, menacing Dark Shadow Bogey-men rolling forward toward him.

'Stop!' Ozzy demanded, holding out his arm firmly, his signal to the Dark Shadow Football team that they should, well, stop.

'Woo!' Sue grimaced, as she saw the Dark Shadows roll straight on, over and then past Ozzy. 'That had to hurt.'

Ozzy was, in a split second, laid flat on his back. Now looking upward at the twinkling ceiling, his arm still held up in a stop position, he now seemed to be seeing a lot more swirling 'stars' hovering above his head than was really normal.

'Not very sporting sorts!' He muttered and blew some dust from his crumpled nose.

Sue, Abdul, Peter and James, all prepared themselves for this wall of horrible Evil to hit them next.

## Times Sword Of Damocles -
### (Fate In The Balance & The Final Countdown)

'Good Grief!' Exclaimed Peter, watching the Shadows roll over Ozzy and become a lot nearer. 'These chaps are going to be rather a hard lot to beat!'

Sue, Abdul and James just nodded silently in agreement.

The long line of quickly moving Dark Shadows, had by now, quite suddenly seemed to fill the entire width of the soccer pitch, and as they grew closer and larger, their dark forms started to blot out entirely, the golden yellow hue of light that still streamed from the 'Hold the Scales and balance' goal posts at the other end of the pitch.

However, instead of just waiting for this wall of Evil to roll over them, the four children, surprising even themselves, all moved together and rushed forward at the same Time.

'Tally ho!' Called Peter at the top of his voice, rushing forward.

'Yahoo!' Cried James, starting to run.

Sue just screamed as loud as she could, but was not really sure why, as she felt that these things did not frighten her all that much now. But then, Sue was still really angry at the way they had treated Ozzy and ran forward as quickly as she could with the others.

'Waha!' Shouted Abdul, running quickly forward and the four children headed on a direct and almost immediate, collision course with the Evil Dark Shadows.

Surprised at the children's response, the Dark Shadows Bogey-men slowed for a moment. Then they became more menacing and louder than ever, lunging forward at full speed.

With a few seconds to spare before an inevitable impact, there suddenly arose the most strange roar of wind.

Sue, Abdul Peter and James, looked up at the Dark Shadows, to see each one of these horrible creatures suddenly fly harmlessly skyward, right over their heads.

'What on Earth?' The four children all exclaimed. They span around to see the whole Dark Shadows football team being lifted into the air, and each being carried by a single flying, smiley mouthed skateboard and it's riders.

The large array of children riding these skateboards, had all bent downward and grabbed one each of these Evil creatures by their collars. Now, with the children carrying them beneath their smiley mouthed skateboards, each Shadow was thrown directly between the 'Tip the Scales un-balance Time' goal posts.

One by one, a skateboard would then suddenly veer upwards after dropping it's unsavoury load, to allow the next to pass. Following the Dark Cavern walls each smiley mouthed skateboard trailed the next, travelling around the large chamber, in a single, unbroken chain.

'Now that really is how things should be in Time!' Said Sandy, helping Ozzy from the floor and dusting him down.

## Times Sword Of Damocles -
## (Fate In The Balance & The Final Countdown)

'Human children of the Planet Earth, helping each other!' Spluttered Ozzy.

Patriot, standing at the soccer pitch edge, looked around the huge cavern, he was searching for and just managed to catch a glimpse of the Evil Furtive Von Flatulence. This odious little creature was still shuffling urgently sideways, in the attempt to make good his escape.

'Hey!' Pat tapped Monty with his elbow. 'That smelly little Evil guy. He is going to get away Buddy!'

Monty looked quickly toward the other end of the soccer pitch and frowned in disdain.

'The bounder!' He muttered, but then he thought quickly. 'I think we should send someone to follow him!'

Monty looked at his mobile phone and pressed the clearly marked 'camera mode' button. A single, small blinking eye appeared directly out of the mobile phones top.

'Listen!' Said Monty firmly, talking to the eye. 'Mobile Buddy phone. Track that Evil bounder for us!'

Monty then pressed another button marked 'walk' sitting right next to a 'talk' icon. Instantly as he did this, two long, hairy chicken like legs with large bulbous knees appeared from the mobile phone sides. Monty lifted the small device and then threw the mobile phone, as hard as he possibly could, toward the Vitamin room doorway.

Just at the same moment Furtive Von Flatulence disappeared through this exit doorway, the mobile phone landed, it's two feet started to run most furiously as soon as they had hit the ground, the mobile phone then ran through the doorway, to closely follow the exiting Dark Voids Evil henchman.

Monty again pressed the small yellow clock on the front of his hat, the lid instantly sprang downward and shut. He turned to look past Patriot and to see how the children were getting along.

'I say old thing!' He said happily. 'Looks like the young sprogs have taken care of those Evil bounders already!'

Pat quickly twisted his head, to observe the last Dark Shadow being thrown unceremoniously into the 'Tip the Scales un-balance Time' goal posts.

'Yes sir re!' He replied and nodded his head in agreement.

Sue, Peter, Abdul and James, also intently followed the track of the very last skateboard to fly above them, and watched open mouthed, as the riders deposited the very last Dark Shadow into the goalmouth.

The dark, inky Void of this long goalpost howled loudly and very eerily, as the last Evil football player merged into it's total emptiness.

'Cool' blurted Sue, watching this last skateboard stop abruptly at the goal mouth.

## Times Sword Of Damocles -
## (Fate In The Balance & The Final Countdown)

The girl watched as a child rider looked curiously toward the small sign painted above this peculiar doorway, then reached out to grab it. It was quickly examined and then turned around, to be placed back onto the cavern wall.

'Trash storage area' read Abdul aloud, looking at the reversed sign hanging above the doorway. He looked quickly upward, watching with a smile on his face as the young rider and her skateboard accelerated skyward.

'Like, of no use to anyone' muttered James, who also read the sign.

Peter looked toward the sign and then turned to the others.

'What is Trash?' He asked.

'Rubbish old thing' replied Monty shuffling up behind Peter. 'It means, things that are no longer of a useful purpose. Master James is most correct in his estimation.'

The Penguin Person looked into the goalmouth that was now, gradually, becoming just a solid, thick wall, as was the rest of this huge cavern.

'You see, Evil' Monty continued. 'Is of no use to anyone, except the Dark Void, who of course, feeds upon it and requires, in it's most strong wishes, that only itself will exist for eternity.'

Monty moved forward, twitched his large red nose and long moustache, then said thoughtfully.

'The Void can and will, use any means possible to effect the aim of releasing itself from banishment.' He turned to the children and scratched his chin. ' And the only thing stopping it from doing so - Is you!'

'And all of those folks!' Interrupted Pat, pointing to the other skateboard riders laughing together and circling the huge cavern. 'Yes sir re - All you young folks, put together!'

'Well -' Noted Abdul, watching the goalmouth now close entirely to a solid wall. 'We must find this Void and defeat it - The Brain or Soul, whatever it's Evil may be made of.'

'Hey! - Where is that little guy?' Asked James looking around.

'Yes' Sue also looked around. 'He was the leader of those Shadow things. 'Where has he gone?'

'Maybe through the place where he entered' pondered Peter, looking toward the strong, golden yellow light still streaming through the 'Hold the Scales and balance' goal posts.

'Ah!' Sandy shuffled behind Abdul. 'But you have scored the goal with History and Wisdom!' He tapped Abdul on the back. 'Where Peace and Hope goes strong. Evil cannot enter!'

'Absolutely!' Agreed Monty. 'Besides old fruit's, we have a chap after him at this very moment.' He shuffled past the children. 'Follow me! We shall see what has developed!'

## Times Sword Of Damocles -
## (Fate In The Balance & The Final Countdown)

The children and Penguin People all made their way to the 'Vitamin Power Library room' entrance.

'Come on down old things!' Called Monty to the children, each flying with a Cartoon Buddy around the cavern as he reached the entrance. 'We will need all your help!'

'Er - ' Enquired James peering through this doorway. 'What is that?'

Sue also looked through the doorway, toward the huge spiral staircase.

'Yes - What is that?' She exclaimed, as she could see two, long, chicken like hairy legs, complete with bulbous knees, sticking out from under a large book.

Monty shuffled quickly forward, entering into an ominous, Vitamin Power Library room and removed the large dark book from the object that lay sprawled under it. Revealing a knocked out mobile Buddy phone that had been half hidden under this book, he bent forward and picked up the motionless device.

Monty's monocle, through which he examined the mobile phones chicken like legs dangling loosely from his hand, twitched, as much as his moustache did in disgust.

'Cecil' cried the small Penguin Person. 'What has that absolute cad done to you?'

'Your phones named Cecil' asked James, looking over Monty's hat and toward the small device. He turned with a big grin on his face and looked at Sue. She just shook her head in disbelief and smiled back at him.

'Hey!' Called Patriot, shuffling forward and standing by the side of Monty. 'Well take a look here!'

Pat bent downward and picked up an object from the floor. He held the oblong shape upward in his hand so Monty could see it, and quipped.

'Looks like an assault and no battery Buddy!'

Monty eyed the oblong battery through his glistening monocle and flipped the Buddy phone over.

'Thank you old thing!' He said with a nod, accepting the battery from Pat and pushing it firmly into the receptacle on the phones back. 'Maybe we can now shed some light on where that bounder has gone.'

Cecil suddenly puffed back into life, the thin hairy legs kicking the air as if he was still trying to run, and his single eye blinking rapidly.

'Relax Buddy!' Comforted Patriot, as Cecil came around from his sudden assault and battery failure. 'You are OK now.'

Monty tilted Cecil the mobile phone, so Pat and all the others could see the small screen on the phone's body. Monty pressed a tiny button and the screen burst into light, revealing the first, of a set of clear pictures.

In the first picture, the Evil Furtive Von Flatulence could be seen from the rear, running at full shuffling speed toward the spiral staircase.

## Times Sword Of Damocles -
## (Fate In The Balance & The Final Countdown)

In the second picture, the dark little character could be seen moving quickly up the spiral staircase.

In the third picture, Von Flatulence had quite clearly noticed Cecil following him as he stared toward the cameras eye.

In the fourth picture, Von Flatulence was seen pulling a book at random from the library wall.

In the fifth picture, this large book became larger in the screen as it hurtled downward toward Cecil.

In the sixth picture, the book had practically covered the small screen as it was imminently about to flatten the mobile Buddy phone.

In the seventh picture, Monty himself was pictured and was photographed sitting comfortably on a deck chair, sitting at the edge of a small hole in the Antarctic ice.

A small fishing rod stood upright in front of him resting on a stick, that dangled a thin line into the water below the hole. Monty was wearing what appeared to be a large pair of Union flag coloured shorts, his equally coloured jacket, dangling loosely from the chairs side. He was holding a glass of lemonade, from which a thin straw protruded and was pictured sipping through this straw while reading a magazine called Penguin People Chill Out Monthly.

'Er - Holiday snap!' Exclaimed Monty in embarrassment. 'From a set of other pictures stored in Cecil's memory.' He turned the screen off, very quickly, by re-pressing the tiny button.

'Looks like that Evil little feller took the stairs Buddy!' Noted Pat, a thin grin at Monty's embarrassment emanating from beneath his large red nose.

'Lets go after him!' Demanded Sue, who, along with the others, watched while Monty replaced Cecil into his Hold All Things Receptacle.

'Yes come on!' Agreed James, moving forward toward the spiral staircase.

Peter and Abdul also rushed toward the staircase and all the four friends started to quickly climb the many large steps upward.

'Wait!' Interrupted Monty shuffling as quickly as he could toward the staircase. 'We must first remove these books from the Vitamin Power library Room. Or the Dark Voids Power, will be far to great to defeat.'

'Yeah' agreed Pat, following Monty closely. He looked upward and strained his neck toward the ceiling, that lay a great distance above the spiralling, book lined staircase. 'We will need a whole lot of folks to do that.'

'Yes' agreed both Sandy and Ozzy, the two Penguin People following Pat and Monty to the staircase.

'But assistance, it would appear, is at hand' continued Sandy and he turned, with a shuffle, to look back toward the packed Vitamin Power Library doorway.

This Evil doorway was by now positively brimming with the faces of many smiling children, each standing with their own Penguin Person Buddy.

# Times Sword Of Damocles -
## (Fate In The Balance & The Final Countdown)

James had rushed impulsively up the spiralling steps to follow the Voids Evil Henchman, then he stopped for a moment, with eyes squinted, James looked upward at the seemingly endless tube like shelving structure that was filled with books.

It surrounded the spiralling staircase, heading skyward above the Vitamin Power Library Room, while allowing just enough of a gap, so as to see the cavern ceiling, far away in the distance.

'I agree!' James said loudly, he turned to Sue who stood on the step behind him. 'How about forming a human chain and passing the books down one by one.'

Leaning forward, James reached over the cold spiralling metal rail of this huge staircase and pulled a book at random from the tube shaped wall.

'If we make a chain!' He called downwards to the others. 'We can remove these books, one by one and pass them along the line.'

'Yes - Seems cool to me' replied Sue, accepting the heavy book from James. She passed it down the next step to Abdul.

'That would seem to be a much more effective way of transferring all these books' replied the boy, accepting the heavy object.

Abdul looked down at Peter and passed him the book.

'Here' he said and gave a nod of his head.

'One agrees! ' Nodded Peter right back, accepting the book.

Peter looked over the cold metal rail and peered downward, holding up the book toward the many smiling faces of all colours shapes and sizes that filled the Vitamin Power Library doorway.

'Come on!' He shouted. 'Pass it on!'

With an enormous and very sudden clamour of shouting voices, all the children rushed forward. With the momentum of moving children rushing past them, Monty, Patriot, Sandy and Ozzy were automatically buffeted to the side of this huge spiral staircase.

'Excellent!' Called out Monty toward the other Penguin People who had all tottered back and forth on their lace less shoes as the children rushed passed and started to clamber up the staircase. 'Excellent!'

'Human Kids working together against the Evil Void!' exclaimed Patriot, finishing Monty's sentence, while his hat slid over a twitching, large red nose and then his hat tilted sideways. 'As a team!' Pat spluttered.

'Quite!' Retorted Sandy, moving his head backward and forward quickly, while observing the many different forms of human children rushing past him.

The small Penguin Person watched them, as each, one by one, followed the other to rush up the spiral staircase toward where Peter and the others were standing.

## Times Sword Of Damocles -
## (Fate In The Balance & The Final Countdown)

With a smile, the first human child to reach Peter accepted the heavy book and passed it down toward the next, that stood on the step, directly behind her.

'Good on yeah!' Called out Ozzy, looking upward to follow the path of a now continuous line of books that were being quickly passed, one by one, down the staircase and along the human chain.

Each heavy book that had been removed from the wall, bounced downward along this hand held human chain and travelled quickly toward the end of it.

Sue followed their path intently between passing the books down.

'But where are they going to go when they reach the end of the line?' Sue asked in concern, while passing the next heavy book to Abdul.

Before the boy could reply, there was an ear piercing scream of a whistle that filled the cavern, and vibrated around the dark walls.

'Ah! - Here we are!' Called out Monty and he twitched his large round red nose toward the noise, that became louder and louder by the second.

'That sounds like -' Spluttered James, hardly believing his own ears.

'Like a steam train -' Interrupted Peter loudly, and unexpectedly agreeing with the unspoken thoughts of James. He watched intently as a beam of light shone brightly through the dark cavern wall entrance of the 'Your Fate and Time is in the balance' room and toward whatever had arrived and screeched to a halt beyond it.

'The Train Of Thought has arrived!' Cried Monty to all the children and he pointed toward a most strange sight. 'There!' He smiled, looking beyond the doorway and into the next cavern where a stationary, sparkling locomotive that positively shimmered with golden light pulled to a halt.

There were no rails that could be seen under this strange locomotive that were set into the stone cavern floor, only the single row of seemingly endless, open topped and equally shimmering carriages that trailed from the locomotive in a straight and dutiful line could be seen.

No driver stood at the controls of this peculiar train, but the train still puffed and grunted with energy and seemed ready to move at a moments notice.

'Fill the Train Of Thought with your books children!' Called out Monty, shuffling forward. 'The Peace Train will only move forward when you have completed your human chain and removed the dark power of hate from these shelves!'

Each of the Penguin People stood back and nodded in satisfaction, all were watching the human children, who suddenly continued their chain and passed the line of books forward toward the Peace Train Of Thought.

Monty's nose twitched and his monocle beamed with light.

'It is powered, don't you know -' he said looking toward James. 'By the pure energy, that only human children working together in Peace can create.'

His moustache twitched, and a thin smile appeared from beneath his large red nose.

## Times Sword Of Damocles -
## (Fate In The Balance & The Final Countdown)

'Yes, a first class effort' Monty muttered, as he heard from inside each of these sinister dark books an eerie cry emanate, as one by one, each book was passed into the golden yellow hue of shimmering light from the Train Of Thought carriages.

As every carriage became quickly filled the train itself moved slowly forward, so that the next and following carriage could also be filled. Within next to no Time the locomotive had slowly travelled so far forward that it, itself, entered through the illuminated Goal-posts Of Justice and each carriage that had been filled, followed it into the light.

Giving out an array of the most painful, and sinister of howls, the Powerful Spirit that had lay within each Evil deed noted throughout History and had then been encased within the pages of each book, to feed the Evil Dark Void, now dissipated, with a trailing eerie cry, as the carriages of light containing them left the dark cavern forever.

'Come on!' Ordered James, who could not see or hear all this happening from where he stood, as he was nearing the top and end of the long spiral staircase.

He called out again to the others.

'I can see a doorway at the top!' James moved forward and raced up the last set of steps.

Sue looked down toward Abdul and Peter.

'Lets go follow him!' She shouted. 'The other kids are doing just fine!'

'OK' replied Abdul and handed his last book to Peter.

'Yes! - We are a team!' Beamed Peter, smiling at Abdul and Sue. Then he handed his book to the next person in line. 'Please finish the last few shelves.' Peter, smiled at the girl who had accepted the book. She smiled right back at him and nodded.

'Hey!' The voice of James now came from the very top of the spiral staircase. 'Quick there is something strange here!'

The footwear of Sue, Abdul and Peter clattered loudly on the spiral staircase metal steps, as they hurried upward toward James.

'Look here!' Exclaimed James excitedly. He turned, allowing the three other children who had by now reached his side, to examine the strange, electronic device which stood in front of him.

'See -' He said, pointing to a large, triangular control panel, that was embedded into the solid cavern wall. 'It is some sort of computer terminal.'

James then moved slowly sideways, toward an ominous, solid and closed metal doorway next to the electronic device, which carried a red, frowning face, with eyes of fire.

'I do not like the look of that' he muttered and James scratched his chin in thought.

# Times Sword Of Damocles -
## (Fate In The Balance & The Final Countdown)

Sue, moving right next to James, quickly felt her feet clatter uncertainly, on the large square platform at the top of the staircase on which James stood.

'What are those controls for?' She asked inquisitively, while at the same moment, instinctively tapping the floor to test how safe the platform was underfoot, which now seemed quite solid enough.

Sue slowly eyed the small, illuminated screens, that flickered with light and a single, large keyboard below them.

'It must open the door' mused Abdul, squeezing next to Sue and also peering at the device.

Peter stopped, then looked past the shoulders of Abdul and Sue. He noted how the screen suddenly flickered with letters and words.

'It may contain some sort of instruction in how to effect entry past that doorway.' Peter then looked at the solid, dark door, that carried the single word, Enter, in blood red. 'One would hazard a guess, that just pushing the door, would prove a most fruitless exercise.'

'Mm -' James agreed and he studied the flickering computer screens. He then noticed and read aloud, words that were now starting to cross a long, thin screen.

'It is for you alone to press your own key, take your own choice. The balance of life is already turned on. With the minutes that only you alone own, you must be a judge only to yourself. Could you choose wisely. Could you choose wrong. Think, be both aware and beware. That within one minute, a minute man's end, levels all, that will have been right, or all, that will have been wrong.'

'That does not make any sense' huffed Sue, scratching her chin in thought.

'No' agreed Abdul also a little bemused. He watched the words trail sideways from the screen and then observed, more words appear gradually from the screens centre. 'Look at that!' He cried.

Abdul read this set of words aloud.

'Times sword of Damocles.' He shook his head. 'What is Times sword of Damocles?' He asked the others. 'Any ideas?'

'Well -' Chipped in Peter, 'We have learned about Damocles in school.'

He remembered back to his school lessons.

'Damocles was a chap in an old Greek Legend. He kept saying how the King, a chap called Dionysius, was always so happy and powerful. Probably was an awful bore and got on the Kings nerves a bit, I suspect. So the King seated him at a banquet and placed a sword over his head, suspended by a single hair. The sword could drop at any Time of course, or not. The King was making the point that there is possible imminent danger, even in Times of happiness. So never be too sure of yourself as to be really self centred and arrogant, I suppose.'

# Times Sword Of Damocles -
## (Fate In The Balance & The Final Countdown)

'I reckon we should push some buttons and get that door open' said James, moving toward the control panel.

Sue agreed and moved forward with James. Peter and Abdul nodded toward each other, then also moved forward.

'Start and enter!' Exclaimed James, looking at a large red button on the control panel that was marked with these words in small yellow writing.

'Stop and Go' read Sue, looking at the yellow words on another red button, directly below the one James was looking at.

Peter, for his part, looked at the large letters above the control panel.

'Enter Gate Of Fate' he read them aloud and thought deeply for a moment, pondering the words that had crossed the screen beforehand.

'So -' He pondered further. 'Although one may choose their own fate, by pressing their own choice of buttons, in the end, everyone is equal and level.'

'Look! - We cannot all just stand here debating things all day!' Interrupted Abdul impatiently. 'We must press on!' He moved quickly toward the control panel. 'The most obvious choice to open the door, is that.' And he pressed a button marked, 'Start and Enter.'

'Stop!' Ordered a concerned voice from behind the four children which made James, Abdul, Sue and Peter all whirl around instantly.

Standing at the top of the spiral staircase was a puffing Sandy, who was closely followed by Monty, Pat and Ozzy.

The Penguin People had all rushed up the staircase, but were not quite in the nick of Time. They moved toward the children and then looked past them, as the dark doorway creaked sideways open and an Evil wind roared from the unseen cavern beyond it.

'The Gate Of Fate has been opened!' Cried Sandy, his nose twitching rapidly.

Before the children could ask the single question, one that was on all of their minds,(what the Gate of Fate actually was) A sinister voice trailed from the control panel and made everyone turn toward it.

With an unfeeling but quite soft tone, the voice began to repeat the same sentence over and over.

'The Final Countdown has begun - The Final Countdown has begun - The Final Countdown has begun.'

'I think I now know what those words meant by a minute man's end, and all that other stuff!' Gulped James, turning his head back from the unfeeling, repetitive voice, trailing from the control panel.

He stared at the cylindrical centre of the spiral staircase which now vibrated, and started to detach itself from the metal steps surrounding it.

'Your own choice to judge whether to create Peace or War - It is a Missile! - And you have just started it.'

# Times Sword Of Damocles -
## (Fate In The Balance & The Final Countdown)

The others standing on the platform, all automatically turned their heads at the same moment to see what James was looking at.

'I think' Noted Abdul. 'That we are all now, in a large degree of danger!'

'Heck!' Exclaimed Patriot Penguin Person, recognising instantly the quite unmistakable, to him anyway, form that was taking shape from the spiral staircase centre. ' I thought those things were history!'

Patriot shuffled forward and twitched his nose toward the long, thin, cylinder shape. Pat then very quickly, reeled off some of his history notes.

'START – Or - Strategic Arms Reduction Treaty - Signed by the United States President George Bush and Soviet leader Mikhail Gorbachev in 1991. It was an agreement between the worlds super powers, designed to reduce the number of intercontinental Ballistic Nuclear missiles.

The threat of both sides retaining missiles of Apocalyptic power, that would destroy the whole planet if ever used, had maintained the balance of World Peace, but had also left the Sword Of Damocles over the entire human world, with a constant and very real threat to all human existence.'

Monty twitched his large red nose and interrupted Pat.

'Previously, in 1989 the 45 year 'Cold War' between East and West, that had been in place since the end of the human second world war ended. The Berlin Wall was removed and the Eastern Soviet Union led Warsaw Pact was replaced by separate, democratically elected governments.

The test of Time was almost on the road to being passed, for the first Time in human history.'

'So - What exactly is that pencil thing?' Asked Sue, looking toward the steaming cylinder.

'That pencil thing -' Answered Pat, twitching his nose. 'Is a Minute man intercontinental Ballistic Nuclear missile - Or ICBM for short.'

He shook his head in contempt for the device.

'With a Nuclear warhead capable of unspeakable destructive power, and a range of about 6300 miles.'

'Still looks like a pencil to me' observed Sue, not impressed.

'No!' Said Monty, shuffling forward and he moved toward the cylinder.

'Er - No what Buddy?' Asked Pat, watching Monty pass him.

'Not a nuclear warhead inside that old thing!' He tapped the side of the vibrating cylinder. 'This is the Dark Voids Sword Of Damocles! - It's own constant threat over the human race!'

'Like what?' Asked Abdul. 'What does it contain then - What sort of threat?'

'Some sort of gunpowder?' Chipped in Peter. 'I would hazard a guess.'

'Well -' Asked James. 'Is it empty, or something like that?'

'Tell us the answer!' Called out Sue. 'The final countdown is happening, we need to know what is going to happen!'

## Times Sword Of Damocles -
## (Fate In The Balance & The Final Countdown)

'I understand' said Sandy shuffling forward. 'The minute man is far from an empty shell.' He moved next to Monty and Pat. 'It is the very spirit of the beast - Is that not so my friends?'

'Quite!' Snapped Monty in agreement. 'You see - The centre of this spiral staircase held together and channelled the very essence of the surrounding Vitamin Power Library Rooms dark books. The Evil spirit of human bad deeds that was contained within the books, ran up the spine of the staircase (this cylinder that is) and moved directly up into the Dark Void, to feed the Evil blighter.'

'So like – Um -' Interrupted Pat. 'When the final countdown ends and that cylinder explodes, the Evil spirit's are kind of released, all in a heap.'

'That has got to be the Time, when, **A**ll **R**ight **M**inded **A**nd **G**ood **E**ducated, **D**issolve **D**iscrimination, **O**bliging **N**ations!' Exclaimed Ozzy, remembering words from the Cartoon Buddy Legend book. 'Look!' He pointed. 'Those initials are painted on the sides of the Cylinder!'

The four children looked intently, as red letters formed visibly from within the cylinders thin walls.

'ARMAGEDDON' Sue read the initials aloud. 'Isn't that the end of the World, or Judgement day, something like that?'

'Yes - The Spirit of destruction or of Peace which is one of human choice!' Answered Monty, twitching his nose.

'However!' He continued. 'The Dark Void uses the wrong choices that humans make to increase it's power!'

'Well the clock is ticking' observed Abdul, feeling a little upset. 'I have pressed the wrong button - Start and Enter - It has set that thing to go off and I feel terrible.'

'Nonsense young human!' Interrupted Sandy. 'All is not lost if you should make a wrong choice.' He moved toward the boy. 'Things are constantly flowing in the wind of change. The ability to repent and alter ones mind for human Peace and Love, is all that really matters in Time.'

'Well' said James, patting Abdul on the back. 'Lets see what we can all do to put things right!'

'Yes!' Agreed Peter and he moved toward the control panel. 'Maybe to press another button may change things.'

Sue felt the platform that had seemed so solid underfoot before, now start to suddenly sway and rock.

'I think we had better move quickly!' She urged. 'This place is falling apart!'

Everyone moved toward the cavern wall as the platform rocked violently sideways, and the huge cylinder became even more detached from it's holding area, it's sides steaming with anger.

## Times Sword Of Damocles -
### (Fate In The Balance & The Final Countdown)

Abdul looked through the Gate Of Fate doorway. He could see a large cliff face, dark and shimmering with red light just beyond the triangular entrance. Another huge cliff face lay far beyond the first, with an endless drop in between.

'We need the skateboards to take us across that gap!' He called hopelessly. 'We have no chance of jumping across it.'

'There is no Time for the skateboards!' Replied Monty, watching the platform at his feet start to drop downwards. 'They are too far away!'

'Doesn't Time fly when you are having fun!' Called out Patriot, being, along with all the others who stood on the platform, tilted roughly into the cavern wall.

'No!' Shouted a definite response from James, who hit the cavern wall painfully. 'You call this fun?'

'Excellent' Exclaimed Monty, who proceeded to pull the small yellow clock from the front of his hat. He watched as Pat, Sandy and Ozzy automatically did like wise.

'Is there really Time for clocks?' Asked Sue, crashing painfully into the control panel embedded within the cavern wall.

The Penguin People, in complete unison, quickly threw the small yellow clocks onto the falling floor at their feet. Although the four children were by now rocking back and forth on the swaying platform, their eyes were all transfixed to the yellow clocks, and the very strange transformation that was suddenly occurring to each of them.

'Now that is cool!' Noted Sue, watching the most strange thing happening.

Each of the small yellow clocks had stopped quite suddenly just before hitting the platform floor. Then, like dry sponges absorbing water, they grew quickly to form four, large round discs.

To the children's surprise, from the sides of these four discs a set of wings unexpectedly sprouted and they hovered, with wings gently outstretched, as birds gliding in flight.

'Hop on folks!' Pat pointed to the discs and hopped onto the nearest one at his feet. 'No Time for fussing!' he said, pulling James gently toward the disc that he now stood upon.

James automatically hopped onto the disc and found, as it had been with the Penguin Persons flying skateboard, his feet stuck fast to the strange, hovering clock.

'Come on chaps!' Called out Monty, hopping onto the disc at his own feet while the platform staggered sideways. He looked toward Sue, nose twitching. 'And of course, Ladies!'

Sue jumped onto a disc hovering above the floor and Penguin Person Ozzy followed closely.

Peter joined Monty on his disc, while Abdul was pulled forward onto Sandy's disc, by a gentle tug of his arm from the small creature.

## Times Sword Of Damocles -
## (Fate In The Balance & The Final Countdown)

It was just in Time, as the platform creaked angrily then hurtled downward, twisting upright, while it headed toward the ground, far below.

'Here we go! - Tally Ho!' Cried Monty and the disc beneath his feet quickly flapped it's wings, heading with two riders on board toward the Gate Of Fate Entrance.

The other three discs moved at exactly the same moment, hurtling toward the triangular entrance. Each rider felt the Evil wind surge toward them from the doorway, as they in turn, surged toward it.

'Duck!' Called out James, feeling Patriot cling tightly to his legs, while his disc flew through the Gate Of Fate. The triangular entrance had seemed to grow instantly smaller as his disc passed through it, almost as if it were trying to close, but could not.

'Duck!' Responded Pat instantly. 'No, I am a Penguin Person Buddy!'

The small creature turned his head back, to see the triangular entrance shrink suddenly.

'Oh - I see what you mean!' He said, feeling a little foolish.

Following James, Abdul and Sue, Sandy and Ozzy quickly ducked their heads to fly through the Gate Of Fate and over the huge drop, between the cliff faces beyond it.

'Stop!' Ordered Peter, a split second before his disc flew through the Gate Of Fate.

Monty was pushed with some force into the legs of Peter as the disc stopped abruptly.

'The other children!' Demanded Peter, turning his head toward the still falling platform below. 'We must help them!'

Peter watched the spiral staircase start to disintegrate and looked toward the huge cylinder. Horrified, he observed the children who had helped move the dark Books clinging desperately to the thin metal railings and staircase steps that had managed to still surrounded it.

'But the countdown is almost complete!' Responded Monty, hearing the unfeeling voice from the control panel continue loudly, but now with numbers. 'You are in danger!'

'Ten! - Nine! -' The numbers, loud and very cold, reverberated around the dark cavern chamber. 'Eight!'

'So are they!' Peter smiled at Monty. 'So are they' he said again.

Monty looked into Peters eyes, nodded his small head, and his moustache twitched. A thin smile appeared from beneath the bushy, dark line.

'So then! - Up and Away! - Save the day!' He shouted.

Their disc hurtled suddenly toward the steaming cylinder, and to where the first of the long spiralling line of children clung desperately onto a disintegrating metal rail.

## Times Sword Of Damocles -
## (Fate In The Balance & The Final Countdown)

Twisting around the huge cylinder Peter and Monty heard the unfeeling voice continue.

'Seven! - Six! - Five! -'

Peter suddenly observed a metal lever at the top of this spiral staircase that had previously been obscured by the platform. Above it, the word 'Down' was painted in bright yellow lettering.

It seemed to call out to Peter, but hurtling forward at beak neck speed Peter looked up, to see the face of the very last person at the end of the human chain, still standing at the top of the crumbling spiral staircase.

As she grew closer Peter could see fear in her eyes, and without a second thought, instinctively, Peter jumped forward, his feet instantly un-sticking from the flying disk.

'Peter!' Called out Monty, feeling the boy release from the grip that he held on his legs. He turned as the disc flew on and saw Peter falling downwards.

'Ah!' Shouted Peter, in some pain. His hands had caught the lever and it smashed downwards, with the force of his weight and gravity.

'Four! - Three! -' The unfeeling voice continued it's countdown, and with a sudden roar, this voice was momentarily drowned out by a huge metallic thud which sent the steps of the spiral staircase shooting forward, linking into a single, spiralling slide.

The children that had been standing on the staircase fell backwards, and all of them quickly slid down this slide, that flung each one, within a matter of seconds, out of the Vitamin Power Library Room and into the carriages of the Train Of Thought.

Beyond the Gate Of Fate, James, Abdul, Sue, Pat, Ozzy and Sandy, had heard the roar and metallic thud. Then the unfeeling voice from the control panel continue.

'Two! - One! -'

'Peter!' Their voices of concern were drowned out by the detonation of the huge cylinder beyond the Gate Of Fate triangular doorway.

An enormous blast of darkness lunged outward through the entrance, across the cliff faces and huge central drop, to crash with a roar into the disc riders beyond it.

'Ah!' The disc riders voices called out in the pitch darkness, and were quickly carried away as the blast enveloped the discs and flung their riders into the unknown darkness, of the Gate Of Fate.

## *Times Planet Wake Up Call - (Classroom Kids)*

In the real world, far beyond this Gate Of Fate and exterior darkness of a massive, all consuming, swirling Evil Void. The effects of an internal and Timeless struggle between Good and Evil were to be felt far and wide.

Immediately following the Sword Of Damocles detonation, a strange and extremely powerful electromagnetic pulse had swept across the planet, temporarily severing all power supplies to Planet Earth's electrical equipment.

In a clear blue sky out at open sea, a small red breasted robin, that was not noticed by busy humans, but like them, had been watching the Void's swirling darkness from afar, fell suddenly downward. Then, fluttering it's wings frantically, the small bird proceeded to hop steadily onto a long metalwork shelf that now lay at it's feet.

This long metalwork shelf was dotted with uncomfortable bulbous rivets and the red breasted robin hopped quickly back and forth to avoid them, while watching with interest, through thick glass window panes, events that were unfolding within a huge aircraft carriers bridge that was only now recovering from the vessels total loss of power.

The small red breasted bird observed that the Captain of this powerful vessel, was extremely concerned. Not least by the power failure, which had affected his entire ship, and the fact it had also rendered the united nations fleet powerless as well. But even more, by the sight of a huge wall of very dark water, that had suddenly spread toward his vessel and the other international fleet of ships that had accompanied it.

'Clear the Deck!' The ships Captain bellowed loudly, as he watched this huge wall of water spread ever closer, while lights now flickered back to the control panels as his ship regained power.

The Captain observed the swirling Dark Void start to visibly shrink upward from the clear blue ocean and sprawling landfall that it had just reached.

'Unfortunately' he thought to himself. 'This upward motion has caused a disturbance in the water that now threatens all the ships.'

The Captain stared again, hard, at the wall of water and thought, just for a moment, that he could see a face materialise in the dark, swirling foam.

'Evil eyes of fire!' He whispered to himself... 'And a grin of anger!'

He composed himself, and said aloud.

'Don't be so stupid man!'

The Captain looked to the deck and saw the last of his men run for cover before the colossal wave hit the vessel.

'We will have to surf this one out!' He stated quite calmly.

'But the other ships!' Exclaimed an officer, fiddling frantically with illuminated buttons. 'They are going to be swamped sir!'

With a rapid movement the Captain moved to one of the vessels windows, and stared at the array of much smaller ships, that followed in line, the huge aircraft carrier. There was no Time for **dis**cussion...

## Times Planet Wake Up Call - (Classroom Kids)

The Captain made an instant decision, it could possibly endanger his ship further, but it may protect those following that had no real chance of weathering the strange dark storm and wave.

'Hard a starboard!' He bellowed, and ordered his huge vessel to lumber to the right, attempting to shield the smaller ships that followed it.

Outside the bridge, a dark shadow suddenly fell behind the hopping, red breasted robin. It spread ominously and quickly across the glass window panel in front of the small bird.

The robin wheeled around and was suddenly confronted by an Evil looking Raven, a bird much bigger than itself, which pushed it's head forward menacingly.

Without a second thought, in an instant, the Raven smashed the robin with it's huge head and the small bird fell downward, to land painfully onto the deck of the huge aircraft carrier.

The Raven then pushed it's head toward the glass and watched the humans intently, completely ignoring the rivets which hurt the dark birds large feet.

While the dark bird watched events unfold on the bridge, a lone sailor, far below, stopped to pick up the stunned robin. Observing the small bird was in no state to fly, the sailor quickly pushed it into his tunic and rushed toward a watertight hatchway. It was just in the nick of Time. The incoming huge wave lashed over the huge vessel and sent it careering upward and sideways like a toy boat.

'Hold onto your hats gentleman!' Ordered the Captain in alarm, grabbing hold of his seat... 'This is going to be a rough one!'

The wave raised upward from the Ocean, and the Evil face that the Captain had seen was quite visible now, as it pounded the aircraft carrier and threw the ship into the air, making it lurch and tilt violently. Then, as suddenly as it had came, the wave vanished, dissipating quickly back into the flat, clear blue sea.

The Captain picked himself up from the floor to where he had fallen and rushed to the water drenched window.

'Strangest darn wave I ever saw!' He muttered, staring through the vessels water drenched windows.

With his eyes straining, the captain quickly searched the ocean and thankfully saw that no ships had been lost. But there were now more pressing things to be thought of, and he quickly demanded.

'I want a status report on damage! - Prepare to assist other ships if need be.'

Within the swirling Dark Void, someone was not so pleased at the events that had taken place.

'My little bird tells me!' Sneered the rather annoyed Evil Spirit. 'That those humans are, yet again, working together and not just thinking only about themselves!'

# Times Planet Wake Up Call - (Classroom Kids)

'Er - Yes Master' responded a cowering Furtive Von Flatulence, looking at a dark screen that was showing the vision through the Dark Ravens eyes as it sat outside the aircraft carriers bridge.

'They have again repulsed my Face of Adversity! - They are draining my power!' Snapped the Evil Spirit.

This face, with eyes of fire, looked directly and menacingly, at the squirming little character.

'What are you going to do about it!'

'I – Um -' Quivered Von Flatulence, not quite having an answer to the Evil Voids question.

The Void peered at him with an angry grin.

'Look!' It said sarcastically. 'The humans are working together to help one another in the Face of Adversity. You know how much I hate that. It is so draining on my will power.' The face with eyes of fire gave a huge huff. 'Find those that have removed my Vitamin Power note books and have removed the Sword Of Damocles from the Planet.'

The Evil Face grew in size and then shouted violently.

'That would be a good start, don't you think!'

'Yes oh master!' Responded Von Flatulence, holding onto his hat as a blast of hot air from the Voids mouth nearly blew him over. 'I shall seek to find them immediately!'

The Furtive little character backed toward the dark cavern doorway.

'And what shall I do when I find them oh Master?' He asked, suddenly thinking back to how he had been defeated at the football, or rather nose match.

The Evil Void grew even further in size, and then bellowed in it's most menacing, impatient voice...

'Destroy them of course!'

'Yes! - Yes! - Oh Master' Answered Von Flatulence and he slowly backed out of the softly illuminated cavern and entered into the pitch darkness of a seemingly endless, darkened corridor system.

While the vile, smelly little characters feet shuffled further into the reaches of darkness, the sound of his shoes echoed around and along the long, inky black corridors. Von Flatulence pondered his next move.

'What does the Void expect me to do?' He said, muttering sarcastically. 'How many bogey-men can one carry up each nostril?'

He pulled the lapels of his cloak further up to his face, protecting himself from a chilly, ill wind, that travelled these dark corridors of Time and Fate.

'I do not even have a skeleton staff to assist me these days!' He snapped, pulling his hat further down his small head.

'But - That is it!' He suddenly exclaimed, the hat movement forcing his single Evil brain cell to crash against the inside of his thick skull.

## Times Planet Wake Up Call - (Classroom Kids)

'A skeleton staff!' Von Flatulence very quickly moved forward.

Further along these long, twisting corridors, other figures moved painfully from the floor and stood to their feet.

'Is everyone all right?' Asked James, feeling a small bump on his forehead.

'AOK' responded Pat, straightening his hat in the half light that emanated from behind each long row of closed doorways, carved into the solid rock of these corridors.

'That was a rough ride!' Called out Abdul, helping Sandy to stand in his small, lace less shoes.

'What happened to Peter and Monty?' Asked Sue, feeling concerned for their welfare after the dark, powerful blast.

'It will all be fair dinkum sport!' Answered Ozzy, being pulled by Sue back to his feet. 'Those guys can look after themselves I reckon.'

Sandy bent down and picked up one of the three clocks that had by now, returned to their smaller size. He placed the small yellow clock that he had picked up from the darkened floor, back into the front of his hat. Then he bent down again, to pick up the remaining two clocks, handing one each to both Pat and Ozzy.

'Time and Fate are both parallel things!' Sandy stated, quite Philosophically. 'Like both Good and Bad. Light and darkness. For who can know what tomorrow may bring, as in Time, the corridors of fate will eventually help decide all things.'

'Right!' Agreed Pat. 'In the corridors of Fate, like everywhere else, everyone has the free choice to be good, or bad. But these corridors can, eventually, take all kinds of folk in strange, unknown directions.'

'Yeah - Even the best laid plans can go array!' Chipped in Ozzy. 'And that is because of the corridors of Fate. But they can also make life interesting and not quite so boring for everyone.'

'Well' said Sue, looking around. 'They are not boring - Dark, yes, defiantly - But where do we go from here?'

James moved toward one of the doors that a frame of light surrounded and emanated from.

'How about seeing what is behind here' he said, reaching out for a protruding key below the large shining door handle, that looked almost like a moon shape that he could just make out in the half light.

'Careful -' Exclaimed Abdul. 'Remember what happened when I pushed that button.' Moving next to James he added. 'We must be certain what will happen when you turn that Key, and open the door!'

Sandy tapped Abdul gently on the shoulder.

'My boy!' He said gently. 'When you pressed a button, the Gate of Fate had decided to open and let us all gain entry into it's corridors.'

He looked intently toward the key that was protruding from the doorway.

## Times Planet Wake Up Call - (Classroom Kids)

'The human choice, is to act upon their best intentions and feelings. The corridors will direct the rest, if they so please. So you did not make the wrong decision.'

The small Penguin Person then continued...

'You acted for Good. But the corridors of fate, seem to have decided another direction, for both Peter and Monty to take.'

He tapped Abdul again.

'If you had chosen 'Stop and Go', that would have meant that you would not have acted at all, then the corridors would have taken the Evil Void and all mankind, in a different, equally unknown direction.'

'So -' Sue broke a small, thoughtful silence, that followed Sandy's words and she smiled at the others. 'Do we turn the key or what, we have to decide.'

'I guess so' replied James, and he twisted the protruding key around and around, until it gave a dull, metallic click. He pulled on the round door handle, until the solid door creaked angrily, in full resentment at being opened.

James took a deep breath of anticipation and along with Abdul and Sue, peered into the brightly lit room beyond the dark corridor.

Pat, Sandy and Ozzy, instantly the doorway opened, shuffled forward, moving between their legs and entered into the light, from the darkness of the long corridor.

'It is a classroom!' Exclaimed the children, each saying their thoughts aloud and together all at once. They hurried forward into the room, following the three Penguin People inside.

'And look - Behind the desks' cried Abdul. 'I cannot believe my own eyes!'

Abdul rushed forward, quickly dodging past the three shuffling Penguin People that stood in front of him.

The boy then stopped, quite abruptly, directly in front of two of the rooms many small school desks, across which, the large figures that had caught his eye, lay dormant. These familiar figures, were both hunched forward in their seats, apparently fast asleep.

'These are my parents!' Abdul exclaimed excitedly. He reached forward to rouse the sleeping couple. 'Mother!' he cried out. Then 'Father!' But, to Abdul's surprise, his out stretched hand just travelled right through both the sleeping bodies. 'What?' He uttered, feeling quite shocked.

James and Sue both followed, rushing into the room past the Penguin People. Then they hurried past Abdul, heading toward other figures that were also sat at school desks in the same manner.

'These are my parents!' Said Sue in shock. She reached forward the same way as Abdul had done, to find that her hand also swept right through the sleeping figures.

## Times Planet Wake Up Call - (Classroom Kids)

'What is going on here?' Demanded James in concern, discovering that his hand, just like those of the others, moved through the sleeping figures that lay in front of him. 'These are my parents, but I cannot touch them, are they real?' He asked, turning toward the three Penguin People.

'It would seem!' Replied Sandy, twitching his large red nose. 'That they are as one would say, 'dead to the world', but to be really all alive and sleeping!'

He moved forward and examined further the figures at the desks.

'The Void would appear to have retained them all within a fifth dimension of measurement, not of real Time and Space, but somewhere in between.'

'Like ghosts you mean?' Asked Abdul, horrified.

'No!' Responded Pat quickly. He also moved forward toward the figures and stood beside Sandy. 'Not at all Buddy!'

Pat twitched his nose in thought.

'They are just held here, sleeping, by the Void. Where Time has stood still. Where it goes, neither forward, nor back.'

'Why?' Asked Sue. 'What could the Void possibly gain from doing this.'

Ozzy moved forward and held Sue's hand.

'To cause tears, and also, maybe, formulate a sense of hopelessness in the World' he said, sniffing the air with his nose. 'In the hearts of those' Ozzy continued. 'That can destroy it's ultimate aim of escaping from the shadows of banishment, by the Great Spirit of Peace and Light, to return and erase all of Time.'

'But!' Added Sandy. 'The Evil Void has underestimated an immense power carried within the very Spirit of hope, that has been given to all humans!' He turned toward the children... 'In you three the power is most strong!'

'But can we free them from this fifth dimension?' Asked Abdul, looking sadly at all the sleeping figures.

'You small humans!' Said Pat, again twitching his large red nose. 'Can do just about anything, if you have a mind and a heart to!'

Ozzy and Sandy quickly nodded in agreement.

'Well I am all for putting and keeping that old Dark Void back in it's cage!' Stated James, looking around this strange room. 'How do we start things rolling?'

He moved away from the desks, sadly, but knowing he could do no more right now.

'We need to get our folks freed from the fifth dimension too!'

Sandy nodded in agreement, and he moved toward the wall and a book case, that was filled with an array, of dusty old books.

'Legends' he said, noting that all the books, were marked with the same, single title.

## Times Planet Wake Up Call - (Classroom Kids)

Sandy then raised his hand and reached toward the books. With a thoughtful 'Hmm' Sandy noted how his hand passed through these books that were also not of the real world.

'Can anyone observe anything in this room that is of a solid form?' He asked, twitching his large red nose.

Everyone looked around and touched everything that they saw. No book, pencil, pen, even waste paper basket was of solid form, and every hand that had reached out to them just passed straight through.

'An odd sort of place sports!' Exclaimed Ozzy.

Sue agreed, then noticed the blackboard and a line words that had been chalked in small lettering there. She read aloud the words.

'Rule One. To measure and make futures path, faith to have the power of courage, love and unity, must be instilled within all rulers.'

'Hey -' Said James, listening to Sue and automatically reaching for an object that he, or anyone else, had not yet tried to pick up. 'This is a ruler.' He then picked up a long, transparent measuring stick, used to make straight lines. 'And it is solid.'

Abdul also picked up a ruler and found it too, was solid of substance.

'Wow!' He exclaimed, as the transparent measuring stick suddenly lit up with a bright, yellow glow of light.

Sue picked up a rule stick too and immediately, it illuminated, as did that of the stick James was holding.

'Cool' she said, twisting the stick, back and fourth to see the light shimmer.

'Kind of strange?' Mused Pat. 'Seems that you folks, have installed some power into those things now.'

Sandy moved forward and looked at the illuminated rulers.

'Yes!' He agreed. 'The measure of the future, will be made from those, that will make the future, the small humans.'

There was a sudden, loud, rippling nose coming from the corridor outside, inside the room everyone heard it and looked at each other.

'Was that - What I thought it was?' Asked James.

'Sounded like someone breaking wind' replied Abdul, turning toward where the sound had originated from.

'The Evil little guy!' Shouted the children, and all together they rushed toward the doorway, rulers still in hand.

Furtive Von Flatulence, shuffling furtively along the long half lit corridor, stopped dead in his tracks.

'So - I have found you!' He sneered menacingly.

The three children bundled from the classroom door, and entered into the corridor to confront this smelly little character that they had been chasing.

'Yes – Well - You have found us!' Snapped James. 'Time to rumble Buddy!'

'Rumble!' Snapped Von Flatulence... 'Indeed!'

# Times Planet Wake Up Call - (Classroom Kids)

The Evil little character ripped a small piece of cloth from his cloak and threw it to the floor. The corridor shook most violently as this small piece of cloth reached the ground, and Von Flatulence sneered.

'Meet my friend... I call him Rag!'

With the corridor shaking all around them, the children looked to the floor and saw the most horrible sight arise from where the piece of cloth from Evil Von Flatulence's Cloak had fallen.

'Good Grief!' Exclaimed James, quickly stumbling backward one step with a look of absolute shock on his face.

'Not Good Grief!' Snapped Von Flatulence, flickering his fingers back and forth, toward an emerging, frightening creature, almost as if playing an invisible piano... 'Bad Grief!'

Through a single, thick and choking dust cloud, that had quite suddenly fallen from the corridor ceiling, everyone in the creepy corridor of fate, blinked their dry eyes and watched on most intensely, as the small piece of fallen cloth grew and grew, to finally form into a hunched, bony and loathsome form, that thrust forward it's menacing, red eyed skull, toward all the children.

'A skeleton!' Cried Abdul, staring from behind the shoulder of James. He also stumbled backward, gripping his ruler tightly and holding it out in front of him, as his only from of defence.

'Not so fast!' Ordered Von Flatulence, laughing sarcastically while watching James, Abdul and Sue stumble away from this rather frightening creature. 'You have yet to meet my other friend!'

The repulsive little odour, reached forward with his hand and ripped a single gleaming rib, from the skeletons bony and writhing structure.

'And here!' Bellowed Von Flatulence most triumphantly, throwing the rib to the floor. 'Is my friend - Bones!'

Dust again fell from the violently shaking corridor ceiling, while this single, shimmering rib, transformed, as had the piece of cloth, into another Evil, red eyed skeleton.

James looked forward with squinted eyes, right through the cloud which whirled around his head, and obscured his vision with a dry, painful dustiness. He took yet another step backward, observing both skeletons raise upward and quite suddenly move forward toward him.

The corridor of fate vibrated most violently and clouds of chocking dust whirled around it's long, dimly lit interior as the skeletons moved.

James, Abdul and Sue coughed the dust away, clearing their eyes quickly as they stumbled backwards. They saw the dust reach the ground at their feet, first to cloak the Earth as a swirling carpet, then most unexpectedly, disappear beneath it.

'My Skeleton Staff will soon have you attended to!' Wailed Von Flatulence and he laughed aloud, an Evil laugh.

## Times Planet Wake Up Call - (Classroom Kids)

The Evil Voids henchman then glared toward his Evil creatures from beneath a crooked hat.

'Teach these humans a lesson in Evil that they will never forget! - Sorry!' He snapped, eyes closing together... 'Survive!'

'Wow!' Cried out James, as he bundled backwards onto Abdul and Sue, and everyone crashed to the floor, just outside the classroom door.

A large red nose appeared from within the doorway and sniffed toward the fallen children.

'You folks going to just lay down and take this?' Asked Pat, leaning forward from within just inside the classroom. 'Or what -'

Another red nose suddenly appeared, sniffed, then sneezed away the dust from the head of Abdul.

'It might be wise' asked Sandy, stifling yet another sneeze from within his bulbous red nose. 'To use ones rulers, in unison... Would it not?'

Ozzy added to the duo, poking his red nose forward toward Sue.

'Come on girl - All you Kids together!' He sniffed.

The skeletons raged forward and lunged toward the fallen children, red eyes ablaze.

'You are finished!' Sneered Von Flatulence. 'Good is defeated! - Forever!'

James, Abdul and Sue looked momentarily toward the Penguin People, just for a second, watching a smile appear from beneath each of these strange creatures red noses.

'Together!' Shouted the children, turning their heads toward the oncoming Evil eyed skeletons.

James, Abdul and Sue, then quickly thrust forward their rulers in front of them with outstretched arms, just as the creatures of darkness came baring down toward them.

Within a split second, the rulers touched together and light filled the corridors of fate.

An unexpected, thunderous crack, followed a sudden and brilliant illumination flowing from the joined rulers. The almost deafening, overwhelming sound, then rolled, like an unstoppable wave, past the doorway where the three penguin people characters were standing.

Pat, Sandy and Ozzy, hit by this powerful vibration, automatically reeled backward on their lace less shoes, and held tightly onto their hats.

'The crack of Doom!' Cried Von Flatulence excitedly, his Evil eyes temporarily blinded by the strong light. He opened them quickly and blinked, fully expecting to see his skeletons having destroyed these intruders of his masters Evil domain.

'Ah!' The children all screamed, and Von Flatulence smiled in a quite loathsome delight.

## Times Planet Wake Up Call - (Classroom Kids)

But then, to his own horror, Flatulence observed an Evil skeleton that had lunged forward onto the outstretched illuminated rulers, stop suddenly, reel backwards, then shatter into many bony, shiny pieces.

'Looks like the Crack Of a New Dawn to me Buddy!' Shouted Pat, poking his red nose from the classroom doorway and twitching it toward Von Flatulence.

'Oops!' He twitched again, as large chunks of useless bones flew past his cap and clattered against dusty walls.

'Er -' Von Flatulence stepped quickly backwards. 'Um - ' The Evil little character uncontrollably expelled a little odour, as he watched his other red eyed skeleton, also lunge forward. It touched the united rulers and violently exploded. Firstly into a shower of scattering bone, then, into a fluttering of flaming rags that fell gracefully to Earth.

'Time... Too!...' Von Flatulence crept even further backwards. 'Hot foot it away!' And he shuffled down the corridors of fate, which flickered with the flaming rags that he crumpled underfoot.

James, Abdul and Sue rose to their feet.

'After him!' Demanded James.

'Wait!' Sandy shuffled his penguin form from the doorway. 'Always use the power of your own rule wisely!'

He sniffed loudly, pushing his head forward into the dusty corridor of fate, his large red nose twinkling in the brilliant light.

'And!' He continued firmly. 'A word, as they say, to the Wise. That united you all must stand with the power of rule. Or Divided you will fall. For the power within any rule that you may hold, can also become a dark, double edged sword, that may be used against it's holder.'

'So stick together human folks!' Added Pat, shuffling next to Sandy and moving behind the children.

Ozzy moved forward.

'Yeah! - I agree' he said, tapping Sue on her leg. 'Don't play into the Evil Voids hands. It wants you all to be separated and divided.'

James, Abdul and Sue just nodded in agreement and with a bound, they all moved forward together heading toward the rapidly diminishing frame of Furtive Von Flatulence, as he fled quickly along the corridors of fate.

For his part, Von Flatulence turned his Evil head to observe the children following.

'Oh Dear!' He snapped, watching with concern as they gained ground on him. 'A most grim day for Evil.'

The Dark Voids henchman, in desperation, ripped more shreds of cloth from his cloak and cast them to the floor.

'More skeletons!' Observed Abdul looking ahead into the corridor, in a quiet, determined and unafraid tone.

'Yes there are!' Replied both James and Sue.

## Times Planet Wake Up Call - (Classroom Kids)

The three children held their rulers forward and in a united effort, rushed toward the arising, sinister red eyed skeletons attempting to block the passageway.

The corridors of fate flashed with light and thunder, as these Evil creatures of darkness were soon cut down by the human children.

Shuffling behind them, the three Penguin People tried desperately to keep pace with these events and stay close to the kids that they had befriended.

'As the saying goes!' Called out Pat, looking beneath the legs of James and seeing skeleton after skeleton block the corridor. 'It looks like all hells let loose!'

Far away, Pats words were being echoed by a sailor stroking the feathers of a small, red breasted bird that was sitting on his arm and who looked skyward from behind a circular glass, door window.

For high above a clear and calm blue ocean, beyond this watertight door, the dark swirling mass of the 'phenomenon' as the military called it, flashed and thundered with a brilliant light show and roaring sound, never before seen or heard in any natural storm.

'Gee whiz - Some strange type of wonderful - Eh bird?' Said the sailor, shaking his head. He opened the doorway hatch and stepped back out onto the ships deck. 'Looks like the oceans calm now my little friend.' With a smile, and examining the scene he added. 'Maybe best you make your way home now, little bird!'

The sailor held up his arm and encouraged the small bird to fly, by waving his hand back and forth. With a calm wind beneath it's wings, the little bird started to soar skyward.

'Take care Buddy!' Called out the sailor. But his words ended quickly, with an ominous... 'Hey!'

A Dark Raven had painfully brushed past his head, flying across the ships deck to attack the smaller bird. But, being much more manageable in flight, The smaller red breasted bird, twisted away from the Raven at the very last moment and headed back toward the safety of the ships doorway.

Quickly following in a full speed dive, the Raven again licked at the heels of the smaller bird and snapped angrily with it's huge beak.

The small bird frantically avoided having it's tail feathers ripped away by twisting and turning, but it seemed that it would immanently be caught be the huge, Evil Raven. However, for the pet of the Dark Void, retribution and justice, was to be at hand.

And retribution came quite instantly, by the quick hands of a lone sailor who, observing this sudden, uneven and deadly chase in flight between birds, swiftly pushed hard onto the watertight door.

With a dutiful creak, the heavy steel plate swung on it's hinges to fly open, and this swift action allowed a fleeing small red breasted bird, to enter the ships doorway, whilst it flowed gracefully in full speed flight and turned sharply to avoid the pursuing Raven.

## Times Planet Wake Up Call - (Classroom Kids)

Almost in an instant, the heavy door creaked again, being pulled forcefully backwards by the sailor, who saw the Raven twist menacingly, then hurtle again toward it's small prey. There was to be an immediate, sickeningly dull thud outside the hatch, with the larger bird smashing quite painfully, into the doors single and circular glass panel window.

'Ouch! - That had to hurt' exclaimed the sailor, who watched the stunned Raven stop instantly, then slide gently down the glass window.

He moved forward, raised his hand and carefully pushed open the door, stepping outside quickly.

Fully expecting to have to tend to an injured bird, the sailor grunted in some surprise.

'Huh -' He muttered, looking around the ships deck and observing that the large Raven had vanished.

'Hey! - What the -' Cried the sailor, who felt a sudden rush of powerful wind emanate from within the ships doorway behind him.

He turned, then moved swiftly sideways, avoiding the small red breasted bird which flew toward and past him at full speed, heading out to sea. The bemused sailor watched this little bird grow even smaller and smaller, the further away it flew from his ship.

'See you little Buddy!' He shouted, his voice trailing in with the wind that followed the small bird. Then, giving one last quick look for an absent Raven, he retired within the ships doorway and shut the steel hatch.

Now, way out at open sea and on outstretched wings, the little bird moved very quickly. It had detected with it's keen senses, a small, circular red buoy that bobbed up and down in the ocean, far beyond this large vessel. The graceful bird headed straight toward the object and just as the small bird landed on this small, bobbing buoy a thin spout of water sprang upward from beneath it.

'Hmm -' A familiar grunt caused the small bird to hop up and down excitedly on top of the red circular object, it's feet attempting to dig downward and find a firm foothold.

With a whoosh of salty water, the red buoy suddenly rose from the sea, to reveal a prone Penguin Person who had lay stunned, just beneath the flat ocean.

'I say old thing!' Exclaimed Monty, twitching his nose painfully, water dripping from his long moustache. 'Please do leave ones beak!' He reached up with his hand to rub his nose. 'To ones self.'

Monty, who was floating flat on his back, looked upward past the bird, into the flashing skies above. The desperate situation that was occurring there suddenly dawned on him, and he came fully around, from his groggy, head numbing state.

'Great Scott, Master Peter!' He cried... 'We must have both been blown clean out of the Void by that dreadful explosion!'

## Times Planet Wake Up Call - (Classroom Kids)

Monty closely examined the numerous flashes and thunderous sounds coming from the skies.

'Master Peter... I wager by that display, that the clock is ticking for the Evil Dark Void! - Your friends must have something to do with that performance!'

Monty turned his head back and forth, then became aware that only he and the bird were in the water.

'Master Peter!' He called out in concern, looking around him. 'Master Peter!... Where are you?' But there was no reply, only a strange, gurgling of the water at Monty's side.

Monty stretched his entire body outwards.

'I say!... That feels like a Jacuzzi - Eh What? -' But a voice cut through his thoughts.

'W... ow!' There was a sudden, violent splash of water, with Peter appearing from beneath a flat blue ocean clutching tightly to a rather wet, red nosed, smiley skateboard.

Grabbing Monty by the moustache, he held on tightly to the floating Penguin Person.

'Are you all right?' Asked Peter, his only concern being for the strange creatures welfare.

'Having a whale of a Time Master Peter!' Smiled Monty... 'Now that you are here and safe, young human.'

There was a massive flash in the sky and a consuming, thunderous crack, that focused the attention of both Peter and Monty heavenward.

'What was that?' Asked Peter, gripping Monty's moustache tightly.

'It would appear... That the Time is ripe!' Replied Monty, his monocle twisting slowly around while he examined the scene above. 'Ripe indeed!'

High above these floating figures, within the dark corridors of fate, the Time was indeed ripe. James, Abdul and Sue, reaching the corridors end, moved forward, linked their rulers and despatched the very last red eyed skeleton that barred the way forward.

'That smelly guy went through here!' Stated James, reaching an apple shaped doorway. 'Let's go on through!'

'Yes' agreed Abdul, stopping to examine the dark centre of the apple shaped doorway.

'Together!' Agreed Sue also, and she turned toward Pat, Sandy and Ozzy.. 'OK?' She asked the Penguin People.

'Wait a second!' Replied Pat shuffling forward. He looked at the apple shaped doorway and the huge, dark, skeleton shaped door handles in it's centre. 'What lies beyond this doorway may be rotten to the very core!'

'Yes!' Sandy agreed... 'It may be the lair of the Evil Void itself!'

## Times Planet Wake Up Call - (Classroom Kids)

Ozzy gently touched Sue on her hand.

'It will be a supreme Test Of Time for you to enter there!' He warned with concern... 'The Void could destroy all of you!'

'Well that my be so' replied Sue, looking firstly at Ozzy, then directly at James and Abdul. 'But are we together on this?'

James looked at Abdul, and Abdul huffed, composing himself. He smiled and James smiled right back.

'Together!' They both agreed.

With a single step forward, the three children all pushed on the strangely shaped doorway, together.

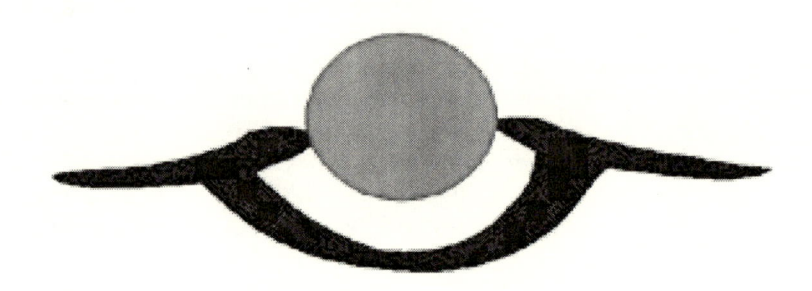

## *And In The End - (The Last Chapter)*

There was an instant, but long and drawn out, loud, agonizing and painful groan from this strange, apple shaped doorway, while it split unwillingly asunder into two, equal half's, creaking slowly, but surely backwards, under the united, powerful force, of children's hands.

Picturing a grim, determined look on their faces, James Abdul and Sue then proceeded to push even further against the skull shaped door handles and each walked forward in unison, as the skulls eyes, burning under their hands, glowed red with rage.

James was the first to look beyond the strangely shaped doorway. He peered, searchingly into the dark core beyond, observing a long, high, tube like structure.

'It is a corridor' he noted, straining his eyes in the quite strange, shimmering darkness, which flickered madly along the tube. Abdul moved to his side, closely followed by Sue.

'The sides - They are cracking!' Exclaimed Abdul. He pointed along the corridor toward what seemed like endless rows, of large, gleaming support columns, that reached skyward and appeared to hold the whole, unseen, dark roof in it's place. But these columns, now strained and groaned, buckling under an unseen force, that pushed most frantically down upon them.

Sue also looked forward and observed the structures condition.

'I do not like the look of that!' She said, noticing one of the creaking columns nearby and watching a dark, snaking crack, slither down it's entire length.

'The Pillars' called out Sandy, staring between Abdul's legs. 'The Pillars of Faith and Hope - They are crumbling!'

Ozzy moved quickly forward, twitched his large red nose and looked past Sues leg.

'Strewth!' He exclaimed... 'Those Pillars are fair crumbling under the forces of darkness!'

Pat shuffled forward, scratched his chin, and momentarily contemplated the scene. The seriousness of the situation dawned on him immediately.

'Hurry!' Pat suddenly bellowed... 'Or the Path to Peace, Time and Light may be lost - Forever!'

'Path to -' Blurted James, looking downward, ready to ask what the strange little creature was talking about. But the small, Penguin Person Creatures all shuffled forward, pushing against his legs.

'Wow!' Cried James, quickly stumbling forward into the tube.

'Lets move!' Called out Sue following him and she rushed forward, ignoring the dirty dust falling from ominous cracks that now quickly snaked down each of the column walls.

'You have to reach the end of this corridor!' Warned Pat in some urgency, pushing against the legs of James. 'Before the Power of Time, Peace and Light is totally extinguished!'

## And In The End - (The Last Chapter)

Abdul stumbled forward, trying to run, along with James and Sue. But the very ground beyond the doorway felt like clinging mud and pulled down on his feet, which now felt like lead weights.

'Moving forward is difficult!' He gritted his teeth and made a supreme effort to move onward.

'Yeah!' Agreed James pulling his feet, one by one, from the Earth and struggling to move on.

'Look!' Sue exclaimed excitedly. 'There is another door!' She pointed her finger forward, indicating a shimmering, circular doorway further along the tube. 'Lets get through there!'

'Yes!' Agreed Abdul and Peter. But the closer the children struggled toward it, the further the shimmering, circular doorway appeared to move away.

'It appears - That the human children will not reach the doorway before the Path is crushed!' Observed Sandy sadly, pushing as hard as he could against Abdul's legs and looking toward Pat and Ozzy.

The other two Penguin Person Creatures nodded, equally sadly, in resigned, uncomfortable agreement.

'Look folks!' James stopped his struggle forward. 'Where there is a Will - There is a Way!' He looked down toward the Penguin People Creatures, who were trying to push the children forward. 'Least Wise!' He continued. 'That is what old grandpa always says.'

An enormous crack rent the air, bringing everyone's attention immediately to the sky.

'The Pillars - They have had it!' Cried Sue.

Along with the others she watched as inky darkness plummeted downward, extinguishing the shimmering light from each column, as it headed toward Earth.

'Excuse me please!' The voice of James, suddenly commanded everyone's attention.

'Er - Excuse you what?' Asked Pat. And his question was immediately answered, when James did the most extraordinary thing.

With a quick thinking, instant movement, James lent forward toward Pat and with a firm, but gentle grip of his hand, pulled the nose from the small Penguin Person creature.

'Hey!' Snuffled Pat, his hat immediately falling forward toward the very spot where his large red nose had previously held it in place. As the hold all things receptacle obscured his very small eyes and wanting to know what James had planned, Pat asked.

'What's the sketch Buddy?'

'Just a second!' Replied James, and he threw the red nose forward.

It landed, with a soft plop, onto the clinging and dark floor in front of him.

## And In The End - (The Last Chapter)

The boy stepped onto the large red nose and it, as he had expected, or rather, hoped, held firm under his feet.
'Great!' He beamed. 'We can use these balls of Wisdom as Stepping stones!'
'Good idea' replied both Abdul and Sue together.
'But -' Added Abdul. 'There are only three noses - Not nearly enough for us to get as far as that exit!'
Sue thought very quickly.
'What about this?' She said, moving forward. Sue pressed the small clock embedded into the front of Ozzy's hat and the top immediately sprang open. 'Maybe -' She continued, reaching into the hat and producing a notepad and pencil. 'We can sketch our own stepping stones.'
Flipping open the notepad cover, Sue proceeded to draw a large circle onto the strange, shimmering paper, beneath the rotating pencil tip.
'Excellent!' Laughed Abdul, watching this circle Sue had drawn, quickly emerge upward from the paper, just like a ball of bubble gum. 'Amazing -' He added, as the large transparent ball then transformed, into the same red hue as the noses of the Penguin Persons.
'This first one!' Sue proudly announced. 'Is for you!' She pulled the red ball from the notepad page and lifted Pats hat, very carefully backwards. 'Here!' Sue smiled, then, unexpectedly pushed the large red ball onto the face of the small Penguin Person.
'Thanks Buddy!' Sniffed Pat, blinking his very small eyes, that now sat either side of his brand new, large red nose. A happy smile drew from beneath it. 'Good Sketch!'
'If you please!' Asked Abdul politely, leaning forward toward Sandy. He pressed the small clock embedded into the Penguin Persons hat and as Sue had done, produced a small notebook and pencil from inside it.
Abdul proceeded to draw a circle into a note book page and smiled himself, when a resulting large red ball emerged quickly from it.
James turned toward Pat, to copy the others. He found Pat had already removed his note book and pencil, holding it forward, in his outstretched arm and hand.
'Make good use of your note books folks' smiled Pat, handing his to James. 'The path forward is in your human folks hands now!'
'Quick then!' James called out urgently, as pall of dust from the dark, rapidly descending ceiling, plummeted downward, making him clear his dry eyes. 'Let's draw on!'
The three children scribbled furiously, each sketching circles on the notebook pages. Then, after a large red ball had emerged, James, Abdul and Sue, threw their creations forward onto the creepy floor.

## And In The End - (The Last Chapter)

With a Cartoon Buddy gripping tightly onto their shoulders, step by step, and jumping from ball to ball, they all thankfully neared the circular, shimmering exit doorway of this rapidly crumbling, tube like structure.

A huge roar erupted along the corridor, as the enlightened support columns finally succumbed to the Evil, snaking cracks, that crawled earthward down them, and one by one collapsed into pieces.

'There is no Time left!' Sue cried as she reached the circular doorway exit and finding it locked firmly shut.

Reading the notice that was etched into the very solid, wooden timbers that flickered with neon light. Abdul huffed in despair, then read aloud.
'No admittance!'

His eyes carefully and quickly examined the doorway. 'And there is a no key for that huge lock!'

James looked back along the tube, to see darkness rushing forward toward where he and the others stood balancing on top of the red balls.

'Where there is a will' he mumbled... 'There is a way.'

James firmly gripped his pencil and sketched a large key onto the page of his notepad. With the drawing complete the key burst from the page, as had the large red noses, and James pushed the key into the lock, giving it a sharp, firm turn.

'Wow!' Everyone exclaimed together, thankfully, as the lock clicked loudly and the large, circular door creaked slowly open. However, within a moment of this event, everyone cried a quite painfully driven... 'Ah!' As the darkness from a collapsing corridor tube finally reached them, and blasted all living things within this corridor forward at speed, to hurtle far beyond the shimmering circular doorway, into the unknown beyond.

It was to prove to be a rather quick journey, for within a space of seconds the three children and their Cartoon Buddy Creature friends had been flung far into the deep depths of the dark unknown.

In a heart pounding instant, quickly followed by an aching, dull thud like sound, all forward movement ended abruptly and violently in a very sudden stop, which left them all dazed and semi-concious. The entire world quickly seemed to spin around and around their heads, making all of them feel terribly sick.

Lying here in an untidy heap, the mists of semi consciousness rose away, almost as strongly as the strong, unpleasant smell, that punctured the clean air.

'Not so much with the smelling salts Buddy!' Grunted Pat, his hat crumpled over his large red nose.

'Yes' agreed Sandy in a stifled voice, his head wedged firmly under Ozzy's back. 'They are most strong and upsetting to the nasal cavities.'
Ozzy raised his small frame releasing Sandy from his entrapment and looked toward the three human children.

## And In The End - (The Last Chapter)

'Are you all OK!' He called out with concern, his head still swimming with the stunned shock of an abrupt halt and his nose twitching from this strange smell.

'Guess so!' Replied James, patting Abdul on the shoulder and then looking toward Sue, as Abdul sat upright on the misty, dark floor.

'Fine!' Added Sue smiling toward James and Abdul. She then added an uncertain... 'I think?'

All now sat upright and cleared their stunned, misty minds. Everyone mumbled the same, unanswered question that was on their very dry lips and in a nose twitching, stomach churning displeasure, they all asked.

'What on Earth is that awful smell?'

A stunned and dazed head, suddenly appeared from the misty, swirling floor in front of them. The face, with it's beady, staring eyes, lay still obscured under a dark brown hat, that now stood upright, but somewhat crumpled, from where six flying objects had inadvertently landed upon the wearer of it.

Von flatulence twitched his own large red nose and glared in anger at both the children and cartoon Buddy creatures.

'That odour -' He growled and snarled with hate. 'Is me!'

With a dark cloak of sinister, Evil foreboding, rising further up an angry face, Von Flatulence rose to his feet.

'Now you shall feel the wrath of my Master!'

James, Abdul and Sue, automatically looked to their left, as a roar of Evil wind reverberated from the flickering, shadow covered walls of this strange and dark misty room. it's source, appeared to emanate from the very centre of a huge circle embedded into the wall, which revolved very slowly, around and around. With each full revolution, a face seemed to appear gradually from the circle, drawn in red and looking decidedly angry, with flaming, hate filled eyes.

James observed the circle closely.

'That looks like a huge full stop dotted onto the wall' he said thoughtfully.

His observation and comment, was met with an immediate angry and very loud response that carried itself easily on the Evil wind, to lick sharply, the ears of everyone in the room.

'I am the ultimate full stop!' Cried the dark circle in an absolute rage, the flaming red face now forming fully within it's centre, an angry frown underlining it's features.

'I am the ultimate Void and Master of Darkness!' It continued. 'I will end all things that begin - All things that are created of light - All things created of wisdom - All things created of good faith and hope - All these things created - Will end with me!'

'Yes Master!' Agreed Von Flatulence, creeping in servitude and answering in his own, sinister voice. 'All things good must be destroyed, only then will you attain the power of an ultimate Evil, full stop!'

## And In The End - (The Last Chapter)

Now this seemed to be the only Time, Abdul observed, that this loathsome little creature seemed to be actually happy, and the very thought of these Evil characters talking about destroying things that they did not like, especially good things, made him feel quite upset inside.

'Hey!' He called out toward the large Evil faced circle and stepped forward. 'Listen you big bully!' He said defiantly. 'Maybe it's your turn now to get – Er - Stopped.'

'Yes!' Agreed Sue and she pulled out her ruler, holding it firmly forward in her hand. 'We will all draw the line to end your Evil here and end your nasty ways!'

James and Abdul produced their rulers also, holding them forward with Sue, together.

'United we will stand against you!' Announced Abdul, touching his ruler with that of Sue and James.

Instantly, a brilliant light buzzed forward from the three rulers, which hit Von Flatulence quite squarely into the centre of his large round nose. The light beam sent the Evil character reeling backwards, where he crashed into an obscured, large, long oblong object that was embedded within the dark walls, and now indicated the point, where he seemed to evaporate from sight.

The children then quickly turned toward the Evil Void itself, grim determination etched into their faces.

'Interesting!' Snapped the Evil Void sarcastically, a smirk appearing from it's Evil frown. It then sneered, angrily...

'But your puny rulers power of light, will have no effect on me whatsoever!' The Void then continued, to huff in absolute contempt.

'They are, to me, like all the creative works formed by the Great Pencil Of Peace And Light, both pointless and quite useless!'

'Well let's see, shall we!' Shouted James in defiance.

Along with both Abdul and Sue, he pointed his ruler toward the very centre of the Evil Void. The rulers touched gently and sent an immediate, brilliant flash of light toward the sinister, smirking, angry face.

Splitting the still, misty air and generating an enormous, thunderous cracking sound, that painfully assaulted the ear drums of those present. This beam of brilliant light zipped impressively forward, to totally envelope the dark circle and it's rather unpleasant, Evil character, that lay within.

'Yes!' Cried out James in a state of jubilant joy, seeing the beam of light strike it's target. 'We hit the monster!'

His happy voice consequently trailed a rather subdued.

'Oh -' As the beam of brilliant light then bounced backwards from the dark circle.

## And In The End - (The Last Chapter)

James, Abdul and Sue all watched with the utmost concern, as their united beam retired quite ineffectively outwards from the dark circle and created a large ring like shimmering misty haze, which reduced rapidly in strength, retaining just enough power as it merged with the shadowy walls to illuminate the strange and very creepy room.

'This is not so good?' Responded Abdul, witnessing the sight of a smirking, sinister and angry face, remain quite intact within it's dark circle. 'Not so good at all.'

Sue agreed. Giving a quick nod of her head and pressing her lips tightly together, she kept her mind in deep thought, while studying the after effects of the rooms illumination.

'This seems to be' Sue said, examining the scene and now observing a seemingly endless, neat row of desks, that trailed far into the distance in front of her. 'Another classroom - Only much larger than the ones we had entered earlier.'

She pointed to a large circular doorway, shimmering with a yellow, golden light, that lay directly opposite the equally sized dark circle spot of the Evil Void.

'And there is the spot where we entered.'

Sue paused for a moment, then continued...

'Those circles -' She said, observing both thoughtfully. 'They seem to mirror each other, in a strange sort of way.'

'The circles - They are the mirrors of creation!' Exclaimed Ozzy, shuffling up beside Sue. 'And this must be the Time of Judgement Class Room!'

Ozzy, twitched his large red nose.

'I thought that this place was only an old legend in our dusty book.'

'Ah – Yes -' Added Sandy, also shuffling tentatively forward, moving toward the side of Abdul.

He examined further the almost mirrored circles and strange, creepy room.

'The place where the final conflict between Good and Evil, Darkness and Light will finally be enacted.'

Pat moved to the side of James, twitching his large red nose and spoke quietly.

'The place where it is said, Time may continue forward - Or the place, where all Time will stop!'

The Cartoon Buddy creatures each picked up his note book and pencil from the floor beside the children, where they had inadvertently dropped them.

Each pushed the button on his hat and when the top had sprung open, placed the notebooks back inside. When the lid of their hold all things receptacle flipped back and shut, each one spoke and said quietly.

'Where no more notes may be taken - Only the final Judgement, on what will be!'

## And In The End - (The Last Chapter)

'And where I shall be the only winner!' Cried the dark Void, it's eyes blazing red. 'All that remains is for me to finally crush all your Spirit's and Hopes!'

There was a violent rumble that immediately resounded around the room and the air chilled rapidly.

Pat looked up at James and the others.

'Have a little faith and keep Hope!' he said calmly. 'The Evil Dark Void cannot physically harm anyone by itself, while it is still contained within the eternal circle. It can only encourage and wish for others to do so!'

'Yeah - It can also offer false bribes and wishes, that will never be fulfilled for any good purposes' added Ozzy. 'Only to serve itself, in it's aim to end all things created by the pencil of good and light.'

Even with these words of comfort and Wisdom, James had now taken a single, tentative step back from the flaming, angry face.

He looked toward Abdul, quickly composing himself, although still feeling a little frightened.

'So what do we do now?' Asked James.

Abdul gave James a semi frightened, half smile back.

'I do not know' he replied, holding his ruler tightly. 'Maybe we could try these again?'

'Somehow, I do not think the light beam will destroy that thing!' Said Sue, looking toward the shimmering, circular doorway that the children had entered through, when escaping from the collapsing tube.

Sue now noticed, that this doorway lay beside a series of seven dark and circular gateways, of which, she noted, each one had a picture of a seal etched onto it, that appeared to be some form of lock.

'Maybe there will be some kind of answer beyond those doors?'

'You think!' Replied James, pointing toward a series of painted crests that portrayed the face of the Evil Dark Void, flickering above each of the seven doorways.

He read the words that were etched onto each and every crest aloud.

'Evil Hate – Selfish – Vanity - Greed.'

'Not really the sort of motto that any good solution could hide behind' said Abdul.

'Evil – Hate – Selfishness - Vanity and Greed... The Crest of every Evil Class of character' Added Sandy. 'But the crest itself might be reversed, but only by a united and strong strength of the right purpose.'

'My favourite crest!' Interrupted the Evil Void, a huge roar of Evil Wind blasting from the Dark Circle. 'And the last thing that your human kind will ever see before you are all erased - Forever!'

Sue stepped forward confidently, now rather annoyed at the Evil Void's tone and only feeling ever so slightly afraid, inside at least, that is what she told herself.

## And In The End - (The Last Chapter)

'You do not frighten us you Evil bully!' She snapped, pointing her finger in reproach toward the Dark Void. 'Let our parents go free and stop trying to erase everything!'

'Oh Yes! - Do I sense anger within the human child!' Responded the Evil Circle smugly, it's eyes flaming red and mouth smirking. 'That would of course, be to my most excellent advantage!'

It then added, even more smugly than before.

'Any others care to create a little hate for me? - Any kind will do!'

'Please be careful' said Pat quietly toward the children. 'Remember - That the Evil Void feeds on any negative emotion!'

Sue smiled toward Pat and the others, then looked back toward the dark circle.

'No - Is your reply!' She answered, even more confidently. 'I do not hate you, or anyone else. You are just a thing to pity! - After all, you cannot enjoy anything good that can be created - You can only live with the emptiness of yourself and your hate of things. If you should ever win over Time, you will be really lonely, in an Evil Space of your own, without any sort of thing to talk to or like!'

'Well said young Sue!' Agreed Ozzy, twitching his large red nose. 'Good on you!'

'Yes!' Agreed James and Abdul, together, in loud voices. James added.

'We think that Sue is right about you!'

'You are a bully!' Shouted Abdul. 'And bullies always lose in the end!'

As the children's words reached toward and assaulted this Evil Void with pity and compassion, it became absolutely furious with these children that had stood in his way. The angry face of the dark circle contorted even more with rage, and the room trembled beneath the children's feet.

'Er - I think we seemed to have upset the beast' quipped Abdul, tottering on his feet as the ground shook violently.

'Maybe we should open those doors! - As Sue suggested' said James, steadying himself.

Pat held the boys leg to help him balance.

'Those doors are sealed – And - If I am correct - The seals may only be broken by the mirror of light, that was created by the Great Pencil, of the Spirit of Peace.'

'Right!' Said Sue hopefully. 'I don't suppose you know where to look for the mirror.'

'The mirror!' Replied Sandy, looking toward Ozzy and Sue. 'Does not have to be found.'

'Yeah!' Agreed Ozzy, nodding his head in agreement. 'The mirror will find you. If you have a little faith that is.'

A huge roar of wind cut short Ozzy's words and light suddenly beamed from the darkened doorway, that the children had previously entered through.

## And In The End - (The Last Chapter)

Under the full force of this howling wind and light the gateway blew open, and a single remaining, enlightened support column, could be seen standing within the long, tube like corridor.

'Well' said Pat, pushing harder on the leg of James as the wind whipped past. 'It looks like you young human folks have kept enough enlightenment power to support that particular column!'

As his words trailed away in the wind, and just before anyone could say anything else, the single remaining pencil shaped pillar of faith that shimmered with the power of golden enlightenment, plummeted Earthwards, heading toward the circular doorway and in a heart stopping instant smashed straight through this gateway, landing with an almighty resounding crash on the dusty, misty ground.

Now pointing directly toward the children, the column instantly exuded a single, brilliant and concentrated beam of golden light, that quickly flashed through the room, enveloping each of the rulers that the three children still held firmly in their hands.

A split second after this contact and with a huge, single bang, the strange light beam became instantly fragmented, splitting into a series of cracking, thunderbolt shaped tracks, that bounced away from the rulers and as if aimed by some unseen force, hurtled toward the seals that had locked each of the seven, dark circular gateways, firmly shut.

With the first of these thunderbolt shaped tracks of light hitting the first seal picture and shattering it into a cascade of thousands of star like small pieces, the sound of an enormous clock striking the hour, reverberated deafeningly, around the room.

With a rush of the strangest, most powerful and strange wind, the first gateway, very slowly opened.

'Great!' Exclaimed Sue. 'The first gate is opening!'

'Maybe not so good!' Interrupted Ozzy, looking forward to the gateway and witnessing the strangest sight arise from within it. 'It looks like - The clock may have now finally stopped, for all you humans!'

Now, Sue really liked horses, but she was quite stunned and felt more than a little frightened, when she saw a rather creepy looking white horse appear from the first gateway. It was ridden by a shadowy, sinister character holding a bow and wearing a crown on it's head, but whose face was hidden by a dark cloak, that billowed in the wind blown from the opened gateway.

'I don't think I like this - Not one bit!' Said Sue nervously.

James nodded, because he also did not like this event, as he watched a 'fire red' coloured horse appear from the second gateway.

The rider of this particular horse held a large, shining sword and it's face, like that of the first, was hidden. It also wore a long, billowing, dark cloak and James really did not like the look of it.

## And In The End - (The Last Chapter)

'I do not think these things are good!' He said, trying not to appear afraid.

From the third gateway, a black horse rode quickly forward, the equally sinister rider of this beast carrying a pair of weighing scales.

'An odd looking bunch' observed Abdul, feeling his mouth dry somewhat, in anticipation. He continued his transfixed stare on the gateways, as yet another horse appeared from the fourth gateway.

This pale coloured horse, made Abdul take a step back. The face was obscured, as was the body, just like the other three riders. But a fierce and Evil wind following it seemed to rip the very air from the room and made the temperature, rise to a quite uncomfortable degree.

'Yes... A really Creepy bunch!' Said Abdul, nervously.

'Well now - That is a sight you do not see everyday!' Interrupted Pat. 'The Four Horsemen Of The Apocalypse!'

'Indeed!' Agreed Sandy, who proceeded to identify these four characters for the children.

'Conquest, with it's bow, the vanity maker. War, with it's sword, the hate maker and Peace taker. Famine, with it's weighing scales, the selfish, greed creator. And, of course, Death, who will follow the paths of sword, famine, beasts and plague and who, is followed in turn, by Hades, it's wind of hell.'

'So! - The seals have been broken!' Bellowed the Evil Dark Void, his thunderous voice reverberating around the room. 'The Four Horsemen Of The Apocalypse have now been unleashed from their gate and here, they will destroy you!'

James, Abdul and Sue moved backwards, as quickly as these Four, strange horsemen moved forward.

'What do we do now?' Asked Sue, stumbling against one of the many wooden school desks, that had stood in neat rows behind her and the others.

As she spoke the seal of the fifth gate, also smashed into thousands of shining pieces and the door hurtled open. A most powerful, howling wind, suddenly whipped past the Four Horsemen, pushing all of them very roughly aside. It then rushed onward, to pass quite gently, toward and over the children, to swirl frantically, but gently, around the entire room.

'This place is falling apart!' Exclaimed Abdul, stumbling behind one of the school desks, while the ground trembled violently beneath his feet like never before.

The sixth seal had shattered, sending a single, blinding beam of light to shine from within the gateway. It lit up the room, as brightly as the sun had lit up the day and then, unexpectedly, seemed to be sucked outwards, then backwards, into the circular opening, where the three children and Penguin People creatures had entered the room. There it stood momentarily, like a beaming torch, to unexpectedly explode, sending a shower of sparkling, shimmering fragments cascading throughout the entire room.

## And In The End - (The Last Chapter)

James quickly grabbed the arm of both Abdul and Sue.

'Move back!' He shouted with some concern, the four horsemen moving forward toward the desks and almost reaching his friends.

'Come on!' Called out Abdul to Sandy, Pat and Ozzy. He was not about to let the Four Horsemen hurt these small creatures, that had helped both him and the others so much, even if it meant standing up, somehow, to the sinister figures.

Sue thought the same way and pulled against the holding arm of James.

'Take that!' She bellowed, and threw her ruler at the four horsemen.

It bounced instantly over their heads, to drop, ineffectively, onto the misty floor. However, the four horsemen stopped suddenly in their tracks.

'Er -' Enquired Sue, surprised. 'How did that work?'

There was a most sudden and unexpected interruption to the proceedings. Behind James, Sue and Abdul, a rather peeved and casual voice announced.

'What an absolutely, ghastly Shower!'

The children turned their heads, to see Monty Penguin Person, his moustache still dripping wet with sea water and nose twitching frantically.

'Away with all you, sinister type chaps!' He demanded, sniffing toward the four horsemen... 'Shoo!'

'When the - What the -' Asked both James and Abdul, spluttering as they spoke, while also seeing the welcome sight of a dripping wet Peter alongside Monty.

Sue peered beyond the sight of her lost friends, now found again, and toward the endless, neat rows of school desks that lay behind them, each one now occupied.

'And who the -' She asked, quite astounded.

With a twitch of his long moustache and a quick revolution of his shining monocle, Monty shuffled toward Sue and answered her questioning gaze.

'These are - All children from the Train of thought!' Announced Monty, still sniffing his large red nose, rather contemptuously, toward the now quite static, but still very sinister looking, Four Horsemen Of The Apocalypse.

'You see -' he continued, looking toward Sue, Abdul and James, while ignoring a deep, angry growl from the Dark Voids circle. 'You children have now entered and are standing between, the Great Walls of the Eternal Clock Circle itself.' Monty, while still speaking, shuffled quickly forward, to join Pat Sandy and Ozzy..

'Inside here, you all stand together, within the very workings and walls, that suspended all of existence itself, that is held between both the Good Front Of Time and the Rear Evil Shadow of Time.'

The small Penguin Person creature twitched his long, damp moustache and held out his arm, to traverse and point his finger, toward all of the human children in the room. In a most serious tone, he added...

## And In The End - (The Last Chapter)

'And all that stands between the Evil Voids Power of Dark Shadow, in it's aim of replacing the Good Of Daylight - Is you - All of you!'

Peter, dripping spots of water onto the misty floor, moved forward toward Sue, Abdul and James.

'It appears!' He said, with an urgent tone to his voice. 'That in the outside world, Time itself is now standing still and that all the people are frozen, quite motionless, because the Eternal Clock has stopped ticking!'

He hugged the other three children, who hugged him back, despite the Victorian boys dripping wet clothes. Peter and the others then smiled at each other.

'Nice to see you all again' said Peter, very quickly adding. 'And that you are all well.'

'But when and how did you get here?' Blurted James, surprised to see his friend safe, after the huge explosion of The Sword Of Damocles.

'Monty and myself were blown from the Evil storm!' Answered Peter. 'The smiley mouthed skateboard came after us, with the train of thought following, but we crashed into the sea.'

He looked toward the many faces of children that sat behind the many neat rows of desks and who were all smiling at him.

'We were then, sort of sucked up suddenly, into some sort of a spiral, that was reaching skyward directly up from the sea and somehow, we were all transported here.'

Peter looked at The Four Horsemen, with an anxious feeling, rumbling right around his stomach.

'One supposes?' He enquired, most politely. 'That, maybe, our united help would be welcome and needed here.'

'Yes!' Agreed Sue, also looking toward the sinister figures. 'But I am not really sure what we kids can do against those things.'

'So then -' Asked Abdul. 'What exactly are they waiting for?' Curious as to why the Four Horsemen had not advanced any further forward, and stood menacingly static.

'Ah -' Answered Sandy, thoughtfully, looking toward the children. 'Maybe - Evil is held at bay, with the presence of so many smiles and happiness?'

'Yeah' agreed Pat, twitching his large red nose. 'For now! - But how do the horsemen get put back in their sealed doors?'

He nodded his head, in a hopeless kind of no fashion.

'I don't think even the Penguin People can help in that.'

'Hmm' thought James carefully and contemplating the situation.

'Perhaps there is a way to rebuild those pillars in the corridor of Time - And maybe that will re-start the clock of Light.'

## And In The End - (The Last Chapter)

'Yes - There must be a way!' Exclaimed Sue, peering toward the long, fallen pillar pencil, that still pointed from the corridor into the clocks workings and reflected a beam of golden light, like a mirror reflecting sunlight, to glimmer around the gloomy interior.

'There is - No way!' Boomed a sarcastic and very angry Voice from the Evil Voids Circle.

'There will be a way - I am sure of it - And we will find it!' Responded Abdul, glaring at the flaming red face in the dark circles centre. 'And we are not afraid of you! - Or of those Horsemen!'

'Oh! - Well said young human!' Monty exclaimed and the small creature positively beamed with joy. Then he clenched his tiny fist toward the Evil Void.

'See that you rotter!' He called out. 'Young humans that are not afraid of you! - They are all working together, almost like the fingers on a hand – And -' Monty thought for a second. 'Like those digit's that work together on a clocks hands at that!'

The Evil Void was filled with the utmost rage and started to roar it's angry reply. But, it was abruptly and quite rudely interrupted when James bellowed a sudden and very authoritative.

'Silence in class!'

An automatic and joyful smile appeared on the faces of James, Peter, Abdul and Sue, as the Evil Void was, unexpectedly, lost for words. Their own happy faces were very quickly, in turn, joined by the smiles emanating from the rest of the many human children that were sat, most amused, behind neatly rowed school desks in this huge and gloomy room.

'Hey! - I think you kids have stumped the old shadow now!' Laughed Ozzy.

'Yes sir re!' Nodded Pat, the small Penguin Person sniffing his large red nose toward the dark circle. 'Guess it is has met it's match - For once.'

The Evil Voids eyes flamed even redder with rage, it's large and angry mouth, at first mimed silently the unpalatable words.

'Met it's match!' But then, the dark, Evil circle, vibrated violently. 'I will have my vengeance!' Cried the Void. 'You shall all be erased!'

The Evil eyes looked again toward the stationary Four Horsemen Of The Apocalypse and bellowed.

'Forward Spirit's! - I command you!'

As the sinister horsemen again moved forward, now empowered by the voice of an Evil Void, without warning, all attention was drawn to a loud ear splitting crack, that emerged from the seventh picture of a seal, painted onto the seventh, strange doorway.

The seal picture quickly and unexpectedly shattered, scattering into millions of tiny, brilliantly lit pieces, and the doorway itself sprang open.

Around the tense room, a loud, screaming wind, rushed forward and hurtled past both horsemen and children.

## And In The End - (The Last Chapter)

It continued, unstoppable and quite frightening, to illuminate, with a single, blinding flash of light, a huge oblong blackboard that was situated on the entire wall length, to the side of the rooms many occupied school desks.

There followed, an uneasy and quite unnerving silence, while this strange, long board, now pulsated back and fourth, with an ominous, neon blue light.

The entire room froze, with an unexpected eerie chill, in a seemingly endless and very quiet, stillness of Time itself, while this strange blackboards light, flickered on and off, to repeatedly illuminate all those present.

'You know -' Gulped Abdul, drawing the cold air into his lungs, while trying desperately to remain calm. 'This situation, could be considered rather frightening.'

Ozzy sniffed the chilly air with his large red nose and poked it and his head, past Sues legs.

'Nah!' The small Penguin Person said, quickly twitching his beak and looking up at the children. 'Come on! - You human kids, are scared of nothing! - Right!'

'Er -' Sue thought for a second, looking toward the illuminated and now flashing in a hue of blue horsemen, who had, again, been forced to stop momentarily in the wind and who now, composed their Evil forms, to move forward again.

'Right!' Sue agreed. 'Afraid of these horsemen, shadow things! - Never!'

'That is correct!' Nodded Peter. 'There is no fear of this Evil Void and all it's doings, from us! - We place our faith in Peace and light, good deeds will rule here!'

Yeah! - OK - No fear! - That right folks, isn't it' replied James, looking toward the many faces behind row upon row of school desks, who, in turn, were looking directly at him.

'Agreed!' Nodded Abdul, forcefully putting his fears behind him.

The boy smiled, as the faces behind the desks also nodded with him. His smile then grew even larger as all these faces smiled back.

'No!' Roared the Evil Void, with the strange, neon blue light suddenly reflecting very strongly around the dark cavern, paling somewhat in hue as it did so.

'You must be afraid and filled with fear and hate! - It is my power! - My will. -My strength - My darkness!'

'It would seem' said Sandy thoughtfully, gesturing toward the blue light, that filled the cavern and gradually illuminated every corner. 'That the blue sky of day light, is now replacing your darkness, with the power from within these young humans.'

'Hmm' Pat looked toward the Evil Void that was filled with rage within it's dark circle. 'Guess that each one of these human folks are each just a single, but very important small cog, behind the great clock face of Time and creation.'

## And In The End - (The Last Chapter)

The small Penguin Person looked upward at James.
'See... Working together,' he said with satisfaction. 'You folks can and will, make the clock continue forward, to tick along the path of light.'
Sandy nodded his head.
'But, if human cogs really do not wish to rotate forward and want to stand still, doing deeds of darkness. Then creation, light and Time, can and will be stopped, to forever favour the Evil Void.'
'So, what we need' said Sue thoughtfully. 'Is for all of us to join together?'
'But we have already done that here!' Abdul looked at the four horsemen who appeared to be ready to attack again. 'I mean, we are all agreed that we must defeat this darkness, but we must need something else, as we have not destroyed it yet.'
Peter bent downward toward Monty and asked.
'Would you have you any thoughts on what is required?'
'Well old thing' sniffed Monty, his moustache twitching below his large red nose. 'What you need? - Is all you need ' His monocle glistened in the blue light. 'And that, old things - Is Love!'
As Monty's sentence ended, a peal of trumpets reverberated forth, at first quite quietly, then very loudly from within the corridors of fate hidden beyond the last, pencil shaped fallen pillar and the fading light of the circular doorway, that it protruded from.
'Yes - Pillars of your own faith and love!' Added Pat, sniffing toward the sound.
Sue, very suddenly, grabbed the hand of Peter.
'Come on then!' She shouted, pulling him forward. 'Lets try to get that pillar, pencil thing upright!'
'OK - Come on folks!' Cried James, grabbing Abdul's hand and both headed toward the children sat behind the school desks.
'Lets help out!' Cried Abdul stretching out his hand, and it was quickly held, to be joined by another and yet another within a chain of kids hands, that helped each other to move up and forward.
Everyone scurried, in a single, unbroken chain, past the four horsemen, with all in the chain, now acting as if these Evil characters did not even exist.
For their part, each one of the four horsemen reeled backwards toward the doorways that they had entered from, helplessly thrashing back and forth from this power chain of light, that pushed them roughly aside.
These many hands, in a chain of hope, reached for the fallen pillar and with a great strength of unity and purpose, lifted and pushed it upward from the ground, to support the ceiling, which it immediately illuminated, in a golden, brilliant glow.
'Ah!' Cried the Evil Void, watching in horror with it's flaming red eyes. 'Stop!'
Monty shuffled forward and twitched his moustache at the raging Evil circle.

## And In The End - (The Last Chapter)

'Time is up for you, you Evil beast! - They have continued! - They have saved Time!'

And continue, they had... The chain of children that had lifted up and held the pillar in place, found themselves gradually glowing brighter, with a golden soft light, as they each illuminated like a light bulb.

The Four Horsemen Of The Apocalypse were forced to retreat, as their united light flowed from the circular doorway, being pushed way back beyond their own gateways, where a shattering of sparkling light, suddenly reversed itself and reformed, to form the solid doors and seals that had originally held the Evil characters in place.

'Good show!' Exclaimed Monty, a smile forming from beneath his large red nose. 'Time is now set in it's rightful place!'

He and the other Penguin People smiled into the circular doorway of light, toward the chain of children that smiled right back.

But, quite suddenly, pitch darkness fell all around, as an alarm bell resounded loudly around the chamber.

Within a second, equally as suddenly, a massive beam of brilliant light burst forward, flowing all around and enveloping the chambers, as the loud, strange alarm bell, abruptly stopped.

'No Time!' A voice shouted urgently from within the brilliant light. 'There is now, no Time!' An ear splitting crack, immediately followed the authoritative voice, that had flowed from the brilliant light.

With a start, this golden illumination that had completely enveloped the eyes of James, Abdul, Peter and Sue, now cleared quickly, as the children awoke, from their very own, individual daydreams.

Sat at their school desks each one now raised their head from the palm of their hand, that had rested, very lazily upon their bent at the elbow arm, while leaning on the desk top in front of them.

'I repeat!' Said the smiling school teacher, picking up the large, dusty book, that he had just dropped onto his own desk top and which, in turn, had caused the loud crack that finally awoke the day dreaming members of his class.

'There is now no Time! - In which to continue our lesson, of old Earth Legends!'

Mr Adams turned, to move his small, portly frame, toward an awaiting shelf of neat, but very old books, that had stood on the long wall behind his seat. He replaced the book that he was holding, back into the space that patiently awaited it, within this neat row.

'And!' He said, with some dissatisfaction. 'Unfortunately children, there is no Time to examine this latest artefact uncovered from Old Planet Earth.'

Mr Adams turned again to his desk and blew a pall of dust from the covering cloth that had obscured a long, decorative object, that was hidden beneath it.

## And In The End - (The Last Chapter)

'Indeed, a most interesting object, from Earth!'
The teacher suddenly looked upward and across his classroom and Mr Adams let fly one of his random questions, that he liked to test his class with so much.
'And how far - Would one have to travel to Old Planet Earth?'
He stared hard and picked a 'victim'.
'James! - Answer!'
'Four light years sir!' Snapped James, his head still a little groggy from his daydream. 'Within the Galaxy formally known as the Milky Way - Now re-named Quadrant 7.'
'Yes!' Very good, replied Mr Adams, again looking around his classroom.
'And what feature did mankind once use to identify a particular tribal area and zone of control?' The teacher selected another victim for his spontaneous test.
'Sue - Answer!'
'An individually designed decorative cloth was used sir, it was known as a flag!' Replied Sue. 'And each flag donated a specific area of land mass known as a country and it would be the representative visual banner, for the particular peoples that would live there!'
'Yes!' Very good, again, huffed the teacher with a quiet satisfaction.
'What event, initiated the first stage of Space exploration, leading to the human expansion and population of various planets, that we know today?'
Mr Adams glared across his class and again picked at random.
'Abdul - Answer!'
'The substance and fossil fuel known as oil, became totally depleted sir!' Replied Abdul, quick as a flash. 'However - The means to measure the exact remaining stocks became available in Time and there proved to be enough stocks left, to begin the Space Ark Vault Enactment - Galactic Population began after this S. A. V. E. program began.'
'Good, very good' replied Mr Adams.
'Maybe, one who daydreams in class, may absorb information after all eh?' He added sarcastically.
'One last question then – Peter! - What were the names of the first Population Vessels to leave Earth and colonise other Worlds - Answer!'
'Er - Faith, Hope and Charity!' Responded Peter, realising the teacher had picked on him and his friends as they had, like most Times, not always been paying full attention.
'Excellent!' Grinned Mr Adams, while looking down, yet again, at the long cloth that was sat on his desk top.
'But I think that there is no one here that could hazard a guess, as to what this particular object is, or it's purpose and origins? - As it still cannot be explained, or opened, by any technique that is known today?'

## And In The End - (The Last Chapter)

The teacher pulled back the cloth, to reveal his hidden object and at this very same moment, James, Abdul, Peter and Sue, stared hard in recognition, toward the desk of Mr Adams.

'We have a long and inexplicably, dusty box, even after cleaning!' Continued Mr Adams.

'With a plain, oblong mirror, embedded into a carved, swirling effect lid. A lock on the side of the swirling effect carved base. Also a riddle, etched on the long lid, below the mirror. And with a key hole, but no key.'

James, Abdul, Peter and Sue, very quite quietly spoke as one, reflecting the words spoken by their the teacher, but, just before he had uttered, each, of these same words.

'That box - It was in a daydream that I just had' said Sue, whispering to Peter.

'Me too!' Whispered Peter right back. 'Did - Did you dream of small creatures too?'

'With large red noses' whispered Abdul, overhearing their conversation.

'And flying skateboards' chipped in James, leaning across the isle, to hear better.

All four children looked at each other, each feeling a little confused, as to how each one, could have had the same daydream.

'Any fool can frown at me. Any person can happy be. Stop think twice before a key you turn. For Time and Peace you have to learn' Mr Adams continued.

'An unexplained riddle, etched into an un-openable box, that has mystified archaeologists throughout the known universes for centuries.'

The teacher re-placed the cloth, then looked toward a large digital clock embedded within the classrooms metallic lined wall.

'However - As Time has run away with us today - We will study this peculiar object on Monday. It is now end of lessons. You may all leave for home!'

Within an instant, as usual, the entire classroom erupted into a frantic, but controlled clamour for the exit.

'Oh for the old days, when clocks were clocks' huffed Mr Adams, glancing nostalgically toward the pride of his antique collection, an old circular clock, that sported a large red dot in the centre, intersected by a smiley mouth and which had been a feature of his personal collection that had been brought to this planetary system, from old Earth, many centuries ago.

James, Abdul, Peter and Sue, had also observed the clock, but rather more closely today than usual, as they too left the classroom.

'Was that smiley mouth, in your dreams too?' Asked Peter, turning his head toward the others.

James, Abdul and Sue nodded a quick, thoughtful yes and all four children then glanced back, toward the long, dusty box, that lay on the desk in front of Mr Adams.

## And In The End - (The Last Chapter)

'Have a good weekend!' Called out Mr Adams, seeing the four children turn back. 'Do though, all remember to make enough Time and write your homework essays of, the values of humanity today and what was wrong with the Old Planet Earth... It must be on my desk, Monday Morning!'

'Yes sir!' Replied the children, giving a quick smile toward their teacher. Or rather, toward the long box, that sat on the desk in front of him. 'We will make the Time!'

James, Abdul, Peter and Sue then turned, giggling to themselves and left the classroom.

Two small, unnoticed figures sat on the classroom window sill, and watched the human teacher follow the four children out side the doorway.

Lifting a tasty fish sandwich toward his small mouth, which remained hidden beneath a large red nose, Patriot Penguin Person sniffed.

'Think they will make Time Buddy?'

Monty finished chewing a piece of his own sandwich and his long, dark moustache stopped twitching back and forth.

'I think' he said slowly. 'That Time may have other plans for them, old thing' he replied, sniffing the air with his own large red nose.

Looking toward the circular clock that hung on the classroom wall. Both Penguin People observed, with interest, the smiley mouth fade and disappear from the face.

Their attentions were then drawn to the long chalkboard, mounted onto the classroom wall and the small sinister voice that emanated from it.

'Mater!... Master!... Your power!... It is regenerating!'

The unmistakable, sinister little form of Furtive Von Flatulence, drew slowly forward from the chalkboards darkness and forced a contemptible twitch from both noses of the small, sandwich consuming, Penguin People.

'Oh dear!' Exclaimed Monty... 'It would appear - That the Evil Void, returns!'


### THE END
- Of The Beginning -

(-: Watch out for the next book in this continuing serial adventure :-)


### Master Of The Four Keys Of Time
### - Sabre Seven -

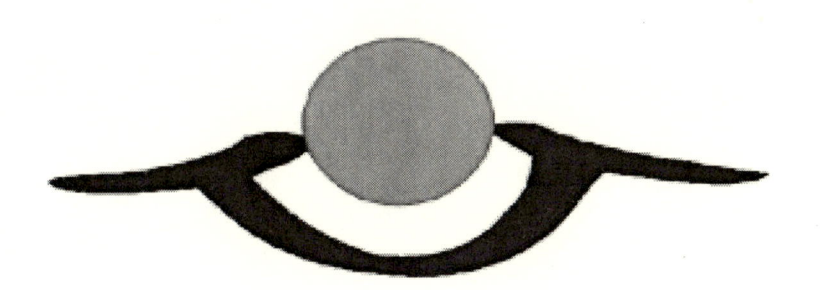

Printed in the United Kingdom
by Lightning Source UK Ltd.
129068UK00002B/11/P